The Shrouded Coast

Frank Hurst

The Book Guild

First published in Great Britain in 2025 by
The Book Guild Ltd
Unit E2 Airfield Business Park,
Harrison Road, Market Harborough,
Leicestershire. LE16 7UL
Tel: 0116 2792299
www.bookguild.co.uk
Email: info@bookguild.co.uk

The manufacturer's authorised representative in the
EU for product safety is Authorised Rep Compliance Ltd,
71 Lower Baggot Street, Dublin D02 P593 Ireland (www.arccompliance.com)

Typeset in 12pt Adobe Jensen Pro

Printed and bound by CPI Group (UK) Ltd, Croydon, CR0 4YY

ISBN 978 1835743 089

British Library Cataloguing in Publication Data.
A catalogue record for this book is available from the British Library.

FSC www.fsc.org MIX Paper | Supporting responsible forestry FSC® C013604

Other novels by Frank Hurst:

The Postmistress of Nong Khai – 2016

The Chiang Mai Assignment – 2018

Mekong Dragon – 2019

The Peccavi Plot – 2020

A Backward Glance – 2021
(a family memoir written under his own name)

The Story of Jett – How He Became A Secret Agent – 2023

The Story of Jett – The Quest Begins – 2024

The Bangkok Betrayal – 2024

The Peccavi Plot– 2025

If you wake at midnight, and hear a horse's feet,
Don't go drawing back the blind, and looking in the street,
Them that asks no questions isn't told a lie.
Watch the wall, my darling, while the Gentlemen go by!
Five and twenty ponies,
Trotting through the dark –
Brandy for the Parson,
'Baccy for the Clerk.
Laces for a lady; letters for a spy,
And watch the wall, my darling, while the Gentlemen go by!

Rudyard Kipling 1865-1936

For Gillian – a much-loved sister and true friend,
who has stuck with me through thick and thin…

Author's Notes – Some Context

This is a work of fiction, although the central character in the novel, Henry Gough, actually lived. He was born in the London suburb of Marylebone in 1835 and was my great-grandfather. My first stories in this series, *The Peccavi Plot* and *The Bangkok Betrayal*, shadow his earlier history. Research has shown us Henry's family life was both scandalous and complicated, to say the least…

We know Henry Gough was less than six years old when both his parents, Charles and Hannah, died. We know he was brought up by his grandfather, Richard, a Haymarket chaff cutter, and there is evidence that Henry started work, aged thirteen, for a baker named James Cummings, who lived appropriately in London's Upper Baker Street. We know also that Henry eventually rose from this highly inauspicious start to own a thriving business, becoming a hansom cab proprietor with stables and forty horses. He lived and worked, for the most part of his life, close to his birthplace in Marylebone. Henry Gough went on to sire twenty-one children – nine with his wife, Hannah, and twelve with his mistress, Caroline, who subsequently became his second wife.

How Henry prospered and managed his life largely

remains a mystery. How he coped with keeping two families concurrently and feeding so many children is even more of a conundrum. We can only guess.

This novel is another whimsical attempt to add further colour to his story.

Given my own working background, it was inevitable that Her Majesty's Revenue and the Excise would enter part of Henry's fictional story. The revenue officers, policemen, civil servants and clergymen are all inventions, although, like Scotland Yard, the Excise Detective Branch at Tower Hill and the War Office Intelligence Branch at Horse Guards Avenue both existed. The Excise Detective Branch was created in 1850 to address the problem of illicit alcohol; it was the forerunner of Her Majesty's Customs and Excise Investigation Division, which has played a key role in recent years to combat drugs smuggling into Britain. The numbers, objectives and methods of the early detective branch are portrayed as accurately in the novels as I have been able. The story, set in 1881, is largely based in North Cornwall, an area, since childhood, very close to my heart – a place, once intimately connected to the smuggling trade, that flourished in the late eighteenth and early nineteenth centuries.

What happens to Henry Gough and the rest of the cast in this story is complete make-believe, although I have made every effort to preserve as much historical detail of the period as possible. Borwenstow does not exist, as such, though its characterisation may seem familiar to some readers. A few of the prominent events of the time are cited, as are some of the lesser characters who were conspicuous in Victorian Britain.

The individuals in Cornwall and London are all fictitious. All are completely fabricated and products of my own imagination. I have appended a cast list of characters at the end of the manuscript to assist the reader.

Henry Gough died in 1912, aged seventy-seven, surrounded by the children and grandchildren of both his marriages. I am a third-generation product of his love affair with long-time mistress and eventual wife, Caroline. My grandfather, James, a man I much admired, born in 1888, was Henry's twentieth and penultimate child.

It has been fascinating to speculate about Henry Gough's life and utterly absorbing to write another novel with him at its centre.

Frank Hurst
West Sussex
March 2025

Prologue

17 SEPTEMBER 1782 – BORWENSTOW, CORNWALL, ENGLAND

The Reverend Jerimiah Forrabury was not a well man. His strength had been in decline for two years – exactly two years to the day, to be precise. Since Christmastide, his parishioners had started to gossip about the changes in him, blethering, as they did, in graveyard whispers.

The truth was, Reverend Forrabury's physical vigour had hardly altered at all. He'd arrived in the parish nearly a decade before as a lean and wiry man – and lean and wiry he still remained. It was the clergyman's intellectual strength that had collapsed, and for his congregation at least, this reduction of life force had rendered their parson an abject shadow of his former self. As to the cause of their parson's emotional ills, many suspected but none would speak of it, certainly not within the precincts of the churchyard.

It was ten minutes before midnight; the church was wholly deserted, save for a few circling bats. Evensong had concluded many hours before, and Reverend Forrabury's congregation had dispersed into the village or back to their farms in the sleeping fields beyond. His beloved St Piran's, which could trace its origins back to Saxon times, had never felt so desolate to Jerimiah Forrabury as it did at that moment. Alone, he knelt in the dead quiet of the chancel and prayed out loud…

'Merciful Father, I come before you with a repentant heart, acknowledging my sins, which are plentiful. I confess my need for your forgiveness and mercy for my past transgressions… and for the sin I am about to commit. Amen.'

He rose awkwardly, clutching a bible in his left hand and his journal in his right. Reverend Forrabury laid the latter on The Lord's Table, placing it directly before the stone cross at its centre, releasing it slowly, almost reluctantly. He genuflected before the altar and collected up the folds of his cassock with his free hand. Once upright, he removed one of the trio of lit candles and, without a sound, departed back down the aisle. On arriving at the font, he turned to face the altar once more, bowed solemnly, then walked towards a knotted wooden door, which he opened and entered. Mounting the thirty-five steps of a narrow circular staircase, which had been hewn in ancient times from solid stone, he arrived in the belfry. A solitary bell, daunting in size, hung in absolute stillness to greet him. After crossing over the boards and wedging his bible safely under his arm, Forrabury stepped onto an iron ladder fixed to the wall. Grasping the rail, he rose the five rungs, clumsily pushed open the ceiling hatch and climbed onto the tower roof.

Outside, the autumn night felt cool and agreeable on his face. He could hear the sea now, churning and crashing against the nearby rocks. While his eyes adjusted to the light, the half-hidden crescent moon seemed to endow the landscape with a strange otherworldly glow – a wraithlike vista such as he'd never encountered in his life before. He removed his spectacles. A perplexing gust of icy air gushed uninvited from the ocean; the candle guttered and was extinguished in a second. 'Twas as if a hidden hand had snuffed the life out of it.

Still clasping his cherished bible, he clambered onto the parapet at the point where a lone flagpole could assist his balance. Here he perched a few seconds, then threw open his arms to the night.

'Redeem this soul, O God, from all of its distress. O Lord Eternal, grant sleep unto this poor mortal sinner and let perpetual light shine upon him. May I rest in peace. Amen.'

And then the Reverend Jerimiah Forrabury jumped.

Chapter One

Marylebone, London, 16 March 1881

It was exactly fifteen minutes past six on a half-dark, half-breezy Wednesday morning when the invitation arrived. Jabbed through the freshly painted front door, amongst a clutter of far less welcome correspondence, it landed on the cockeyed Hindustan rug that overlapped the skirting boards of Henry Gough's tiny hall.

For occupants of the mews, the clattering of wooden letter boxes signalled the start of yet another working day, and the Gough household was no exception. The neighbourhood seemed to come alive at this hour – Sundays excepted, of course. For most, the arrival of the morning post was ignored; the pandemonium of their preparations decreed there were always more pressing matters to tackle. Put simply, the Royal Mail could wait. With its habitual demands, shrill reminders and tedious brown envelopes, there was no appetite for it either. But on this particular squally morning, with the wind gusting under the door, the sound of fluttering papers in the hall prompted Henry to drop his half-polished boots and leave the parlour. Stooping low, with grunted grimace on account of a lately inflamed knee, he searched amongst the fallen correspondence. After a hurried reshuffling, he found it! A broad smile took hold between the whiskers of his jagged yet pleasing forty-five-year-old face.

The special communiqué had been expected – indeed, it had been long-awaited.

If evidence were needed as to its source, the pair of Penny Venetian Reds, complete with their ink-smudged silhouettes of Queen Victoria, bore the mark of the Borwenstow Post Office – proof enough of its Cornish origins. Confirmation of its author was even more swiftly achieved. Henry instantly recognised the artistic hand of his eldest daughter, Elizabeth, whose embroidered lettering seemed to waltz across the face of the crisp cream envelope. As to the contents, Henry calculated this was no mere letter. The weight and palpable rigidity of the enclosed parchment, and of course the extra cost of the stamps, were sufficient clues. This was *the* invitation, to be sure, no doubt accompanied by a missive from his firstborn, with perhaps some directions to follow or a hand-drawn map... Henry's heart missed a beat at the thought of opening it, and almost in the very act of clasping the envelope, he was already calling out towards the parlour.

'Caroline, my love, it has arrived!'

Caroline was holding George's chubby legs against the Belfast sink at the moment her partner cried out. Preoccupied by her three-year-old's constant writhing, she let out a strained sigh and attempted to force a pair of red woollen socks around the boy's ankles.

Henry dashed into the parlour and, as if brandishing a prize, exclaimed more vociferously than was strictly necessary at that hour, 'Let me read it out to you, Carrie!' Exasperated by his son's incessant wriggling, he lowered his brow to address his next remarks directly to the boy. These were sharply delivered. 'George, please do as your mother says, for a change!'

Much to the surprise of all, the lad halted his performance in an instant, and with bowed head and trembling lip, he blinked repentantly towards his papa. The ensuing calm lasted a full three seconds. Henry used the hushed moment to gather himself, and with as much gravitas as he could muster, he slid open the pregnant envelope.

'Very well, now hear this...' He cleared his throat. 'The summons is addressed to Henry Gough, Esquire and reads as follows –

'The honour of your esteemed company is requested at the wedding of Elizabeth Charlotte Gough and Samuel Snuggs at St Piran's Church, Borwenstow, Cornwall on the morning of Saturday, 7 May 1881 at 11 o'clock. Reception to follow at The Parsonage, Borwenstow.'

'Oh, sweetheart, 'tis good news indeed!' Caroline seemed genuinely excited. 'At last! Perhaps now you can cease all your dreadful fretting.'

Henry leant forwards and planted an adoring kiss on her brow. In receiving his embrace, she momentarily loosened her grip on the infant. Taking full advantage, young George squirmed out of her arms and tumbled to the floor. Unscathed, he made a happy escape towards the bedroom he shared with his two older brothers, Arthur and Walter.

'You won't mind if I go alone, Carrie? You can see the invitation is just addressed to me.'

'Goodness, of course not, my love. This will be your day – yours to cherish forever. Elizabeth has always been a kind and loving soul, but my attendance at her wedding would stretch even her charity. And in any case, your wife would never allow it. Forbearance of just *your* presence at the ceremony will be enough to tax whatever remains of Hannah's compassion. But to ask her to accept her husband's mistress would be the final straw, and in her shoes, I would feel exactly the same. No, Henry, you must go alone, and believe me when I say, I am truly glad for you. My mother has offered to help tend the boys, so all will be well until your return.'

Henry took her fingers and put them to his lips. 'The day I first clapped eyes on you was the best of my life, I swear. I do not deserve you, for all I have done.'

'Nonsense, Henry,' she replied softly. 'You fell in love, that's all – as did I.' She pressed his hand to her cheek. 'And you should not feel the least smidgen of guilt. Goodness, you take responsibility for your wife's welfare as seriously as any man ever could. You are both a dependable husband and an affectionate lover.' She caressed his neck. 'An honest man, Henry, who holds fast to his pledges.'

'Am I truly that to you, my love? If you say 'tis so, it would make my heart sing.' Henry was beginning to sound like an actor in a Gilbert and Sullivan operetta.

Caroline frowned. Perhaps she'd been too effusive. 'If you will allow me to speak plainly, my love...' She withdrew his hand from her face and raised the pitch of her voice by a degree. 'Our tiny apartment here in these miserable mews is testimony to the sacrifices you have made to keep Hannah and her children prosperous. There are times when I wish you were less generous with the money you earn, for it is me and *my* boys who have to suffer for it!' Then, sensing his disquiet, she resumed her soothing tone. With the addition of a distinctly suggestive smile, she added, 'But listen, Henry... the inescapable truth is, I find I love you all the more for each of your bountiful imperfections.'

Henry's eyes glistened. 'What would I do without you, Carrie? You give me strength indeed.'

Their minor brush now amicably resolved, there was a subtle change of mood around the house. With a reflective sigh, Henry returned to his discarded boots and the solemn task of their polishing.

* * *

Henry's eldest child, Elizabeth, had been born nearly twenty-three years before, during the autumn of 1858. Elizabeth was the first of nine children to rise from his marriage to Hannah. The union with his lawful wife had, for the most part, been contented. For upwards of fourteen years, it had become increasingly prosperous too. But then Henry had met Caroline, eighteen years his junior, on that fateful winter afternoon when she had first entered his Marylebone stable yard. Caroline had been recommended for employment by her father, James Buchan, a Scotch coachman in Henry's service.

'Her reputation as a first-rate bookkeeper is second to none!' old Buchan had gushed.

And so it had proved. But the relationship between proprietor and accountant was to blossom. Beyond the formal scheduling and tedious columns of the counting house, the pair gradually became close – and eventually, inseparable. Then, one chill February night, after two years keeping tally for Henry's business, Caroline had pronounced her love for him. All self-control collapsed in that moment as he held her icy hand and returned the love she offered. Now, seven years and four children later, their bond was stronger than ever.

Henry's separation from Hannah had been hard, to say the least. He lost his business to his wife, in return for his freedom, and had to start another, almost from scratch. But for his part, he had been as good as his word and had kept to the bargain he'd made. Through thick and thin, he had always managed to generate sufficient to keep bodies and souls together in both his families. This had meant working all hours, in all weathers, but eventually, he'd managed to claw his way back into profit.

Such had been his poverty during the autumn of seventy-five, he'd been drawn briefly into crime to make money. But his naivety and artlessness had soon led to his capture. In hindsight, his arrest by the excise detectives for keeping an illicit whisky still and selling the alcohol to the inns of East London had been wholly inevitable.

Yet, life has a strange way of revealing its hand. For, bizarrely, it was this graze with the forces of law and order that had led to surprising doors being opened for him. The doors released into wood-lined corridors and the offices of some of the shrewdest men in the land. Incredibly, five years after his arrest, and after many exciting adventures, Henry Gough now found himself measured amongst those citizens most trusted and prized by the metropolis's law-enforcement officers and even by certain powerful government servants. His dashing exploits in Siam's enigmatic capital, Bangkok, in the service of the Crown but a year earlier, had brought further approbation, albeit ephemeral and now largely forgotten by the proletariat. But most importantly of all – for him, at least – the oriental escapade had marked a turning point. He had fully rejoined the ranks of law-abiding inhabitants in the greatest city in the world, his beloved birthplace, London.

* * *

His boots now gleaming, and with laces neatly tied, Henry kissed each of the children in turn and took the familiar fifteen downward steps to the cobbled yard and into the embrace of the crisp morning air. He decided to head east on his first trot-out of the day, and after his head groomsman, Jock O'Keefe, had hitched the newest hansom to the best grey mare, he turned the cab towards the entrance to Wellington Road.

The wedding invitation, Henry decided, was the perfect excuse to visit his old friend and former "partner in crime", Albert Woodward, who, for the last fourteen months, had occupied the rather splendid Tower Hill office belonging to the head of the excise detectives. Encouraging his horse forwards with a guttural click of his tongue, he made a deft yet harmless swish of the whip, and the cab started to rumble over the cobbles. A minute later, the hansom, bereft of passenger, had jolted into the Marylebone Road, and Henry set a course towards the great Norman fortress that was the Tower of London.

Henry Gough and Albert Woodward had first crossed swords five years earlier. It was Albert who had arrested Henry for his excise crimes. When Henry had been brought into custody one fateful wintry morning, he'd been questioned at length by the gnarled old detective. But such were the frustrations of law enforcement in tackling the problems of illicit alcohol that flooded the taverns and dives of the great city, Henry had found, to his surprise, that his luck was in. Instead of incarceration, the authorities offered him a deal. Deciding to make a bold and novel move to tackle the problem, they abandoned their outmoded and increasingly unsuccessful methods to capture the manifold still makers and traffickers.

Albert persuaded Henry, partly on account of the latter's previous good character, to turn agent for the Excise in return for his probationary freedom and the promise of future cooperation. It was this fortuitous arrangement that saved Henry from gaol, disgrace and certain penury. Within a few short months, it also brought the greatest success in stemming the illegal trade the Excise had enjoyed for over ten years. But most significant of all, Henry's easy access to the drinking houses and hidey-holes of East London had allowed him to stumble into a clandestine plot that would imperil England itself. His bold and perceptive interventions on behalf of the Crown against a maniacal Russian anarchist, in the case the press dubbed "The Peccavi Plot", demonstrated a natural talent for the work of intelligence and sealed his fate amongst the great and the good in secret government circles.

From then on, his status transformed, Henry's star had risen to a point where he had been approached by the British Foreign Office and Scotland Yard, no less, to help solve the crime of political murder. When a passenger's life had been brutally cut short in his cab by an oriental assassin, Henry had been dispatched, with Albert as consort, to faraway Siam to uncover the truth of the matter. This affair, which became known in London as "The Bangkok Betrayal", had become much celebrated amongst the general population, not just in the capital, but in all of England too, and Henry's reputation had been bolstered by exaggerated stories of his derring-do. It was a week, at least, before the newspaper reports subsided, and only when the press found new dramas with which to enthral their readership.

A scant wash of sunshine crept through leaden clouds as Henry's horse approached the Monument and turned to face the familiar lines of Lower Thames Street. The hansom drifted past the London Custom House and climbed the slope towards Tower Hill. It was not yet seven thirty, but Henry fancied it was the perfect time to catch Albert alone at his desk. He had a question for his old friend, one he'd been meaning to ask for some months, and he was sure that now was the perfect time to ask it.

Chapter Two

The revenue constable at the gate, shielded in part by the pall of mist and in part by an over-ornate portcullis of solid wrought iron, rose from his narrow bench. He greeted Henry's arrival with a smart salute and an open-hearted chortle of recognition. 'Good to see you back again, sir!' he beamed as Henry dropped down from his cab to secure the horse. 'Our first visitor of the day! May I enquire, sir, have you come to see Mr Woodward?'

'I have indeed, Jim. Is he in harness at this hour? I hope I am not too early.'

The constable's face lit up on hearing his name remembered by the celebrated morning visitor. 'Too early, sir?' he laughed. 'You know well enough that our chief is not one for idleness. He arrived more than thirty minutes ago. Shall I escort you up, Mr Gough? Is he expecting you?'

''Tis just a speculative call, Jim. I was passing without a fare, and if truth be known, I am craving a cup of Mrs Ayling's sweet tea.'

'Ha-ha! No harm in that on such a blustery day. Just go up, sir. There's no need for my protection. You know the stairs as well as any man. Fear not for your horse. I shall keep an eye on the animal while you conduct your business.'

Henry touched his cap and slid past the checkpoint railings. Walking briskly, he crossed the courtyard, mounted the broad stone stairs and entered the grey building via the heavy door he'd come to know so well over the last five years. Three flights of wooden steps later, he'd arrived in a polished passageway where a door, complete with brass plate, announced "Chief Investigation Officer, HM Excise Detectives".

'Enter, if you must...' a deadpan voice came from within, two seconds after Henry's knuckles struck the door.

Albert Woodward was not a small man by any measure, but he appeared strangely dwarfed behind the huge rectangular desk he had acquired and shipped from Siam two years earlier. "Secured for the Excise" was how he'd explained the expense to the commissioners at the time, in the full knowledge that the giant teak table would suit his office as the new leader of the detective branch perfectly. Fortunately for Albert, the commissioners had sanctioned the purchase. In truth, they'd had no alternative after his thrilling successes in the Orient. It was small reward for his service, but one, they reminded him with the typical zeal of true bureaucrats, that would have to be surrendered, one day, to his successor.

'My goodness!' Albert rose from his reproduction Chippindale with a look of cheerful amazement. 'Why, it's Henry Gough – and before eight too! Shouldn't you be mucking out the stables at this time, my man?' He rounded the great expanse of burnished wood in a flash and offered up both hands in greeting. 'Come, sit. Whatever brings you here, you are most welcome. I was just going to call for tea. Good timing, sir!' Before Henry could utter a word, Albert reached towards the corner of his desk and picked up a silver handbell, which he rang vigorously. 'Mrs Ayling will be with us in an instant. Her hearing is better than mine, I'll be bound. Now tell me, young man, what brings you to me at this early hour?'

'I travel in the hope of seeing you in fine health and to offer up my belated good wishes for a prosperous New Year. I fear my visit is long overdue. Why, I think the last time we supped a draught of ale together was in the *Cheshire Cheese* on Christmas Eve.'

'I know you better than that, Henry. You always have some intent in mind – although I'll admit it's usually for the common good. Why, you are as predicable and as purposeful as our recently restored prime minister, Mr Gladstone, himself. Come, tell me, what do you have in mind?'

At that moment, there was the sound of movement and clattering crockery on the other side of the door.

'Enter, if you must, Mrs Ayling…' Woodward bellowed with a mischievous glint in his eye.

The familiar figure of Liz Ayling stumbled in, all flushed smiles and dainty curtseys. She addressed her first remarks to Henry. 'I took the liberty of bringing two cups, sir, on seeing you pass from the scullery hatch.'

The tea was served thick with sugar, as usual, while the pourer offered up her interminable red-faced good wishes to Henry, whom she'd imagined she hadn't clapped eyes on "for a whole year – maybe more, as God is my witness". In due course, Mrs Ayling departed, wiping her hands on her apron, and Henry could finally respond to Albert's question.

'Do you know a man of your service, a Mr Samuel Snuggs?' he said simply. 'He's an exciseman, an officer of revenue from Borwenstow in Cornwall.'

'Aha! Straight to the heart of it! And what if I do?'

'He is to marry my daughter Elizabeth in two months. Perhaps I should have spoken to you earlier on the matter, but I knew only of the engagement recently, and 'twas just this morning I received the wedding invitation. You see…' he faltered… 'I heard some gossip a while back about a certain scandal in the county of Cornwall involving a revenue officer from those parts and wondered if you could cast any light.'

'Have you met this man Snuggs?'

'I have not, Albert. I have never ventured further west than Oxford. But something nags… Elizabeth tells me she is in love and he is a good man. I am truly happy for her and will attend the wedding, but I recall there was something in the newspapers a while back which I cannot place, or remember correctly – some event – some horror… I believe it involved an exciseman, in part. I may be misplaced. Samuel Snuggs may have no connections whatsoever, but I thought you might be able to enlighten me, as you and he are of the same profession.'

'I see…' Albert fixed Henry with a look that might have made others feel uncomfortable. There was a sparkle though, which Henry recognised as affable, maybe even playful. 'Well, Henry, my good fellow, I always said your memory was sharp. You are not mistaken on this occasion either. Samuel Snuggs is a man who, like you, I have never met. But as a fellow officer of the Crown, I do know *of* him, and one of his late exploits did indeed come to my attention. Regrettably, it came to the ears of the prattling proletariat too – all this about six months ago. I'll wager his story, with all its supposed horror and unearthly claptrap, has sold more than a few penny dreadfuls since then…' Albert shook his head like a sullen Labrador. 'All now forgotten by the masses, I'll be bound.'

'Unearthly claptrap, supposed horror?' Henry advanced.

'Those are my words, Henry. Many others thought differently at the time. Some of the locals, both great and small, believed in everything they'd heard – or more likely, been told by others. Malicious gossip flies fast in closed communities. 'Tis a story all right – and not one for the fainthearted. But I am a man who likes to ask questions, and on this occasion, it was not my place to ask them. All I know is the hearsay of the matter, and you and I both know that hearsays cannot secure a conviction.'

'And Snuggs – what was his part?' Henry leant forward in his seat. 'Pray, tell me the story, so I may be the judge. Is Snuggs complicit in some wickedness?'

'The answer is, I do not know for certain... But my understanding, and that of my fellow officers, is that Snuggs played his part as an exciseman honourably and acted according to the law. There was an enquiry. Officers from Exeter were dispatched. They found nothing wanting in Snuggs. But mud sticks, and in those parts, the mud of Bodmin Moor sticks fastest. I will tell you the account I have heard and hold to the official record where I can, but beware aspects of the wretched penny version. I may stray unavoidably into tittle-tattle and anecdote for greater effect...' Rather unexpectedly, Albert made a sudden, weird, ghoul-like face, complete with jutting teeth and wild eyes. Henry nodded back with a wearisome smile to show he understood. He knew his old friend was relishing the thought of telling another one of his tall tales.

Albert continued thus: 'You will be travelling into those parts soon enough, Henry, so you will have a chance to examine the terrible events for yourself. If Samuel Snuggs is to be your son-in-law, you will see things at firsthand. You can come to your own conclusions, and when you return, I will be most interested to listen to your findings on the matter. In fact, I insist you dig as deep as you can – get to the bottom of it, eh? 'Twas a rum affair, in more ways than one, and the matter is still not settled in my book.'

'I would be delighted, my dear friend. If I can be of service, pray, tell me your Cornish yarn and then send me on my way!'

'Very well. Have you heard the legend of Captain Honey's ghost tunnel?'

Henry shook his head. 'I have not.'

'Neither had I until last September, so our ignorance of the matter makes us equals.' Albert clapped his hands in mock jubilation. 'So, the story goes as follows... This fellow, Captain Jake "Heartless" Honey, was a smuggler back in the days of mad King George – more than a hundred years ago. I have consulted the library in the London Custom House and the offences he committed are manifold and proved beyond doubt. The brandy, tea and other contraband he and his buccaneers brought onto the beaches of Borwenstow became the stuff of legend. The smuggling was so widespread over many years, particularly around 1780 or thereabouts, it fattened the population of upwards of a dozen parishes, by all accounts. Heartless Honey was a giant of a man, nearly seven feet tall, some said. Whether this be true is uncertain, but without doubt, he was a daring seafaring fellow who became a true terror to the local inhabitants. Woe betide anyone who crossed him. He was wont to capture innocent men and force them, like slaves, to his cause. Some of the unfortunates became crew to work his boat, the *Sea Vixen*. Once, he lured the revenue cutter *Swan* into a shallow channel near "Cow and Calf" rocks; it went aground and all souls perished. Honey amassed such a fortune that when he bought a farm and land above the cliffs at Borwenstow, he paid for it, lock, stock and barrel, entirely in gold coin. The papers written at that time speak of *dollars and ducats, doubloons and pistoles, guineas – the coinage of every foreign country with a seaboard*. We are told the transaction was only finalised after the lawyer was forced to weigh the gold as payment.'

'This Heartless Honey sounds like a most scurrilous cove, for sure,' Henry intervened. 'But if he lived a hundred years ago, what of his connection to the matter at hand?' It was clear that Albert's audience was beginning to show the first signs of edginess.

'Patience is a virtue,' came the crisp reply. 'You will learn soon enough. The Custom House papers have revealed a lot more besides. Your man Snuggs will enter the story in time…' Albert Woodward raised the palms of both hands as if in supplication.

He continued. 'Now, it seems suspicion also fell on the parson of Borwenstow, the Reverend Jerimiah Forrabury, who many thought was in cahoots with the smugglers. You see, our holy reverend wrote a diary that was discovered on his death in 1782. It revealed that the suspicions against him were well-founded – in part, at least. His journal, which reads more like a Newgate confession, speaks to his own culpability not just for the illegal act of smuggling but for much more. For it was his personal guilt – his anguish in the extreme – that was to torment his suffering heart for the rest of his mortal days. He went to his grave a broken man as a result.

'A single act of despicable malice was to bring about the change I speak of. This occurred during a busy night of smuggling, two years earlier, in September 1780, when one of the local revenue men accidentally fell upon the gang in the act of transporting their contraband. The movement of goods was made via a secret underground tunnel that originated from a concealed spot deep within a dank and dripping grotto under the cliffs. This led directly into the warm sanctuary of the crypt beneath St Piran's Church – a matter of over 120 yards, no less. To be sure, 'twas a construction of no small undertaking, as it was wide enough to accommodate a pony or two fully standing men in line abreast. This clandestine passageway had been furtively fashioned over two long years – with Reverend Forrabury's express consent – for the purpose of bringing the "harmless merchandise" safely ashore. On the night in question, the aforementioned revenue man was kneeling inside the church, in the act of praying for his recently deceased mother, when he heard strange noises from beneath his pew. Exploring further, as is the custom of a steadfast officer, he hit on the crypt, and following the sound, he soon encountered the secret tunnel hewn from the rock beneath the church's very foundations. But then, on seeing the advancing smugglers, who out-numbered him by at least ten to one, the hapless fellow tried to make an escape in the direction from whence he came. He was sighted in the attempt, chased and captured by the blackguard Honey himself, who brutally cut him down with a single stroke of his cutlass. Then, in a deliberate and reprehensible act designed to warn others who might interfere with future trade, the officer's skull was hacked from his shoulders. The headless corpse was carried by the gang back out to the beach and tossed into the waves, where it was left floating in its own blood. The body washed up along the coast some days later, a menacing portent to other revenue officers, warning them to turn a Nelson's eye in future. The severed head of the unfortunate officer was placed in a recess within the tunnel as if in the act of staring seawards – arranged deliberately as a second reminder to those who might wish to interfere. Heartless Honey's reputation as the evilest man in Cornwall was sealed from that point.

'When he discovered what had happened, the Reverend Forrabury was appalled but found he could do nothing. What, at the time, had seemed like a whimsical adventure, to bring "harmless merchandise" to the space under his vestry, had backlashed badly against him. He'd foolishly imagined that the free trading would bring uncomplicated and undisruptive gains for all and sundry; he thought it might even bring "divine benefits" to his blessed community. And now, he'd been made to think again, brought down by murder, no less, from his lofty perch. He felt as involved as the next man in the band of ruffians who made their living at this wicked business. In an attempt to make pitiful amends, Reverend Forrabury later recovered the rotting skull and laid it to rest, with all pious and holy solemnity, under the exact spot in the tunnel where the man's appalling death had occurred. The library transcripts record that Forrabury had written in his journal that day, *I prayed for his soul – nothing can save mine now, I fear.*'

'My, 'tis quite a tale. This man Honey, was he ever caught for his vile crimes? Was justice served in the end?'

'I fear not, Henry. By the time the parson had flown to heaven and the true events became known, a local legend had already been created, fostered by the smugglers themselves… a haunted beach, ghostly caves, the spectre of a screaming skull that could be seen hovering about the tunnel entrance on dark moonless nights… The career of Captain Honey blossomed, naturally, as the coast was made clear for his criminal business to flourish. No God-fearing man or woman wished to approach the beach at night for fear of encountering the troubled spirit of the aggrieved revenue officer – thus the smuggling continued unabated. The parson was a weak man, a man who lost his faith. So scared was he of both Honey and God, he knew not which to favour. His indecision led him to allow the business to continue under his very church, but not under his feet, as on contraband nights, he would absent himself and retire to the parsonage. Folk said that he never took any personal bounty from the shipments after that. He spent the rest of his days in prayer and mental torment, until one night, on the second anniversary of the officer's death, he threw himself off the church tower and ended his own life. The locals believe the church has been haunted by not one, but *two* lost souls since Forrabury's fall.'

'And Honey, what of him?'

'He was knifed by one of his own men in a fight over a woman, just three years after the parson's death. He died screaming that Borwenstow would be cursed for ever. His ancestors kept at their brutal trade for a while, but by the turn of the century, duties were slackened, and the illicit trade declined somewhat. Most of Honey's gang returned to their fields and their cows. Honey's only son settled down at the same clifftop farm which his father had once bought in gold coin, and the boy's descendants continue to live there even now.'

'And Snuggs? You have still not mentioned him.'

Albert shifted uneasily in his chair. At length, he replied, 'Samuel Snuggs is the great-great-grandson of the murdered revenue officer. Like Honey's tribe, his family have not moved away from those parts in all these years, and Samuel's line of ancestors have followed in excise footsteps to this very day…'

Henry blanched. 'And what of recent events?' he enquired as an involuntary tremor ran between his shoulders. 'Tell me, Albert, what caused Snuggs to come to the attention of an excise enquiry?'

'He was accused of murder.'

'Murder?'

'Yes, the most disgraceful of all crimes. But his accusers were few – just certain folk from the village, from one family, in particular… The authorities were informed, but no action was taken against the officer. There was not even a court hearing. The accusers' claims were dismissed out of hand by the magistrate. To make sure the judgment was sound, the Exeter Excise sent down two of their most experienced officers to make further enquiries, and after a week, they came to a similar conclusion. The evidence against Samuel Snuggs was not even circumstantial. He had witnesses not only to prove he could not have committed the foul deed, but of his good character, to boot. The allegations were seen to be utterly false – the product of a monstrous grudge – yet, to this day, the crime has still remained unsolved.'

'And what was this crime *exactly*? Tell me, Albert. Give me all the facts. What was the terrible act for which Samuel Snuggs had been blamed?'

Albert paused before replying. At length, he said, 'Of murdering a local dairy farmer... a man known as Ignatius Honey... and decapitating him outside the lychgate to St Piran's Church.'

Chapter Three

Henry Gough had always been fascinated by steam engines. The haughty leviathan locomotives, all smoke and bluster, that bullied their way into the London terminuses had captivated him since youth. He knew their names, their numbers, their ages, their carriages, their various outputs of power and their routes. Indeed, it had been this mind-numbing knowledge of all things steam that made him appear an outright dullard at times, and there had been many occasions when Caroline had been forced to intervene in conversations amongst friends to allow discussions to veer towards a more stimulating course. Chief Superintendent Jack Grieve of Scotland Yard, on the other hand, had reason to be grateful for Henry's irrefutable and impeccable knowledge, for it had been this otherwise tedious accumulation of intelligence that had once rescued all from a most calamitous situation and thence saved the day.

So, for Henry, the planning of a 250-mile railway journey from London's Paddington Station to Launceston was going to be a real pleasure. The journey would necessitate a change of trains. The London and South Western Railway could take him as far as Plymouth, where he would board a Launceston and South Devon Railway service directly to Launceston itself. From here to Borwenstow and Cornwall's rugged north coast was a matter of about eighteen miles, which could be managed by horse and carriage – a journey, he estimated, of about three hours. He resolved to arrive on 5 May, a full two days ahead of the wedding, and in his reply to Elizabeth, he accepted her suggestion of taking a room at *The Gauger's Return Inn*, situated at the centre of the village, but a short distance from St Piran's Church. If he caught the first LSWR train of the day from Paddington, he calculated he could conduct the whole journey in daylight. He would spoil himself – with the help of the paltry five shillings advance provided for expenses from the Excise's petty cash, in expectation of his future report, Henry decided he would travel first class. With an air of contented inner contemplation, as he was driven in one of his own cabs to Paddington Station, he realised he would be unpacking his suitcase at the inn in Borwenstow well before dark and certainly in time for a hearty supper.

Elizabeth had been living in Cornwall for just over a year, employed as governess for the notable land and tin-mine owners, the Pennycrocker family. The Pennycrockers could trace their Cornish lineage back to the thirteenth century and the reign of King Edward I. Their wealth was based on land leases made possible by a fortuitous decision by a distant ancestor to ally himself with, and fight for, the King's uncle, Richard, Earl of Cornwall, against the usurper Simon de Monfort, in a struggle which the Royalists eventually won. The Pennycrockers had become exceedingly rich over successive centuries and owned houses in London, in addition to their grand Cornish estate, which had been largely established in the mid-eighteenth century, amounting to over 2,000 acres in the parish of St Piran.

Elizabeth, who had undergone a proper education,

including attendance at finishing school at no small expense to her father, had first been employed as a junior governess for the Pennycrocker children in their largest London home in Regent's Park. When Agnes, the senior governess, fell pregnant, the children (all little girls under the age of six) pleaded with their parents, Sir William and Lady Kathleen Pennycrocker, to allow Elizabeth to take on the role full-time – so popular had she been with them as understudy-in-chief. When Sir William decided, for business reasons, the family were to spend more time in Cornwall, Elizabeth followed them into the fine country house.

In her letters to her father, Elizabeth had spoken of her great excitement of living in the countryside and the joy of attending to the needs of the children, who she described as "utterly delightful in every which way possible". However, she had been remarkably reticent about the man she was about to marry. Clearly, she loved Samuel with all her heart, but initially she had avoided mention of his occupation, describing him only as a man of high standing, good family and education – "a pillar of the local community". The two had met in church, apparently. It was only after some pressing from her father that Elizabeth had eventually revealed her husband-to-be's excise calling in life – and this, when it came, was with noticeable diffidence.

With the inside knowledge in Henry's possession, courtesy of Albert's dramatic monologue, he now found his daughter's shyness of speech only partly explained. For him, it was still puzzling... It was true that Elizabeth knew well enough of her father's long association, indeed friendship, with London's excise detectives, so the fact she had withheld her future husband's occupation for so long had been all the more thought-provoking. Perhaps she had wanted to give her father a pleasant surprise; maybe she had been trying to shield him from something... It was possible, of course, that in all the early excitement of marriage preparations, she hadn't made the connections and had been careless in her letters to her distant parent. Perhaps it was the now allayed suspicion of Samuel's part in a grisly killing she'd wanted to conceal – but surely, she must have realised all would out, in the end. *Which was it?* Henry found himself asking this question over and over as the train puffed past Newbury and into open countryside.

The carriage had been full for the first hour, but as the well-ordered fields and paddocks of rural Berkshire gave way to the industrial charms of the Kennet and Avon Canal, his fellow passengers started to thin out. Travelling onwards towards the ancient landscape and uninterrupted skies of northern Dorset, Henry found he had space to stretch his legs and long periods of solitary time for reflection. He knew once he arrived in Borwenstow, he would have to confront his wife, and he hoped it would be as convivial as possible. He had no wish to hurt her; the truth was, a part of him still loved her. He had made his bed and was happy to lie in it, but there was guilt – *his* guilt to cope with. The reunion would not be comfortable for either of them. He and Hannah had been separated for nearly six years. He had sired three further children in that time. He had even travelled halfway across the world on a government assignment, and as a consequence, his story had become a minor talking point of the gossiping gentry for a few weeks. A lot of water had passed under Tower Bridge since he'd last seen his lawful wife. He loosened his collar with a damp index finger as the carriage slowed on the outskirts of Newton Abbott.

* * *

It had been the spring of 1875 that had brought the great change to Henry's life. A proverbial crossroads had been reached and he'd found he could no longer defer the most important decision of his then thirty-nine years. He'd had but two options, each with life-changing consequences. He could spend his remaining years in domestic union with his lawful and loyal wife or continue to nurture the ferocious love affair with his adoring mistress. He still admired Hannah; she was a thoroughly good woman in all respects who had done him no harm. Their children were devoted and well raised in every way, and he loved each of them equally. But Henry's infatuation for Caroline had become so acute it knew no bounds. Once, he'd attempted to make a clean break and part from her. For a full three months he abandoned his lover, returned to Hannah and resumed his duties as the family patriarch – in all respects.

But this attempt to staunch his passion for Caroline and occupy the moral ground, so expected of him as an aspiring Victorian gentleman, had proved utterly futile. The fraught months away from his mistress had only produced the purest form of loneliness he'd ever known. A vile temper, brewing resentment and gut-wrenching sickness soon followed. His business suffered; he became increasingly reckless with his money. Quite what brought him to his senses he could not recall, but after over a hundred days parted from his Carrie, he came to the certain conclusion that this was no way to lead his life. The brink on which he then teetered loomed like a chasm, and it was but a short while after this moment of epiphany that he'd been drawn back into the tender embraces of his mistress. He knew also that the time had arrived when he'd have to make a clean breast of his affair.

Unsurprisingly, Hannah had been outraged when he had confessed. Of course, she had every right to her angst, although he believed she'd known for some years their marriage had become less than idyllic. As if to make the point, she even admitted she'd suspected his affair a year previously; this, despite the birth of John, their last child together, just months before – an ill-starred product of Henry's hopeless attempts to make his marriage work in every sense. Naturally, divorce from Hannah had been out of the question; the scandal and cost were beyond both their emotional and financial means. So, a deal had been struck. In return for his freedom, Hannah would take four-fifths of the business and expect financial support from her wayward husband for their remaining children. Despite these harsh conditions, Henry knew he had no alternative. In his heart, he was actually surprised by his wife's generosity. She could have demanded the entire business in return for their separation. He warranted no less, but the charitable offer of three horses and a pair of cabs allowed him to continue working, and in time, he would become eternally grateful for this small bounty.

The last words Hannah had spoken to him had never been forgotten. They had returned to Henry in his dreams many times over the intervening years, as if they'd been hot-branded on his forearm –

You may visit the children as often as you desire, but please send notice ahead so I can absent myself. I wish to ensure that the pair of us never confront one another again.

How demonstrably reasonable his wife had been; how little he'd deserved her.

By the time the train pulled into Plymouth, it was just after midday. He bought a hot meat pie from a vendor on the platform and then crossed the tracks to find the Launceston train, the *Kernow Queen*, hissing gently at the buffers. Twenty minutes later, with a full head of steam, the locomotive wheezed her way out of the station to start her journey north-west. If all went to plan, Launceston would be reached by three o'clock. The compartment was mercifully empty, so armed with his copy of *Great Expectations*, he'd taken a seat facing forwards by the window, and his thoughts turned to the legend of Captain Honey's ghost tunnel, as told so colourfully, weeks earlier, by his old friend Albert.

What was he to make of it? What of the ghosts of Borwenstow? Henry was not a spiritual man, but neither did he reject out of hand matters of which he knew nothing. It sounded much like hocus pocus to him – Albert had dismissed it as such – but in Henry's experience, you could never be sure until you'd weighed up the facts. There were more things in heaven and earth that any man alive knew – of that Henry was certain – and the cruel killing, eight months earlier, outside the "haunted" church must account for something. At least his future son-in-law had been cleared of all charges. He was glad of it, but at what cost? Henry reminded himself he was a rational man and, in any event, he would find the truth of it all soon enough.

A delicious feeling of expectation gripped him. It was reminiscent of his mood on encountering Siam for the first time. Much lay ahead to be discovered, and he sensed the next few days would be stimulating, at the very least – and not just because his eldest daughter was about to be married.

Shortly after the train had pulled out of Bodmin, he found himself gazing pensively into the desolate and rocky landscape, which he imagined must the edges of Dartmoor. Suddenly, the carriage door slid open with a thump and a middle-aged man bustled his way in. His arms were full of sundry bags and boxes of different sizes, strange-looking nets, and what looked like a series of long poles. He made quite a sight and Henry could not prevent himself from staring. The interloper was slight of stature, all flapping limbs and noticeably unsteady on his feet. As the vicar – which Henry assumed he must be, due to the recognisable dog collar around the man's gaunt neck – started to lift the first piece of assorted luggage onto the rack above the seats, the train lurched around a tighter than usual bend in the track. Completely off balance, the clergyman tumbled headlong into Henry's lap.

'Oh mercy! I'm so sorry. I must have lost my footing,' he explained as he picked himself up from the carriage floor while in the act of disentangling all his equipment. 'Please excuse me, sir. I'm afraid I'm not as sound on my pins as I once was. I played cricket for Cornwall once, you know... Hard to believe it now, what?'

'Let me help you, Reverend. Can I assist with your luggage?'

'Oh, bless you. You are taller than I,' the man of the cloth replied as he offloaded his paraphernalia onto the empty seats beside them.

Henry rose to his feet, and with exaggerated care, he lifted the boxes and bags one by one onto the webbed luggage rack above his head. They were surprisingly light, he thought, if a trifle unwieldy. He saved the nets and poles until last and laid them out carefully on the rack opposite, which faced the rear of the train.

'That should do the job nicely. They are safe now and won't fall. May I enquire, Reverend, is fishing your hobby? These nettings appear most unusual.'

'Ah – "Come ye after me, and I will make ye fishers of men". Perhaps I am, in one respect, sir,' the vicar hummed back. 'But not in the sense you mean. Who do I have the honour of addressing? I am Studley, by the by, Clarence Studley. I have the honour and privilege to be the rector of St Geraint's, in Trevilla.'

'I am most pleased to make your acquaintance, sir. My name is Gough – Mr Henry Gough, of Marylebone, London. This is my first visit to your lovely county, and I find the landscape so wonderful – rugged and wild, and to my fresh eyes, it appears both ancient and mysterious. It's a mighty change from the clatter of the Euston Road, I can tell you!'

'Good gracious, there's a coincidence! My older brother has a residence in Marylebone. A military man, once of the Madras Light Infantry. Served under General Malcolm. I don't suppose you know him – Colonel Rupert Studley? He has a villa in Bentinck Street.'

Henry frowned amicably. 'I'm afraid I don't recall his name. Marylebone is twice the size it once was. So many folk, these days. It's hard to keep track.'

The Reverend Studley slumped his near skeletal frame into the seat by the window directly opposite Henry and crossed his spindly legs politely towards the centre of the coach, so as not to inhibit his fellow passenger. 'To answer your question, I am not an angler, but I see how you came to that false conclusion. These are butterfly nets. I am a lepidopterist – only a layperson, you understand, but active whenever I have the time.'

'I see. That is most interesting. And is Cornwall famous for its butterflies?'

'Why, yes. Would you like to see some specimens?' Before Henry could reply, Rector Studley had leapt to his toes and was fumbling for one of the wooden boxes above his head. 'Fritillaries are my speciality. I'm particularly fond of the Heath variety – *Melitaea athalia* – part of the *Nymphalidae* family. Becoming quite rare these days. Would you like to see one?' The polished box was opened in a trice to expose a rather small, distinctly uninspiring exhibit of brown, white and yellow chequered wings. 'Utterly delightful, isn't she?' Reverend Studley gushed. 'Quite the prettiest of all the fritillaries, in my view.'

'Charming,' Henry replied, not quite knowing whether to smile with pleasure or frown in fascination.

'Of course, my greatest goal is to find evidence of *Phengaris arion* in these parts. Some say it is already extinct, but I shall keep searching. What a coup that would be, eh?'

'I wish you luck in your quest, sir,' Henry replied as he opened the book on his knee. The tale of Pip's adventures had become particularly absorbing, and the story's setting in London was so wonderfully familiar.

The parson did not allow him to read for long. 'And you, sir? What is your greatest love? What gets the blood flowing through your veins?'

A playful image of Caroline at her boudoir came instantly to Henry's mind, which took him longer than a few seconds to erase. At length, he replied, 'Oh, for me, I am a man attached to the technology and power of steam. In particular, I have a fixation for locomotives, and the like. Our engine today, the *Kernow Queen*, for example, has nearly—'

Suddenly, the specimen case on Reverend Studley's lap clapped shut with an authoritative crack, in such a manner as to indicate both the simultaneous closure of the box and the subject under discussion. 'I have no interest in such matters, I regret to say,' he muttered. 'The ghastly fumes and clouds of exhaust from modern machines are, in my humble opinion, one of the reasons why counting our country butterflies has become so terribly vexatious. Where there are railways there are fewer of God's creatures, it seems to me.'

Henry was sorely tempted to say something about hypocrisy – of the churchman's easy use of the "stinking" train to transport him wherever and whenever it suited his purpose. But restraint won through in the end, and he thought better of it. Instead, he mildly offered, 'Do you travel this route often? 'Tis my first time, as I say, and I wonder if the service is reliable. I am keen to reach Borwenstow by suppertime.'

'Borwenstow, indeed. A most interesting choice... You will be there before sunset, have no fear. There are traps waiting at Launceston who will eagerly transport you, providing they can return before dusk,' Studley replied steadily. 'The roads can be pitted, but you should make decent enough progress. Beware, however,' he paused, 'most drivers will insist on getting away from the village before dark…' His words seemed to tail off as he turned to gaze out of the carriage window. At that moment, the locomotive screeched into a tunnel. In the ensuing blackness, the cleric spoke once more in tones which Henry perceived to be distinctly gloomy. 'I've had cause to deliver sermons at St Piran's, from time to time, though I have to say not much lately – not for three years or more. I leave that to the parson. A good man. He knows the lie of the land there, and its people, better than I…'

'It's the parson I will be meeting. My daughter is to be married on Saturday at the altar at St Piran's, and I expect he will conduct the service. You must know him well.'

Having conquered the tunnel, the train broke through in a blinding flare of afternoon light, which illuminated Reverend Studley's lined face in an instant. There was no doubting it, the parson was looking distinctly troubled. 'Yes. Of course. Parson Rosewarne is a good man, a man of principle and a quiet man of the cloth,' he mumbled. 'He troubles few and keeps his church well. He will conduct the service with good grace. You will not be disappointed. A godly man indeed…' His voice tailed off, and he fell into silent contemplation.

An opportunity now presented itself for Henry to delve a little deeper, to discover more about the recent goings-on in Borwenstow; Reverend Studley could be a mine of information. But Henry sensed any inner vigour his fellow passenger had possessed when he'd first entered the carriage had somehow drained away. Was it their talk of Borwenstow that had brought about the change? The priest before him now was no longer the effusive, eccentric, chatty, if slightly disjointed, arrival of ten minutes earlier. It was as if the juices had been sapped from his inner workings – along with his very spirit, perhaps...

The train rattled on for a full fifty minutes as the pair sat in silence. Henry reached again for his copy of *Great Expectations* and read for a while, but his concentration was lacking. He gazed over at the lean, dozing figure opposite. Reverend Studley appeared crumpled, limp – rather like a hot air balloon with the air released. Despite the moment being less than opportune, Henry decided he could wait no longer. The train would arrive in Launceston in less than half an hour; he simply had to ask the rector what he knew before it was too late. He may never get another chance.

Henry slapped his Dickens shut. The sudden noise had the desired effect. Studley's eyes opened with a start. He gazed around the carriage in mild confusion while dreamily licking his lips as if in search of moisture.

'We should arrive in Launceston soon, by my reckoning,' Henry announced in a not-to-be-ignored voice.

The Reverend Studley fumbled in his waistcoat for his pocket watch, nearly dropping it in the process. 'Umm... in twenty-eight minutes, if I'm not mistaken,' he replied, his bearings somewhat regained.

Now was the time to dive in. 'Tell me, Reverend... I heard stories of a dreadful murder last year in Borwenstow. Close to the church, by all accounts. Do you have any insights into the events that caused the crime? Do you know if the culprit has been brought to account?'

'Is that your true purpose for visiting there, Mr Gough?' the reply flashed waspishly back. 'Are you in search of some ghoulish story? My guess is you are a man of the press. Am I right?' If Studley's spirit had temporarily vacated his frame, this was evidence of its certain return.

Henry felt distinctly affronted. He knew the profession of cab proprietor came with certain negative connotations – he had experienced the prejudice all his working life – but to be accused of being a pushy journalist... Well, that was almost libelous! 'No, sir, I believe I mentioned...' the condescension in his voice was not easy to miss, 'I have a wedding to attend. My eldest child, Elizabeth, is to marry an officer of the Excise by the name of Samuel Snuggs. I am no penny dreadful reporter looking for a cheap story, sir. I find the assertion a hint ungracious. You are a man of the cloth; therefore, I must bow to your greater education, but my profession is an honest one. I work with horses, sir. I own thirty of them, all told, and carriages, besides. I am a London cab proprietor and proud of it.'

The speech must have struck its mark, for after an uncomfortable interlude of maybe five seconds, the parson replied. All the stridency contained in his previous pronouncements had disappeared. 'Mr Gough, I must apologise. I meant nothing by it. It's just that we have become so accustomed to the lower orders of the press – gutter correspondents of late, I believe they are known colloquially – all probing for a story in these parts. It has become more than tiresome, and none ever reports the truth of it. It seems some will go to any lengths for a few lines of salacious print. And I will not dwell on the ghastly images their illustrators have dreamt up! Sheer folly and hurtful in the extreme. Please forgive me, and let me put the record straight. Your daughter is to be married to Samuel Snuggs, you say, in St Piran's. Well, let us rejoice together, for I am sure it will be the happiest of occasions.'

'Your apology is accepted, sir, and please accept mine, if I appeared rather abrupt in my latest remarks. But if you are able, can you shed any light on what happened? 'Twas last September, as I recall, wasn't it? If my Elizabeth is to be married in a place where unholy acts have been performed, I need to prepare myself for it. I am not a spiritual man, Reverend, I confess. It is only the truth I seek. I'm sure you understand. Our meeting today appears to be most fortuitous – a divine intervention, you may describe it…' Henry realised he had gone too far with his last sentence as the expression on old Studley's face altered appreciably. He hoped the new goodwill between the two of them had not fractured once again.

'"Divine" it certainly wasn't, Mr Gough. As for our meeting today, I should put that down to good fortune on both our parts. You have helped me; you have been candid. I will tell you what you wish to know of everything that happened. Pray, commence your interrogation!'

Henry took a few moments to settle himself. 'My first question is of a personal nature. This man, Samuel Snuggs, who is to marry my daughter, what have you heard of him? I have learned he was falsely accused of a most terrible murder.'

'I have known Samuel since he was a boy and his father before him. He is a bright young man, industrious and with a loving nature. He is a fair man in each of his actions and did well at school. Your daughter has chosen well, Mr Gough.'

'And what of the allegation?'

'As you seem to know already, the allegation was maliciously brought and easy to disprove. The idea that your future son-in-law has committed murder is utterly preposterous.'

'Then why, and by whom, were these false charges brought?'

'That is simple, sir. Samuel is the eldest child, who followed his father in a long line of Cornish revenue officers. To be employed by the Revenue in these parts brings great respect, but it also harbours loathing and hatred from certain quarters. As an officer of the Excise, in charge of men, Samuel has an even greater burden to bear. I will not beat about the bush; smuggling continues in these parts. 'Tis not the wild trade it once was, but there are profits to be made for those who engage in the game. Cheap tobacco and alcohol remain in high demand all along the coastline, and the art of smuggling in local parishes has been a common pastime over the centuries. Samuel has made it clear to all that he sets his stall against them. He is a fine man with high principles, but with principles come enemies. It's no coincidence that his accusers came from amongst those he would seek to obstruct.'

'The Honey family, by any chance?'

Reverend Studley harrumphed. 'You know more about this than you let on, sir. Why yes, the Honey family is at the root of it. Their lineage in the trade of owling goes back further than most.'

'But the murder – the victim was a Honey.'

'Precisely, Mr Gough. Ignatius was the younger brother of Cassius Honey, the patriarch of the clan. All the more reason for the Honeys to accuse a man whose avowed intent is to bring their family down.'

'But if not Snuggs, who *did* kill Ignatius?'

'Ha-ha! If you ask the customers of *The Gauger's Return*, they will tell you 'twas the *spectre* that murdered Ignatius in revenge for his own death, a hundred years before to the day, when he himself was cut down. I assume you have heard the tale of Abel Snuggs. He was Samuel's great-great-grandfather.'

'I have heard an account. The poor man was beheaded while doing his duty, his skull removed as a warning to others. His ghost is said to haunt the tunnel under the church.'

'All blather, of course, but 'tis a convenient and sensational supposition, and folk love to gossip and spread frightening stories of the eerie world of the spirits.'

'And you, sir, what do you believe?'

'I have no opinion, Mr Gough. If truth be known, I *wish* to have no opinion also. But if you ask me to speculate, I should say a feud of some kind between rival smugglers was the cause of it, but I cannot say… One thing I know is that the head of unfortunate Ignatius has never been found. His body lies in the graveyard *sans* skull.'

Chapter Four

The journey by open trap from Launceston Station passed without incident. The roads were, for the most part, flat, save for a section where his driver took a shortcut via a rutted track to bypass the moor. As predicted by Reverend Studley, the young coachman was anxious to set off quickly, which did not allow Henry any time to find sustenance for his onward road trip.

'I will take you to Borwenstow, sir, but I wish to be on my way back and beyond the parish boundary before darkness falls. I have a place in mind to bed down on my return, but it is some three miles from the village. We should leave now, sir, if you please.'

'Would you not prefer to rest at the inn? There will be lodging and stabling, I'd imagine,' Henry enquired.

'That's as maybe, but I'd prefer not, sir, thankee,' the sprightly driver replied with the hint of a scowl. 'I'll be on my way home as soon as possible after I've dropped you. Better all round, for sure.'

The route took them via Hallworthy, a tiny hamlet at a lonely crossroad, where they rested a while and watered the horse. Henry was able to purchase a couple of boiled eggs and half a pint of milk from a farmhouse window. These supplies he consumed voraciously before reboarding the trap. Two hours later, as the western sun sat low and yellow in the sky, the village of Borwenstow hove into view. From the rolling pastures that dominated the high ground above the village, the scene was as picture-perfect as one could imagine on such a temperate May evening. The dramatic backdrop of rolling blue Atlantic waves crashing onto the north-facing coastline that lay behind the extended cluster of crouched houses, gaping stores and assorted farm buildings, further accentuated the bucolic beauty of the scene. From this high vantage point, Henry could see the square tower of St Piran's quite clearly. It overshadowed the lesser buildings of the community by quite a margin, appearing, as they did, as indistinguishable smudges of grey slate under the high cornices of the upright twelfth-century church.

As he shaded his eyes with outstretched hand to absorb the lines of the tower all the better, an image of a tumbling cassock and fluttering surplice came suddenly and uninvited into his mind. That was the spot where the conscience-stricken parson, Forrabury, had plunged to his death nearly a hundred years ago. He squinted again at the church, and with an involuntary nudge of his head, he shook the vision from his mind to focus instead on the skylarks that chirruped and pirouetted high above in the cool blue evening air.

Henry had arranged to meet Elizabeth in *The Gauger's Return* at about seven o'clock. As the little carriage descended into the shadow of the village, leaving the sun-drenched pastures behind, he glanced at his pocket watch. It was a few minutes after six. *Perfect,* he thought.

'Won't you tarry a while, my man?' Henry enquired with a genial smile when the luggage had been offloaded. 'You have driven carefully and quickly. I am a coachman myself, by trade, and I know when a fellow has worked hard and worked well.' Henry thrust the agreed coinage into the driver's palm. 'Allow me to reward you a little further. What's your name?'

'Joshua, sir.'

'Well, Joshua, I'll warrant this inn serves mighty fine beer. Let me buy you a pint of their finest ale to set you on your way.'

'I'll be heading off, sir, thankee.'

Henry gave him an exaggerated frown. 'Very well then, but I hope to renew our acquaintance soon. I shall send word to Launceston when I am ready to return. Perhaps you can come to collect me.'

'If you travel at midday, sir, I'm your man,' Joshua replied as he flicked the reins. The weary horse peered over his harness with a look of equine indignance. A further brush, this time more insistent and with a cluck of the tongue, was enough to encourage the animal to turn and trundle back up the lane towards the hill they had recently descended.

At that moment, the bearded innkeeper bustled onto the scene. Henry thought him to be unusually slender for a man of his calling.

'You'll be Mr Henry Gough,' the fawning proprietor announced in a curiously high-pitched voice. 'Your daughter told me you was coming… I'm expectin' her any second. You're earlier than what we thought – but welcome all the same…' The innkeeper gave a shallow bow and waved carelessly towards the pub. 'My boy will take your bags,' he piped. 'Your room's on the first floor. Our best – you can gaze on the sea and the church from it.' A young fellow hurried up, nearly tripping over the caked mud in his efforts to assist the newly arrived visitor. 'My son. He'll take your bag – he's stronger than he looks, ain't cha, lad?'

The reunion with his eldest daughter, forty minutes later, was exactly as Henry had hoped. Elizabeth blushed when he opened the door to greet her at the threshold of his newly occupied apartment, and when he swept her up in his arms, she wept.

'Oh, Papa. It is such a blessing you are here. You have been in my thoughts all day. I was worried you might miss the train or lose your way or—'

'Tut! 'Tis your papa you are talking to. A man who went to faraway Siam and returned to tell the tale.'

'All the same, you must be tired, and all that bumping in the waggon at the end. I always hate that part.'

'You forget, my dearest, I am used to horses and carriages!' he laughed. And Elizabeth, wiping her eyes, started to laugh with him. 'When am I to meet your betrothed?' he asked her lightly. 'I have heard nothing but good reports of him. Why, even my fellow passenger today knew of Samuel Snuggs and what an upright good fellow he was.'

'A passenger on your train?'

'Yes, a holy man – a man of the cloth. The rector of Trevilla, I think he said. Not far from here, I imagine. The Reverend Clarence Studley, no less.'

'I have heard the parson speak of him as his superior, but I have never met him. How does he know my Samuel?'

'Oh, since a boy, apparently – he knew his father too. Spoke very highly of them both and offered up his best wishes for your wedding. But enough of the old vicar… I have to say, Daughter, I am so pleased for you. I am fit to burst with pride.'

'Will you dine with us tonight, Papa? I have a place for you at the table, if you will join us. I know you need your rest, but if you have the energy, we dine at eight. I have a private room arranged here at the inn. The food is better than passable if you avoid the pilchards.'

'Will your mother be joining us?'

'Yes, Papa. She has agreed.' Elizabeth took her father's

hand. 'I think you will find her forbearing. She has promised as much. Will you come, Papa? Please say you will. Samuel and his mother will join us too. There will be five at table if you come.'

'I will have to reacquaint myself with your mama sooner or later.' Henry smiled with the air of genuine benevolence. 'It's been nigh on six years.' He squeezed her hand. 'Why, of course I will come. And I promise to be both as contrite and generous as any man you have encountered in this fair county. I'm sure you have much to tell us, and my plan is to listen to every word you and your mother utter and speak as little as possible.'

After Henry had washed – vanity dictated he had to trim his beard and clip his moustache in the process – he dressed informally for dinner, with a fresh white shirt and winged collar, silk cravat and a double-breasted waistcoat of black satin with notched lapels. There was no mistaking his nervousness, and efforts to attach the cravat to his neck suffered from fumbling fingers and thumbs. Satisfied he looked better than he had in many months, he creaked down the narrow staircase to the inn's ground floor. Here, he spotted an array of bright candlelight at one end of the broad oak-lined chamber. A fire blazed and crackled in the hearth. This was obviously the venue for dinner. He noticed Hannah instantly, seated at the table with her back to him, but unmistakeable all the same. On seeing her father's approach, Elizabeth, dressed adorably in ivory satin, sprung up to greet him.

'I see I am the last to arrive – not too late, I hope,' Henry found himself apologising already. 'This tie has been a damned nuisance.'

'No, Papa. In fact, you are slightly early. We have yet to hear the chime for eight—' At that moment, the rustic timepiece above the hearth commenced its clockwork ritual of striking the hour, and the whole assembly chuckled and tittered out loud. It seemed this timely intervention had broken the ice, for most, at least, but Henry could not be certain of Hannah. The back of her royal blue evening gown remained turned against him.

'I am so pleased to make your acquaintance at last.' A taller than average, fair-haired, slim-hipped man stretched out his hand. He had an open face and a pleasant countenance. 'I am Samuel, Samuel Snuggs. This is my mama, Constance.' The attractive auburn-haired lady opposite smiled and offered her silk-gloved hand, which Henry took in his own.

'Mr Snuggs, I have heard much about you. And your mother too. Constance – such a lovely name.' Henry made an exaggerated bow. 'Henry Gough, at your service.'

A period of awkward silence followed. The air seemed stiff with expectation as a frisson of anticipation gripped the room. The tittering and small talk had suddenly died.

Henry realised it was for him to make the next move. Rounding the table, he turned to face his wife.

'Hannah, it has been a long time. May I be so bold – you look to be in glowing health.' He meant what he said. Hannah did look splendid, and his voice caught at the sight of her again. 'I, err…' He coughed lightly. 'I, err… am so happy to see you looking so fine. And on such a wonderful occasion as this, our daughter's wedding day,' he blethered.

Hannah offered her hand, and Henry found himself bending to kiss it.

'The wedding is on Saturday, Henry,' she chided. 'You look to be in good fettle too. The extra weight suits you…'

Henry smiled the most benign and generous smile he could offer. *Touché. Hannah has not lost her wit,* he thought to himself.

A bottle of *Carrells* Irish whiskey appeared on the table, followed quickly by decanters of red wine. Glasses were raised, and a familial toast of welcome was delivered by Samuel after all had taken their seats. Elizabeth had set the places around the table in advance, and Henry found himself sitting between his wife and daughter. To his great relief, it was not long before the convivial hubbub of friends and relatives eating and drinking as one filled the room. During the next hour and a half, Henry became aware that he was conversing more with his wife than with his daughter – *much* more, in fact – and to his relief, he found the exchanges both stimulating and affable. Hannah spoke of her business and how it had grown in the last few years, a subject Henry much enjoyed discussing, for he was able to compare his own recent successes with hers. They had more in common, on the commerce front, at least, than he had imagined.

But it was hearing the family news that gave Henry the most pleasure. His regular visits to see the children had meant that he was up to date with most of their activities, but the little insights Hannah was able to provide gave him much delight, so much so that at one point, the pair found themselves laughing uncontrollably at a story she told of their youngest, seven-year-old John, and his antics with a stray kitten that had wandered into the yard one day. It felt, in that moment, as if they had hardly been separated. It was with a degree of unease, Henry found his feelings for her returning, feelings of fondness and respect he never imagined would surface again. Despite the veneer of jollity, he felt a deeper ache in his heart. How he had wronged her… He had no doubts he'd made the right choice at the time, and even now, he knew it had been inevitable. His regrets were none the less painful. His decision could not have been fudged; the outcome was wholly inescapable, so binary, so black and white, and ultimately, so divisive.

They did not talk about Caroline. Hannah did not enquire; nor did he ask of her whether a loving man had entered her own life, though he knew from Elizabeth that this was not the case. Instinctively, for both of them, these subjects were taboo – certainly not for discussion on their first encounter after six years.

After dinner, which had consisted largely of assorted meat pies, sweet pastries and dumplings in sauce – Henry had taken his daughter's advice and had avoided the starry gazey pie – the group withdrew from the table and recharged their glasses from the decanters of port and brandy. Henry wondered absently if the liquor had been smuggled...

He had a chance to speak briefly to Constance Snuggs, a woman who giggled a lot, but all the same, he judged, a person of considerable intellect and charms. But he was keenest to speak privately with his future son-in-law, and as the party reshuffled, Samuel seemed to have the same notion. As soon as Henry took his seat in a vacant wing-backed armchair close to the fire, he came alongside and, with the broadest of grins, offered up a newly filled glass. Meanwhile, the ladies settled into a group of their own, close to the arched window, and as if relieved to be freed from their formal duties with the menfolk, they fell to chattering ten to the dozen amongst themselves.

'By all accounts, you have led a most exciting life, sir. Elizabeth tells me you have travelled to the Orient, no less,' Samuel opened.

'I have indeed, and I've had a few brushes with the law on the way,' Henry replied with a candidness that Samuel found most disarming. 'But I'm pleased to say, those desperate days are past me now. I confess, however, that while I have voyaged far to the east, this is the most westerly point I have reached in my entire life.'

'Welcome to Cornwall, sir. 'Tis a wondrous and magical place, all things considered, despite what you may have heard. My family settled here nearly 150 years ago. Originally, we were Devon folk – mostly sailing people from Dartmouth – but now I feel a Cornishman through and through and am as proud of St Piran's flag as the next man.'

'I understand you are from a long line of revenue officers; your father was one and his father before him.'

'And more besides.' Samuel looked wistful. 'You are well informed, sir. Indeed, I must appear to you as being practically married to the Excise, but I pledge I shall not act the bigamist when I take your daughter's hand!' he exclaimed with a flourish. 'Why, I love her so dearly. Since the first day I spied her last year, in her pretty Easter bonnet, sitting but ten places from me in the pew ahead, I have thought of no one else.'

'That is very reassuring, I'm sure...' Henry replied with a steady gaze, his thoughts, predictably perhaps, drawn to the word "bigamist" that Samuel had just uttered. He lit his pipe and with the first puff indicated to Snuggs to continue.

'The first of the Snuggses, Alfred, was sent to this parish as a riding officer by the Revenue, back in the days of the second George, and we have remained here ever since, all of us in the service of the Crown. The numbers of revenue men are much fewer these days, of course, but our work along this coastline, in particular, continues to be of great value to our government. The defence of the realm and protection of our hard-won empire must cost the Exchequer a pretty penny. Our enemies abroad are manifold. My resolve, and that of the brave men under my command, is to protect the Revenue at all costs. This resolve has on no occasion diminished since I took up my commission, and I vow it never will as long as I hold the office.'

Clearly, this young man imagined he had a true vocation – a divine calling, almost. Possibly he had... Henry mused. Whatever his motivation, the speech made Henry want to know him better. The passion in Samuel's voice was clear for all to hear. To Henry's ear it bordered on the evangelical. He suddenly felt a desire to regale his young confidante with yarns of his own exploits for the Crown and of his adventures with the excise detectives of Tower Hill, but he quickly realised now was not the time. There were more important things to discuss. He came straight to the point. 'Tell me, young man, I hear tell you have been falsely accused of a vicious murder. Are you able to shed any light on the matter – to me, as your prospective father-in-law, that is?'

Samuel Snuggs drew his chair an inch or two closer. 'I had no part in it,' he murmured. 'I swear on my life. I was patrolling at Beacon Point when Honey's body was discovered. I had bivouacked with my squadron at dusk, and we remained in position for the whole night, expecting a consignment of kegs to be landed in the early hours. We did not return 'til midday, by which time the rumours had started to circulate.'

'Rumours?'

'Yes, the wild allegations that I had been seen, cutlass in hand, while in the act of severing the despicable Ignatius's head from his body. His brothers swore they saw me commit the deed at precisely midnight – exactly the hour and in the very manner that tradition says my great-great-grandfather met his end. The so-called witnesses said they gave chase, but according to them, I "rose up like a shell from a cannon and disappeared into the night sky". What poppycock! According to the mob, I had revenge as my motive, and half the village believed them – until, of course, I returned twelve hours later with half a dozen of my men to vouch for me.'

'But if not you, Samuel, who?'

Samuel Snuggs drew closer still. Into Henry's ear he whispered, 'It's my firm belief the Honey boys were engaged in smuggling brandy that night and had sent out false intelligence to lure us away to Beacon Point. The old parson's tunnel, supposedly haunted by my ancestor and which had been blocked for more years than anyone could recall, had been reopened and showed evidence of recent use when later inspected by my men. I am a spiritual man, sir, a man who holds to his faith, but as I sit here now with you, as God is my witness, I'll be damned if it wasn't the ghost of old Abel that had returned.' The earlier conspiratorial whisper had disappeared, exchanged by degrees into a seething outburst. 'Risen again,' Samuel fumed, 'to dispense rightful justice on the vile spawn of the man who took his life three generations ago – Captain Jake "Heartless" Honey.'

Chapter Five

Despite arriving in his bed at nearly midnight, Henry found he was awake again just a few hours later, and try as he might, he was unable to induce his body into sleep once more. At first and instinctively, he reached out for Caroline, but only cool sheets met his grasping fingers. He lit a candle and checked his pocket watch. It was twenty-seven minutes after four. A tawny owl kee-wicked and hooted in a faraway wood, its calls interrupted only by the profound stillness that seemed to envelope the entire village. The sea, so close to his window, must have died in the night, for there was no sound of it, not a whisper of incoming waves, though his bedroom faced the shallow cliffs that overlooked the broad strands of silver sand beneath. As he lay awake, straining to catch the noises of the night, he realised that something was troubling him. He fumbled for *Great Expectations* on the bedside table and opened it, but the spitting candle and bible blackness of his close surroundings made it almost impossible to read, and anyway, he told himself, he had no appetite for Miss Haversham at this hour.

There was only one thing for it. Knowing the sun would emerge just after five thirty, he decided he would steal a march and rise before it. Henry relieved himself in the stone chamber pot he found under his bed, sluiced water over his face and neck, and dressed. A bracing walk before breakfast, he decided, would be as invigorating as it would be instructive. As he tiptoed, candle in hand, into the inn's shrouded salon, the clock that had caused so much amusement the night before chimed five. Henry let himself out into the courtyard. The half-moon was high, appearing glossy in the cloudless sky, and provided more than sufficient illumination for sure-footed navigation. As his eyes adjusted, the dawn light seemed to fall first on the lonely church tower, and in the chill morning air, he trembled at the sight of it. Clutching the trusty swordstick presented to him years earlier by Albert Woodward, he entered the village square, and with fixed gaze, he set a course towards the outline of the lychgate on the other side.

Before they had retired for the night, Samuel had drawn Henry a rough map of the surrounding area, with the village as its centrepiece. The farm belonging to Cassius Honey and his family, aptly named *Doubloons*, lay in the top right corner, adjacent to the line that defined the beach. Henry decided there was no better time than the present to see it for himself. According to Samuel's description, it could be found just over a mile away. All Henry had to do was follow the footpath that coiled past the ancient yew tree at the eastern corner of the churchyard. This would take him directly past the Honeys' farm gate, which protected the hotchpotch of close-knit structures and stumpy chimneys of the farmhouse itself. This could be reached, if he dared to make the journey, by negotiating the gate and taking a short march down a private track. At first, the path was level and the ground firm, but then it descended sharply towards a babbling stream. He crossed over a rustic bridge and found the path rising in a steep incline back to the top of the cliffs. At the summit, brushed forwards by a gentle breeze, Henry made good progress. The flatter ground made walking much easier, and as the slanted rays of the newly rising sun cleared the hedgerow ahead of him, the dark silhouette of Doubloons rose up from the fields like a man-of-war sighted on a distant horizon.

From nearby meadows, the sound of contented lowing could be heard; morning birds chirruped a fresh dawn chorus as Henry, now bathed in shallow sunlight, approached the farmstead. Standing outside the broad wooden gate, he could see the farm buildings closer now. They presented both a peaceful and yet somehow forbidding picture. Perhaps it was his newfound bias against the Honey clan that produced the latter reflection. He decided to walk a little further down the easterly footpath, and after about a quarter of a mile, he found a soft hummock of grass a few yards from the path that commanded an all-encompassing view over the Atlantic Ocean and its wheeling gulls. Here, he sat down and lit his pipe. For a few moments, the breadth and beauty of the landscape were overwhelming. Gazing out to sea, his thoughts lost in the sweeping vista, he became suddenly aware of a brisk movement to his left, in the direction of Doubloons. He turned his head westwards and spotted a horse and rider at about 200 yards distance. They were approaching at some speed – at an extended canter, for sure. The horse, which was exceedingly large and blessed with a white snake-shaped blaze on its forehead and muzzle, slowed upon approach and came to a full halt about twenty feet from Henry's grassy knoll.

'What is your business here?' the rider barked in a tone that was distinctly unfriendly.

'My business? I have no business, sir. I have just my pipe for company – and this wondrous morning, of course.'

The man seated astride the chestnut stallion was broad-shouldered, of about thirty years of age, Henry judged, maybe younger – his ruddy complexion and the lanky black hair that swept over his hatless forehead masked his features somewhat.

'You have no business here. This is private land. If you wish to rest a while, pray, stick to the footpath.'

'I am sorry if I have offended, young sir,' Henry said as he got to his feet with an indulgent stretch of his shoulders, 'but I am new in these parts and saw no sign to show I was trespassing. Who do I have the honour of addressing, sir?'

'I am Gabriel Honey. My family owns the farm beyond and the land hereabouts. I saw you pass. You walk to Dizzard, I presume.'

'I walk to no such place. I walk for recreation only.'

Gabriel Honey looked confused, as if the thought of walking for the purpose of pleasure was utterly bewildering. 'If I see you stray from the path in future, I will be forced to act. We do not like trespassers in these parts, and I am in my rights to remove you forcibly, if necessary.'

'I am here for a wedding, Mr Honey,' Henry replied lightly. 'Just that. I am a London man who has travelled far to be here.'

'A wedding is none of my business.'

'Yes, a wedding at St Piran's tomorrow, in fact,' Henry persevered in the hope of drawing the man out.

A hint of recognition appeared on Gabriel's face. 'If you speak of the marriage of Snuggs, what is your connection? I thought his father was dead long ago.'

Henry was getting somewhere at last… 'Why, I am the father of the *bride*. 'Tis my daughter who is to marry the man Snuggs. Will you be attending yourself, perchance?' he asked with an innocent smile.

'Snuggs is no friend of this family. Now, be off with you and pay attention in future. I have the cows to attend.'

'I'm grateful for your advice, to be sure, but before I depart, and to make certain I do not transgress in future, pray, outline the extent of your land holding. I would not wish to breach any boundary the next time I venture out.'

'Just stick to the path,' came the short reply. And with that, Gabriel Honey pulled on the reins, turned his horse and within seconds had entered into a thumping gallop back towards Doubloons.

Breakfast in *The Gauger's Return* was a fine affair, much better than Henry had anticipated. The eyes of the silver pilchards laid before him seemed to wink invitingly, but he remembered Elizabeth's advice and ignored them. Instead, he tucked into hot porridge served with local honey, and a plate of eggs, ham, bread and butter, which the shrill innkeeper, who went by the name of Isaac Trewint, informed him had come from a local farm. As the farm where he'd recently trespassed had been of the dairy variety, Henry presumed some of his feast might have originated there, and he munched away contentedly at the thought of it. There was hot coffee too, and after he'd drained his second cup, he retired to his room to prepare for the wedding rehearsal that was slated for ten o'clock.

Holding hands, Elizabeth and Samuel greeted Henry in the salon at ten minutes to ten, with Elizabeth unable to prevent herself from throwing her arms around her father's neck once more.

'We must not keep Parson Rosewarne waiting, Father. 'Tis but a short walk, but even now, I am sure he'll be waiting.' With that, Henry obediently positioned his hat, adjusted his tie and collected his silver-topped excise stick. A minute later, all three were marching in happy purpose towards the now familiar stones and pointed arches of the village church. As Elizabeth had predicted, the parson had obviously been waiting in the nave for a while, for as soon as the heavy door was shoved open, there he was, standing as if on stage, his back to the font, licking his lips in costumed readiness for his audience. In full regalia he made an impressive sight – black cassock, white surplice and emerald-green chasuble, complete with expansive gold embroidered cross.

The Reverend William Rosewarne was of plump and pink disposition, a short man with an effusive smile. His physical appearance set him apart from the rest of the inhabitants of Borwenstow, who had looked universally lean to Henry's eye since his arrival the day before. The holy man greeted his visitors with arms outstretched and unctuous welcome. Appearing to salivate and licking his lips once more, he gushed, 'Greetings all ye who enter, in the name of our Lord.' For all the world it looked like he might break into song. As Samuel opened his own mouth to speak, the church door widened once more with a clunk of ancient iron. Hannah and Constance entered shortly after, appearing to be deep in conversation, with Constance's recognisable giggles to the fore.

'Excellent,' Samuel announced with a gentle clap of his hands. 'We are all gathered.' He made the introductions one by one, ending with Constance. The parson touched his neck and cleared his throat. He responded to each in turn with a slightly unsteady bow of the head, reserving what Henry imagined was an exceptionally wide-eyed beam of acknowledgement for the last. Constance must have been known to him as a parishioner for many years.

It was at this moment that something extraordinary happened.

Without warning, and as the others watched on helplessly, the Reverend William Rosewarne clattered to the floor. Clutching his collar in a squall of cassock and surplice, he emitted the most dreadful wail of distress Henry had ever heard. On its way down, the parson's skull collided with the ragged edge of the font with such a forceful snap that it bounced back to near upright. With startled open eyes that were most horrible to witness, the cleric's head fell once more and struck the flagstone floor – a further resounding blow but a second later. The twin sounds of bone on stone echoed down the aisles in a most alarming and ominous fashion. The noise danced through the arches, along the vacant pews and reverberated into the deserted corners of the nave as if the devil himself was making his exit.

Henry knew the man was gone even before he'd turned him over. The first awkward crack had broken the parson's neck – dead in an instant. The priest had met his maker even before his earthly body had crashed so horribly and unceremoniously to the ground. If further proof of death were needed, the bubbles of foam and the line of blood around Rosewarne's generous mouth provided it.

As Henry tended to the stricken priest, there was an eerie silence for a few seconds. No one could quite believe what had happened. Samuel appeared as if the eyes would pop from his head. Then, almost as if it had been rehearsed beforehand, the three ladies let out such a chorus of shrieks their voices might have been heard in Launceston. Samuel moved to comfort his mother, then put his arm around Elizabeth to drag her gaze away from the terrible sight. Realising there was nothing he could do for the dead man, Henry got to his feet and embraced Hannah, pressing her head gently against his neck as she wept uncontrollably. He could not remember the last time he had embraced his wife in such a fashion.

At this moment, the door from the vestry swung open with a thump. It was Isaac Trewint, the lean innkeeper of *The Gauger's Return*. With him were two other men whom Henry had not seen before. Henry hadn't realised there were others inside the church – he'd certainly not heard anyone, but this was no time to draw conclusions.

'We heard the screaming,' Isaac said with a look of obvious surprise on seeing the others, his worn-down features fitting the mood perfectly.

'You had better call the physician,' Samuel offered. 'But I doubt there is anything he can do for him. The vicar fell like a stone, just as we—'

'He is dead,' Henry interrupted with a bleak expression. 'I have checked.'

The new arrivals gathered around, wringing their hands, but none dared to touch the body of the sprawling priest. They just gawped, open-mouthed. Rosewarne's pallid face stared back – an instant portraiture, if they needed one, of their own mortality. At length, one of them spoke. 'I'll go fetch Dr Plymswood, all the same.'

'Very well, Jago. Tell him we will not move from this spot until he arrives, and there is a drink for him at the inn if he gets here within the hour.' It was Isaac who spoke. Jago hurried to the main door and was gone in a flash.

'We had better call the constable too,' Samuel said, disentangling himself from his wife-to-be. 'I will send one of my men to bring him here.'

'Are you sure that is wise, Mr Snuggs?' It was Isaac's high-pitched voice once more. 'You being a witness and all... Maybe 'tis better you remain here until the constable arrives. *I* will send for him – 'tis no problem.' Before Samuel could respond, the innkeeper added quickly, 'Amos, go find Constable Poundstock. I'll warrant you'll locate him at his usual place at this hour. He will be with the postmistress, Miss Chadwick, I'll be bound. Run along now to the post office and be quick, before the doctor arrives and messes things up.'

Samuel concurred with a simple nod. It seemed the wisest course of action. As Henry bent to cover the parson's ghastly face with his 'kerchief, he said, 'We'll all wait and give our statements to the constable. Now, let us remove our eyes from this terrible sight and take our places in the pews until either he or the good doctor arrives. Maybe 'tis a time for some quiet reflection.' They all did as suggested, and it was not long before the entire church had descended into a deep yet most unnatural silence.

Chapter Six

The next few hours were spent in waiting for the police to arrive. On seeing the body of the vicar inert on the church flagging and grasping the possibility that a grievous crime may have been committed, Constable Poundstock decided to call for reinforcements. After taking a brief note of events, as seen through the eyes of the five witnesses, the heavy-jointed policeman released them all to appear at four o'clock at the church hall, where they would be further questioned by an inspector drawn in by telegraph message sent to Launceston by Miss Chadwick.

Doctor Plymswood arrived in the nick of time to earn his gratis drink from Trewint, but it was clear to all who watched him go about his business, he was drunk already. 'The man is dead,' he announced with a hiccough, after an examination that had lasted less than ten seconds, 'from wounds to the head. His heart was weak, a factor that would have contributed to his sudden passing.'

Henry ventured an enquiry. 'What caused him to collapse, sir? That must surely be the question.'

Dr Plymswood did not like being put on the spot. 'Why, 'tis as I said. The man had a weak heart. These things happen to one so much blessed with belly fat, don't you know!'

'Will there be an autopsy?'

'If the coroner in Launceston orders it.' The words were noticeably slurred.

'Will you recommend one, Doctor? Given the circumstances, it would appear to be necessary.'

'I expect so…' Plymswood looked flustered, 'and now if you wish, I need to retire. I have business to attend. Please arrange for the body to be taken to Lych House.'

The Lych House was a small stone building on the perimeter of the churchyard which had served the village as a temporary resting place for the bodies of departed souls for nearly 250 years. The tiny mortuary had been filled to overflowing only once – when it had been used to lay out the bodies of six drowned sailors, following the wreck of a West Indiaman with a cargo of Barbados sugar in December 1760.

'I will make the necessary arrangements,' Dr Plymswood added deliberately. 'Good day, ladies and gentlemen. I bid you farewell.'

Once the doctor had lurched away and his instructions for the removal of the body met, the next few hours were passed by all at *The Gauger's Return* in trying to recover their composure, but the animated conversation that ensued made any relaxation almost impossible. Elizabeth sent word to Lady Kathleen at Pennycrocker Hall, explaining events and that she would be detained a while longer in the village until all formalities had been completed. She undertook to attend to the children's lessons as soon as she returned.

After taking a light lunch on the premises, the five witnesses moved, as instructed, to the village hall, only to find the visiting inspector had not yet arrived from Launceston. Constable Poundstock found them a dusty table and pulled up a few bedraggled chairs, and they were asked to wait, which they did, for the most part, in contemplative silence. Fortunately, they did not have to linger too long. For as Henry's pocket watch showed eighteen minutes after four o'clock, the sound of a carriage drawing up outside could be heard, and it was just a few seconds later that a balding shambles of a fellow hastened into their presence. This was none other than Inspector Austol Halwill Barton, unceremoniously arrived from Launceston. Some yards to the rear, followed the uniformed figure of Police Constable Marshgate, who impressed all by his obvious youth and a distinct appearance of anxious bewilderment.

Inspector Halwill was a naturally impatient man and not in the habit of being late for his appointments. One of the wags under his command had dubbed him "Hasty Halwill" for that reason, and it was not long before the name had stuck. At first his men, and then his superiors began to speak of him thus, using the exact same moniker. Hasty Halwill was a man who always seemed to be in a rush, forever dashing hither and thither on some mission of one sort or another. His less important colleagues at the police station were left feeling befuddled most days, and many others were wearied by their attempts to keep pace with the inspector's latest undertaking. Whether it be routine task or perilous assignment, to each and everything, Halwill applied the same quality of precipitous endeavour. But Halwill was no fool. Apt to be clumsy at times, on account of the speed he attacked each problem, he was nevertheless one of the shrewdest detectives in south-west England, with a reputation for getting to the heart of matters and solving cases quickly. Devon and Cornwall had no finer man in that respect, and his colleagues in the service, whether of high or low rank, generally afforded him his little eccentricities, as a result.

"Time and tide wait for no man" was the trite expression

that passed his lips often – so often, in fact, that both friend and foe alike had ceased to remark on it any more. Halwill even spoke the sentence at lightning speed – in a hail of words, as if delivered from an American Gatling gun.

Constable Poundstock jumped to his feet as the distinguished inspector pitched into the hall. 'Sir, I am Constable Poundstock, at your service,' he saluted. 'I have made the arrangements for you to speak to the witnesses. They are here now and will do your bidding.'

'You've taken down statements?' the inspector asked sharply, with a face that appeared all bent out of shape.

'I have, sir. They are in my pocketbook.'

'Let me see.'

Without uttering another word, Inspector Halwill snatched the offered pocketbook from Constable Poundstock's outstretched hand and strode briskly, as was his wont, to a quiet corner of the hall, where a stockpile of old church furniture lay stacked neatly in rows, waiting for the next meeting of the parish council. Here, he pulled out a tattered folding chair, sat down and commenced to examine the notebook with a keen eye. As if by some hidden instinct, the two constables silently took up positions either side of the church door, for all the world as if they were preventing the rest from escaping. A full three minutes of impatient flicking through the pocketbook followed, while the others, with the exception of the constables, who remained resolutely stone-faced, gazed quizzically at one another in mild, almost amused, puzzlement. At length, the inspector gestured for Poundstock to approach.

'Are these notes contemporaneous?' he bristled.

'Yes, sir. I wrote down exactly what each of the witnesses told me in turn.'

'Then, pray *sign* the pocketbook as such, Constable! If the magistrate ever gets to see your book, he will take you to task if it remains unsigned… Very well.' Halwill moved swiftly to the next matter at hand. 'Bring Mr Henry Gough to me. The others may return to their lodgings. If I need them, I will call them accordingly.'

The twin constables did as instructed, and all but Henry were ushered from the hall. Henry called out to Hannah that he would like to meet her and Samuel at *The Gauger's Return* as soon as his business with the inspector had been concluded. As she nodded her heard acquiescence, he heard Constance let out a fit of giggles while they were being shepherded away; he presumed the outburst to be a product of some nervous exhaustion, for the day, until then, had certainly been no laughing matter.

'Mr Gough?'

Henry nodded.

'I am Inspector Halwill Barton, sir, Cornwall Constabulary. I have been sent to investigate. The local constable is concerned that foul play might be involved.'

'The parson's sudden death appeared most unexpected, for sure,' Henry replied.

'I have read all your statements. They concur. I am satisfied for the present, apart from the need to conduct a search of the immediate area. Further questions are pointless until the post-mortem examination.'

'Will there be one?'

'Most certainly. In light of the circumstances, I informed the coroner before I left Launceston. Surgeon Lesnewth has been instructed. He will be here in the morning.'

'I am pleased to hear it. Dr Plymswood seemed uncertain.'

'I will speak plainly, sir, because I know you are to be trusted. Plymswood is a drunkard. My past dealings with him have never been of any value. His diagnoses are mistaken more often than not.'

'You know *I* can be trusted? That is quite a claim!' Henry said with a careless laugh.

'I am a man who devours facts, Mr Gough. I have known the Snuggs family these many years. They are good people. As a clan of excisemen, our professional paths have crossed many times. When I heard from Samuel of your attendance at his wedding tomorrow, as father of the bride, no less, I made some enquiries. Samuel's slim intelligence concerning your reputation needed to be checked. Enquiries in my hands have a habit of producing facts, sir. I have contacts at Scotland Yard, and I used them. I now believe I have all I need to know about you, sir, and thus, I can say, with all confidence, that I trust you. Do I make myself clear?' Henry found the way Halwill made a compliment sound like a reprimand slightly unnerving. 'Indeed,' the inspector continued, 'I too was to attend Samuel's wedding tomorrow, so my arrival this afternoon has merely been brought forward by a few hours. Of course, the wedding cannot proceed now. There will have to be a postponement.'

Henry's head was suddenly filled with a host of questions. Which one to ask first? 'Postpone the wedding?' was the best he could offer.

'Naturally. Three reasons. The church may be the scene of a crime, the autopsy has to be concluded—'

'And there is no cleric to conduct the service.'

'Precisely. In fact, it may be weeks before the ceremony can be rearranged,' Halwill said in a matter-of-fact tone, appearing to take no umbrage at Henry's interjection. 'And now, Mr Gough, I seek your assistance. My constables are fine young men, no doubt, but greenhorns, all the same. Will you help me search the church? We need to be thorough, mind. The reports of your good character tell me you are the man for such a task.'

There was one question Henry had been aching to ask since all but he had been dismissed by the inspector. Now seemed the right moment to ask it. 'Why not involve Samuel Snuggs, Inspector? He is a senior revenue officer, after all, and is used to searching for contraband. You have spoken highly of him, yet you have dismissed him to his lodgings without a word and chosen a man you have never met to assist in your endeavours.'

'I do not search for bulky contraband but for tiny clues, sir. And in any event, Samuel has his bride to consider. She must be fair startled by events. And…' The inspector's voice faltered for the first time.

'And…?' Henry asked.

'And… his involvement in certain other matters of late may cloud the case if I involve him now.'

'You mean the false accusation of murder.'

'I do, sir. I may be known as "Hasty Halwill" in some quarters, Mr Gough, but my reputation for speed of action does not extend to making impulsive judgements. I like to keep all possibilities in mind. Do I make myself clear?'

The search was to take nearly two hours. After they had walked the short distance from the hall to the church, the verger was sent for. He must have been expecting the call, for just minutes later, a hunched man with a wooden leg hobbled into the vestibule.

'Penrose Polrunny is my name. I am verger here,' he announced with a surprisingly cheerful leer, considering his master's recent fate. 'I lost it down Wheal Beeney,' he told the assembly before anyone had time to ask. 'I was under 'undred ton of rock and ore for nigh on a week 'afore I was dragged out. Spitting blood, back then, I was! Must be ten-year ago, at least. Been a follower of the Lord since that day, for as sure as eggs is eggs, 'twas the Lord God Almighty what saved us.'

'Do you have keys for every room – the vestry and the like, Polrunny?' Halwill was looking restless.

'I do.'

'Then, pray lead my constables into every chamber. I will stay with this gentleman and conduct a search here in the nave. When we have concluded, we shall come to find you.'

'Very well, sir, if your officers would follow me, then. Look lively! This way, gentlemen.' And with a clutch of clanking keys in one hand and a crutch, wedged under his shoulder, in another, Verger Polrunny shambled off. Poundstock and the other officer followed in his wake.

'I propose we start at the point where Rosewarne fell,' Halwill barked as soon after the others had departed. 'Can you point it out to me? Then you take one side and I the other. When we have finished, we shall switch over and repeat the process. Is that clear?' The tone was insistent.

In this manner the search began. Henry was not really sure what he was looking for. There was a smudge of dried blood where the parson's head had struck the ground. Inspector Halwill scratched a sample from the flagstone and placed it into a clean 'kerchief. All else seemed to be in order, as far as Henry could see. The church looked neat and tidy, clean and ordered in every respect – just as it should be. The open font appeared unscathed, with just a hint of clear blue holy water at its base, oblivious as a carved rock to the part it had played in the poor parson's death. A line of oak shelves was examined. It was set against the whitewashed wall, lined with prayer and hymn books neatly stacked. A bouquet of dried flowers sat on a wide plinth close to the door, next to a more recent arrival – a vase of freshly picked spring blooms. The floor looked clean. The marble statues all about seemed to gaze at him with stony benevolence, as did the walls themselves, in their own flinty way. Nothing seemed out of place.

Nearby, there was a knotted wooden door that looked like it might lead to a passage and a bell tower beyond. It was on Henry's chosen side, and to his surprise, when he turned the handle, he found it unlocked. Indicating to Halwill that he was going to enter, he mounted the narrow circular staircase hewn from ancient stone and counted thirty-five steps before he reached the belfry. Here, he found a shuttered room and, in the centre, a solitary bell, daunting in its size, age and its absolute stillness. It hung with simple gravitas, attached to a single rope that descended through a cavity in the floorboards towards the nave beneath. The atmosphere here felt dank, somehow solemn, with an air of neglect and desolation, save for a scattering of old wooden chairs and a single rustic table that lay, apparently abandoned, directly under the giant bell. Henry spotted a hatch in the ceiling. Leading towards it was an iron ladder fixed to the wall. Grasping the rails, he climbed the few rungs and pushed the flap open. From here, he was able to climb out and escape from the belfry's bleak claustrophobia onto the parapet and into the cool zephyrs of clear evening air. A flagpole, as tall as three men combined, was located at one edge, fixed by metal braces, but on this day, there was no flag flying at its head.

The view from the parapet was stunning. The tide was out and the rock-strewn beach seemed almost within touching distance. Under the early evening sun, it appeared to stretch for miles. The distant horizon and surrounding hills could be observed curving away for a full 360 degrees. A whimsical thought entered Henry's head – that this would be an ideal place to spot the approach of men, horses, waggons, even boats. The perfect smuggler's lookout, in fact. Abstract images of cut-throat pirates swiftly followed, but then he concluded, with simple if rather dull logic, that the high ramparts were an equally fitting hiding place for the forces of the law too. The broad-booted buccaneers brandishing cutlasses were quickly replaced by the no less romantic vision of a ghostly huddle of revenue officers in faded uniforms playing Brag around a bottle-strewn table as they waited for the events of the night to unfold. He would like to have tarried longer and let his imagination take him further still, but then he remembered the urgency and precision of Halwill's instructions and he was persuaded otherwise.

'I have concluded my search, Mr Gough,' were the words that greeted Henry as he returned to the nave. 'We should swap over now. Was there much of interest in the tower?'

'Nothing I could see, save for a colossal bell and a glorious view of the sea and sky. Your trained eye might reveal more,' he added respectfully as Halwill passed him to ascend the narrow staircase.

Henry went about his business on the other side of the church but found nothing of any consequence. Fussing that he might have missed something the intrepid inspector had already detected, he went round once more, just to be certain. An accusation of carelessness would have been intolerable. As he waited for Halwill to emerge from the belfry, he wondered what was taking the man so long. Then he heard the sound of descending footsteps, and when Halwill reappeared, he was holding an empty bottle made from thick black glass which, by the look of it, must have once contained rum.

'I have nothing to report here, Inspector.'

'This may be of some consequence,' Halwill replied as he placed the rum bottle onto the plinth next to the vase of fresh flowers. 'It appears the belfry may have been used for activities other than bell-ringing—'

'That was my conclusion too,' Henry replied quickly. 'My guess is the tower was once a lookout. Back in the day, smuggling was rife in these parts, so I am led to believe.'

'And still is,' came the abrupt reply. 'And now, if you will excuse me, I have to complete my search.'

Henry watched from a polite distance as the policeman nosed around the shelves, wandered down the aisle all the way to the altar, and poked fingers into crevices in the wall opposite. He even mounted the pulpit and felt for papers – a task Henry had, embarrassingly, not considered. After a few minutes of detailed rummaging, and slightly to Henry's relief, Halwill reported that he could discover nothing untoward.

'Let us now find the others,' the inspector declared. 'The main object of our search awaits us beneath our feet.'

Henry thought a moment before responding. 'Do you mean the crypt and the owlers' tunnel that is supposed to lead to the sea?'

'You are well informed, Mr Gough – just as I expected.'

'The passage is supposed to be haunted, if local legend is to be believed.'

'Indeed, by the ghost of Abel Snuggs, no less.' The inspector looked grave.

'Do you hold to such claims, Inspector?' Henry asked respectfully. 'That the skull of the murdered exciseman can be seen floating in the ether on certain nights?' Henry tried not to sound dismissive and judgemental, but it was hard not to display his scepticism of such a tall story.

'In such matters, I believe only what I witness with my own eyes and nothing more,' Halwill said as they approached the vestry door.

Henry could not disguise his relief. 'Your proficiency as a policeman shines through, sir. These notions of phantoms and spectres are purely homegrown – invented years ago by local folk to discourage those who wished to thwart their business of smuggling. 'Twas but a pretence to hide their crimes.'

Henry's affirmation stopped Inspector Austol Halwill

Barton dead in his tracks. 'I'm sorry, Mr Gough, I fear you misunderstand me... You see, I *have* witnessed the spectral skull of which you speak. With my own eyes, I have seen it. 'Twas an experience I shall never forget.'

Chapter Seven

Henry Gough had been stunned into near speechlessness by the inspector's sober revelation that he had actually seen the phantom skull of Abel Snuggs. If there had been questions to ask before, now there were dozens more of them. Instead of asking them, he uttered some inconsequential mumble in response and tamely followed the policeman to the vestry door.

He had only met the outwardly severe Halwill Barton a few hours earlier. So far, he'd liked what he'd seen. Even the inspector's no-nonsense style smacked of competence, and it was quite possible that his feelings were reciprocated – Henry had been singled out to help the man, after all. In that moment, Henry imagined Halwill probably respected him, but he needed time to get to know this man better. He was nervous of making rash judgements that might come back to haunt him – possibly, quite literally! He knew nothing of the policeman's reputation as an impulsive but insightful detective, other than the single remark made by Halwill himself that others had once dubbed him "Hasty". Now was not the moment to ask awkward questions, but in his heart, Henry resolved he would have to ask them sooner or later. It was all about picking the right moment.

Upon entering the vestry, Gough and Halwill followed the sound of voices towards what appeared to be an open cellar door. Here, they lit candles and descended the dozen or so ragged steps into the chill and shadowy basement, which served as the crypt of St Piran's. The chamber was lit in part by the candles of Verger Polrunny and his twin custodians, who were still engaged in their exploration, and in part by a rounded skylight high on the upper west-facing wall. This aperture garnered the sun's now slanted rays from its position just above ground level in the outside churchyard. The crypt was fairly typical of its type and age. About a quarter the size of a modern lawn tennis court, its ceiling was supported by six low-slung pointed arches, each held up from the floor by stumpy stone pillars topped with capitals of plain design.

Embedded into the stone floor were rectangular gravestone slabs. Henry counted six ledger stones in all, plus three raised tombs topped with disintegrating effigies. Of these, there was a pair of thirteenth-century crusaders, complete with carved helmets, scarred chain mail and crumbling stone swords. The other prostrate sculpture was of a skeletal holy man – a cadaver monument, probably of a former bishop or abbot. Henry imagined the ledger stones must have marked the mortal remains of former parsons, perhaps the most notable and pre-eminent of the line of clergy who had once served the Lord in this place. There was a sense of rank amongst the stones. In all, there were nine memorials. This had Henry wondering which and how many of the previous vicars – there must have been many – had missed out on a resting place amongst the great and good of the hallowed crypt. He pondered if the Reverend Jerimiah Forrabury had made it to the top table and then quickly dismissed the thought as absurd…

It was a few minutes past six o'clock and the crypt was surprisingly light and airy, considering its underground state and the paucity of candles. Constable Marshgate spoke first. It was good to hear he possessed a vocabulary – of sorts.

'We 'ave located the burrow ye spoke of, sir,' he drawled in the respectful dialect of a farmhand speaking to a duke. ''Tis by the tomb yonder.'

'Show me.'

'It appears all bricked up, sir, as you said it would…'

The "burrow" Marshgate spoke of could be seen on the north-facing edge of the crypt, next to a yellowed stone tomb bearing the name and effigy of Oliver Pococke, with the dates 1713–1777 discernible. With light-accustomed eyes a difference in the nature and construction of the wall became quite noticeable. Where whitewashed stone had once been, there was a distinct patch of rust-coloured brickwork, which suggested the previous presence of a low rectangular door. Halwill's first impressions told him the brickwork was not ancient; it was of a type and size currently popular and still in use. The facade hinted towards a concealed entrance into another room, one which, by the look of it, had been recently bricked up.

'Well done, Marshgate,' Halwill said steadily, doing his best to look enthusiastic.

'It was Mr Polrunny who showed us, sir.'

Inspector Halwill Barton bent down and held a candle against the chipped lines of bricks. 'You are right, Constable. It looks like this entrance has been recently closed.'

Polrunny decided it was his turn to explain. 'The Revenue and their men were here nearly a week repairing the wall. 'Twas last year, just after we'd celebrated the Nativity of the Blessed Virgin Mary, as I recall. And they had a gang of men down on the beach piling rocks and sand up at t'other end.'

'Remind me, when is the Virgin Mary's feast day?' Halwill said quickly.

'Why, 'tis in early September, the eighth day, as I recall. The revenue men were all over us, poking here, poking there. Mr Snuggs can tell you all about it. It was a week after the body of Ignatius Honey was found murdered in the churchyard.'

'We know the story, sir. No need to hear it once more,' Halwill rasped.

'Indeed,' Polrunny persisted, ''twas a lot of excitement for folk back then, I can say.' The verger was clearly not going to be put off his stride. 'Between the village and the local farmers, there was much gossip about clifftop spectres being seen and ghostly spirits roaming abroad in the graveyard. Many testified they'd seen these unearthly things with their very own eyes... There was a lot of bad feeling, to be sure, and some who made wild accusations too – if you get my meaning—'

'Enough, Polrunny! We have heard enough!' Halwill's eyeballs bulged noticeably. Then, once quiet had been fully restored, he turned to Marshgate and resumed as follows, 'Now tell me, Constable, have you discovered anything else of interest or value during your search?'

'Nothing we could describe as "of value", sir – save this fresh blocked entrance!' The young policeman forced a chuckle in an attempt to return some lightness to proceedings.

'Did you search the vestry and the other rooms?'

'We did, sir.'

'Still nothing?'

'Nothing. But I would like to add that Mr Polrunny has been a most helpful and instructive guide, sir.'

'Excellent. I have seen enough,' Halwill said with an air of finality. 'Mr Polrunny, I am grateful for your assistance today. Pray tell me, how many sets of church keys do you possess?'

'I have one set, and the vicar holds the other. I mean, he used to...'

'Very well. I request you keep your keys close. I wish you

to lock the church for the next few days – until I tell you otherwise. Is that clear?'

'Yes, sir. And the wedding tomorrow?'

'Postponed,' the policeman replied flatly. 'We will speak to the rector. He will have to fix another date and another parson.'

'The rector is in Trevilla,' Polrunny advanced.

It was Henry who spoke next. 'Reverend Clarence Studley is the man in question, if I'm not mistaken.'

'Sir, you are correct!' Polrunny fairly blinked with surprise. 'Reverend Studley had been a good friend of the parson... for some time...' He paused and thought a while. 'He will be shocked to hear the news.'

'You say "had been... for some time", Polrunny. Is there any significance in that?' Halwill spoke with marked edge returning to his voice.

Polrunny became suddenly flustered and would have shifted the weight between his feet, had he been able. Instead, he just gripped his crutch and shrugged his shoulders.

'Speak, Polrunny. If there is something to tell, you must tell it.'

'Nothing of consequence, sir. I have been employed as verger here these last eight years, and in the beginning, Reverend Studley was a frequent visitor to this parish. He was a most popular speaker, too. He and the parson were once the best of friends... until lately... well, until about three years ago, when he stopped coming altogether. When I enquired of the parson whether the rector was suffering with his health, he was most displeased and told me not to mention his name again. Word has it that the two fell out.'

'Was any reason given?'

'None that I know firsthand. Some say 'twere to do with the farmers over at Doubloons – the Honeys – and the parson refusing to marry their Prudence.'

'Prudence?'

'Prudence is the youngest – a most lovely girl indeed…' he said with the look of a man fleetingly transported by his thoughts. 'She and her brothers had to go all the way to Trevilla for the service.'

'Trevilla – the rector's parish?'

'Yes, St Geraint's. The wedding was well attended, by all accounts, and by all around, despite the distance.'

Henry asked, 'Did *you* attend the wedding, Mr Polrunny?'

'Why, no. The parson forbade it. He said I'd forfeit my job if I did. What with my leg and all, I couldn't afford to cross him, so I stayed put. By the by, did I tell you about my leg, sir? How I lost it and all?'

'Thank you, Polrunny. You may leave us.' Halwill sucked his lip. 'Pray, leave your keys with me for the time being. We will lock the church when we leave. Constable Poundstock will return them to you within the hour.'

After they had returned to the nave and watched the verger limp away, Halwill turned to the others and said, 'We have an hour, gentlemen. An hour to find the parson's keys. Then, I wish to visit the Lych House and view the body in person.'

'I spotted some keys hanging in the vestry, sir,' Constable Marshgate proclaimed brightly. Inspector Austol Halwill Barton let out a heavy sigh but refrained from uttering a word.

In silence, all four made their way to the vestry and soon after, as described, a bunch of ancient iron keys, eight in number, was located on a hook behind the vestry door, just beside the parson's discarded hat.

'Constable Marshgate,' Halwill was clearly vexed, 'have you thoroughly searched the parson's desk and his cupboards?'

'The desk was locked, sir…'

Halwill struggled to contain his frustration. 'Would you try again, please?' he harrumphed while dangling the newfound chain provocatively in Marshgate's face. Henry Gough coughed lightly. Even the ancient portraits of former parsons that hung around the vestry walls seemed to add their disapproval.

After some embarrassed fumbling with a series of the smaller keys, Marshgate declared, with a face as long as shame itself, that he had managed to open both drawers to the desk and to a locked cupboard next to it.

'Very well,' Halwill said as if he were talking to a pair of seven-year-olds. 'I wish you both to go through every item you find and have them laid out for my inspection when we return. Mr Gough and I are going to the Lych House while the light holds.'

After a brisk march through the churchyard, a miserable grey slate-roofed building, befitting its calling, greeted them from under a giant yew. Henry remembered seeing the structure earlier that morning when he'd ventured out on his morning walk to Doubloons. He'd wondered then what its purpose might be. The memory of his hostile encounter with Gabriel Honey came flooding back to him – an unpleasant vision, indeed.

'Before we enter, Inspector, can you tell me what you know of the farmers hereabouts – the Honey family, in particular?'

'They are rogues of the first order – all of 'em,' was the instant and harsh repost.

The inspector was clearly not in the mood to say any more, but Henry was not to be deterred. He wanted more facts. 'One of them, Ignatius Honey, the man Polrunny spoke of, was murdered close to this spot only last year. Is that correct?'

'Ignatius got what he deserved. Now, if you will forgive me, Mr Gough, this is not the time to be discussing such matters. There is urgent and grim business that awaits us.'

With that, Halwill selected one of the larger keys from

the tarnished bunch and turned the ancient catch. The lock opened at the first attempt. As the door creaked ajar by degrees, the final shafts of twilight lit up the interior of the tiny, windowless morgue inch by golden inch. At that springtime hour, the angle of the evening light fed through the western-facing entrance and illuminated the chamber perfectly. Happily, therefore, the lighting of candles was not required. Along each side of the morgue lay recesses, four in all, each of which was empty – there being no others awaiting burial at that time. A simple oak cross stood on the unadorned altar at the eastern end. Reverend Rosewarne's ample frame lay in singular isolation on a raised platform right at the centre. The corpse was protected by a plain white shroud that draped over the body, its hems almost touching the cold stone floor. The head was facing west, towards the entrance, which was the custom for laying out members of the clergy. Gough and Halwill fell into a curious hush as they entered the tiny morgue. Creeping forwards, appearing almost on tiptoes, they approached the catafalque guardedly and with due reverence – in such a manner befitting those arriving in the quieted presence of the dead.

After a few seconds of gazing at the shroud that evidenced the upturned face of the deceased priest lying beneath its furrows and folds, it was Inspector Halwill who spoke first. 'Do you see that?' he whispered, pointing at the creases in the shroud around the head. 'Under the projection of the nose, where the mouth lies.'

Henry bent down and peered closely at the white fabric. 'Do you mean the black stain above or these yellowish marks lower down?' he replied in a stifled tone.

''Tis the stain of ochre...' was the simple reply. This was followed shortly after by, 'Let us see what has caused it. We must remove the cloth.'

Without any ceremony, Halwill reached forwards and swiftly drew back the shroud. Reverend Rosewarne's previously plump face, now drained of its natural colour and pinched around the cheekbones, looked unnaturally at peace. The once bright eyes were mercifully closed, but the sockets around the lids appeared deep-set, dark, almost hollow. There was an obvious gash, about two inches across, planted on the disfigured upper forehead. Marked by its congealed, desiccated blood, it presumably indicated the spot where the tumbling parson's head had clattered against the font. But it was not this that had attracted Halwill's immediate attention. Almost instantly, he pointed to the rather puffed lips of the dead man, and with a slightly raised voice and a pointed finger, he uttered, 'See, look there. The vicar has vomited. The yellow glue around his lips is evidence of it. There appears to be a mild rash around the mouth also.'

From his jacket's top pocket, Halwill quickly withdrew a white handkerchief. With a dexterous, gloved hand, he used it to remove a small sample of the dried drool from the vicar's mouth and then wrapped it carefully and placed it back in his jacket.

'Just enough for analysis, in case the evidence might be missed or lost by others...' he said in a distinctly wary tone. 'It's always best to be prepared for unforeseen events and to protect any evidence as soon as it is discovered. Now I want to see his hands.' Halwill instantly drew the shroud back towards the body's waist. He wasted no time before lifting each hand from their crossed positions over the parson's heart. These he put, one at a time, close to his face and examined them with care. 'You see here, on the right hand, the three centre fingers and palm are reddened slightly. There is a small but noticeable difference in shade from the rest of the skin. If I'm not mistaken, the fingers here look slightly swollen too. What do you make of it, Mr Gough?'

Henry screwed up his eyes and scrutinised the lifeless hand presented to him by Halwill's gloved embrace. 'You may be right, Inspector, but I am no judge of such matters. If there is a change in colour, it is but a small one and largely indecipherable to a common man such as I.'

Without any further ado, and with a swift and deft movement worthy of his nickname "Hasty", Halwill returned the shroud back into its original position, and the awful image of Rosewarne's lifeless cadaver was abolished in an instant.

'I will try my level best to hasten the inquest,' Halwill explained once the pair had returned into the comparative fresh air of the graveyard. 'It is my view the parson's death was not an accident, nor did he die from natural causes. An autopsy may reveal much… But until then, what of your movements, Mr Gough? Is it your intention to remain in Borwenstow, or do you have plans to return to London?'

'Unless you wish it otherwise, I will return. I have seen and heard things here I must report to the excise detectives in London. I have the honour to be one of their trusted agents.'

Halwill smiled. 'Indeed, I have heard as much. I understand that you are a confidant of Mr Albert Woodward, no less, the man at the head of their service.' The inspector's ability to surprise and confound set Henry back on his heels once more.

'You are well informed, sir. It is to Mr Woodward I shall report. He is most interested to learn if smuggling still continues in these parts. I shall tell him what I have seen in that regard. He will have little interest in the other matters here, which must be your duty to resolve. I'm sure you agree, Inspector, murder and smuggling are two very different crimes. And with my daughter's wedding postponed, I cannot dally here. I have a business to run, after all, and my wife and family will be anxious.'

'Maybe they are connected…' Halwill retorted.

Henry frowned.

On seeing this look of mild bewilderment, the policeman added, 'For clarity, I refer only to the murders and the smuggling. Perchance, they go hand in hand. Solve one and we solve both… What do you think?' Inspector Halwill tapped his chin. 'At any rate, I will let you know if I learn anything to assist your investigations, Mr Gough. Until then, I wish you Godspeed and a safe journey back to the smoke-filled streets of our wondrous capital city. A quiet word of advice before you depart… I rely on your discretion, sir, and would appreciate it if you could keep the matters we have witnessed and discussed today close.'

'You have my pledge on that, Inspector, but do I have your permission to discuss the details with Mr Woodward? I believe he will benefit from knowing the full story.'

'Of course – a most reliable man, I am told. You have my sanction on that score but, please, no idle tittle-tattle… For my part, I will be informing Chief Superintendent Grieve at Scotland Yard as soon as the results of the parson's autopsy are known. In any event, I suspect our paths will cross soon enough. After all, your daughter's wedding cannot be postponed indefinitely. I shall see you in next to no time – of that I feel quite certain.'

Chapter Eight

It was nearly dark by the time Henry pushed open the door of *The Gauger's Return*. He had been in the company of the police for a full three hours, and he wondered if Elizabeth and Samuel would still be waiting for him. To his great relief, he spied them almost as soon as he crossed the threshold. Together with Hannah and Constance, they were seated in soft, candlelit armchairs around the hearth, silently absorbed by the activities of one of the inn's boys. He was kneeling before them as he placed fresh wood on the open fire – the inevitable evening chill had begun to steal in under the doors, through the casements, and now drafted upwards by way of the gaping floorboards.

'Oh, Papa, you have been such a long time!' Elizabeth cried as she sprung up from her chair. 'We have been fretting all the while – Mama thought you must have been taken into custody.'

'No such luck, I'm afraid, Hannah.' Henry produced a wicked smile which he aimed directly at his long-suffering wife. 'As you can all see, I have returned unscathed, and I believe my dignity and reputation are still intact.' Hannah returned the speech with a tut-tut and a knowing grimace of her own, but it was clear she meant her husband no harm by it.

'Tell us, Papa, what news do you have? You must speak plainly to all of us.'

'Concerning the death of the parson, there is to be an inquest. The police wish to expedite matters for reasons of their own. In respect of the wedding, unfortunately this has to be postponed. There is no alternative. Reverend Studley, the rector at Trevilla, will be informed of events and asked to officiate as soon as the police have completed their formalities.'

'But when might that be?' Elizabeth looked particularly downcast.

'It may take some time – some weeks, perchance,' Henry replied. 'I have resolved to return to London until a new date is decided. I would be happy to accompany you, Hannah, if it is your wish to return also.'

'In anticipation of your news, Elizabeth and I have already discussed the matter, and it is my wish to remain here until a new date can be fixed. I will not be missed in Marylebone, such is the way of things, and the prospect of unending travel is irksome to me. Our daughter will ask her employers at Pennycrocker Hall if they can accommodate me for the duration. If they refuse, Constance has kindly offered a bed in her cottage.'

'Oh, Mama, I've told you – Sir William will be happy to offer you a place. The servants' quarters are plentiful, and he will probably never clap eyes on you. He may have the reputation of a firebrand, but I believe him to be a good man at heart. And if he grumbles, Lady Kathleen will soon turn him to our cause, for she is indeed a good woman, without exception. Why, Mama, you will be able to help me with my chores. We shall have such fun. 'Tis all for the good, to be sure.'

'Then that is settled.' Henry looked pleased with the outcome. 'I will send for the carriage to collect me tomorrow morning, in time for me to catch the afternoon train to Paddington. Perhaps we can dine together tonight. What do you say? I shall be the host. Can we agree eight thirty? I will speak to Mr Trewint directly. Are we all content?' The assembly murmured and nodded their agreement. 'Before I dress, may I have a word or two with you in private, Samuel? I'm sure the ladies won't object.' The ladies didn't hear the request or Henry's subsequent observation, such was the animation of the conversation they had already commenced amongst themselves.

Samuel, who had been remarkably reticent until then, replied in the affirmative. 'Would you like to come to my office, Mr Gough? 'Tis but a short walk from here. I would like to take some air, and a short stroll will do nicely. I have the keys; we shall be quite alone.'

With the ladies still chattering ten to the dozen, and after Trewint had agreed to lay a table, the two men took their leave; their departure was hardly noticed. The walk to the Custom House was indeed a short one – a matter of less than 150 yards, in fact. The building was tucked away along a narrow, cobbled passage full of tiny, whitewashed cottages that seemed to topple forwards into the street. Such was the restricted width between opposing neighbours, there seemed barely enough margin for a horse and cart to pass through.

'It's not ideal, in my opinion, Mr Gough,' Samuel said as he turned the key to the front door.

'Ideal?'

'I mean this apology for an office… It's nought but a pair of simple fishermen's cottages converted to its new purpose.' Samuel pushed the heavy wooden door open and entered first. 'There is stabling at the rear, which is a mercy, I suppose.' Once he'd lit a candle, lifted from a nearby table, he invited his guest to follow him in. At the moment Henry's feet became planted onto the hall floorboards, a violent gust of air caught the door, slamming it back into its frame with such a crash as must have been heard down the entire alley as far as the inn.

An omen, perhaps? thought Henry idly.

After securing the internal bolt, Samuel turned to face his future father-in-law once more. 'You see, 'tis too small by half, this place. The revenue commissioners closed down the old Custom House on the quayside nearly three years ago and sold it to the Pennycrockers. They have transformed it into a modern home – all plush hangings and silver platters, so I am told. The word is, there are walnut chairs and oriental rugs in every room. Servants are brought from the Hall when the house is occupied. The family use the place as a sort of refuge and "somewhere to escape the rigours of Pennycrocker Hall" – Elizabeth has told me as much. She's had cause to visit on the few occasions when the children are allowed, but Lady Kathleen prefers to use it as a creative retreat – she writes love poems, apparently – without the tiresome noise of chattering infants. Goodness knows the building is hardly in use these days, save for Her Ladyship's spontaneous breaks and some random comings and goings when the mood takes them.'

'I see. You must be downcast to see a historic public building used in such a fashion.'

'Precisely, sir. Now my staff, however paltry in number, and I have to squeeze in here. The Queen's Warehouse at the rear is much smaller than before too – barely enough room to store fifty kegs. The commissioners, in their wisdom, tell me "smuggling is not the problem it once was", and they wish to save on costs. But I believe different. It may be true for other parts of our country, but not here in Cornwall. Smuggling runs like blood through the veins of the folk in these parts. It's always been the preferred trade for as long as I can remember.

Like wrestling and hurling, the art of owling has been a Cornish pastime for centuries.'

'That may be the case, but do you seize much contraband these days?' Henry was not afraid to ask difficult questions from time to time.

Samuel Snuggs sighed. 'I grant you, our seizures have fallen; the Queen's Warehouse is most times empty – but the reasons for this are as clear as the Crystal Palace, to me. My situation is so much reduced now. I don't have the men to patrol the cliffs and coves satisfactorily, even for one night a week, let alone *every* night, as it should be.' Samuel wrung his hands as he spoke. 'The main problem is that folk won't speak of it – they won't take me into their confidence. I offer rewards and promises of protection, but nothing will draw them out – nothing! 'Twas ever thus, by all accounts, but now the shame of failure has become unbearable.'

'And what of the villagers? Are they hostile towards you?'

'In honesty, they are mostly respectful these days, but in a knowing kind of way. The men are inclined to chuckle lightly while doffing their caps, and the girls always give me shy but calculating smiles whenever I pass. Lord, I should be thankful, I suppose; gone are the days when the rank and file would want to kill a revenue officer as soon as look on him. But it grates, you see… I am a respectable officer from a long line of revenue men and I shudder to think what my ancestors would make of my lamentable performance. Each and all around here seem to have their separate, sly ways and hidden secrets. I just know if I had more staff to watch the coastline, I would have more success. I also wish the revenue cutter would pass by from time to time… or even take a berth on the quayside, just to show we still have a presence. To be feared in these parts is half the battle. But no, the crews have bigger fish to fry, by all accounts… The last time we saw the *Vigilant* must be a year since! Now, I hear talk that the commissioners have plans to close down even this pitiful place, such is their lack of enthusiasm for our work. It is their intention to move us all to the Custom House in Port Isaac!'

Henry quickly realised he needed to offer up some intelligent yet sympathetic analysis, just to stem the flow of accusations and complaints pouring out of his son-in-law-to-be. Samuel Snuggs was beginning to fulminate and this did not bode well for the future. Was he obsessed by his supposedly hopeless situation? Maybe he was just wedded to his work. Maybe he felt victimised. Perhaps Elizabeth held the key to his future sanity. Maybe Henry, on the contrary, should advise his daughter to steer clear of a man so utterly fixated by his condition. Henry decided if he was to unravel the set of conundrums set before him, he would need to start by asking some simple questions.

'How many staff do you retain here, Samuel? The property does indeed look cramped,' he advanced with a benevolent smile.

'Three officers, one of whom is a drunkard, and a single clerk – that's all they give me. But if I get wind of an imminent event, they will dispatch others to help. I can usually muster half a dozen or so if there is a shout on.'

'And the Honeys? Do you believe them to be still involved in the trade?'

'They are without doubt the vilest blackguards in all Christendom!' Samuel Snuggs exclaimed. Henry was immediately reminded of a similar utterance made just hours before by Inspector Halwill – clearly the Honey clan had an ugly reputation, certainly universal amongst the law-enforcement fraternity.

Samuel continued, 'The skirmish last September proved it to me.' The lines on his face appeared to become even deeper under the soft candlelight. 'The ruffians broke down the tunnel into the St Piran's crypt and brought in contraband while my back was turned. I should have known better. I thought for once I'd received intelligence I could trust, and it had me and my men scurrying over the clifftops at Pentargon. 'Twas nearly two miles from here. It's clear we were sent to watch the wrong cove. Since then, I've searched everywhere for the consignment but with no luck. All I have gained is more enemies than before, if that were possible. Many believe I overplayed my hand by conducting the searches. Rummaging private property with a writ of assistance has always brought howls of anger from those who must suffer it. You should have heard the depraved abuse I received from Cassius Honey at Doubloons Farm! But I had to find the goods.'

'What goods did you suspect had been smuggled?'

Samuel Snuggs shook his head. 'I had no leads then, nor do I have any now. That is the problem. Brandy and tobacco, most likely; rum from the West Indies, perhaps; lace from Ireland... To be honest, I have no idea. The only thing I am certain of is the goods have been all got away.'

'Why are you so sure that contraband came in that night?' Henry ventured, still doing his best to sound fatherly.

'Why else would the old tunnel into the crypt be crashed through, if not for smuggling?' Samuel cried. 'Answer me that, if you can. I'd thought that route to be a thing of the past. The passage had been blocked up for nearly all my lifetime. It took my men, and others drawn in from Bude, nearly a week to jam the shaft once more. We've obstructed the seaward entrance too. It will take a mighty effort to reopen it in future!'

'And what of the presence of Ignatius in the churchyard the very same night? Was that a coincidence?' Henry was sounding distinctly conspiratorial.

'Precisely, Mr Gough! You have it! That fact alone speaks

directly to the Honeys. But I have a theory in that regard. My guess is Cassius or Gabriel, or in unison, most likely, killed their own brother! A squabble over money, perhaps – or the share of booty. They left his headless body all cut up to incriminate me. They will go to any lengths, that family.'

'Do you have a stratagem to capture them?'

'In short, I do not… but I will never lower myself to seek revenge in any *criminal* way. I have law and order on my side. I have a Crown commission in my pocket, and I intend to use only my official powers and to play by the rules laid down to me in order to bring them to heel. And, by God, I will, if it's the last thing I do.'

'Would it be impertinent for me to ask who was your informant? I have experience of such delicate matters. You have my word that your reply – if you choose to give it – will go no further.'

The creased valleys on Samuel's brow suddenly appeared even deeper than before. The candle flickered, and his hand seemed to waver. There was no doubting it, Henry was witnessing a visible change wash over the officer of revenue, both in his demeanour and countenance.

'I feared you might ask… If you must know,' Samuel paused as he took in a gulp of air, 'it was your eldest child, Elizabeth, no less. She told me of the Honeys' plans that night. One of the staff at Pennycrocker Hall had wanted to get news to me without alerting the suspicion of others. Elizabeth was brought into confidence purely because of her association with me and the desire of the informer to pass on the intelligence. Because of my love for Elizabeth, my eyes were blinded to the trap being set. I wanted to impress her so much – to rein in the Honey family once and for all. This was my chance to become a hero in her eyes. But, alas, look at me now… Distracted from my true purpose, I have allowed the Honeys to deceive me, and to their eternal shame, they then accused me of killing their brother, no less. Great Scott! How mad I was when I heard I had to present myself before the magistrate to answer those trumped-up charges!'

Henry decided he'd heard enough. It was time to ask the questions he'd planned to put all along. He wanted his own answers. It was time to be blunt.

'Mr Snuggs… are you innocent of all these allegations?'

Samuel glared back in utter disbelief. At length, his reply was tremulous, to say the least. 'Why do you question me thus? Of course I am innocent!'

'A father has to ask such questions. Do you swear by it?' Henry looked his future son-in-law directly in the eye.

'By all that is holy, I swear on my life!' Samuel's voice was stronger now – clearer and more compelling. 'I had nothing to do with the murder of Ignatius… or any other crime, for that matter, in case you choose to ask.'

Henry glowered into Samuel's face for a full five seconds. Satisfied by what he saw, he put out his hand in a gesture of compliance. 'Very well. That is what I wanted to hear from your own lips. I believe you, Samuel. Here, let's shake on it. You must understand I had to know. Your emphatic declaration of innocence brings me to the reason I wished to talk with you tonight.'

Samuel stared back in quivering silence for a number of seconds. With tear-filled eyes he gradually, almost reluctantly, offered up his hand to complete the handshake. 'Very well, sir. A father has the right to know his future son better. You may ask me what you will. I presume you want my repeated avowal that I love Elizabeth… To save your further probing, I can tell you, not only do I love her, but I worship her with all my heart and will honour and protect her for all my life.'

'That is not in any doubt now, Samuel, but I am grateful

for your assurances, all the same. To be candid, my reasons for wanting to speak to you in private were to ask if you would bring me into your full confidence and accept my help. You desire to bring this gang of smugglers down – so do I. Together, we might achieve it. If we can disentangle the riddle of smuggling and get to the culprits, my guess is the rest will follow in short order. We shall solve the murders and the fantastical fables of wandering phantoms that have plagued Borwenstow for many generations. I believe the police inspector is of the same mind – the two go hand in hand. What do you say? Will you confide in me and tell me all you know so that we can work as a band of brothers?'

'You wish to help me?'

'I do. Allow me to lay matters out as plainly as I can. You have a problem you cannot alone resolve. I have powerful excise friends in London who would like to know more of your situation. If you agree, I believe I can persuade them to support our cause. If you want this matter ended, this may be your only chance. I pledge to be as true a friend and colleague as you will find in the whole kingdom. Will you let me in, Samuel?'

Samuel Snuggs's waterlogged eyes blinked three times before he replied, 'I will, Mr Gough. I will indeed.'

Chapter Nine

The following morning, Henry rose early and decided to take another walk along the cliff path. He wanted some exercise before his departure, and the idea came to him that gazing upon the area of cliffs Samuel had spoken of the previous evening, around Pentargon Cove, might be a worthy expedition.

The night before, he'd enjoyed a quieter than normal supper with his family and future relations, making sure to avoid any further consequential talk with Samuel. The ladies seemed a little off colour, which made for a rather sombre occasion, and all were in their beds by ten o'clock. Before dinner, he'd sent word via the innkeeper for the trap to meet him at *The Gauger's Return* at noon the following day. Isaac Trewint had seemed jollier than normal. Perhaps it was the news that his inquisitive London guest was about to depart that had cheered him.

'Joshua will be 'ere on time, sir. He is a reliable man, during the day, at least.'

As Henry settled his account, he asked, 'Tell me, Mr Trewint, why is that? Joshua told me himself he doesn't like being in Borwenstow after sunset. Do you know the reason for it?'

At a stroke, all the newfound jauntiness seemed to drain from the innkeeper's countenance and his squeezing tones seemed to raise another octave. 'Must be the legend that makes 'im afeared, sir… Some folk here swear by it.'

'And you, Mr Trewint? Do you believe the story of the spectre?'

'Which one, sir? There are two spectres, if truth be known.' Trewint stretched his gaunt neck, curiously reminding Henry of a turtle.

'I was thinking of the revenue officer, Abel… err—'

'Snuggs, sir,' Isaac Trewint completed the sentence in a flash. 'Yes, that's one of 'em, and t'other is the old parson what killed his-self.'

'And do you hold any store by them?'

'There's much in this mortal world which is not clear to us, sir.'

'So, you think there are ghosts abroad, here in Borwenstow?'

Isaac Trewint looked askance, and after sucking his teeth in a most disagreeable manner, he replied with a question of his own. 'Will ye be returning to Borwenstow, sir? I can keep a room for ye if you like…'

Henry decided not to press any further. Clearly, there was nothing to be gained by badgering the man. 'Thank you, Mr Trewint. You have been both a generous and kind host. I would be delighted to rest here again. You will learn of the new wedding day soon enough, I'm sure. Perhaps you can reserve the same room for me two days in advance of the slated ceremony. My plan is to return in good time to see my daughter married.'

'Very well, sir. I shall see to it.'

It was a quarter past seven o'clock when Henry stepped through the hall to commence his exercise. There was no sign of the innkeeper of the previous evening, or anyone else, for that matter. It was as if he had the place entirely to himself. Much the same could be said of the first hour of his walk; there was not a soul in sight. In order to reach Pentargon Beach, Henry had to pass by Doubloons. He made sure to observe and note what he could while striding boldly and adopting a deliberate air of self-confidence as he cut by the farmhouse. He took extra care not to transgress as before, but as far as he could ascertain, there was nothing stirring on the land or within the buildings – no sounds of life at all – even the cattle must have been sleeping or otherwise hidden from view. The remainder of his hike to the cove required some energy – more, in fact, than Henry had bargained for. The cliff path was acutely steep, in parts, and descended and climbed again as each new inlet was encountered. Henry dropped down and scrambled up the sides of three boulder-strewn coves before he reached Pentargon. On each occasion, his feet almost touched the level of the beach before being forced to grind their way back upwards again to reconquer the clifftops once more. The whole process took him over an hour from the time he'd left the inn. The term "Cornish mile" suddenly came to him, and despite his exertions, he grinned to himself. He realised the old adage had proper weight, one borne, perhaps, from ancient experiences of clambering between apparently nearby outcrops.

When Henry eventually stumbled into the little bay – Samuel had helpfully marked its position on a map the night before – he wondered if the trek had been worth all the effort. Each cove looked much the same! But on regaining his breath, and with closer inspection, he realised that Pentargon's beach was a little broader and less rocky than the others he had traversed. He assumed these features might make the place more suitable, perhaps, to bring shallow boats ashore in the dark. And the path into the cove was less precipitous than the others – maybe another reason why Pentargon Cove would have made good sense as a place to carry out business – for both smuggler and revenue officer alike.

As he pointed to face the upward path, Henry took one last look at the heaving sea as it crashed white foam onto the rocks around the northern margins of the cove. He wondered at the daring of the men who brought goods ashore in such conditions – and behind the shield of darkness, too. The owler's famous dislike of the moon must have severely hindered navigation. Even in broad daylight the risks were obvious.

It was time to head home; he had an assignation with timid Joshua in just a few hours. As Henry steeled himself for the stomp back up the track, the first human form he'd seen all morning appeared high on the clifftop above him. To be accurate, the vision was both human and animal, as the shape against the leaden sky was a figure seated on horseback. As he squinted further, the image appeared to be engaged in the rather lonely occupation of gazing northwards and far out beyond the tossing ocean, towards the line of dark water that marked the distant horizon. There was nothing for it... Henry would have to pass that way to return to Borwenstow, so he resolved to start his ascent forthwith, knowing that an encounter would be inevitable, unless the individual moved from the spot. Soon the distance between them had shortened to less than a hundred yards. Each time Henry took his eyes from the path ahead to peer upwards at the skyline, the motionless character on horseback had drawn closer by a few further yards. He could see it was a man now – a man of considerable stature – his back upright, riding boots firmly planted in the stirrups. The fellow seemed to be completely unaware of Henry's approach, still fixated was he by his unwavering study of the sea.

'Good day, sir!' Henry said cheerfully while touching his hat. 'This is indeed a fine morning for a stroll.'

As soon as the sentinel spun his horse to face him, Henry distinguished who it must be, and with recognition came a brief but shuddering pang of anxiety. Henry knew his horses, and the animal before him was one he'd seen before. The sheer size of the animal, plus its unique snake-shaped blaze, marked the horse as the same he'd seen Gabriel Honey astride just days before. If he was not mistaken, the hulk of a man who now turned to speak to him was none other than his brother – Cassius.

'Good morning, Mr Gough! It is Mr Henry Gough, if I'm not mistaken…' Another shaft bore down Henry's spine – how did this fellow know of him? 'I am most pleased to make your acquaintance, at last,' the man smiled.

Leaning forwards amiably from the saddle, the rider extended a leather-clad hand to shake Henry's own. 'Allow me to introduce myself. I am Cassius Honey, the master of Doubloons, the farm you have just bypassed on your way to this remote corner of our coastline.'

Henry took the offered hand, gripped it firmly and nodded in gracious recognition, while noting the surprisingly educated manners of his new interlocutor and the unusual, and rather proprietorial, use of the word "our" when referring to the coast thereabouts.

The character who loomed above him was indeed a substantial human being. Though seated on horseback, his standing size was not difficult to imagine. Henry, who was normally a good judge of such matters, estimated Cassius to be about forty years of age and at least six and a half feet tall – a man who looked to have been created in perfect proportion. Powerful looking in every respect – from his biceps to his calves, his bull neck to his broad chest – all the dimensions appeared to be in impeccable symmetry. The head was the perfect size for the body, the face high-boned, well chiselled and striking. The prominent Roman nose at its centre was entirely fitting and gave its owner the natural look of a patrician. The eyes, like beads of blue light, flashed from high-browed sockets. Above the square chin were lips full and conspicuous. Cassius Honey was a fine-looking fellow – of that there was little doubt. In his mind's eye, Henry had fashioned an imaginary vision of Cassius Honey based on the many ugly reports he'd received of his wayward conduct and bad character. Henry had half expected the man to have but a single eye, a wasteland of sun-scarred skin, an army of blackened teeth and a chin plentifully covered in half-shaved stubble – in short, the veritable spawn of his ancestor "Jake the Heartless". But Henry's imagination had clearly been an unreliable informant, for here before him appeared a man of polish and style. A giant amongst men, perhaps, but nevertheless an accomplished individual who took great care of his personal appearance. Without doubt, Cassius Honey had the facade of an authentic gentleman.

'I'm pleased to meet you, sir,' Henry replied. 'As a matter of fact, I had the good fortune to speak to your brother, Gabriel, just a few days ago. He pointed out the perimeters of your land in these parts. His message to me was plainly delivered, but welcome all the same, for I am not one who wishes to trespass on another man's property. I am a law-abiding soul – or, at least, I like to think as much.'

'Ah-ha, Mr Gough, think nothing of it. And, please, accept my apologies if Gabriel was rather plain-spoken in his conversation with you. He has a tendency to be rather hot-headed and overprotective of our family and our rights, at times. You may have already heard folk speak of us and, my guess is, not kindly, either. Such is our reputation, which I regret most deeply. It seems the unending legacy of those who hold the name of Honey, in these parts, is to shoulder the sins of their forebears.'

Henry was once more struck by the man's eloquence. Again, this was not what he had expected at all. Gabriel had delivered his remarks in short, rough sentences. This bear of a man, contrariwise, had the manner of a prosperous farmer – and a cultivated one, into the bargain.

'Thank you, sir, I am obliged for your clarification. Think nothing of it. Your brother was, no doubt, doing his best to impart a difficult message – which, in truth, he did most marvellously!' Henry let out a forced chuckle, which had the desired effect, for Cassius beamed back with a most friendly, open expression and a full set of perfect teeth.

'I hope you enjoy the remainder of your stay in our humble parish, sir,' Cassius exclaimed from high on his stallion. The combination of huge animal and tall man continued to make a most imposing sight – not an image for the fainthearted. 'I understand it's your intention to return to London at noon. If that be the case, I wish you a good journey, although I confess it is not a prospect I would contemplate with a happy heart. I cannot abide the city. I went to Bristol once and the place nearly did for me. I'm a countryman at heart and always will be.'

'Farewell, sir, and I thank you for your good wishes.' Then, after a short pause, Henry added, 'I plan to return to Borwenstow as soon as my daughter's new wedding day has been announced.' He wanted to test exactly how much Cassius Honey already knew of his business and intentions in Borwenstow. It was clear the fellow's intelligence was unnervingly accurate – but what was the full extent of his knowledge? Henry hoped his open revelation that he would be returning soon might provoke a reaction of sorts. This, indeed, it did… but when Cassius's almost instantaneous reply came back to him, Henry was not, on any account, prepared for it.

'Excellent, Mr Gough. Then I look forward to seeing you towards the end of the month. I'm told the wedding has been fixed for the twenty-first of May – another Saturday, as I understand it. Good luck, sir, and now I must away. I have important business to conclude with the owner of the nearby estate!' And with that, Cassius Honey reared his horse, pointed its head southwards and galloped away across a wide grassy field. He was gone in a flash. In the distance, the stone tower of St Julitta, which marked the village of St Juliot, beckoned.

Had Henry noticed a trace of derision in Cassius's otherwise affable farewell? Perhaps there had been even the hint of contempt... Or had he imagined it because he'd half expected to find it? The brief encounter certainly left him with food for thought. If it were needed, this was yet another illustration that not everything in Borwenstow was quite as it seemed. A sensation of unease crept back inside of him. He would have to think it through later; but for now, he had a train to catch.

* * *

By the time Henry got back to *The Gauger's Return*, Molly, the comely kitchen maid, was tidying the tables after breakfast. Noting his late arrival, she rebuked him with an amiable scowl before fetching him a mug of hot, milky tea and two chunks of bread. A boiled egg and a fillet of locally smoked fish swiftly followed, for which he was especially grateful, considering all his morning exertions.

'Ah, Papa, there you are!' a voice called to him. Henry looked up to see Elizabeth, fully dressed for the road, with a valise at her side. 'We missed you at breakfast. Have you been exploring?'

'I took a walk along the cliffs towards Pentargon.'

Elizabeth seemed not to hear him. She looked preoccupied and slightly befuddled. 'I have to leave, Papa. I must return to the Hall. Her Ladyship has sent word; I must resume my duties before midday. She heard the wedding has been postponed and wishes me back as soon as possible. I am in a rush now. Mr Trewint is finding me a carriage.'

'Where are the others?'

'Samuel and Constance returned home immediately after breakfast – Samuel will be locked into the Custom House by now, I expect. Mama is upstairs. She will remain here until I get word to her that she may reside at the Hall until the new date is set. By all that is good, I hope that is soon.'

'Have you not heard?'

'Heard, Papa?'

'I encountered Cassius Honey while walking. He told me all is fixed for the twenty-first of May, which is just two weeks hence. I assume Rector Studley at Trevilla must have given his consent.'

'You spoke with Cassius Honey? How could you, Father? The man is an unbridled rogue – worse, in fact.'

'Hush, Daughter. Despite his reputation, I found him to be a most amiable fellow. He spoke plainly and with degrees of wit and charm.'

'Oh, Father, I fear you have been taken in by him. Even Lady Pennycrocker speaks to me of his wicked ways. His monstrous reputation is known to all gentlefolk in these parts. As for the rest… why, they know 'tis best to keep their own counsel, rather than suffer the man's wrath.'

'And the wedding?'

'I've heard nothing, Papa. But I am not surprised to hear it has been fixed – the way things occur in this parish is confusing to me at the best of times. If Cassius Honey says it, then the twenty-first it must be. I will make further enquiries, but I hope Lady Pennycrocker will look favourably on the new arrangements. Now, if you will allow it, Papa, I must start my journey. Rain is forecast and the roads can become difficult.'

Henry embraced his daughter and murmured gently in her ear. 'May we speak just a little further?' Gently taking her by the arm, he led Elizabeth into a quieter, more private part of the dining salon, away from the stairs and the entrance to the kitchen. 'Before you depart, my dear,' Henry advanced in a hoarse whisper, 'I spoke with Samuel last night, man to man, so to speak, and he told me you had supplied some information to him concerning some recent smuggling activity at Pentargon Cove. 'Twas around the time of Ignatius's killing.'

'Yes, 'tis true,' Elizabeth muttered almost inaudibly in return. 'I regret it now, but I was merely passing on a message I had received. I thought it might help poor Samuel. He is so much in the dumps, at times. The activities of the damned Honey family seem to preoccupy all his waking moments.'

'The information you gave turned out to be false...'

'Yes, and I am deeply shamed by it!' In speaking these words, her frustration seemed to mount and her voice rose for a second. Then, on hearing a scuffling noise from the pantry, she returned to her previous low tones. 'Samuel told me he'd been up all the night looking in the wrong place,' she whispered. ''Twas fortunate in one respect, mind. When the magistrate asked for his testimony, he had witnesses to say he'd been nearly two miles away when Ignatius was murdered.'

'Who gave you the message, Elizabeth? It's important I know.'

'Why, 'twas Lady Pennycrocker herself. She said she'd heard it from one of the other servants, who was too afraid to share it with the Excise. Knowing my association with Samuel, she wanted me to pass it on.'

'Did she tell you who had given her the information?'

'No, Papa, and I didn't ask. It would not have been proper for a governess to ask such a question of her employer. No, Her Ladyship told me in good faith, and I promised I would share it with Samuel. When Samuel asked me the same question, wanting to know the "identity of my source", as he quaintly put it, I didn't tell 'twas Her Ladyship who'd spoken to me. I merely informed Samuel I'd heard directly from one of the servants, and even when pressed, I refused to name the person. I had no idea anyway, and I didn't want to complicate matters. I hate gossip at the best of times. I know it was a minor falsehood, but I passed on the information, and that was enough for me. Goodness only knows, I wish I had never become involved.'

'You did right, my daughter. Be not afeared that what you did was wrong. And now, I have a request to make of you. A most personal request, which I hope you will look kindly on…'

'Speak, Papa. I will do anything.'

'But you must tell no one. Not Mama, not even Samuel. Do you agree?'

Elizabeth withdrew her arm from her father's gentle grip and stepped back further into the shadows. 'You are scaring me, Papa… what do you want of me?'

'I just ask that you pay attention to what you see and hear while at Pennycrocker Hall these next few weeks. Someone there must know something of the smuggling in these parts – the very fact you were approached, albeit by a go-between in the form of Lady Pennycrocker, speaks to it plainly. Keep your ears and eyes open. I must tell you I have agreed to help Samuel get to the bottom of the affair, and your help will be of the utmost value to us. There should be no risk – just listen, watch and remember. Take notes, if you wish, but hold them safe. I will return well before your wedding day. Keep any facts you learn to yourself and only divulge them to *me* when we meet again.'

'And Samuel?'

'For the time being, I wish you to tell Samuel nothing of this. I will bring him into the fold when the time is right.'

'Very well, I will do as you say.' She kissed him on the forehead with a tenderness Henry had not expected. 'I am so glad you are here with us, Papa. You must know, I bear you no grudge for what you did. I admit, I wish it hadn't been so, but I know a little about love these days – and how it is capable of warping the very essence of us hapless humans. They say love will conquer all. Let's hope they are right, for both our sakes.'

Chapter Ten

The journey to London was not without incident. Joshua was waiting for Henry before the appointed hour, and they set off together a full fifteen minutes ahead of programme. Unsurprisingly, given his well-flagged reticence to be in Borwenstow any longer than absolutely necessary, Joshua was keen to get moving, even if it *was* the middle of the day. The weather was closing in, apparently.

'The skies will open soon, sir, and the clouds tell me it will be fair streaming in a few hours. Best we get moving afore it arrives.'

Driving briskly, they encountered very little rain, in fact, just some light drizzle as they clipped past the edges of the moor. They spoke hardly at all until Joshua pulled the trap to a halt at the Hallworthy crossroads, where they took refreshments. Henry purchased eggs and milk, as before, and in addition, he bought a small, crusted loaf, still warm from the oven. These provisions he shared with his driver, who seemed most grateful for the gesture. As he and Joshua tore into the bread, Henry took the opportunity to probe his companion further. Joshua's knowledge of the local residents and any recent happenings was of particular interest to him.

Henry reasoned, as he now knew some of the main players and had visited a few of the nearby places, he could be more objective in his questioning – more incisive, more to the point, so to speak. He decided the way to draw his man out would be to share some sensational information with him *before* asking for any in return.

'I take it you heard the parson collapsed dead in the church, my man? It was quite shocking to witness. It occurred before my very eyes. He dropped like a stone, don't you know. 'Twas indeed a dreadful sight!'

'I 'eard it so,' came the gruff reply.

'And what do you make of it?'

'Make of it? The parson is dead, ain't 'ee?... That's all I need to know.'

'Do you wish to learn more of what happened? The police were called. Came all the way from Launceston...' Henry offered, unable to disguise a certain eagerness in the telling.

'That, sir, I do not. I wish to 'ear nuthin. The place is cursed – that be the long and short of it. 'Tis enough for me.'

'But *why* is it cursed, Joshua? Have you ever thought on it? What have you heard that makes the place so afflicted?'

'I know nuthin and I speaks nuthin to no one. I keeps meself to meself on the matter – as I do for all matters, sir. 'Tis better not to fret about things what's weird to me for which I have neither the force nor the wit to shape... And now, sir, I think we'd best be off. The rain is sure coming, and I don't want you to miss your train.'

An image of Reverend Clarence Studley surrounded by butterfly nets suddenly came into Henry's mind. He recalled the rector, when pressed for his opinion on the Borwenstow hauntings, had replied in a similar vein, if in a rather different vernacular. "I have no opinion; I *wish* to have no opinion" had been the clergyman's initial response. Isaac Trewint had been equally unforthcoming. Clearly, the desire to disassociate from the legend – to distance oneself from the goings-on, to refrain from interfering – had common ground across all the classes. The idea made Henry smile to himself. There was some unity in this, at least, he mused.

The threat of rain proved to be erroneous, and nothing of note passed between driver and passenger for the remainder of the journey. Not a single word was exchanged on the patently thorny subjects of weather forecasting or the unhappy struggles of Borwenstow folk. At a quarter past three, the trap trundled into Launceston Railway Station twenty minutes ahead of time. Henry bade his long-suffering driver farewell with a generous tip and advised him he would be returning in a few weeks.

'I hope you'll be available to carry me back to Borwenstow the next time I arrive, Joshua,' he advanced with a friendly grin. In return, his driver looked at his shoes, grunted something indecipherable and touched his cap with a grubby forefinger.

Alas, the *Kernow Queen* was not so punctual, arriving a full hour late from Plymouth. The stationmaster said it was something to do with a "snapped water connector". As a result, the train's return journey was delayed by nearly forty-five minutes. Although Henry was keen to get back to London and tell his story, he was beginning to feel weary with all the exertions and intrigue of the day, and the idea of the long forward passage was having less and less appeal. He found the prospect of arriving home well after midnight particularly disagreeable. So when, on arrival in Plymouth, he received the almost inevitable news he'd missed his onward connection to Paddington, it came almost as a relief. His mood actually brightened as he resolved instead to enjoy a tranquil dinner and a glass of whisky alone. He would use the quiet time to enrich the scribbled notes of his recent encounters, while resting a night in the *Railway Inn* on the nearby Embankment Road. He undertook to be up early, and fully refreshed, he would catch the first train the following morning. With luck, he'd be home to surprise Caroline at lunchtime.

* * *

London, when it arrived, looked exactly as he'd left it. It even smelled the same. As he stepped out of the hansom to confront his rooms above the yard in Bolton Street, an unusual and sudden gust of wind blasted through the mews. It fair lifted the rim of his bowler, which Henry was forced to seize mid-air to prevent it flying into Regent's Park. Holding on to his hat, he braved the squall and mounted the familiar scratched steps towards his front door. As he reached the top, the thought came to him he'd been away only a matter of a few days. It felt like a small lifetime, such had been the intensity of his interlude in the countryside.

To his great disappointment, Caroline was not at home. He presumed she'd taken the children to see their grandmother, so he cut some bread and made a pot of Assam tea. Lighting a freshly-filled pipe, he settled down with *Great Expectations* and waited. It was not until the mid-afternoon that he heard the turn of the latch, and soon the place was full of noise and infants running hither and thither, all thrilled to see their father back in his favourite armchair. Despite the chaos of children, Caroline was looking particularly enchanting. The breeze had evidently battered her hair during the afternoon excursion, giving it and her a rather tousled, even wild, appearance. But her natural loveliness seemed to shine through all the more. Henry reflected that whatever the weather, however many new challenges she had to handle, and during their times of mutual anxiety, she always found a way to remain herself – Caroline –

quietly composed and utterly beautiful. She was, in all respects, a woman beyond compare. How much he loved her.

While sitting alone, Henry's mind's eye had anticipated the joyous moment when she would rush to him as soon as she looked upon him and then enfold her soft arms around his waist. So, when her first words of welcome came as she pinned back her hair and jostled with the children, he found it difficult not to mask his feelings of mild rejection.

'I didn't expect you until Tuesday!' was her opening remark, rather bluntly delivered. Clearly, Caroline had lost none of her directness during the days he'd been away, and if truth be known, he adored her all the more for it.

'My love! Is that a proper welcome for a man who has hurried back early to be at your side?' he chided with an allusive smile. Caroline dipped her head and wrinkled her nose. One of her special all-embracing sunbeams soon followed.

'Oh, Henry, don't tease me so. I was just surprised to see you, that's all... Now tell me all your news. Did Elizabeth look radiant on her wedding day? How was your wife? As delighted to see you as I am now, I expect!' she giggled deliciously.

As Henry commenced to tell her the story of his adventures, Caroline's eyes widened in visible amazement. She was not distracted in the slightest by the jiggling of their youngest son, who fidgeted playfully around her ankles. Instead, she listened in evident wonderment to the unfolding tale. George, on the other hand, seeing his mama so preoccupied, became jealous of the attention she was giving to the interloper, notwithstanding this being his very own father. He made a lunge to clamber onto his mother's lap and seek her unbridled attention. This was too much to bear. Caroline shooed him away with a commanding yet gentle swish of her hand.

'Please, George, go play with Walter this instant. Do not bother your papa. We have important events to discuss.'

The boy did as he was told, and with a sullen look directed only at his father, he toddled off towards the bedroom. When Henry had concluded his narrative, which took a full ten minutes to recount, Caroline seemed genuinely dumbstruck.

'What now?' she asked at length. 'You must return for the wedding. The expense will be great, but you have given your word.'

'I can do no less, Carrie. Elizabeth needs me now more than ever – and so, in truth, does her husband-to-be. I fear Samuel is in a pretty fix. But before I intervene, I mean to speak with Mr Woodward. Albert is certain to have things to say on the matter. With luck, my news will encourage him to dip his hands into the Queen's purse once more, to assist my costs. I believe I've discovered much of consequence to him, and if I know the man at all, I expect he'll ask me to revisit the scene – and offer to pay for it, too. Until then, I plan to rest and reacquaint myself with my own loving sweetheart. I have brought us Cornish honey and a flagon of a strange beverage the local folk call "scrumpy". 'Tis a type of cider, I'm told. They say 'tis a potent brew – much like your Henry!' he chuckled. 'Perhaps we can partake this evening, once the children have gone to their beds?'

'Oh, Henry. When will you ever change?' she retorted with a mocking yet irresistible heave of her bosom.

'I hope I never. At least, as far as thou art concerned, my love,' was his straightforward answer. 'I hope I never...'

* * *

The following morning, Henry rose at daybreak to conduct his customary tour of the stables. Despite the gusting wind during the night, the tender and loving embraces of Caroline had meant he'd slept as soundly as he could remember – more soundly, in fact, than any man on earth had the right to, he reflected. Relaxed and fully restored, his step was sprightly as he crossed the yard. Jock O'Keefe greeted him on the dot of seven with a respectful doff of his tartan cap.

'Good morning, sir, and welcome back. You look in fine fettle, if I may be so bold, considering the long distances you have travelled. I trust the wedding was a success and all went as it should.'

'Unfortunately, there were some minor hindrances. A postponement is the regrettable result, but it's just a short delay – no more than a few weeks. I will reveal all in due course…' Henry did not wish to waste any time narrating his adventures once more, especially to his head groomsman, who was known to be a dreadful chinwag, so he changed the subject. 'Jock, can you prepare a cab? I need to take a trip to Tower Hill. Edward can drive me. I'll take breakfast now. Seven thirty, if you please.'

It was just before a quarter past eight when Henry stepped from the hansom. A hint of yellow-white mist hovered, like a funeral veil, over the dead-snake body of the most exalted river in the kingdom, the once mighty Thames. Its khaki-brown mudbanks, for ever consumed by rotting filth, appeared very much on the cusp of death, in fact. Henry watched as the slow stream of water slouched past the contrasting white parapets of the Tower of London towards the aptly named Gravesend. Tilbury, on the opposing bleak bank, beckoned the sludge too, as did the wide expanses of estuary and the promise of new life in the open sea beyond. Henry noted the smell of London once more. Illogically, his mind was drawn back to Borwenstow with its flawless air and scent of heather.

'I will make my way from here, Edward. You may go about your normal business and be sure to bring every penny you collect back to Marylebone!' he called up to his driver with a friendly yet knowing gesture of his head.

Jim Jones, the always smiling revenue constable, made a note of Henry's name in the register and pointed to the familiar stone staircase that led to the office of the chief investigation officer. As they parted, Jim gave his visitor a friendly wink. 'You'll find Mr Woodward is at his desk, sir. He arrived nearly an hour back. The office boy should have the fire lit by now.' Violently clapping his shoulders with both hands, he added, 'Summer may be coming, sir, but it's certainly taking its time to get here, eh?'

Jim's prediction was entirely correct. Albert Woodward was to be found in precisely the same spot he'd occupied the last time the two had met – behind the vast rectangular desk of polished Siamese teak he'd "appropriated for the Crown". A freshly lit fire crackled in the hearth. Albert was perceptibly pleased to see his "special agent", as he was wont to call Henry from time to time, even rising from his chair in affectionate greeting. In the course of some frivolous chit-chat about Cornish miles, Cornish weather and Cornish pasties, Mrs Ayling lumbered in with a brew of her legendary sweet tea and a most welcome plate of chocolate sponges.

'Special for you, Mr Henry, since I see you so little these days – more's the pity!' Only after she had finally departed, all affected airs and graces, did the two men set about their business in earnest.

'I must say, you have excelled yourself, Henry,' Albert cried once the full story had been laid out and his copious interruptions for questions had been satisfied. 'To have achieved so much in such few days is indeed a marvel. A better snooper I have yet to meet!'

Henry wasn't sure whether to take the remark as a compliment, so he glossed over it. 'But what now, Albert? The matter needs to be investigated properly. My "snooping", as you call it, will not take us far. You have told me, more times than I can recall, it is only hard evidence that convicts a man. Maybe my limited enquiries have offered up a prima facie case, of sorts – sufficient perhaps to bring a case to answer – but surely that will not wash, especially in the crafty courtrooms of Cornwall. I believe the services of a true detective will be required, one selected from the top drawer. Such a man, seconded to our rightful cause, is our only hope of securing a conviction against the Honey strain and their many accomplices.'

'Out of the question, Henry!' Albert slapped the table. 'I have no such man – and if I did, I would not offer him. These cruel murders you speak of are a matter for the constabulary, in any event, not the Excise.'

'But what of the smuggling? If we stop the night landings, maybe we can close this whole Pandora's box of wickedness once and for all.'

Albert Woodward looked distinctly uncomfortable. 'You have spoken of Halwill, a local inspector of impulsive but shrewd temperament. I have no doubt that with your help, he will solve the murders in no time at all, and the problem of smuggling will cease forthwith. Mark my words, this man Halwill sounds as if he is born to it. No, Henry, there are times when it's best to allow matters to take their course and refrain from interference. Let the police handle it, I say. And I will use my staff to attend the matters that concern me here in London. Also, the commissioners would not wash it. Imagine! One of my precious excise detectives scratching around in Cornwall in the hope of exposing a fraudulent phantom. They'd go mad at the very idea. Why...'

As the diverse reasons for inactivity flew from Albert's lips, Henry became increasingly disconcerted. Apart from their unfortunate first encounter, back in seventy-six, which had marked Henry's arrest at the hands of the man before him, he could not remember a single occasion when Albert, now a much respected and trusted friend, had been so obstructive – so cantankerous, even. He tried to reason with him one more time.

'My old friend, pray, hear what I have to say. Allow me an opportunity to put my case again, for I fear I have been clumsy in my approach and have taken your high office for granted, for which I humbly apologise. I am willing to add my weight to resolve this matter, but by necessity, the next time I am in Cornwall will be brief. My appearance at my daughter's wedding is expected, but once the celebrations are concluded, I will have no further reason to be in Borwenstow – in all of the West Country, for that matter. Any extended presence on my part will be swiftly suspected. Added to that, I may say, I have plenty of reasons to be *here*. My horses, my business, my children – my dear Carrie, to name but a few. As for the commissioners, you need tell them nothing. Send an officer on a fact-finding mission alone. You *are* the chief investigation officer, are you not?'

'I am.'

'With full powers to act in hot pursuit?'

'I have.'

'Then, pray use them, Albert. We have won, in the past, by being bold. Your ledger with the commissioners is much in profit. Why, they have told you as much. "We are in your debt, Mr Woodward". Were those not their very words?'

'They were.'

'Then I urge you to reconsider, Albert. Surely there is *someone* in your company who would fit the mark. The man need not present himself as an officer of the Excise. In truth, it would be better if he did not. A much sounder proposition would be if he travelled incognito in some fashion.' Henry was thinking fast. 'He could pose as a wandering fisherman, or a farmer from Devon, perhaps. Or as an itinerant salesman peddling soap or some such household item – medicines, maybe.'

'He could…'

Albert Woodward's disposition seemed to be altering slightly. The prospect of some support might now be possible, after all. Sensing a change of mood, Henry pressed on.

'It might be dangerous, of course. You'd need to take care who you chose. The man would need to have his wits about him.'

'He would.'

'What do you say, Albert, are you with me? I will offer all my support and counsel while I am in Borwenstow – this would have to be achieved in a clandestine manner, naturally – and I'd be happy to work with the man here in London, before he departs – to provide briefing, show him the local ropes, so to speak.'

'Could work…' Albert said dreamily.

In a matter of seconds, the ambiance appeared to change yet again. From being one of wistful concentration, it turned to one of unadulterated, genuine enthusiasm.

'In fact, it can!' were the triumphant words Albert spoke next.

Something must have clicked in Albert Woodward's brain. To Henry, who knew the man so well, it was almost as if the celebrated excise detective had found a way to proceed which truly appealed to him – conceivably one that might resolve an issue with which he was presently struggling. There was no doubting it. Albert, chameleon-like, had changed from detractor to benefactor in less than two minutes flat. Henry was starting to become suspicious.

'Or perchance – a cartographer!' Albert announced with eyes all lit up. 'We could send a map-maker! You said the tracks and paths around those parts are roughly hewn, and the boundaries between the farms are ill-marked.'

'I did.' It was now Henry's turn to reply in two-word sentences.

'Then, my dear friend, I think I have the very man. One to solve *all* our problems.' Albert fumbled for the silver handbell buried amongst the confusion of papers on his desk. He picked it up and promptly dropped it, such was his excitement and the patent desire to ring it as fast as he was able. The bell fell to the floor with a jingled clatter. As Woodward bent to retrieve it, a soft knock could be heard at the door, followed shortly after by the tottering entrance of a rather elderly man, small of stature, and apart from a slight paunch, lean of body. His plain, dark dress was remarkable only by the thin blue tie and the high collar that enclosed his reptilian neck.

'Ah, Browning, I had hoped you might have graced us with your company by now... Will you send for Mr Jarvie, please. Mr Jacob Jarvie. Tell him to wait outside until I call him.'

Chapter Eleven

Once old Browning had departed, Albert Woodward leant back in his chair, tilted his chin towards the bright-lit window behind him and took a few seconds to straighten his tie.

'Before my officer arrives, there is something we must discuss,' he said in steady tones. 'I must bring you further into my confidence, Henry. In normal circumstances, I would never discuss the merits, or otherwise, of my staff. They are matters that should perforce remain between me, as their superior, and my personnel – the men I task each day to perform their duties. But I have no wish to deceive you, and this state of affairs is unusual in the extreme. This is why I must be candid with you now...

'It is a matter for the excise commissioners to recruit who they choose. It is they who set the standard, and for the most part, the bar is set high. In respect of my detectives, I have a say, naturally. I'm constantly reminding our esteemed leaders of the qualities I seek. I persistently stress the work of an investigator is most singular. I grant the profession requires education – I am in agreement with the commissioners on that matter. But an officer under my command needs much more besides. Dedication, loyalty and intuition rank high amongst the virtues I esteem... but above all, Henry, I require my men to have courage; I want fellows with fire in their bellies who will take risks when the situation demands. Lamentably, however, there are occasions when my pleadings go unnoticed...' Albert let out an affected sigh, loudly discharging the air from his lungs between puckered lips. 'Such is the way of the world these days. You see, there are other factors at play. These allow the commissioners, from time to time, to make certain appointments as a favour to others... Do you get my drift, sir?' he grunted.

'You mean some bias exists in their choices, a degree of partiality... some favouritism, perhaps?'

'I would go further, Henry; I would call it simple nepotism!' he snorted.

'And what of Jacob Jarvie? I take it he is a case in point...'

Albert shuffled in his seat and fiddled with his tie once more. 'In a word – yes.'

On seeing Henry's fallen expression, he added hurriedly, 'But bear with me, for not all is bad news. Young Jarvie came to me via the Office of Ordnance Survey – a gift from his father-in-law, who happens to be the deputy chairman of the Board of Excise, Sir David Whittington, no less... Sir David's reasoning for the appointment has not been disclosed to me directly. I only have the utterances of his son-in-law to guide me. Apparently, on hearing his father-in-law boast of the excitement and shadowy activities of London's excise detectives who worked under him, young Jarvie, being dissatisfied with his dull station in life, pleaded to be given a chance to prove himself. I assume Sir David's only daughter had some say in the matter too. To be fair, Jarvie is a fine and likeable fellow in many respects. An impressionable man, though – twenty-five years old, he's been with us for nigh on six months.'

'If he is so agreeable, where does your difficulty lie?'

'Jarvie fulfils some of the qualities I seek – but not all. He is educated, a grammar school boy from Exeter who was top of his class. Such was his desire for adventure and his hope of gaining an army commission, he continued his studies at the Royal Military Academy in Woolwich, before being appointed to the Ordnance Survey. Here, he spent the next three years. During his time in Woolwich, he was introduced to, and fell in love with, Sir David's daughter. Jarvie is loyal and dedicated, as far as I can ascertain, but he lacks depth, appears wholly lacking in intuition, and worst of all, seems to be scared of his own shadow, most times. I suspect this was the reason he was overlooked for the front-line army and found himself in the mapping department – an occupation, Jarvie confided to me just a few short days ago, that was "tedious beyond description".'

'I see. And what if I say no to him?'

'Henry, you alone must decide if Jarvie fits the bill. You will meet him soon enough, and I will allow you to ask him whatever questions occur to you. Tell him as much of the matter as you see fit. On paper, at least, the lad is well qualified for the task – his many bookish certificates speak to it. His map-making skills and his knowledge of the West Country will be a boon. Goodness me! He's practically a Cornishman! Posing as an Ordnance Survey official will come naturally to him and offer the cover and protection you believe is required. Why, we may find you can bring out the man in him, and all will rejoice if that arises!'

'Is he the only option, the only man you can spare?'

'He is,' thus came the plain reply. 'If you are prepared to take him on, I am content to release him in the next few days. You can have him for one month – no more, mind. The Crown will pay all his expenses – and I will ensure we are generous to you also, especially if you can halt the resurgence of smuggling in those parts. If Jarvie makes a good fist of it, I shall review his appointment here with benevolence. I trust you to report fairly on his performance and in every good conscience. If he fails to deliver the goods, then I will have a conversation with Sir David and see what can be done. I offer this as much to you as I do to him. If you agree, you will have your man – albeit one only passably formed. For his part, 'tis a final chance to satisfy his aspirations, his last opportunity to pass his probation and become truly one of us.'

Henry had seen this bulldog look before, and he knew what it meant. Albert Woodward was not for budging. It was to be Jarvie or nothing! 'Very well,' he replied at length. 'You'd better let him in...'

Albert made sure not to drop the silver bell this time, and within seconds, the dependable Browning appeared once more. 'Sir!'

'You may bring Mr Jarvie before us now.'

Quite what Henry had expected, after listening to such a lukewarm commentary of the man he was about to meet, might have been anyone's guess, including his own... But even those nascent visualisations were entirely confounded, as the figure who now presented before him was different in every way. Jacob Jarvie must have been well over six feet in height – by at least three clear inches. Perhaps Henry had expected a much smaller fellow; a clean-shaven man with thin mouse-coloured hair; a pale, shrinking fellow of freckled complexion and scholarly glasses perched atop a short stub nose.

But Jacob was quite the opposite, exhibiting a neatly trimmed full beard below a shock of wavy dark hair that receded from a broad, confident forehead. Tall and lank, he would have qualified as the mind's eye image of a perfectly imagined police constable – minus the blue serge uniform, of course. Jarvie's physical impact was impressive indeed, but Henry soon noticed a certain reticence in the man's outward bearing. Jarvie appeared pale, his movements agitated – uncomfortable, even. Perhaps it was Woodward's presence and his imposing office that had given the fellow such a thin pallor. His footsteps, as he approached, were hesitant and rather ungainly, and he seemed to stoop slightly, as if in the act of imminent prostration.

'Ah, Jarvie, good of you to come at such short notice. I'd like you to meet Mr Henry Gough. You may have heard stories of his previous and most supportive associations with our office. Mr Gough is a leading light in the hackney carriage trade and knows London like the back of his hand.'

Henry stretched out a welcoming arm to greet the newcomer and did his best to look his man firmly in the eye. But this quickly became a struggle, as Jarvie seemed determined always to glance sideways and avert his gaze – *either that, or he has a terrible squint,* Henry mused. Much to his relief, the handshake was returned with all the strength one would expect of a man who must have weighed in at upwards of thirteen stones. Once introductions were made, Albert encouraged the assembly to sit around his petite but elegant conference table, and all duly obliged. He then indicated for Henry to speak first.

'Mr Jarvie, I am very pleased to make your acquaintance.' Henry tried his best to sound friendly. 'Mr Woodward tells me you have knowledge of maps and the like.'

'I know how to produce them, if that is your meaning, sir. Before I had the good fortune to join this happy band, I was engaged with the Ordnance Survey Office, who are masters in the field of cartography.'

'Excellent. And what do you know of Cornwall, sir? Have you ever been there?'

Jacob Jarvie looked mildly bemused, perhaps by the directness and outward irrelevance of the question, but he soon recovered enough to answer.

'Why yes, sir, as a matter of fact, many times since I was a child. My ancestors are from Glasgow, but my grandfather moved to Bude as a boy. We would visit his family on the north coast from time to time. 'Twas but fifty miles from our home in Bodmin – could be done in a day. My parents and a sister returned to Bude when I moved to Woolwich and still live in the town. My father is now a magistrate, sir.' As Jarvie spoke these words, a hint of bashful pride could be seen. 'And my grandmother resides just outside, in a hamlet called Upton Cross. She is eighty-eight years old now but still has a strong disposition, so I'm told.'

'All the sea air, I expect,' Henry offered affably.

'I expect so, and the gin she partakes most every day!'

For the first time, Henry saw signs his interlocutor might be relaxing a little, and he welcomed it. 'Jarvie, 'tis an interesting name – to me at least,' he said. 'As a cab proprietor myself, it suggests your ancestors might have been hackney carriage drivers, perchance...'

'There was some talk of it,' Jarvie replied, 'by my grandfather mostly, but I have nothing more to offer on the subject, I'm afraid. For the last fifty years my family have been tradesmen, latterly as grocers. My father now has upwards of a dozen shops in the West Country. He used to say 'twas the humble cabbage that had made our fortune!'

'And you? If the business was so profitable, why did you not join yourself? Did your father not wish it?'

'Yes, sir, he most vehemently wished it – with all his heart.' Jarvie's face dropped. 'But there is no adventure in cabbages, sir, to be honest...'

Henry chuckled. 'There may be some truth in that!' He was beginning to warm to the young man. 'And during your time with the Ordnance Survey, did you ever have cause to visit the area? I mean Cornwall, in particular.'

'No, sir, but I confess I oft wished it. There is much good work yet to be done in those parts, and I'd hoped to be given some challenge in that regard, but unfortunately nothing ever came of it. My position was fixed in Southampton, where the headquarters has been based these last forty years. But then I was found new work in London. I entered Mr Woodward's service and joined his excellent company of men…' Jarvie glanced briefly towards Albert Woodward, as if seeking some signal of approbation. When none came, save for a steely stare in return, he continued briskly. 'My wife is from Woolwich, you see, so the move has made me very happy, sir. Of that, there is no doubt.'

'When did you last visit Cornwall, Mr Jarvie?'

'I fear I have not been back these last three years.'

'Why is that?'

'When I was married my parents came to London for the wedding. 'Twas the last time I saw them, and since then 'tis been all work. Especially since my change of occupation, there has been no thought of Bude, as I am keen to make my way here and do well for my superiors. I should like to return to Cornwall someday, if truth be known, but I expect it will be a while afore such an event is possible. You see, there is another matter. My wife is with child. I was meaning to inform you, sir,' he added while looking at Albert once more, 'but 'tis just announced. I expect once we are blessed with littluns, all such excursions shall be more difficult.'

'When do you expect to see the first child?'

'Oh, not 'til nearly Christmas, so the nurses say.'

Henry decided he'd heard and seen enough. There was no doubting he was beginning to like the look of Jacob Jarvie. There was something about the man's manner that strangely appealed. Without doubt, Jacob had grown in confidence during their short conversation, and glimpses of an inner strength had begun to shine through. In short, he was almost certain he could work with him. The fact that he was the only officer offered up by Albert seemed less important now. It was time to bring this conversation to a close and open up a new one. With a knowing nod of the head, Henry indicated to Albert Woodward that he was satisfied. Albert understood his meaning instantly and took up the discussion.

'Mr Jarvie, I should like you to undertake a short intelligence assignment for me in Cornwall. The task will involve you working closely with Mr Gough and the local revenue officer, Mr Samuel Snuggs. I do not deny there may be some danger involved, and you will be required to work incognito and alone for long periods.' Albert looked Jacob squarely and uncompromisingly in the eye. 'I take it you accept—'

'I am at your command, sir.' And then, as if to show he already knew his present situation was somewhat precarious, Jarvie added, 'I am grateful for another chance to prove myself, sir.'

'Very well. I'll ask Mr Gough to brief you. He knows more of the matter than anyone, and I shall enjoy hearing his story once more. You may start from the beginning, Henry. I have both the time and the inclination to listen.'

For the next ten minutes, Henry unfolded the narrative, commencing with the murder of Abel Snuggs, a century before, and the suicide of the Reverend Jerimiah Forrabury. He decided to withhold some of the finer details for another time. He did not wish to clog Jarvie's brain with minutia. All Jarvie needed to hear now were the bare facts – the story in outline; the names and occupations of the main actors; the crimes that had been alleged; and those amongst the cast who were suspected. Jarvie learned of the long history of Borwenstow smuggling, the St Piran's tunnel and of the alleged complicity of local folk, including the clergy, in its pursuit. He heard about the feud between Snuggses and Honeys, about the rich landowners – the Pennycrockers – and about all the gossip of ghosts. Finally, as this was the only event Henry had actually witnessed, he was informed in greater detail about the sudden demise of Parson Rosewarne at the font of St Piran's, just a few days earlier. When all was concluded, Albert Woodward asked Jarvie if any further clarification was required.

'No, sir. I have heard the story and knowing what I do of Cornwall, it doesn't surprise me; I understand matters to be both delicate and convoluted. I have all the facts I need, save one.'

'Tell me.'

'Pray, sir, can you instruct me what you wish me to do?'

'Do... Mr Jarvie?' Woodward boomed. 'Why, I would have thought that to be as clear as the nose on my head! We want you to find out the truth of the matter! We want you to nose about Borwenstow in the manner of a scholarly cartographer, fresh from the Ordnance Survey Office in Southampton – a young academic who measures fields and ditches, who records the dimensions of farm buildings and the distance between boundary posts. But above all, we want you to listen and watch. Make yourself known, put on a friendly face, get the locals to like you – they may even confide their secrets, if they see you pose no threat. But you must never ask questions directly, save for the simplest. Do you understand? You must play the part of innocent greenhorn, a stumbling, stuttering kind of fellow who the community might take to their hearts. I think you are perfectly fitted for the part... what say you?'

Jacob Jarvie looked around uneasily, as if lost for words. As he tried to form a suitable response, he became preoccupied by whether his superior's final remark had been intended as a barb or an accolade. At length, he managed to utter a few words. 'I will endeavour to—'

His faltering speech was almost immediately interrupted

by a sharp rap on the door, and the awkward moment passed in an instant.

'Enter, if you must!' cried Woodward.

It was the obsequious Browning once more. 'A message has arrived from Scotland Yard, sir, from the office of Chief Superintendent Grieve. He apologises for the intrusion and suggests if you can pay him a visit before noon, you will learn something to your advantage. He has added a postscript, sir… *If your man Gough happens to be in your company, bring him too. I'll buy you both lunch.*'

'Thank you, Browning. Would you please prepare a carriage for Mr Gough and myself?' When the acolyte had departed, Albert leapt out of his chair. 'I say, if we leave now, we can easily meet that deadline. Lunch at the Yard – what do you think, Henry? I just hope the cook is on form. His steak and kidney pudding was one of the best I ever tasted last time I popped in to see old Jack.'

'Well, err, we have much to discuss here, Albert. Perhaps today is not the best—'

'Nonsense, we can resume our monkey business when we return. Mr Jarvie, you are relieved, for the present. Please be back here at four o'clock. And pray, tell no one of our conversation. On pain of death, mind. I mean it, sir. Nobody outside this room must know of our plotting. Is that clear?'

'Yes, sir. I will await your return.'

'It will give you time to come up with some stratagems for us to consider. You are going to Cornwall, Jarvie. Think on it. And take care to make all proper preparations.'

* * *

The hansom ride to the gates of Scotland Yard took less than twenty-five minutes, and it was well before noon when

Henry and his mentor had reacquainted themselves with their old policeman comrade in back-slapping salutations. Chief Superintendent Jack Grieve came to the vestibule to greet them personally and welcomed them in his typically provocative fashion.

'I am glad to see you looking so fit, Henry. That fetching wife of yours… I'll wager she's keeping you on your toes, eh? – Or most likely off 'em… ha-ha! Shame the same cannot be said about our old Welsh colleague. His expanding midriff increasingly brings to mind an image of Mr Pickwick – and *he* ended up in gaol! What a sorry state!'

Before Albert could register his exasperation, he was beaten to the punch. Even by Grieve's standards, the remark about his waistline was bordering on insult. It may have been mere banter, but to Albert, the blow was struck very much below the belt. 'Fear not, old friend,' Grieve cried, 'I have lunch arranged for us all. But before we dine, I have a remarkable revelation for you… and a most interesting man for you both to meet. Two for the price of one!' he jested. 'Though, I believe Mr Gough has already made the fellow's acquaintance. Come, follow me, and the curtains to my little mystery will be opened for you all.'

The two trailed the chief superintendent up the wide staircase and into the great man's familiar office. The aforementioned mystery fellow was seated in a comfortable armchair as they entered, and as soon as Henry clapped eyes on him, he recognised him immediately.

'Why, Inspector Halwill, how wonderful to see you, sir! My, you have journeyed far to be here today.'

'I travelled up by the morning train. I arrived just two hours ago. They don't call me "Hasty" for nothin', you know!' A thin smile broke out on Halwill's angular face. 'But it was Mr Grieve who insisted I came, once I'd given him the news.'

'You bring tidings from Cornwall, Inspector?'

'I do, Mr Gough.' He hesitated and looked towards Grieve, as if to gain his approval to proceed.

'Go ahead, my man, tell Mr Gough all. Then we shall have lunch.'

'Very well. Thank you, sir.' Halwill turned to face Henry. 'You see, Mr Gough, the priest who collapsed at your feet just a few days ago, the Reverend William Rosewarne, was indeed a victim of murder. The autopsy has confirmed it. It was none other than the poison cyanide that took the parson's life. It is irrefutable.'

'Great Scott, Inspector! 'Tis as you suspected – foul play, indeed.'

'There is more... The verger at St Piran's is sick. Old Polrunny may die soon enough. I was told he may not last the week. Doctor Plymswood, though he be drunk most days, suspects poisoning too – perhaps even from a lesser dose of cyanide, or so he says.'

Chapter Twelve

Jacob Jarvie had been waiting obediently, under Isaac Browning's watchful gaze, in the anteroom outside the chief investigation officer's study for nearly an hour by the time Henry and Albert rolled back into Tower Hill House and hurried up the staircase to meet him. The jolt of hearing that Rosewarne's death had been confirmed as murder most foul had much affected Henry's mood, which had become sober and reflective. Albert was in more jovial spirits. Doing battle with Scotland Yard's finest always made him feel uplifted. His plate of steak and kidney pudding and the jug of Scotland Yard's best claret may have also contributed to his contented disposition.

Based on Inspector Halwill's evaluation of events while in the nave of St Piran's, now officially categorised as a scene of crime, Henry had half expected the pronouncement of murder, but when the revelation came, it stunned him all the same. More concerning, by far, was the news that Verger Polrunny had appeared to suffer the same fate – and only a matter of hours later, by all accounts. During their meeting in Grieve's office, the assembly agreed the two incidents must be linked in some way, but each struggled to find the connection.

Who would want to kill both the parson and his verger? It was certainly a most vexing conundrum.

In the absence of a solution, they had moved the discussion on – to examine ways to tackle the investigation as a whole. Inspector Halwill had been outspoken on the subject. He wanted to conduct house-to-house searches and use whatever staff he had in watching the coastline day and night, for like the others, he had come to suspect the smuggling and the murders must be connected in some way. But Albert Woodward had disagreed.

'With due respect, Inspector, one rarely comes across a smuggler engaged in his free trading by randomly watching the coastline. Prior intelligence holds the key to catching these fellows red-handed. If we know in advance when and where they plan to land, we can position our forces and be prepared for them.'

'I concur, sir,' Halwill had retorted, 'but, pray tell me, how do we come by such intelligence? The folk of Borwenstow have never chosen to speak to my men – certainly not in my lifetime, at least; nor, for that matter, have they informed to the revenue officers under Mr Snuggs's command. Paraphrasing the words of the prophet Jeremiah, how can a leopard change its spots? If I had sufficient resources, we might make a difference.' Halwill turned to his superior officer. 'Sir, can you spare me some men from Scotland Yard to join with us in this hunt?'

Chief Superintendent Jack Grieve appeared unprepared for the request, such was his look of surprise. 'I am afraid I cannot,' he replied with an involuntary scratch of his ear. 'I have already spoken on the subject. 'Tis a problem for the Revenue. I cannot dabble in matters which are lawfully assigned to them. They are the experts, after all, borne of many years' experience. Smuggling is in the veins of every Englishman, it seems, and I believe the Revenue have the tools and methods to catch and convict those who offend. Would you not agree, Mr Woodward?'

'I cannot deny it.'

'But what of the murders?' Halwill persisted.

A look of irritation now appeared on the face of Chief Superintendent Grieve. 'The murders are for you to resolve, sir. I cannot interfere with the affairs of the Cornwall Constabulary,' he growled.

'Then, sir,' Halwill was not in any mood to give way, 'if the matter of smuggling falls to Mr Woodward, when can *he* give me some of *his* men to station in the watchtowers?'

'I can do better than that...' replied Albert Woodward with a fixed expression. 'Mr Gough and I have hatched a plan – one which involves subtlety, not brute strength. I have assigned one of my best men to the task. He is an intelligence officer of some repute, who will be deployed to Borwenstow within days. I have no doubt he will provide us all with the information we require so that we may knock on the proper doors when the time is right.'

This revelation took a while to sink in, even for Henry, who regarded the head of the excise detectives nervously. *Has he overplayed his hand?* he mused.

It was Grieve who spoke first. 'There you have it! Ha-ha! The Revenue know their business. Bravo, Albert. I believe your stratagem has much merit.'

Halwill looked anxiously around before asking the inevitable question Henry was dreading... 'This man you speak of, your intelligence agent, may I know his identity? If he is to be roaming my constabulary, I should know of it. He may need the protection of my officers, should he fall into deep waters.'

The reply, when it came, made Henry sigh with relief. 'I regret I cannot divulge that information,' Woodward announced. 'I have no doubt all your officers are sound in every way, Inspector, but the fewer who know the name of my agent, the more secure he will be, as will our enquiry. We are practised in such operations, sir, having worked in this manner on countless occasions, with much success to show for it. It is a question of "need to know" and in this setting, I regret, sir, you do not *need* to know.'

'But...' Halwill looked imploringly at the chief superintendent, who sat across the table from him.

Albert did not wait for a response. 'You have my assurance; you will be kept informed of every development. Each strand of newly acquired intelligence shall be shared with you. I give you my word, sir. When Mr Gough arrives in Borwenstow to attend his daughter's wedding, he will act as intermediary. My man will report all the facts he has amassed to him, and you shall learn of it from Henry Gough all in good time.'

'This is most irregular!' Halwill blurted.

'No, sir, 'tis most proper and 'tis the way it shall be done,' Woodward fired back.

'And what of my murder investigation?' was the tetchy response.

On rare occasions, Albert Woodward's demeanour could alter in a flash. Sporadically, especially when vexed, he possessed the tactless ability to appear disdainful – distinctly *superior* even, and much to Henry's frustration, he saw this moment had turned to be one of them. 'I suggest you proceed as you normally would, Inspector,' the old exciseman offered haughtily. 'Ask what questions you wish, visit whoever you choose, search as you please. That way, you may get to the bottom of things even before Mr Gough returns. If you manage it, all shall rejoice, I'm sure. But as for the smuggling, sir, please leave that to the doyens in the field...'

As Halwill stared back with incredulous and bulging

eyes, Chief Superintendent Jack Grieve decided it was time to intervene. The atmosphere was verging towards the antagonistic, and it was the moment to apply some soothing balm.

'Gentlemen, may I propose a truce? We have two separate lines to follow, and I have no doubt we all wish the same success in both of these endeavours. Am I not correct?' The other three nodded in sullen agreement. 'Very well, I suggest we come to a gentlemanly accommodation. We agree to share what we learn of each other's investigations. In short, to work together to achieve a common goal. What say you?'

Henry reckoned it might be a sound idea to step in quickly and fire the first shot in response. 'I should be delighted to help all I can, gentlemen, and contribute my knowledge with both Inspector Halwill and Mr Woodward's chosen man – whosoever he may be.'

'Hear, hear, and I concur! Whatever my agent discovers shall be shared. Mr Gough's offer of assistance is most welcome,' exclaimed Albert in short order. 'He has been a boon in the past, and so shall he again.'

All eyes then fell on the Cornish policeman. 'And what say you, sir? Are you in with us too?' Grieve questioned with a hopeful grimace.

'I am, sir...' Halwill replied at length and with a surprising smile, to boot. 'I have no alternative, so it seems... but I'll happily accept the proposal to collaborate in all things. You have my word, sir. In return for these promises, honestly given, I will not withhold anything from Mr Gough when he next returns to Borwenstow. Together with Mr Woodward's mystery man, we will fathom this case once and for all.'

* * *

Elizabeth Charlotte Gough sat under the light of the vaulted Gothic window that graced the nursery of Pennycrocker Hall surrounded by her three charges – Wilhelmina, aged five, Clodagh, three and a half and baby Maeve, who was barely two. Engaged in embroidering a set of pure cotton napkins, adorned with dainty yellow roses, Elizabeth released a shallow sigh of frustration. Studying the trio of little girls at play had always been a constant joy, and their bond could not have been closer – but she longed for the day when she would be married and for the chance to have a pretty daughter of her own. She loved her employment as the household's governess more than she could describe and had spoken to Samuel on the subject many times. Elizabeth had held her position for nearly a year, since the time her predecessor, Agnes, had fallen pregnant and had been obliged to leave service. This very thought brought on mixed feelings, for Elizabeth knew she could not have both – her situation required she remained childless, a stipulation made at the confirmation of her appointment by no less than Lady Kathleen Pennycrocker herself.

Her Ladyship had been so kind since then, so thoughtful, so unreservedly generous, and the way she talked, in her softly spoken Irish way, was as attractive as a flawless Dublin sunrise. When there was something to accomplish, a task to complete, some function to perform, Lady Kathleen always requested it done in such a gentle, pleasing fashion as to make the necessary duty a real joy to undertake. She was a fine-looking woman too, in every respect – an authentic raven-haired beauty from the Emerald Isle. When she heard of the circumstances of Elizabeth's tragic wedding postponement, Lady Kathleen seemed almost brought to tears with the emotion of it all – such was her compassion and the gracious nature she bore.

Sir William could be gracious too, for most hours of the day, at least... In appearance, save for a conspicuous scar on his left cheekbone caused by a hunting accident and the fashionable clothes he wore, there was little to distinguish him from most other men. Elegantly dressed, perhaps, but of middling stature, average height and ordinary looks. A prematurely receding hairline made him look older than his forty-two years. A daily-trimmed moustache nestled beneath a somewhat hooked nose gave his face a touch of bohemia. A slight paunch could not be disguised, even by his up-to-the-minute Gieves & Galt waistcoat. Sir William's persona was of a confident, self-possessed man of business. But he could make trouble sometimes too, though his tempers were typically transient in nature. On occasions, the couple's raised voices could be overheard from Elizabeth's top floor room at the Hall, positioned as it was, obliquely above her employers' own bedchamber. But the soothing attentions of Sir William's adorable wife usually brought her husband back from the edge and into blessed sanity once more. On such tempestuous days, Elizabeth always sought refuge in the servants' quarters below stairs, where she scurried for sanctuary and where the enraged outbursts of Sir William and his wife's tender entreaties could be heard no longer. Out of privacy, as well as her loyalty to Lady Kathleen, Elizabeth wished no part of it and made every effort to close her ears to the troubles that went between them. But Sir William had a kind disposition at heart; Elizabeth was sure of it. This made her personal forgiveness of his intermittent flare-ups easier to give.

Some of the servants, the first footman included, saw the worthier side of their master, too. A few told that Sir William looked vulnerable and remote at times, and the chief housemaid once said how much she'd wanted to hug him for it. This made the rest fall into fits of laughter, and Elizabeth had quietly scolded them for it, whilst seeing the funny side all the same. She also imagined there might be a certain truth in their appraisal. Sir William did look like a hunted man, from time to time – perhaps he had some business worries that brought him down. Elizabeth did not wish to know, but...

Certainly, when not in drink, he could be a true gentleman. On the evening following her return to Pennycrocker Hall, just two days before, Elizabeth had encountered Sir William as she herded the children out of the nursery.

'I say, Miss Gough, I heard the news,' he declared, nearly coming to attention before her. 'What a dreadful business, indeed. Please accept my respectful commiserations to you and your betrothed.'

'Thank you, sir... Your comfort is much appreciated. With good fortune such a thing may not happen again.' The three children crowded round the hems of their governess as she spoke to their father, almost as if they sought shelter behind her bustle.

'Lightning striking twice, eh? That's the spirit! I understand you will not have long to wait – the twenty-first is fixed, I believe. Good luck to you both – *bona fortuna*, as Virgil might have it, what?'

Agreeably surprised that Sir William actually knew the revised date of her wedding, Elizabeth gave him an undisguised smile in return. 'Why, thank you, sir. You are most kind. Now, say good night to Papa, girls. It's time for our bedtime story.'

'Good night, my little darlings, another day tomorrow, eh?' Sir William waved self-consciously at his offspring. 'Now, do as our dear Miss Gough instructs, won't you... and no noise, mind...'

As he started to turn away, a sudden thought must have come to him, and he spun around on his toes. 'I say, Miss Gough, do you have a carriage to transport you to the church? Every bride needs the perfect carriage, don't you know!'

'I believe Mr Trewint is making the arrangements, sir.'

'Damn that scoundrel of an innkeeper – why not take mine?' he blurted. 'It's a Shelburne Landau, no less. I have a pair of fine Arabs too, you know, ready schooled and as obedient as lambs. You may have the services of my coachman too. Hawkes is a good man, as reliable as my billiard room clock. Should do the trick, eh?'

Elizabeth hesitated much longer than she wanted. Mouth slightly parted, she didn't know quite how to respond.

'No, I insist, Miss Gough,' Sir William gushed. 'I wish to hear no more on the subject. I'm told your father is a horseman, of sorts. Well, we can't have him coming all the way from distant Marylebone to gather you up behind a couple of rough old Bodmin ponies with Trewint's lackey at the helm, now can we?'

Goodness! Elizabeth thought. Sir William must indeed be a knowledgeable man – such a grasp did he have of local events and the goings-on thereabouts, conscious even of the business of those who were mere fleeting visitors to the parish.

'Accept it as our wedding gift, from Her Ladyship and me. My Kate speaks very highly of you, very highly indeed.'

Elizabeth flushed. 'Well, sir, if you insist. I'm sure my father would be honoured as, of course, am I. Shall I inform Mr Trewint that his services will no longer be required?'

'Ha-ha, tell the old skinflint what you must, Miss Gough. But promise me one thing – you must report back to me his reaction. Knowing him as I do, I expect you will find it as entertaining as I will, for sure!'

* * *

Days later, as Elizabeth was in the vestibule placing sun hats onto the children's heads in preparation for a nature walk in the grounds of Pennycrocker Hall, she spied a man stepping down from a carriage onto the front drive, directly before the portico. The weather was warm, summer had come early to Borwenstow, and as the man gazed upwards to engage the lofty columns of the grand house, he wiped his brow with a 'kerchief drawn hurriedly from his morning coat top pocket. Heath, the first footman, hastened past Elizabeth and the children to open the front door and greet the newly arrived gentleman, and as the breach grew wider, she was able to get a better look at the new visitor. A tall, rather gangly yet quite handsome man in his mid-twenties approached and introduced himself.

'Jacob Jarvie, Esquire, Ordnance Survey Office. Here to meet Sir William Pennycrocker. We have an appointment at ten.'

'Will you come this way, sir?' Heath bowed in a much-practised movement of neck and shoulders. 'Sir William is expecting you...'

Jacob Jarvie had arrived in Borwenstow the evening before. On Henry Gough's advice, he had followed the exact same route from Paddington, even employing the same coachman, the ever-timorous Joshua, to transport him from Launceston to the northern coastline. As Jarvie stepped under the glittering high ceilings of the hallway, the words of Albert Woodward seemed to ring in his ears:

"Make your acquaintance with the lord of the manor first, Jarvie. He will want to know of your presence and your purpose thereabouts. Sir William Pennycrocker is very well connected and must be your first port of call. Do you understand?"

For Jacob, the previous three days had been spent in rushed, and at times rather frantic, preparation. Henry had briefed him in detail concerning the characters and places he would encounter at his journey's end. Albert Woodward had ordered that false identity documents be drawn up to show his invented occupation and his mission for the Ordnance Survey Office. Jarvie had been pleased to make a contribution in this regard, and by providing the names of trusted officials in Southampton who might help their cause, he was able to obtain some grudging approval from his superiors. This was enhanced still further when, to the relief of all, the counterfeit documentation was produced within twenty-four hours, under strict secrecy, of course, and in precisely the approved format. Now armed with all the tools of his former trade and the papers to prove his cover occupation, he was about to have his very first encounter.

Jacob was ushered into Sir William's wood-panelled study and offered a relaxing chair by the vacant fire. Heath said, 'If you would wait here for the present, Mr Jarvie, Sir William will be with you very soon.' The first footman then departed with a suitably compliant gesture, closing the door with a gentle click. Jacob found himself all alone. The study clock on Sir William's mahogany desk ticked noisily on for a full five minutes while Jacob surveyed the room. With each tick-tock, he became increasingly restless. From his seated position, all he could see were crammed bookshelves, half-drawn curtains, acres of polished wood and vast swathes of oriental carpet.

As he sat in silence, he was reminded once more of the instructions given to him by his chief investigation officer. "Nose about, man! Make yourself known, put on a friendly face, get the locals to like you – they may even confide their secrets if they see you pose no threat."

The thought came to him that an opportunity now presented itself – a chance to be courageous. The time seemed right to start to "nose about". He listened for noises emanating from the long corridor directly outside the study and realised if he was attentive, he might hear the approach of another well before the door actually opened. He gingerly got to his feet. He would commence his sleuthing in earnest at Sir William's desk. The thought struck him any rummage would probably yield little, but at least it would be practice if similar opportunities arose in the future...

Sir William did not appear to be an orderly man, for Jacob's first impression was of a cluttered paper-strewn bureau with little semblance of organisation. From the desk, Jacob could see the garden better and took a few moments to cast his eyes down the neat borders, wide lawns and trimmed hedges to ensure no one was approaching the window from the outside. Standing as still as possible, he cocked his ear once more. All seemed deathly quiet in the corridor. Making sure not to ruffle the papers unduly, he started to examine the first pile, one sheet at a time. His heart was pounding, but this was no time for impatience. He knew he had to keep a cool head and not rush his search. There was a lot of correspondence – *only to be expected,* he mused. There were bills too, from Sir William's tailor in Savile Row, the village grocer, and from the vet, who appeared to be owed a decent sum of money – in excess of ninety guineas, in fact. To his surprise, he came across a letter from Miss Elizabeth Gough, dated the previous summer, confirming the terms of her new appointment as governess of the household. He chuckled to himself – to be sure, this must be Henry's daughter, the very same as Henry had spoken of during his Tower Hill briefings, perhaps the same lady he had glimpsed walking out with a group of little girls as he'd arrived.

Jacob delved deeper. In the first drawer he slid open, he found a ferry timetable for the City of Cork Steam Packet Company, with the route "Swansea – Cork" underlined in black ink. Pinned to the timetable, there was a bill for two yards of lace from a Cork dressmakers and a short note: *If you could settle this, I would be obliged, K.* This made Jacob's dark eyebrows meet in consternation – *a very curt missive from his loving wife,* he thought…

At the bottom of the same drawer, he felt something bulky. Feeling for it further, he lifted it away from the back. He knew what it was before he saw it. When a Webley two-and-a-half-inch Bull Dog revolver appeared in his hand, he was not surprised. Jacob knew about pistols; he had fired many types during his Woolwich cadet days, and without doubt, this was his favourite. He could not help a smile as he moved the pistol between his fingers, feeling its snub nose of burred, cold metal and its ivory handle once more against his skin. As contented reminiscences flooded into his head, there was the unmistakeable sound of a door opening!

Jacob had heard nothing from the corridor to alert him, so a mild panic set in. He hurriedly pushed the drawer shut, but in his haste, he forgot to replace the Bull Dog. Positioning himself to face the window, as if in the innocent act of admiring the garden, he slipped the revolver quickly into his pocket. There was nowhere else to hide it at that moment. As he heard the door shut with a noticeable crack, he turned to greet the new arrival. To his surprise, he was confronted by a lady – and a most beautiful one, at that.

Chapter Thirteen

The sudden appearance, as if from nowhere, of Lady Kathleen Pennycrocker – for surely, it could be no one else – had startled Jacob to the core. He was confident he'd managed to conceal Sir William's revolver in the nick of time, but now, as he lifted his head to address the interloper, the pistol felt strangely heavy in his pocket.

'Ah, you must be Mr Jarvie, visiting from the Ordnance Survey Office. My husband informed me he had plans to meet you today,' she trilled. 'I had expected to see him in your company, in fact. For it was he, begging your pardon, sir, not you, with whom I wished to speak.'

'It's a pleasure to meet you, Your Ladyship.'

'But what of my husband?' she looked perplexed… 'Have you not spoken with him yet?'

'Not a word, I'm afraid. I suspect he has more pressing matters to attend to than my humble visit. But my wait has been a most pleasant one, Your Ladyship. To amuse myself, I have been admiring your marvellous grounds. The lawns seem to carry on for ever. I imagine one can see right along to the coast from here, if one knows which way to look.'

'Not quite, Mr Jarvie,' she smiled, 'but from the rooms at the top of the house one certainly can.'

Jacob had not noticed the Irish lilt at first – such, perhaps, had been his earlier preoccupations – but now he could hear it clearly. My, how charming it was. Indeed, how enchanting *she* was… He suddenly became aware of thumping noises coming from the corridor outside.

'That'll be him now, I expect,' she said softly, adding a coy smile. And sure enough, five seconds later, the door flung open and Sir William, looking for all the world as if he'd swallowed a bee, stormed in.

'Sir, please accept my apologies for keeping you waiting,' he blurted as soon as he crossed the threshold. And then, on seeing his wife, whose slim figure seemed almost to disappear amongst the background of assorted drapes and exotic fabrics, he added, with perhaps a too wide smile, 'My dear, so good of you to join us.'

'William, I hadn't meaned to interrupt. It was just that I wanted to tell you that I am about to take a ride into the village with the children. Miss Gough has just returned from a woodland walk with them, and I thought while they were still dressed for the outdoors, a ride in the carriage might do us good. It would be so nice on such a day as this to spend some time with the girls, and it will give Miss Gough a much-deserved break.'

'The carriage? Which one?'

'Oh, don't fret,' she chastised him gently, 'not the Landau. The old Brougham will be sufficient for the four of us. 'Tis only a brief shopping trip.'

'Very well. I'm most obliged, my dear. Now, if you will excuse us, this gentleman is here to tell me about some new maps which are being produced of these parts – not before time, what!'

'Excellent. Then I'll leave you both to it.' And with yet another gracious smile, Lady Kathleen turned and, for some inexplicable reason, walked towards a bank of high bookshelves. Jacob's befuddlement did not last long, for it was there she turned a brass handle, one he'd completely missed when he'd entered, and a narrow door, disguised within the shelves, opened. Her Ladyship was gone within seconds.

Thank goodness! Jacob thought to himself. *I'm not going deaf after all. So that was how Her Ladyship managed to creep up on me!*

'Sir, what do you have to tell me?' Sir William poured himself a drink from a silver-topped crystal decanter as soon as his wife had disappeared. 'You have come from London, I assume,' he added, indicating they should sit down. 'Would you like a whiskey, by the by? I find it helps me concentrate in the mornings.'

'No, thank you, Sir William, but I appreciate your offer of hospitality... Actually, our offices are now located in Southampton, so the journey has been all the shorter for it. The London and South Western Railway provide a first-class service these days.'

'I see. Jolly good... So, what brings you to Pennycrocker Hall, precisely? A new series of maps is being drawn up – is that my accurate understanding?'

'You are correct, sir. My office suggested I pay you a visit as a matter of courtesy, to explain my intentions, as I will be spending many hours scoping and surveying hereabouts.'

'Snooping around, eh?' Sir William's lightning repost took Jacob rather by surprise.

'Not in detail, you understand. That work is for others to undertake, who will follow in due course. My purpose is to look at the lie of the land, record whatever changes I discover, make some measurements and—'

'Tell me, is old George Atkinson still there?' Sir William interrupted.

'Where, sir?'

'In the Ordnance Survey Office, man, where else? He must be more than sixty by now, maybe older, if my memory serves. My father knew him, spoke very highly of him. They were at Sherborne together.'

'I know of a much younger man by the name of Arthur Atkinson who is one of the administrators in the drawing office.'

'Do you really? How interesting! Must be his son, I suspect… some relative or other.'

'I expect so.'

'Very well, I think I have learned enough for now.' Sir William got to his feet. 'It has been very good to meet you, Jarvis. Please call again if you wish anything, but be sure to send notice in advance. Thank you for taking the trouble, but I am a busy man, what!'

Bemused by the brevity of their conference and anxious to delve a little deeper, now he had the chance, Jacob decided it best not to correct the nominal mistake. Instead, he plucked up courage to pose a question. 'May I ask, sir, is there anything you know that might assist my work here? I only ask as I am new to these parts and any local knowledge might help.'

'Such as?'

'Oh, matters concerning contested land, boundary disputes – that sort of thing. Such information might be useful to learn in advance. I wouldn't wish to cause any trouble, as I expect to be asking questions of folk from time to time.'

'Ha, I see. What can I tell you?' he muttered to himself. 'Steer clear of old Trewint's pilchards! Ghastly things – hate 'em!' he laughed. His complexion altered slightly. 'And I'd take care when you survey the land around Doubloons Farm, if I were you.'

'Doubloons Farm… yes, I recall seeing it on the chart. Is there a bog nearby or some such hazard?' Jacob asked innocently.

'I'd say so,' Sir William snorted. 'The farmers there go by the name *Honey* but don't be tricked by the sweet-sounding name. Be aware, Mr Jarvis, they are a touchy bunch at the best of times, and if they catch you on their land, there'll be hell to pay.'

'But I have a warrant, sir.' Jacob retrieved a tight scroll from the inner pocket of his jacket.

'Let me see.'

Jacob unfurled the document and placed it in Sir William's palm.

'Show the paper, by all means,' he said after a cursory examination. 'But if they trouble you, it would be best to tell them we have spoken. You see, the Honeys and I… well, we have a certain understanding – of sorts, at least. But they are rogues, sir. Pay no attention to their chatter, for it is designed to intimidate and deceive honest young fellows such as you. And don't let the high-flown ways of Cassius fool you, either.'

'Cassius?'

'He is the head of the family, at least for now… He is a most pretentious fellow with high ambitions, but a blackguard at heart.'

Jacob gulped perceptibly. 'It's fortunate you and they have an understanding, of sorts, then,' he offered tentatively.

'Did I say that?' Sir William grunted as Jacob blinked back. 'What I mean to say is a man has to go about his business. At times, perforce, this may be conducted with others he despises. Messrs Honey and I have an occasional acquaintance built around commerce. Let's leave it at that, shall we? And now, sir, please allow me to retire. I have matters to attend. Heath will show you out.'

'Before you depart, Sir William, may I have a final request?' Jacob had to find a way to return the revolver to its rightful place. 'Would it be too much to ask if a glass of water could be brought to me? I am fair parched, and it would quench my thirst before my onward journey.'

Sir William was noticeably taken aback by the petition. Perhaps he considered it to be rather presumptuous. He pretended to appear apologetic. 'Oh, Mr Jarvis, my humblest apologies. I should have offered refreshments. I will ask Heath to bring some to you directly.'

Sir William walked purposefully to his desk and tugged the cord that hung down nearby. He then pulled out the chair from under his desk and, much to Jacob's consternation, sat down. Pulling back his cuffs, he commenced to arrange the chaotic pile of papers that lay before him. Together, he and Jacob waited in stony silence, with the latter looking on with increasing unease, unable to take his eyes off Sir William's hands as they flitted from one place to the next. At one point, Sir William opened a drawer, not the hapless gun drawer, thank goodness, and stuffed some papers inside. Jacob was unable to utter a word; his stomach seemed to drop a few inches inside his belly. This was not what he had planned at all! Now the pistol felt like a veritable anchor in his pocket, tying him to the spot. He crossed his legs and self-consciously adjusted his dress, becoming aware, in the process, of the weapon's smooth tooled outline once more. After what seemed like an eternity, with only the agonising rustling of papers to break the mood, Heath finally appeared.

'Ah, Heath, would you please escort young Mr Jarvis to the door? Our meeting is concluded. Perhaps you can ask Cook to provide him with whatever he needs from the kitchen on his way out. Good day, Mr Jarvis. It has been most enlightening.'

'Good day, Sir William. Thank you. You have been extremely accommodating…' Jacob tried not to stumble as he made for the study door and felt huge relief when he set foot in the corridor and Heath closed it behind him.

'If you would follow me, sir. I'm sure Cook will have something to satisfy you.'

Jacob was now in a real predicament. If the pistol drawer was opened and its contents examined in any depth, he would be done for and his secret mission would come to an abrupt halt – a wretched faller at the first blessed fence! He wanted to scream. But then, to his temporary relief, as Heath led the way to the kitchen, he heard the study door open and close behind him. When he glanced over his shoulder, he glimpsed Sir William heading down the corridor in the opposite direction. At least he had not been discovered yet. There was still time to make amends. But how? He wracked his brains, but a mild panic had set in, and he couldn't think in straight lines.

Heath turned a corner, then another, and after descending a flight of steps, they arrived in the immense kitchens of Pennycrocker Hall.

'Sir William has asked we offer Mr Jarvie some sustenance, Cook,' he called as they entered. Mrs Hennessey was stirring something unrecognisable over the stove. The request did not seem to sit well with her.

'Give me a few moments; I have to mind this a bit longer,' she grumbled – a hard Irish accent immediately noticeable.

Heath departed without a word, clearly content he had done his duty by Sir William. He hurried away to deal with other matters presumably more urgent.

'Actually, I was only looking for a glass of water,' Jacob offered, trying to look as undemanding as possible.

'Perhaps *I* can help you with that?' a pleasant feminine voice spoke from behind him. He spun around, and to his joy, the unmistakeable figure of Elizabeth Gough stood before him. 'You must be Mr Jarvie,' she smiled. 'We nearly bumped into one another this morning as I was taking the children out. You are a man of maps come to meet Sir William, so I believe.'

'That I am,' he beamed. Then he had an idea. The idea that he'd had an idea shocked him slightly, but there was no time to reflect on his newfound quick-wittedness. He had to act fast. Making sure Mrs Hennessey was still stirring her pot and there was no one else in the kitchen, he asked in a low whisper, 'Am I correct in thinking you are Miss Elizabeth Gough?'

'Goodness, sir, how do you know that? I am the very same.'

'I know your father well,' he replied with a conspiratorial grin.

'He has never mentioned your name…' she darted back.

'You see, I only got to know him recently, but these last few days I have spent a lot of time in his company.' His tone lowered still further. 'I need to speak to you as a matter of grave importance. It concerns your father. Will you allow me to do that? I guarantee I am a man to be trusted. You may ask me anything you wish, and you will see I am no Tipperary corner boy and will come up to proof.'

'Let me get that water, Mr Jarvie…' Elizabeth's intuition, an attribute she relied on often, had quickly shifted into full steam. 'It's a fine day. We can talk in the yard. It will be more private there.'

After the water had been fetched and Mrs Hennessey relieved of her irksome duty, Elizabeth led Jacob to the outside yard, where a few tables had been arranged under a canvas awning for the purpose of sorting fruit, but which now lay bare. A couple of rustic chairs were found, and Jacob dragged them across the cobbles.

Elizabeth wasted no time. 'Now, tell me, sir, you say you have news of Papa. Do you know when he might next come to Borwenstow?'

'He plans to arrive three or four days before your wedding on the twenty-first,' Jacob replied after taking a gulp from the flask – he was genuinely thirsty now, and the draught almost felt life-giving.

'I'm impressed! It seems you may know my father after all, but let me ask you another, just to be sure. How many children does Henry Gough have?'

'I fear 'tis a trick question, madam. I know you are his eldest child. He speaks of "his Elizabeth" often, and he worries for your safety. As for the rest, I would have to speculate, but I have heard him talk of family in London. So…' he paused, 'if I were to hazard a guess… I'd say he had *seven* – don't ask me why, but 'tis a lucky number, so some believe.'

Elizabeth laughed back. 'You are wrong, sir! There are more of us than just a mere seven! But you're close enough. If you'll allow me, I have one further question. Who is his greatest friend?'

'Why, 'tis an easy one! 'Tis, without doubt, Albert Woodward, my superior officer.'

'Now you have me truly confounded, Mr Jarvie, if that be your real name, for although 'tis true Mr Woodward is indeed Papa's dearest acquaintance, he is with the Excise, and you have announced yourself today as an official from the Ordnance Survey. I heard you this very morning when you made your entrance. What must I make of that, sir? Are you being untruthful to me… or to Sir William and this household? Whatever your answer, you appear to be a liar, sir.'

'Miss Gough, please, I must cut to the chase. I have to ask for your indulgence and to do so, I must bring you into a very grave confidence. I can assure you my credentials are sound in every way. 'Twas Albert Woodward who introduced me to your father. I work not for the Survey, but for the Excise and that be the honest truth of it. Let me prove it to you… Do you have knowledge of a policeman by the name of Inspector Austol Halwill Barton?'

Elizabeth nodded her agreement.

'Halwill and Woodward have a plan to finally halt the crime of smuggling in these parts and bring to justice those who, in the late course of their free trading, have committed murder in Borwenstow – your future husband, Samuel, was once villainously accused, was he not?'

She nodded once more, now hardly daring to speak.

'I have been sent by them on a clandestine assignment to establish the truth of the Borwenstow curse and to glean intelligence about the wicked trafficking that has blighted this community for over a hundred years. I have been instructed to remain incognito, to gather the facts and report them to your father when he next arrives. You father is a most trusted agent of the Excise, do you know?'

'So he continually informs me—'

'Well, Mr Gough has been tasked likewise, and we are to work together. It is his intention to bring Samuel into our confidence as soon as he arrives in the next few weeks. Until then, my job is watch, listen and record. That way, I can ask straight questions under the innocent guise of a scholarly cartographer.'

'You say you wish a favour of me.' Elizabeth's head was reeling now.

'I have a pistol in my pocket, madam.'

If her head had been reeling before, it was positively spinning now. Elizabeth was lost for words.

'I wish you to take it and return it to its rightful place in Sir William's study desk – top right drawer, mind, and push it far to the back. Will you do this for me?'

'But how… how did you come by it?'

'It was an error on my part, I confess. I was waiting for Sir William's arrival when I came across the revolver.'

'You "came across" it, indeed! That is a most interesting euphemism, Mr Jarvie!' she cried.

He pressed on while looking about the yard for potential eavesdroppers. 'I was surprised by Her Ladyship before I could return it to the desk and was forced to conceal it about my person. 'Tis a British Bull Dog, no less – a very fine firearm indeed,' he added, much to Elizabeth's utter bemusement. 'Will you do this for me, Miss Gough?' he pleaded. 'I ask only this favour. But it has to be done quickly, mind. I have no wish to bring danger to you, but I can see no other way out of this pickle that I have so foolishly brought upon myself.'

'But how... I don't know... I—'

'It should be a simple task, once the coast is clear. I fear if I cannot return the pistol, I will be suspected soon enough, and my covert mission here will have ended before it has properly started.'

'But a revolver, Mr Jarvie! If I am caught, I will be dismissed instantly... worse, no doubt... brought before the magistrate for theft, and then I shall be a fallen woman, indeed!'

Jacob Jarvie looked reflective for a few moments. 'I fear I have overstepped, Miss Gough. I should not have asked. 'Twas most ungracious of me. I should account for my own sins and bear the responsibility for my hapless actions. I will return to the house now and declare myself to Sir William. 'Tis the only course, I fear.'

'Wait! I shall do it!' she blurted. Even Elizabeth was astonished by her sudden change of tack. 'I will ask Cook to prepare a plate of cold chicken for you,' she said excitedly. 'Stay here and eat until I return. Now, give me the gun.' She slid her handbag across the table. 'With luck, I shall find Sir William in the morning room, and Lady Kathleen and the children are out in the Brougham. That will give me sufficient time.'

Jacob obeyed instantly. The relief was almost tangible. Within seconds, the Bull Dog had been rescued from his pocket and lay contentedly in the petite embroidered handbag of Miss Elizabeth Gough. 'I promise to wait for you. Should things go awry, I shall take the blame for it.'

Pressing her hands against her skirts, Elizabeth rose from the table and walked steadily towards the kitchen. Clutching her newest possession closely to her side, she disappeared into the shadows. Two minutes later, a grumbling Mrs Hennessey appeared in the yard.

'Would ye like to eat out here or in the servants' dining room, sir?'

'Here will do. Err, I say, you are most kind... The chicken looks so appetising...'

His words sounded strangely strangled to Mrs Hennessey as she put the plate of meat before him. ''Tis direct from the hen house,' she replied. 'I have given ye some spuds for balance, sir, and here's some milk, fresh from the dairy.'

This time, he never properly heard the cook's voice, such was the sound of his heart beating nineteen to the dozen. The wait was intolerable. At any moment, he expected to see Heath appear, closely followed by a red-faced Sir William himself.

The next ten minutes, spent picking at his food and ruminating on his utter incompetence, were sheer purgatory. The expectation of feeling the executioner's noose around his neck at any second seemed to grow with each fork of boiled potato. Then, without warning, the door from the kitchen flew open. It was Elizabeth, and she appeared to be alone. She approached him cautiously, taking careful, tiny steps on the cobbles. She was still clasping her handbag to her waist.

'I have done it!' she declared. 'I have done it!'

Chapter Fourteen

By the time Jacob stepped back into *The Gauger's Return* it was already past lunchtime, and the young kitchen maid, Molly, was scrubbing down the long refectory table under the leaded bay window – a task she seemed to perform at least three or four times each day. Without speaking to the girl, he scurried up the stairs to his room, where he poured a couple of pints of cool water into the washbowl and took a few moments to bathe his face and hands. What a morning it had been!

He hadn't wanted to tarry at Pennycrocker Hall any longer than absolutely necessary, but once again, his plans had been subverted. By way of farewell, he'd thanked Elizabeth for her courage and offered up yet another abject apology. 'It wasn't my intention to seek your assistance today, Miss Gough, nor even speak to you on this matter; so please accept my humble assurances that it shall never happen again.'

As he'd risen to go, she'd called him back with an insistent wave of her hand. 'Oh, but you must! If you need my help, you must ask it.'

The look of surprise was clear in Jacob's face as he'd slumped back onto the rustic chair. 'That's very kind, Miss

Gough, but your safety must be uppermost from now on. I insist. What would I say to your father if you came to any harm on my account?'

'But you see, I already know something of this matter. Papa took time to speak to me on the subject before he departed, and I am supposed to be keeping my eyes and ears open. Each day, I note down the comings and goings at the Hall and any gossip I hear, for when he returns. I believe Father may suspect Sir William in some way, so it appears...' She produced a slim green leather-bound pocketbook, about the length of her fingers, from her handbag, where it had earlier been nestling innocently beside the now departed revolver. 'See, I have your name in my book already!'

'Goodness, Miss Gough, you truly amaze me...'

'You may call me Elizabeth from now on. "Miss Gough" is too formal, now I have made your proper acquaintance. You have been introduced to my father, after all! And...' she offered up a wicked smile, 'we have already survived our first escapade together. If it suits, may I call you Jacob?'

Such an overture, so amiably offered, was impossible to resist. 'Very well, Miss Elizabeth, I accept your brave and generous proposal. It will be good to have a confidante while I remain in Borwenstow.'

'Yours is a solitary assignment, indeed,' she replied quickly. 'At least I have Mama for company at the moment, until the wedding is behind us.'

'Ah, yes. Hannah is your mother's name, if memory serves. Your father mentioned that it might be possible for her to find a temporary lodging at the Hall.'

'Lady Pennycrocker was so kind. I had intended to speak to Sir William to seek his blessing, but he was not himself that day – all melancholy and glum – so I raised the matter with Her Ladyship instead, and she gave her approval instantly.

She told me *she'd* speak with her husband but not to fret and to bring Mama from the inn straightaway.'

'Is there anyone else who resides permanently at the Hall, apart from the family and servants… and you, of course?'

'Only Rose, Sir William's sister, a most troubled lady, indeed. But she has since departed from here for Italy – 'twas well before Christmas – accompanied by her cousin, Daniel, and some knowledgeable tutor from Oxford. They call it the Grand Tour, apparently. When she will return is anyone's guess.'

'Such Grand Tours can last for years, so I'm led to believe.'

'I only hope it makes her happy,' Elizabeth said with a sullen look, 'for nothing could make things worse.'

'Why was she not content to stay here? Was she sick? Tell me about her. The more I know of the ways of folk around here, the better. That's Mr Woodward's oft spoken refrain – "seek and ye shall find!"'

'There is nothing to tell, in truth. What happened to her is long past now. She is a spinster, Jacob, a bookish woman, approaching forty years of age. I'm told she has lived here at the Hall all her life and chose to stay on after Sir William inherited the estate. Like her brother, she suffers with states of depression from time to time. Hers could be truly soul-destroying, mind, and some weeks she'd never come out of her rooms.'

'Is that why she has gone to Italy – an attempt at a cure? The thermal baths at San Pellegrino are beneficial in such conditions, I'm told.'

'Ha-ha…' she smiled. 'Your knowledge of ancient Italian therapies is impressive, and your supposition well considered. But you are only partly correct. Rose's constitution seemed much improved last summer. I knew her less than the rest, but for sure, everyone rejoiced to see her carefree and gay once again.

It was the talk of the servants' hall. In short, she had become a different woman entirely. The *reason* for her transformation was clear to all but the ignorant and indifferent. You see, Rose had finally found a man to love – and one who loved her in return. Regrettably, the romance was short-lived, and by late autumn, the black dog had returned – without doubt, worse than ever. Sir William, weary of her mood swings and anxious to do what he could for her, packed Rose off to Venice – "for her own good" – such was the gossip back then…'

'There was a lover, you say?'

'A full-blown suitor, by all accounts. I only met him once. Quite a charming fellow, in truth, given his reputation hereabouts, and at least five years younger than her. Sir William did not approve of the match, but Rose is her own woman, and she fought her cause. She did not *need* Sir William's permission for the marriage, but she cherished her brother's blessing and dogged him constantly for it. Beneath Rose's gentle persona, there lies an obstinate woman. Despite the bouts of melancholia, behind those studious spectacles, there is a doughty spirit, indeed. Regardless of all her chivvying, Sir William was adamant, by all accounts, and would not yield. But then fate took hold. In an instant, all her life's hopes were dashed against the rocks.'

'So, you knew Rose's lover?'

'You're not listening, Jacob… I said I'd met him on just one occasion. 'Twas at the country fayre, last July. I shied away at first, knowing of his family's reputation, but when he caught up with me at the *Punch and Judy*, he surprised me by his gracious ways. I remember he started with, "You must be Miss Gough from the Hall. I'm honoured to make your acquaintance". He spoke very lah-di-dah and gentlemanlike – not as a true farmer might. Not at all.'

Just then, the door from the kitchen jerked open once

more. It was the stout Mrs Hennessey come to fetch Jacob's half-emptied plate. She approached the conversing pair much in the manner of a sailor walking the deck of a heaving brigantine. 'I see you have no appetite for my food, sir. More's the pity, as you look like you need a good feed.'

'It was most appetising, Cook. It's just that I've started to feel unwell. It came on a while back. Miss Gough has suggested I remain until my head has cleared. I suspect it must be all this sea air. I'm not used to it. I fear my constitution is altered somewhat.'

'More likely the stinking train, sir,' Mrs Hennessey harrumphed. 'The smoke those locomotives belch out is enough to turn any man's stomach. I, for one, cannot abide them. No wonder you were seeking water earlier, poor man. Can I get you something stronger, perhaps?'

'No, that's very kind, but I feel my force returning. And now, I must cut along. I have much work to be done – many acres to visit.'

'A dram of whiskey, perhaps?' she pressed. 'We have some fine old *Carrells* in the parlour. I can fetch it if—'

'Please, Mrs Hennessey, I know you mean well,' Elizabeth interrupted, 'but the last thing Mr Jarvie needs now is Irish whiskey. He's feeling much revived anyway, aren't you, Mr Jarvie?'

'I am, Miss Gough. Another minute perhaps... Allow me to take some deep draughts of air before I depart – kill or cure, eh?' And with that, as Mrs Hennessey took her leave, shaking her head as she wobbled away, Jacob rose from the table and inhaled a great and very apparent gulp out of the atmosphere. When the cook had fully disappeared, he resumed his seat opposite Elizabeth and said through slightly clenched teeth, 'I fear it might be difficult for us to converse in future. It would be improper for you to enter the inn unaccompanied, and the open countryside, where I shall be spending most of my time, will be a most inconvenient meeting place.'

'We can meet at St Piran's.'

'But the church remains locked, so Mr Trewint has informed me.'

'Certainly it is, but not the *churchyard*. There is an iron bench outside the northern wall of the nave which faces the sea. It's where I take my novel, from time to time. A most pleasant spot, shaded from the bright sun, and secluded too. I rarely see another while I am there, save perhaps for the parson or Mr Polrunny. Lamentably, neither will trouble us now. I have Friday afternoons to myself. Let us gather there in two days, on the thirteenth. Meet me at four o'clock, and I will show you my little book again. Who knows what it might contain by then!'

'I agree! And who knows what I might have learned also!' Jacob beamed. 'Four o'clock it shall be, on Friday. Before I go, you mentioned the verger... Do you have any news?'

'Only he is still sick and expected to die any day. He may be dead now, for all I know. Mr Trewint or his friend Jago will comprehend more than me. The walls of Pennycrocker Hall confine me most days, but I shall ensure that if I hear any whisper from within them, you shall be the first to hear of it.'

'And so far...' Jacob advanced, 'have you learned anything of note?'

'I regret to say *nothing*. Your arrival this morning has been the most noteworthy event thus far,' she giggled. Elizabeth put her finger to her temple and looked suddenly thoughtful. At length, she added, 'But there may be something... something weird... which could be connected in some way.'

'Tell me.'

'The pistol in Sir William's desk brings to mind an occurrence some months back, maybe seven or eight, when I heard a single shot ring out. It was late, and I'd already retired, but the blast seemed to come from *inside* the house. When I enquired of Mr Wilks the following day, he told me Sir William had killed a fox from his study window, one that had strayed too close to the house.'

'Mr Wilks?'

'He is the butler. You will not have seen him. Sir William has given him leave to visit a sick relative. His father in Plymouth is poorly with the gout, evidently. Mr Heath has taken his place for a while. The butler left us at about the same time as Papa returned to London.'

At that point, the outside kitchen door opened yet again and Esther, the scullery maid, pushed a ginger cat into the yard. 'Shoo! Away with you! You're getting fat – catch your own food for a while. It'll do you good!' The animal skulked off and disappeared behind a mountain of wooden kegs stacked in a distant corner of the yard. When Esther had returned into the kitchen to resume her place at Mrs Hennessey's side, Jacob took up the conversation once more. This time, much to Elizabeth's concealed amusement, he did so with an exaggerated attempt to lower his voice.

'Why should the discovery of the revolver bring this incident to mind, Elizabeth? Do you think Sir William used it to destroy the fox?'

'At the time, I thought it a strange business because Sir William does not keep firearms in the house. He has told the staff he despises such things. There are a pair of Purdeys gathering dust in the servants' quarters – put there by Sir William, as he could not bear the sight of them. Some terrible accident in the past, so Mr Heath says – apparently Sir William's young brother was killed as a result – has turned him away from them. They were his father's, by all account. But you see, the shotguns are held by Mr Wilks himself, who has the only key to the cabinet. I'd wondered how this fox had been dispatched at the time, as I had no idea Sir William possessed such a handgun. Maybe 'twas that he used to kill the creature.'

'A strange weapon to use for killing a fox, all the same…'

'I hadn't given it much thought, in truth.'

'But now,' Jacob rose once more, 'I really must not overstay my welcome. Mrs Hennessey will be back soon with more of her advice and boiled potatoes.'

'I look forward to our rendezvous on Friday. Don't be late.' She wagged her finger. 'I'll ask Heath to arrange the carriage to meet you at the entrance.'

As she began to stand, Jacob touched her arm gently. 'There is one thing you forgot to mention, Miss Gough. You remarked that Rose had an admirer and things had ended badly – "fate took hold" were your words, I recall. But you did not give me his name. You said he was a farmer who spoke like a gentleman.'

'Yes, just like his older brother, Cassius.'

'Forgive me, Miss Gough. I am completely at sixes and sevens.'

'Rose's suitor was none other than Ignatius Honey, the man my poor Samuel was falsely accused of murdering. Now do you see? It is little wonder that the poor lady's spirit was broken… after half his body was discovered on the steps of St Piran's! I just hope the healing baths of San Pellegrino live up to their reputation. Unquestionably, poor Rose will require all their curative powers… and more besides…'

* * *

The verger of St Piran's, the one-legged former tin miner of Borwenstow, was dead. It had taken Penrose Polrunny five days to die, and the process had been painful and unpleasant in the extreme. He'd first complained to his wife of a rash on the fingers of his right hand and a mild headache soon after returning from an inspection of the church. These symptoms were quickly followed by dizziness and a terrible shortness of breath. When the vomiting commenced, Polrunny was confined to his bed and Dr Plymswood called. The doctor, who suspected poisoning at the outset, did what he could for the man, by the applying of hot poultices and by the giving of medicines designed to further discharge the stomach. These remedies were most violently effective, but regrettably, the verger's condition did not improve one iota as a consequence. Plymswood, his diagnosis now firmly set on poison, ordered that the windows be flung open to allow his patient to breathe better. Despite the accumulation of all these treatments, the battle to save him was in vain. After a series of distressing seizures, Polrunny lost all consciousness. The outcome, from that moment, had been inevitable. On the fifth day of sickness, at five o'clock in the afternoon, Polrunny suffered a heaving cardiac arrest and was pronounced dead just two hours later by a surprisingly sober Dr Plymswood.

During his tenure as verger, it was customary for Penrose Polrunny to conduct twice daily surveys of both the interior of St Piran's and its exterior grounds, including the graveyard and the sombre Lych House. After the Reverend Rosewarne's untimely passing, all entry to the church had been barred under the strict instructions of Inspector Austol Halwill Barton. In order not to upset the locals unduly, Halwill had allowed the graveyard and its gated surrounding to remain open. This protected state of affairs continued for three whole days, but on completion of the parson's autopsy, permission had been received from Launceston that normal dealings could be resumed, and the church reopened to its congregation once more. By then, Polrunny was already sick and could not be raised from his bed, so the holy building had perforce remained secured and inaccessible for any form of worship, unless it be carried out within the churchyard.

The fact was, Polrunny had already broken the locked-up sanction by that time. On the evening of Parson Rosewarne's death, less than twenty minutes after the police officers had dispersed and while the reverend's body lay lifeless, embraced within the gloomy walls of the Lych House, Polrunny had let himself back into the church. He'd been alone. This transgression he performed in the full knowledge he was breaching the embargo imposed by Inspector Halwill just hours before. Polrunny had explained to his wife he could not bear the thought of Parson Rosewarne's blood lying uncleansed on the font's flagstone floor.

'It's my duty, dearest. Whatever the mortal powers that be have said on the matter, I must return to clean up this disorder. My higher calling exceeds anything a policeman might decree,' he reasoned.

'Very well, my love, if you must. I promise not to tell a soul.'

This was to prove to be Verger Penrose Polrunny's final visit to his house of worship, for the first symptoms of itchy hands and mild dizziness presented within minutes of him locking up and commencing his short walk home. His death, when announced, caused great consternation amongst the already troubled folk of Borwenstow. Two poisonings in less than a week were difficult to bear, even for such a community as theirs, so used, as they were, to calamity and unexplained happenings. Polrunny's wife, Lena, when questioned by Constable Poundstock as to what might have caused the affliction, could come up with no answer, save to say the illness had arrived suddenly, without any advance warning.

Her husband, she told the young policeman, had been in fine fettle, excepting some soreness around his missing knee where the wooden leg had chaffed.

On hearing the news, Inspector Austol Halwill Barton ordered the body of Polrunny to be removed to Launceston for an autopsy and decided it was time he paid Borwenstow another visit. Only days back from London and Scotland Yard, it was time to commence his travels once more, but this time the outbound journey would be much shorter and almost due east.

On arriving outside *The Gauger's Return* the following day, accompanied by the faithful Constable Marshgate, he made straight for St Piran's. Using the keys he had appropriated, which had formerly been the Reverend Rosewarne's personal clutch, he let himself into the nave and set about a thorough examination. Everything appeared as it had at the moment of his departure, six days before – save one thing. Where dried blood had once stained the stone floor around the font, there was now the very faintest trace of blush to mark the spot on the cold slabs where Parson Rosewarne's head had first rested in death.

'I gave instructions for this church to remain locked, did I not, Constable?'

'That you did, sir, but you released the restriction once the victim's cause of death had been proven – some days ago, in fact. I think 'twas Monday, before you set out for London.'

'I did so, but no one else had the keys to the church, save for the unfortunate Mr Polrunny. Am I not correct?'

'Yes, sir.'

'And he was sick, nearly unconscious, before I gave that order, was he not?'

'I believe so, sir.'

'Then, pray tell me, who cleaned this blood from the flagstones?'

'Perchance, it evaporated into the air...' Constable Marshgate heaved a sigh. This conversation was clearly taxing his brain.

Inspector Halwill did not honour the baleful suggestion with a response. Instead, he got on his knees and brushed the floor with his hands, his face less than twelve inches from the ground.

As he swept, Constable Marshgate, though he knew not his inspector's purpose, looked on in undisguised admiration. Halwill's hands reached the base of the font and started to rise up, feeling its curves all the time. His fingers reached the blunt edge which had collided with Rosewarne's skull as he'd tumbled from above. The inspector stroked its contours, muttered something indecipherable, and now crouching, he moved on upwards.

'Here's another thing, Constable,' he announced on reaching the top, 'the font is empty of holy water. How did that happen, may I ask?' Halwill looked at Marshgate and blinked, the mischief in him hoping to receive the same inane response as before. Inspector Halwill was not to be disappointed.

'Evaporation, sir... I believe that must be the answer.'

'Ha! Evaporation of blood that hardly leaves a stain – and the same for half a pint of holy water? I think not!' Halwill cried. 'Someone has been visiting without my sanction... But who? And why would our mystery individual take the trouble to clean so thoroughly?'

'Perhaps it was Mr Polrunny, sir.'

'But he was sick, was he not? He fell ill the very same day and was soon incapable of lifting his remaining leg from the bed, according to our doctor friend. And since then, the church has been locked, and he was the only one holding keys. I have the only other set.'

Constable Marshgate scratched his chin. 'Maybe he gave the keys to another?'

'I think not. According to the local constable… what's his name?'

'Constable Poundstock, sir.'

'Yes, thank you… According to Poundstock, Polrunny's wife swears her husband slept with the whole bunch under his pillow every night, so devoted was he to them. The sensible constable relieved her of them the day her husband died. They have remained in his possession since then.' Halwill's face brightened. 'I think I have it,' he announced. 'There can only be one solution. You have been right all along, Marshgate. Old Polrunny must be our man. He must have entered the church *just before* he became sick. It must have occurred sometime after we'd departed, for he was already ill by eight o'clock, according to the doctor.'

'I'm glad to be of assistance, sir.' Marshgate was looking suddenly triumphant.

'But why?' Inspector Austol Halwill Barton frowned. 'Why would old Polrunny go against my strict orders so quickly? What was he trying to achieve here? 'Tis strange indeed.'

Chapter Fifteen

That evening, as he pushed his empty plate away and swallowed the last remnants of cider, Jacob Jarvie resolved to greet the rising sun in person the following morning. It was time to start his quest in earnest.

The afternoon following his return from Pennycrocker Hall had been spent in walking around the village for a few hours in a deliberate attempt to make himself known. His first call had been to the post office, where he'd dispatched a letter containing a report of his findings thus far, including all that he'd gleaned from his meetings with Sir William and Lady Pennycrocker, and of particular interest, he imagined, his encounter with Miss Elizabeth Gough. In the ogling presence of Eliza Chadwick, the postmistress, he addressed the despatch to *The Ordnance Survey Offices, Southampton, C/O Albert Woodward, Esquire,* in the sure knowledge it would be forwarded the same day to Tower Hill. This had been the agreed method of communication with his chief investigation officer. The letter would take half a day longer to get to its recipient, but this was a small price to pay to secure his cloak of pseudonymity.

'Good day, madam. I'm recently arrived in Borwenstow –

Jacob Jarvie of the Ordnance Survey, at your service. I wish to send this letter to Southampton and require a postage stamp.'

'Of course, sir. I'm pleased to meet you. Will you allow me to weigh it?' He handed her the sealed envelope. 'That's nearly two ounces, sir, so you'll need a Venetian Red and a Ha'penny Green. A penny-ha'penny, if you please.' He handed her three jingling ha'penny pieces. 'Will you be here long, sir? In Borwenstow, I mean.'

'I expect to remain in your delightful village until the end of the month, at least. I have much work ahead of me and a lot of walking to do, no doubt. Ha-ha! Employment as a surveyor for the Ordnance Survey is guaranteed to keep my legs moving, that's for sure.'

'Shall I put your letter in the post bag, sir? The next collection is in an hour. With luck, it will reach Southampton by tomorrow.'

As luck would have it, at that very moment the post office door swung open to the accompaniment of a tinkling bell, and Constable Poundstock entered. This was an opportunity Jacob knew he had to grasp… but how? While he thought of a way of engaging the recently arrived policeman, he said to the postmistress, 'Perhaps, on second thoughts, I should purchase another pair of stamps. My superior at the Ordnance Survey requires me to send him daily reports, and a few spare will come in handy, should you be closed the next time I am passing.'

'Of course.' Miss Chadwick peeled away another one of each, and in exchange for a penny-ha'penny, she handed him the stamps.

'Good day, Constable,' Jacob offered as he passed her the coins. 'Would you happen to know if the weather will turn tomorrow, as I plan to rise early? I am Jarvie, by the by. Jacob Jarvie, at your service – recently arrived from Southampton.'

'Mr Jarvie means to remain in Borwenstow for all of May,' Miss Chadwick twittered helpfully. 'He is with the Ordnance Survey, no less.'

'Pleased to meet you, sir.' Constable Poundstock extended his hand. 'I see no reason for any change – for a few days, at least. I expect tomorrow morning will be fine again.'

'Good, I'm pleased to hear it. I plan to survey the church and its grounds at first light, before entering the nearby fields to the north-east.'

'Sir, the church is locked until further orders. But you may walk the graveyard, if you wish.'

'Locked, you say? My, that *is* a pity. Will this be the case for much longer?'

'I await instruction from Launceston. You see, there were two fatalities connected with the church only last week, and we have no vicar, either, to conduct the services.'

Jacob's feigned surprise came more easily to him than he'd ever imagined – he felt truly *in the part*. 'Oh, how terrible. *Two* deaths, you say? A pair of tragic accidents in such a short time. 'Tis most extraordinary indeed.'

'You say you are a surveyor, sir?'

'Yes. Ordnance Survey Office, Southampton.'

'Are you travelling alone?'

'Yes, quite alone,' Jacob blinked back.

'In that case, I shall enquire if I may allow you to visit St Piran's so you may conduct your lawful business. If you can wait a few days, you shall have your answer. I hold the keys, so if 'tis approved, I will allow you special entry.'

'That's very kind, Officer. Where may I find you?'

'I have an office not far from the docks, the other side of the crossroads. There is a sign. You may reach me there most days.'

And with that, and feeling mighty pleased with himself,

Jacob made his excuses and departed. He next visited the dry goods store, where he purchased a quarter pound of sugar; then the greengrocer, where an apple took his eye; and finally, he obtained two ounces of tobacco and a box of matches from a dingy store on Fore Street. In each establishment, he spread the news of his purpose in their village. This he managed with increasing confidence and aplomb. He strolled down to the quayside and noted the thick stone construction of its walls. He nosed around the fish market a while and lit a pipe. The old Custom House stood sentinel-like overlooking the harbour, and he remembered the words of Henry Gough, days earlier, informing him the stout building was no longer Crown property and now in the hands of the Pennycrocker family.

Satisfied he had truly made his presence felt, he retired to the inn, where he did much the same touting amongst the local clients until dinner, which he partook alone. A plate of stewed mutton washed down with two mugs of local cider saw him to his bed and a dreamless sleep. As he closed his eyes, he told himself he would start his intelligence gathering in earnest at sunrise the following morning. First on his list, he determined, would be a visit to Doubloons.

* * *

As predicted by Constable Poundstock, the next day dawned much as its predecessor had – clear and calm. As daybreak approached, the inn began to wake with the sound of shuffling feet and the clash of cutlery in the kitchen. Jacob tiptoed downstairs. Armed with a tripod in one hand, plus a theodolite and a brass spyglass secreted in a canvas rucksack, he stepped into the still cool air of the high street. The village clock had yet to toll five o'clock, and there was not another soul to be seen. In his pocket, he carried a copy of the current Ordnance Survey map of Borwenstow and its environs. All the above had been kindly leant to him, thanks to the kind offices of an old friend from his previous employment. It did not take him long to reach the yew at the eastern corner of the churchyard, and from here, passing the Lych House and using his map as a guide, he took the footpath that led steadily upwards towards a broad expanse of fields at the top of the rise. To his right, the sky was brightening, and Jacob stretched his young legs in an effort to reach the summit before the sun overwhelmed the eastern horizon and bathed the village beneath in its ochre, life-giving energy.

But it was not to be, for he had miscalculated on a number of counts. By overestimating his stamina and underestimating the strength required to attain the place he sought with all his baggage in tow, he'd missed his target by as much as five minutes. The sheer distance to his goal was much greater than he'd calculated too, so by the time he had a clear view of the eastern landscape, the orange ball of light had already risen by degrees above the distant spire of St Juliot's.

He cursed and threw down his hat in exhaustion. Laying his tripod on the tufted grass and relieving himself of his rucksack, Jacob lay on his back and gazed into the ever-brightening sky. Some distance away, he could see silhouetted shapes, a cluster of dark buildings which his map told him marked the spot where Doubloons lay. *I'll have to rise earlier next time if I am to keep my promise with the sun,* he smiled to himself.

He was now at the highest spot on the cliffs, and the land fell away gently on all sides, save one. There, the drop to the rocks, 500 feet below, was near vertical. He got to his feet, and on an impulse, he approached the precipice. To the north, the sea below looked as smooth as a silver platter – unruffled, serene, with hardly a ripple on its glassy surface. He drew closer still, at first crouching, then sliding his elbows on the grassy bank to reach the drop. Just as his head poked over the edge, and a feeling of vertigo began to reach into his midriff, Jacob spotted a movement.

It came from directly beneath him – a jolly boat, close in, hugging the shoreline, for the tide appeared to be in flow. He discerned the craft was travelling south-westerly, in the direction of Borwenstow. He could see there were four figures aboard. He reached into his canvas bag, fumbled for the spyglass and directed it towards his target. The two fellows who sat amidships and faced towards him were woollen-hatted and rowing steadily, stirring their oars through the still ocean in regular, unhurried movements. The other pair had their backs turned away; one sat in the bow, the other, a particularly large man, occupied the stern, which seemed to sink a little under his weight. Jacob lay prone on the clifftop, eyes bulging and stock still, hardly daring to breathe, despite the distance between them. Something told him there was mischief afoot, and his chin pressed yet deeper into the tufted grass at the very thought of it. The occupants of the vessel were clearly not fishermen. They did not look like they had come from another vessel either, as none could be seen offshore in deeper water for miles around. The day had hardly begun; 'twas barely five thirty and the light only lately sufficient for safe navigation between the rocks. *They must have freshly set out…* he mused. *What are they up to?*

Jacob waited and watched until the little craft had cleared the headland to the south-west and resolved to track its movements a little further. He desperately wanted to learn its destination, which he assumed might not be far distant. When the vessel was completely out of sight, he collected his paraphernalia and retraced his steps downwards, past the lower headland, until he reached a point above Borwenstow where he could see the tower of St Piran's, still 200 feet below. Here, he approached the cliff edge once again in the same crawling, cautious manner. Much to his relief, as his head nudged over the edge, the sighting of the jolly boat was immediately re-established. She lay close in, as before, as she rounded the headland. From her angle of progress, she appeared to be heading towards the village and a landing at the harbour wall. He watched as the jolly boat drew ever closer, but his view from this position was not as expansive as before, and soon the craft disappeared from view, so close was she to the shoreline. Jacob decided the only course was to hurry to the harbour and await her arrival – out of sight, if he could manage it. With luck, he might be able to identify these suspicious early-morning voyagers.

After a helter-skelter chase down the hill, still clutching his equipment, he soon reached the little dock, which lay practically deserted, save for a few herring gulls that dived into the sound to peck at scraps. Here he waited, concealed, in part, by the corner of the fish market. From his position, he could see the police office on the other side of the crossroads and made a mental note to pay Constable Poundstock a visit the following day. He lit a pipe using the newly purchased tobacco he'd procured from the grimy Fore Street store... Then he lit another... but there was still no sign of any arrival on the quayside. The village clock chimed six. He counted each clang carefully, and with every strike, his feelings of uncertainty grew. *Where have they got to?*

By half past six, folk started to mingle about, going about their daily business. Jacob rose, let out a contemplative sigh and decided it was time for breakfast. He collected up the tools of his ostensible trade, took one last doleful look at the still deserted harbour wall and ambled back to the inn.

* * *

The amiable Molly produced two boiled eggs, a slice of ham and a flask of milk for his breakfast. With Henry Gough's advice ringing in his ears, Jacob turned down her offer of steamed pilchards – a refusal Molly seemed to half expect, as she batted not an eyelid when it came.

'Tell me, Molly, when might I meet the innkeeper? 'Tis Mr Trewint, is it not? I should like to pay my compliments. These last two days, I have yet to clap eyes on him!'

'He will be here soon enough. He's a busy man, of late. 'Tis some other business elsewhere that takes his-self from us from time to time, but 'tis usually a matter of just a few hours, no more. He soon returns. Don't fret, sir. I'm sure ye'll see him this very day and find him most agreeable, too.'

'Thank you, Molly. I'll look forward to it.' He gave her one of his best smiles. 'I say, would you oblige me with another slice of ham, perchance, and a chunk of bread? My exertions this morning have left me quite famished.'

She nodded in compliance. 'Will that be all, sir?'

A sudden impulse came to Jacob. It concerned a matter that had been troubling him while he'd been waiting for the jolly boat to appear against the harbour wall. 'One thing more!' he beamed. 'Do you happen to know about the tides in these parts? Their times and suchlike...' The moment the words left his lips, he knew he shouldn't have asked the question of her.

'Oh, no, sir. I knows they comes and goes, up and down, so to speak. Would you like me to ask Mr Trewint for 'ee?'

'No, it's of no consequence,' Jacob replied hurriedly. 'I'll ask him myself, if I need to.'

After he had eaten – good-natured Molly had been obliging enough to bring him a further *two* slices of ham, a large hunk of bread and another mug of hot, sweet tea, into the bargain – Jacob decided he would pay Constable Poundstock an early call. The matter of the tides needed to be settled, and he was sure the policeman would have the answer.

***

'I'm afraid I have no reply yet from Launceston, Mr Jarvie,' the policeman said as soon as Jacob approached the counter.

'I'm grateful for your asking, Constable, and I can wait, but it's not that I have come to speak about.'

'Sir?'

'Perhaps you can help me. My job of surveyor is to ensure the coastline is accurately portrayed, and I realise I have failed to bring a tide chart of these parts, with the various timings and levels, etcetera… Would you happen to have a copy? One which I may use to make some notes…'

Constable Poundstock looked relieved. This was a question he could answer easily.

'I can do better, sir. I am provided with booklets of the yearly tides, marked with each day and the hours of ebb and flow. I can let you have one, if you like.'

'That would be excellent.' A thought suddenly flashed into Jacob's head. 'And, perchance, if you have a copy of last year's offering, that would be most helpful – for comparison purposes, you understand.'

'Yes, sir, I'm sure I can find one for you. Would you wait a minute? It shall not take long.' Poundstock disappeared into the rear of the office.

'I'm glad to be of service, sir,' the policeman said on his return, while handing over a pair of diminutive publications. 'By the by, if you are passing the same time tomorrow, I may have the answer to the other matter we discussed.'

Equipped with the tide books, each of which was no larger

than the size of his palm, Jacob was soon able to discover what he wanted. High tide in Borwenstow for that day occurred twice, first at 6.58a.m. and then about twelve hours later, at 7.10p.m. He noted the difference in water levels with interest – as much as twenty-three feet, on occasion… maybe more, if he delved further into the books. That surprised him mightily, as the variance surpassed the height of four grown men. The times of ebb and flow altered with every passing day and shifted forwards daily by about half an hour. High tide tomorrow morning would be at 7.27a.m., the following day at 7.56a.m., and so on.

With his new reference books secured amongst the contents of his canvas bag, and once again reunited with his tripod, Jacob spent most of the afternoon up on the high pastures close to Doubloons Farm, where the seaward vista was starkly different from the one he'd experienced at dawn. Gone was the vast expanse of leaden-blue ocean lapping against the base of the cliffs. Now, a panorama of myriad sharp-angled red-grey rocks beckoned. For nearly as far as he could see, shallow pools had appeared all about like craters on a lunar landscape, interspersed by mini deserts of white sand, limpet-encrusted boulders, and what seemed to be acres of dripping green and black seaweed. The water thereabouts had been all but sucked away. *A potent reminder of the force of the moon, if ever one was needed!*

The lapping ocean now lay over a hundred yards distant and to reach the new shoreline on foot would have been a dangerous and abrasive task indeed, even if it were possible to find some passable route downwards into the cove. He set up his theodolite within visible range of Doubloons Farm and took a few random readings. He observed that the land beneath the farmhouse to the north dipped gently at first but then followed a much steeper incline towards the sea, where it seemed to vanish behind a line of sycamores in the distance. Curious to know what lay beyond and closer to the rocks, he packed up his equipment once more.

There was a downward track that led from the farm gate, past the farmhouse towards this lower wooded area, and Jacob set out to walk it, in the full expectation of being challenged at any second. This was Honey land, after all, and he'd been warned to tread carefully. In the comforting knowledge that his Ordnance Survey commission rested securely in his pocket and was ready to be shown at a moment's notice should any aggrieved party approach, he commenced his descent. The path led steadily downwards until it reached the wood, where a fork appeared. The first trail seemed to follow the contour of the incline in a sideways direction, while the other dropped away still further towards the sea. He decided to take the latter. He soon realised his current whereabouts must have been largely hidden by the trees and bushes, and with a modicum of relief, he felt less exposed than before. But still, his heart seemed to beat like a steam piston, and the restless need to look over his shoulder from time to time had not perished.

The track, which appeared well worn, came to an abrupt halt after just a few minutes, and Jacob could see water once more. The sea remained some way from his position, but the faint line marking the progress of the incoming tide was unmistakeable. Much to his great interest, he realised he must have stumbled upon a hidden cove at the foot of the valley. A waterfall could be heard higher up, hidden from view by a wide bank of scented lily of the valley, as it gushed its contents onto the rocky beach below. Directly ahead of him, partly concealed by overhanging branches and camouflaged by dappled sunshine, there appeared a low-roofed building constructed on three sides with ancient oak. A raised jetty led along the side of one of its timbered walls. Jacob stopped for a moment and listened warily, but the waterfall and the droning of the countless creatures that swarmed about his head defeated his attempt to hear anything of value. The insects seemed more abundant here, in this dank Dingley Dell of a place. Quite suddenly, the boughs of a nearby sycamore heaved and cracked as a chilling gust of air swept in from the north. This sudden rattle of leaves and branches instantly conquered the noise of tumbling water and even seemed to silence the cove's entire population of creepy-crawlies for a few moments.

Jacob Jarvie propped his tripod against an old tree stump and gingerly climbed the wooden steps leading to the platform. Making the least sound possible and taking care not to slip, he hauled himself up and made his way towards the open entrance of what he imagined might be a boat shed, of sorts. The tide, being near full out, meant he could observe the complete length of the pontoon, stilts and all, from tip to toe. He comprehended the timber pillars and half the walls must be consumed under many feet of water within a matter of a few hours, but for now, at least, the braces and side walls of the structure could be clearly seen, sunk as they were into the man-made foundations at their base. The jetty wobbled slightly as he lifted himself onto the narrow walkway.

Curving his head around the final stanchion, he peered into the opening. What he saw nearly made his heart miss a beat. For there before him, beached on a purpose-built surface of flat Portland cement, were a pair of jolly boats, identical in every way to the one he'd seen earlier that morning.

So that's it – I was correct! He held his breath again. That morning's boat must indeed have been launched just minutes before he'd spotted it at daybreak, for the boathouse where he now stood was a mere 500 yards distant from the very spot where he'd lain sprawled on the clifftop just hours before. There was no doubting it. One of the jolly boats must have been the same craft he'd seen that morning, and presumably, the large man seated in the stern was none other than Cassius Honey himself – Henry Gough's description of the giant fitted to a tee.

He couldn't wait to hurry back to the inn to compile his second "survey report", but first, he had to run the gauntlet of Doubloons once more. Emerging from the wood, he gazed up the track that bisected the field ahead of him. From here, not even the roof of the farmhouse could be seen. As he ascended the path, the first chimney stack came into view, stark against the eastern sky. The windows of the upper floors soon followed. Now he could be observed from the house, and he knew it. It was important to appear casual, not to show any anxiety in his body movements. He tried a swagger, stumbled and dropped his tripod. Humiliated by unseen eyes, he picked it from the dirt and continued his stamp up the hill.

When he reached the top, there was still no sign of activity, though the house itself seemed to take on a character of its own, staring down at him accusingly. The open footpath and blessed sanctuary were less than fifty yards away. Then, from the rear, he heard the unmistakeable click of a shotgun being cocked.

'Stop, sir, or I'll fire!' It was a woman's voice and a fierce-sounding one, at that.

Chapter Sixteen

Jacob Jarvie turned to face the challenger. 'Apologies, ma'am. I am the official surveyor, come from Southampton. I mean you no harm. I was just taking a few measurements.' The woman before him was slight of figure and about thirty years of age. The shock of unruly hair that fanned an intense and striking face was the colour of an autumn harvest. Without saying another word, she took two threatening steps forwards while targeting the weapon directly at his heart, her unwavering hands held high against her right shoulder. Jacob noticed, with some unease, the shotgun she was gripping was one of the newer types – a model with two barrels. He'd only seen one before in his life, an American design, while he'd been at Woolwich, but the sight of the twin black tubes, set side by side, was as unmistakeable as it was disquieting.

'Madam, please lower the gun. I am the surveyor,' he repeated, holding up his arms, 'come to see the lie of the land for the Ordnance Survey. I am defenceless and of no threat, I guarantee.'

The woman took three further menacing steps in his direction while indicating with both barrels that he should back off. Jacob stood his ground. Quite *why* he did was even a mystery to him, but maybe the sheer tension of the moment had given him the courage to resist, a quality he'd often doubted he possessed.

'My name is Jacob Jarvie, madam,' he said, deliberately lowering his hands. He could see his antagonist's freckles now, vivid and bristling on her pale cheekbones. 'I arrived in Borwenstow just days ago. I have a warrant in my pocket. All I wish is for you to allow me on your land so I may carry out my lawful duty.'

'You should have come to the house first.' Her voice sounded hoarse, as if she, like him, might be in a condition of extreme strain.

'Please lower the gun, madam. I am a man of books, not used to such frightful occurrences as this.'

Further unnerving, unyielding seconds passed before the young woman finally let down the shotgun. 'Very well, but we cannot have strange men trespassing, uninvited, on our land. Now, go quickly. If you wish to continue your business here, you may return tomorrow and speak with my husband. You can show him your warrant then.'

But Jacob wasn't going to skulk away without asking a few questions. This newfound resolve might put him in danger, but somehow, he was beginning to thrill to it. 'My records tell me this land is owned by a Mr Cassius Honey. Is that correct?'

'He is my husband.'

'May I speak with him now? It would greatly help my cause if I could.'

'He is resting.'

'Then his brother, perchance… a Mr Gabriel, so my papers say.'

'He, too, cannot be disturbed. Come at noon tomorrow, and you shall find them both here.'

'Thank you. I shall do as you say… And who do I address

now? I have given you *my* name, madam. Pray, what is yours?'

'I see no reason to speak any further. You have my directions. Now, please leave our land. Come tomorrow if you wish to explain yourself fully.'

Jacob touched his hat and moved to go. As he let himself out of the gate, he spun his head to regard the house once more. The wife of Cassius Honey, whatever her given name, had remained fixed to the spot, defiantly staring back with shotgun half raised. Clearly, she wanted him out of her sight before ceasing her sentry duties. He obliged with a submissive smile, and taking the south-westerly path towards the church, half a mile distant, he took his leave.

As he descended gently towards the now visible tower of St Piran's, his thoughts turned to the events of the early morning. The mystery of how the jolly boat had disappeared near Borwenstow still remained. The little craft had certainly not arrived at the quayside, as he'd so confidently expected, so where, indeed, had it landed? Then a thought struck him. Perhaps there was *another* hidden cove, similar to the one he'd just discovered at Doubloons, between his last sighting of the jolly boat and the Borwenstow harbour wall. With mounting excitement, he realised such a spot would be adjacent to the church, and all the talk of hidden tunnels and hovering spectres started to ring in his head. He decided to leave the path and explore the clifftops once more. Only this time, he would start at the point where the land started to sink sharply in the direction of the churchyard.

Jacob reached the area soon enough. As before, his fear of heights got the better of him, and he was forced to lay on his stomach to crawl the last few feet to the very edge. Here, he extended his head, like a tortoise from its shell, and looked down. It was approaching 4p.m., and the exposed rocks and crevices beneath looked sharp and unfriendly against the angled rays of western sunlight. The tide was once again in flow, its vanguard waters now approaching to less than thirty yards from the foot of the cliffs. To his right, he could see the bluff of land behind which the jolly boat had disappeared at first light that morning. To his left, he half expected to glimpse the harbour of Borwenstow, but instead, another bluff of coastline, much shallower than the first but obstructive all the same, hid the harbour wall from view. His heart raced. This was indeed another concealed inlet, and the mystery of the missing jolly boat appeared to have been solved. *This is where it must have berthed!* He stretched out still further, craning his neck for a better view. The queasy feeling of vertigo returned, but his fortitude was soon rewarded, for now, stretching at maximum safe extension, the very base of the cliffs could be seen directly beneath, still dry from the tide, but not for long by the look of the fast-approaching water. More importantly, the vaguest outline of a fissure could be seen – its entrance bathed in the light of the dipping sun. *This must be it!* he fair shouted to himself. This had to be the seaward entrance to the ancient passageway which, if the stories were correct, led directly into the crypt of St Piran's.

But he could look no more. He half contemplated using the spyglass in the hope of revealing more of the opening, but the thought of peering through it while unable to use his arms as a balancing counterweight was repulsive. The giddiness had become too much to bear, and anyway, he'd seen enough. Very tentatively, he withdrew his body and rolled away from the precipice. Here he lay for a few minutes, gazing into the deep blue sky, half panting from the exertion and half with the excitement of it all.

But what... he pondered, as he lay on the soft grass, *were Cassius Honey and the rest doing in such a lonely and inaccessible place at six o'clock that morning?*

It occurred to him that any tunnel entrance, set deep in the cliff face, might only be reached safely by boat when the tide was high, as had been the case that morning. There was absolutely no way to reach the entrance from the land, so an approach by sea was the only route. But he quickly dismissed the thought as irrelevant – he remembered being told the tunnel had been blocked by Snuggs's revenue men way back in September. It had taken them a week to do the work, so Henry Gough had said. *So why would the Honeys wish to take the boat there?*

Then, another dart of an idea came to him, and he smiled to himself at the thought of it. Not only was he braver than he'd imagined, but now his reasoning was showing real promise! Maybe a true investigator he might become after all! Clutching onto this new theory, he resolved to remain a while longer on the clifftops. If he was right, all would be revealed in two hours, maybe less... It would be sunset at eight o'clock. All he had to do was linger where he now lay and observe what he saw. As cover for his surveillance, he set up his tripod and fixed up the theodolite once more. Then he resumed his place about three feet from the brink and waited.

About half a mile offshore lay the aptly named "Cow and Calf" rocks. Indeed, they resembled as much, particularly on clear days such as this, when the sun sank into the sea behind them, thus consigning the maternal pair into sharp relief.

What an afternoon it was! Skylarks sang high in the firmament as gulls wheeled effortlessly between the crags, capturing the upward draughts of warm sea air. Lone buzzards circled, sharp-eyed, over ragged lines of hedgerow. And all the time, the irrepressible ocean lapped ever closer to the shoreline. At about ten minutes past five, he detected movement out to sea and dipped his head still further. He was becoming used to lying face down on the grass and had even begun to take some pleasure in it.

The boat that rounded the headland from the north-east was the one he'd been expecting. Jacob's theory was beginning to crystallise. He observed closely as the jolly boat containing the same four figures approached. After ten minutes of watching the approaching oars dip in perfect rhythm into the flat calm sea, the vessel and its occupants were practically beneath him. It was time to stretch out once more. He slithered to the edge – any fears he may have held of falling into the abyss temporarily repressed by this moment of high drama. As he'd predicted, the craft drew ever closer to the spot where he believed the hidden cave must lie. The water, less than two hours before high tide, now touched the base of the cliff face. From this vantage point, he could see the scarred landscape clearly. Save for a few prominent boulders, it was now all but submerged under the great weight of sea, which continued its relentless advance to the shoreline. The jolly boat, navigating easily between the larger rocks, drew closer and disappeared under his eyeline. The occupants were as before, with the giant Cassius Honey seated in the stern. Jacob pushed his head out to see better, but it was to no avail. The vessel had simply vanished. Clearly, the tunnel entrance must be its destination, but the question remained… *Why should these fellows want to visit a cave and tunnel already obstructed, and why so furtive about it? Their purpose must be a dark one, but what?*

Jacob decided there was no alternative. He would have to continue his surveillance until dusk, at least. So he hunkered down, eyes fixed on the spot of coastline where the jolly boat had disappeared. By his calculation, the tide would turn in about ninety minutes, and with sunset just an hour later, there was sure to be some further activity before much longer. The jolly boat and its occupants would risk stranding on the jagged rocks unless they used the remaining high water and daylight to make their escape.

Jacob strained his ears in case some sound reached him from the hidden cave, but his efforts were hopelessly drowned out by the sound of the surf and the wind across the cliffs, which appeared to be picking up somewhat. This solitary vigil continued for another three hours. Then, just minutes after the sun had sunk into the western sky in a blaze of yellows and reds, leaving the Cow and Calf forsaken in the midst of the ocean, there was movement…

The jolly boat reappeared beneath, all four of its sailors intact, but with two seated at different stations. One of the outbound rowers, a bearded fellow with a black woollen hat, now occupied the bow where another, who Jacob presumed must be Gabriel Honey, had previously sat. This man was now rowing for all he was worth. The two had clearly exchanged places. Though the sun was gone, the blood-stained glow of dusk still remained as the little ship steered into deeper waters. It was headed north-east, towards Doubloons Farm and the cove that lay amongst the trees at its base.

As the jolly boat reached the bluff, Jacob rose to his feet and retraced his steps back up the hill. It took him ten full minutes of hard walking before he conquered the slope beyond the outcrop and reached a spot where he could see onto the farther side. The light was deteriorating fast, but his efforts were rewarded for, sure enough, he recaptured the jolly boat once more, a lamp lit in the bow. Much to his expectation, it was heading inshore and appeared to be but a short distance from the landing stage at Doubloons, which remained hidden from his view.

Then, he could see it no more. It was time to go home. With luck, the inn would still have food and drink, for he had such an appetite!

It was nearly nine by the time he pitched into the saloon. A few lights remained, but the place was completely devoid of customers. As luck would have it, he espied Molly almost immediately, engaged in her habitual drudge of clearing and cleaning tables. Before he'd said a word, she cried out, with a noticeable twinkle in her eye, 'I have only eggs and ham, sir! That is all, in case it's food you be wanting at this late hour...'

'Oh, Molly, you are a true saviour!'

''Tis only food then, Mr Jacob... Does nuthin else take yer fancy?' Molly drew closer and gazed up at him with a flirtatious shuffle of her hips. The proposition was unmistakeable.

'Why, yes, of course! I should like that very much...' he teased. 'Some of Mr Trewint's finest ale to wash it down would be most appreciated. I have a terrible thirst, you know.'

'I too...' she flashed back while looking theatrically downcast by his reply. 'All have gone to their beds, sir. 'Tis just thee and me awake in this whole house...'

'Not even the landlord?'

'Mr Trewint has yet to return, and his wife and son were abed long ago. 'Tis where I should be too, methinks – you also, I should say. 'Tis the best place for the both of us.' She gave him another engaging, fluttering smile.

Jacob could not deny it – the impulse was strong to forgo his plate of eggs for the other fruits being so unashamedly offered. Molly was a curvaceous beauty indeed. But he did not dwell on the temptation for long. Apart from all the moral teachings that now swam like sharks around his head, he had work still to do, and such a dalliance might risk exposure... or maybe worse. He could jest with her no longer. It was time to speak plainly.

'My dear Molly, you are a most desirable woman, but I fear I have ties that bind, and I must retire to my bed alone tonight. But if your offer of food and ale still survives, I should like that very much.'

She answered with the most affected sigh he'd seen in

years… really, she should have been on the stage at Drury Lane. 'Very well, sir. If that's yer wish. I shall be in the scullery, if you need me.' Her disappointment obvious, she departed with a cheeky grin and sang back, 'If those ties should ever break, Mr Jacob, put me in the line, would you?'

The food arrived shortly after, all piping hot and served up with another wicked wag of waitress hips, lest he forget. There were *three* eggs not two, and he thanked her for it. As he downed the last dregs of beer, the door to the inn swung open with a clang. A bearded man, lean of build and haggard of appearance, entered looking rather unsteady. On his head was a black woollen hat. When he spied Jacob, the entrant looked as surprised as he was bedraggled. Jacob noticed the unmistakeable sheen of damp around the man's trousers, especially below the knee. A bloodstained bandage was wrapped around his right hand.

'Molly!' he cried in a high-pitched screech without first engaging Jacob in conversation. 'I need you! Where are you, girl, when I want you?' The man hurried across the saloon, clutching his wounded hand and cursing all the while. He threw open the kitchen door as if he owned the place and disappeared from view. Only the sound of his raised voice, remonstrating with the girl, identified his presence.

There was only one conclusion to draw from this unexpected and illuminating turn of events. The innkeeper, Isaac Trewint, had returned home. And, by the look of things, in injured condition, to boot. But of more interest to Jacob Jarvie, as the slightly startled onlooker, was this was one of the men he'd seen rowing the jolly boat that very day. Twice that day, in fact… for on the last occasion, his place at the oars had been taken by another – Gabriel Honey, if Jacob's hunch was right. Another piece in the puzzle had been joined. Jacob now believed he knew the identities of three of the four crew he'd seen at sea that day. Such was Jacob's growing confidence, he told himself it would be only a question of time before he uncovered the last member of this heinous quartet.

* * *

Jacob Jarvie woke early the next morning with a noticeable spring in his step. As the clock in the square chimed the half hour, signifying it was thirty minutes after five o'clock, he rounded St Piran's ancient yew and took the now familiar path to the heights above Borwenstow. The sun had risen by degrees by the time he reached the spot he'd vacated less than ten hours before. Yet another idea had formed in his head – when would they ever cease?! This hypothesis came to him, in part, at least, from the sight of Isaac Trewint arriving back in the dark the day before, all torn and weary, looking for all the world as if he'd just swum out to Cow and Calf rocks and back. If Jacob's notion was correct, his morning's expedition would go a long way to proving it. And if he'd timed his departure properly, he would be in plenty of time to witness the spectacle once again – only thirty-five minutes later than before – a repeat performance of the events of the previous day. As if on cue, the jolly boat rounded the bluff within minutes of the expected time and made its way into its hiding place under the cliff beneath him. His beating heart told him he'd seen enough. It was time to return to his room and complete his report.

After breakfasting on yet more eggs – this time with a couple of slices of local cheese, as well as the customary bread and milk, served once again by a very coy Molly – Jacob put the finishing touches to his latest despatch. Once complete, he decided to pay an early visit to the delightful Miss Chadwick at the post office. It was essential he met the morning deadline.

Here, he used his remaining stamps to remit the weighty missive to Southampton and beyond. He imagined it might set more than a few hares running, back at Tower Hill. His grin on handing the postmistress the letter must have been substantial for she chirped almost at once, 'My, my, Mr Jarvie, you look as pleased as punch this morning. I'm thinking the sea air must be to your liking!'

Jacob touched his forelock and thanked her. *Such a kind young woman!* Feeling on tip-top form, he resolved to take a leisurely stroll by the harbour, chat affably to a few locals, pop in to see Constable Poundstock, and take in some more of that famous coastal air. He'd follow this with a spot of lunch at the inn, then maybe a well-deserved afternoon nap. He had an assignation with Miss Elizabeth Gough at four o'clock, and he wanted to be fully refreshed. He had a lot to tell her...

And then he remembered! His heart sank to his boots. He had a previous appointment to keep – at noon, with Cassius Honey, no less – one he simply could not duck. Suddenly, the prospect of lunch was far less appealing.

* * *

Albert Woodward sat behind his Siamese desk and opened Officer Jarvie's latest despatch, just arrived amongst the afternoon post. As he scanned the lines, he did so with mounting interest and an emerging sense of admiration. His man Jarvie seemed to have achieved much in the few days he'd been cut adrift in Cornwall. Woodward gave himself a cerebral pat on the back.

'I knew he'd come through... an inspired choice of mine,' he muttered.

The truth was, the executive part in him actually believed it so. He reached for his silver handbell and rang it vigorously.

It had been a parting gift from Major Callaway on the day Woodward had replaced him as chief investigation officer. For once, this symbol of authority stood proudly on his desk unencumbered by the usual piles of multifarious correspondence.

'Ah, Browning. Please send a message to Mr Henry Gough in Marylebone. Tell him I wish to see him. Tomorrow morning at nine would be convenient.' Once Browing had made his sycophantic exit to carry out his master's command, Woodward relaxed back in his chair and read the letter from Borwenstow once again – line by line. *Well, I never!* he chuckled. *Who'd have thought it?*

Chapter Seventeen

At the appointed hour, it was Cassius Honey's belligerent wife who received Jacob at the farm gate. As he approached along the coastal path, she seemed to stare him down with his every approaching step. Without the hint of welcome, let alone the glimpse of a smile, she swung the gate open and allowed him onto Honey property. Thankful for small mercies, he noted the lady was no longer in possession of a firearm, so perhaps some minor accommodation had been reached. Without speaking a single word, she led him along the track right to the front door of Doubloons, which was already ajar. She bade him enter, and leaving him standing awkwardly in the cramped hallway, she disappeared into another room.

The vestibule had a surprisingly high ceiling and was much airier than he'd expected. It certainly felt considerably cooler than under the midday sun outside. Here he stood and waited... and fidgeted... and waited. A herd of cows lowed moodily in the adjacent field, and close by, despite the lateness of the hour, a strident cockerel discharged a combative shriek. At what seemed an interminable length, the door opposite, behind which Mrs Honey had vanished five minutes earlier, pushed open, and the colossal figure of Cassius Honey hove into view.

'Mr Jarvis, I presume.' A hand the size of a cauliflower was extended towards him. Jacob grasped the offering, instantly aware of the callouses and rough texture of the fingers and palm.

'It's Jar*vie*, actually, sir – Jacob Jarvie, at your service. I am sorry to disturb your rest, but your wife suggested I should call to explain my purpose here in Borwenstow.'

'Yes, Mr Jar*vie*, Flora did mention you may pay us another visit. You were on my land yesterday, were you not?' Cassius glowered down the full length of his Roman nose.

Jacob, at six feet and three inches in height, was not used to addressing a man taller than himself, and he was finding the situation difficult to handle. *No wonder the ceilings here are higher than most. 'Tis a house for giants.*

'I apologise if I caused any distress, but my purpose hereabouts is to check measurements and provide the latest geography, both physical and structural, for a new map which the Ordnance Survey plans to publish within the next two years.' His words sounded stilted, like the foreword to a prepared lecture.

'You have a warrant, my wife tells me.'

Jacob had to fumble in his inside pocket for a while before handing over the now rather crumpled document. To his horror, he noticed that the scroll, having long rested under his armpit, had suffered a disfigurement as a result. The edges now looked distinctly moist, sticky and frayed – testament, if it were needed, of his long strides up the hill and the anxiety he'd endured during the last half hour.

At this point, the door to the parlour swung open again. A man entered, swiftly followed by another. The first, Jacob instantly recognised. It was Cassius's brother, Gabriel – there could be no mistaking it, as this was the same fellow who'd taken up the oars earlier that morning. The second man looked familiar too, and it did not take long for Jacob to realise why. It was the other in the boat – the last, as yet unnamed, oarsman. Now, all four had been pinpointed, and his heart leapt at the thought of his accomplishment. But Jacob still had no name for the fourth man, and without thinking, he heard himself saying, with a cheerful grin, 'Good day, gentlemen! My name is Jarvie, the surveyor from Southampton. 'Tis a pleasure to meet you both.' He offered his hand to Gabriel. 'You must be Mr…?'

Neither of the men said a word in reply; Gabriel scowled back with an ugly grimace that might have terrified the very devil himself. Conveniently, it was Cassius who came to Jacob's rescue. 'This is my brother, Gabriel, Mr Jarvie, and the other is Amos, who helps us on the farm from time to time.'

'I expect you will see me around the paths and byways for a few weeks, Mr Gabriel, Mr Amos,' Jacob continued brightly, adding a slight bow, 'as I have work here to discharge.'

Gabriel ignored the introduction, and with a departing glare, he pushed insolently by his older brother in search of the front door. Close on his heels, a gnarled-looking Amos, smirking like a buffoon, followed his leader to the exit. After a few chaotic seconds, the pair pressed their way past and launched themselves into the front courtyard. Jacob and Cassius were alone once more.

The unexpected interlude appeared to distract Cassius somewhat, for his initial tone of hostility seemed to diminish with his next sentence. 'Very well, you have your work to do, I suppose, Mr Jarvie,' he pronounced as he returned the sodden warrant without even a cursory glance at its contents. 'But I insist you call at the farm if you wish to enter my property in future.'

'I doubt if that will be necessary, sir. I have seen all I need, for the moment, at least,' Jacob replied with breezy self-assurance.

'I take it I shall lose none of my land as a result of your peregrinations.'

Peregrinations indeed! thought Jacob. Then he recalled Henry Gough's words evoking his own encounter with the big man of Borwenstow and how struck he'd been by Cassius's unfarmlike airs and graces.

'Certainly not, Mr Honey,' he replied, 'the ownership of land, or otherwise, is not in my bailiwick. I merely record what I see and ensure the lines are drawn as accurately as possible. There can be no dispute, in any event, as I understand your forefathers purchased the acreage hereabouts over a hundred years ago—'

'And how, pray, do you come by that intelligence, sir?' Honey's late good humour appeared to transform in an instant. 'Is my presence here of such particular interest to the Ordnance Survey that such a history is known to one of their lowly surveyors?'

Jacob realised he'd overreached himself and now regretted his foolish insouciance. Cassius Honey was right. If the ownership of land was *not* the preserve of the Ordnance Survey, why should he know such a fact, and in the act of knowing of it, how did he acquire the intelligence in the first place? He had to think quickly!

'I paid a visit to Sir William Pennycrocker at the Hall just the other day,' he started, 'to introduce myself, much as I do to you now, sir. I believe the matter of your ownership of this farm was mentioned in passing. I gave it very little thought at the time, being of no relevance to my assignment here, but as you raised the matter of possession, the conversation came back to me.'

'I see. So, you have been to Pennycrocker Hall.'

'I have, sir. To pay my respects. Sir William was a most gracious host.'

'So, the subject of *my* land was discussed between the two of you?'

'I believe so...' Jacob could hear himself faltering. 'As one of the prominent landowners hereabouts, you understand...'

Cassius Honey chewed his lip, and the lingering glower returned once more to his face. At length, while Jacob's guts turned cartwheels, he growled, 'I have no more to say on the matter. You may go, Mr Jarvie. And pray, do not trespass here again without my personal sanction.'

* * *

The walk back to Borwenstow gave time for Jacob to clear his head. He had run a fine line, and he knew it. He promised himself to choose his words more carefully in future. *Pride always comes before a fall.*

His next assignation should be much less challenging. Indeed, he was positively looking forward to a reunion with Miss Gough. Without doubt, any swagger he might have fleetingly possessed had been diminished by the encounter at Doubloons Farm. His newly found confidence needed some repair, and he hoped the engagement would provide it. But, as with any imagined situation, happy expectation is often trumped by raw actuality, and his meeting with Elizabeth would prove to be such a case in point.

His hunger completely gone, he bypassed Molly and the kitchen and made straight for his room, where he set about putting into writing the account of his meeting with the Honey family. There was the muffle of distant thunder. It was another warm afternoon, and he rose to look out of his narrow sash window. There were dark clouds building in the west, suggesting the approach of Atlantic thunderstorms. The same bedroom window afforded him a view of the church tower – it seemed so close. Jacob gazed at the belfry in quiet contemplation for a few seconds, trying to imagine what it must have been like to throw oneself from its high parapet. He shuddered at the thought of it, and a frightful image of the tumbling parson, starkly focussed against the full moon, came suddenly to him. He drew the curtain, and the image went with its closing. He returned to the table and picked up his report, the completion of which took him less than twenty minutes. Then he lay back on his bed. He resolved to postpone the planned "affable chat" with the quayside locals and his assignation with the constable to another day. He closed his eyes instead.

The sound of rumbling clouds greeted his departure from *The Gauger's Return,* and this made him wonder whether Elizabeth might have opted to stay within the confines of Pennycrocker Hall, rather than meet him as arranged. But he need not have concerned himself, for as he rounded the corner of St Piran's nave, a full five minutes ahead of the appointed time, there she sat on the perfectly described iron bench, book in hand and with a courteous smile to mark his approach.

'Good day, Miss Gough. I feared the impending storm might keep you indoors,' he opened as he took his seat at a respectful distance beside her.

'I had to come! I have so much to tell…' Elizabeth looked to be in a state of high excitement.

'I also,' he beamed back. 'Too much, in fact, I know not where to start… But, pray commence. My account can wait.'

'There has been another flare-up at the Hall!' Elizabeth launched into her report without further prompting. ''Twas the very day you left the house – and I have been bursting to tell you ever since. You see, I have a room above Sir William and Her Ladyship, not *directly* above, you understand, but by some quirk of construction there are occasions when I might overhear conversations held within their bedchamber, particularly if voices are raised.'

'A quirk of construction?'

'Yes, I believe that must be the reason. Maybe 'tis the plumbing or the upwards route the ventilation takes, but when the two of them are squabbling, which of late has been commonplace, I can hear their exchanges. In the past, out of deference to their privacy, I have always closed my ears to their talk. A pillow crushed against my head usually suffices, but sometimes during the day, I have been forced to remove myself to another room altogether – to the gossip of the servants' hall, mostly. But since my father spoke to me and put me on alert, and especially now, as we have made our compact, I have been less sensitive and more inquisitive.' She paused for breath and looked at Jacob in a manner of one seeking affirmation.

'Very good, Miss Elizabeth.' Jacob looked at her approvingly. 'And have you heard anything that might assist our investigations?'

'I shall allow you to be the judge. You are a true detective, after all…'

Jacob could feel himself redden, partly from embarrassment and partly with pride. 'I will do my best.'

'This event took place the night before last, an hour before midnight. I'd bathed and packed the girls off to the nursery a long time before and was reading my Trollope when I heard voices from below. Sir William had been drinking alone in his study since dinner, and Lady Kathleen had retired to her chamber. I'd imagined all the servants to be abed too, but I was proved wrong, as one of the voices was none other than Mrs Hennessey, come to Her Ladyship's chamber. You must understand, this is a most unusual occurrence; for the cook to venture into that part of the house at that hour is exceedingly uncommon, especially when there are others to do Lady Kathleen's bidding, should she call for service.'

'Pray continue.' Jacob was transfixed.

'I could not decipher much, at first, but forgive my soul, I got out of bed and crept closer to the corner of the room where the sounds could be heard better. God bless me if I didn't actually lay down and put my ear to the floorboards! This is when I recognised Mrs Hennessey. Her County Cork accent is so distinctive, as is Her Ladyship's, but in a much more refined way, of course. I was shocked by what I heard, for it sounded as if the cook was berating Her Ladyship in a most disagreeable fashion! I could hardly believe it. I heard Mrs Hennessey say quite clearly, "It must be done – or there'll be all hell to pay." Then Lady Kathleen replied, "But my husband is having second thoughts. He tells me he wishes no further part of it. He says he has done enough already." Or words to that effect… The discussion carried on much in the same vein, with Mrs Hennessey's voice rising still further. At one point, I heard her cry, "You must remind him of the consequences. He will agree soon enough. You must be firm with him." … And suchlike…'

'And then?'

'And then, horror of horrors, Mrs Hennessey said words I can hardly utter…'

'You must tell me…' Jacob could barely breathe, such was the anticipation of her next reply.

'She said… "He has blood on his hands." It was as simple as that. "He has blood on his hands." After which, Her Ladyship remained as silent as the grave. Then Cook said, "The day is set. It will be the *twenty-fifth*." She was most insistent.' Elizabeth continued, 'Cook said, "Patrick has sent word from Cork." Those were her very words – "Patrick has sent word from

Cork." To which Her Ladyship replied, sounding contrite all of a sudden, "Very well, I shall do it. 'Tis for the best. Trust me, it shall be arranged." … Or suchlike…' Elizabeth Gough's eyes widened. 'Look,' she said, 'I have written it all down in my pocketbook. I scribbled as I lay on the floor.'

Jacob flicked though the copious pages of almost illegible jottings. He was pleased to see these were followed by what must have been a summary, drawn out in neat, artistically formed words. 'Did they say *what* must be done?' he asked.

'Nothing more, for at that point Sir William himself entered. I heard the door crashing as if it were my own. Then, all hell let loose, and there was little need for my ear to be pressed so tightly against the skirting board.'

'Was he angry?'

'I should say so! "Get out, vile bitch!" he cried. "Go back to where you belong." Those were his very words. Then I heard the door close. I presumed 'twas Mrs Hennessey departing.'

'And after she'd left? Did Sir William and his wife speak further?'

'They did, but 'twas not long before he stormed out once more. I imagined he went to sleep in the Green Room, where he has a bed also.'

'What did he say?'

'*He* said nothing. 'Twas Her Ladyship who spoke. She talked softly to him, so I may not have caught it all. But it sounded like she said their hands were tied, and he must obey. That was the gist, as far as I could tell. Then I heard the door slam once more, and silence reigned again. Goodness, my heart was so aflutter I could hardly write. 'Twas well into the small hours before I fell asleep.'

'Is that all?'

She looked indignant. 'Is that not enough? You have heard everything.'

'You have surpassed yourself,' he reassured her. 'And since? What of their demeanour? Has it changed as a result?'

'The next time I saw the pair of them together, there was all sweetness and light between them, as if nothing had happened.'

'And Mrs Hennessey?'

'She has remained hitherto her normal irascible self, all moans and groans about the rest of us and how easy our positions are compared to hers – particularly mine, for she believes the care and education of three little ones is insignificant compared to cooking each day for the household. Nothing changes with Mrs Hennessey; her mood these last two days has been exactly as before.'

'You say she is Irish. I thought I noticed an accent when our paths crossed the other day.'

'Oh, yes, but I have heard her put on airs when amongst others she does not know. For a fact, she is from County Cork. She has a son, Michael, there. She talks about the lad all the time – he's truly the apple of her eye. She's continually comparing him favourably to poor old Heath, whose name is also Michael – it's always a source of amusement to us all to hear her carry on about how different two "Michaels" can be – one being so perfect and the other the hapless Heath!'

'How long has Mrs Hennessey worked at the Hall?'

'I was told she was taken on at Her Ladyship's behest soon after the marriage. Both Mrs Hennessey and Mr Wilks arrived together, some five or six years ago – before my time, for sure. The servants jest that it was as if the two of them had been a second payment of her dowry! The previous cook and butler had to go, such was Her Ladyship's bidding, but according to Heath, they were tired and old, and both received handsome payments in return for their early retirement.'

'And Patrick? There was mention of a Patrick in your narrative. Who might he be?'

'I'd thought, at first, that must be Mr Wilks himself, the butler – Patrick Wilks – but he has been away in Plymouth for quite a few days, or so everyone says. I'm rather confused. Maybe there is another Patrick…'

Jacob scratched his chin. 'Or maybe the two are one and the same and the butler is in Cork after all.'

Elizabeth's face brightened. 'You know, I think you must be right. Mr Wilks hails from Cork, in fact – that makes better sense… But why should he lie to us about his true destination?'

'That's a question for another time, I suspect,' Jacob replied. 'You have done so well, Miss Elizabeth. I thought I'd be the one to surprise *you* with *my* news, but your revelations have been truly illuminating.' He paused. 'I mean to say, they *could* be "illuminating" if only we knew what these conversations meant.'

She blushed. 'And you, Jacob, tell me your news.'

Jacob tried to put things into order, but somehow the history arrived in increasingly muddled form. His discovery of twin hidden coves less than a mile apart, his obdurate encounters with the Honeys, the brush with a waterlogged and scarred Isaac Trewint, and his lonely vigils high on the clifftops overlooking mysterious locations where boats came and went at strange times of the day, seemed to merge as one. He made sure to avoid mention of his dread of heights for fear it might make him look fainthearted. Through it all, it was clear Elizabeth had struggled to follow the narrative at times, such were her alternating expressions of enthusiasm, empathy and sheer puzzlement.

Just as he was trying to explain his theory of why the Honeys were visiting the cove under St Piran's so regularly, there was a noise of movement in the churchyard. The clock had just struck five, and until then, their conversation had been conducted with hardly an extraneous sound, save for the song of blackbirds and the chitting of wrens in the undergrowth. A gate closed with a thump, and footsteps could be heard clipping up the stone path. As Jacob and Elizabeth listened out intently, there soon followed the noise of grating keys and the creaking of a door being pushed open.

'I hear the church door opening,' Jacob whispered. 'What do you say? Shall we follow in their wake, whoever it might be? I have been anxious to see the interior for some days. Now seems as good a chance as any.'

'But should we be seen together? Perhaps I should take my leave now. We can meet again at the same hour on Monday, if you wish. I can make an excuse. You have my story; I have the kernel of yours... I will keep my ears low and listen, as before.'

'Very well. It has been a true delight, Miss Elizabeth. Two sleuths are better than one, eh?'

Elizabeth Gough beamed back.

'And our purpose is greatly advanced, as a result,' Jacob added. 'One word of advice, before you go. I urge you to keep the pocketbook safe. I should like to share your excellent notes with Mr Woodward, when the time is right.'

She nodded her understanding and rose to go. 'Same time on Monday, then...'

He watched her diligently as she rounded the corner of the nave and waited a full minute after he'd heard the sound of the churchyard gate opening and closing. Then he followed in her path. On turning the corner and seeing the door to the church open to the air, he ventured towards it, and pushing it fully open, he crossed the threshold. To his left was the font, where he knew Reverend William Rosewarne had collapsed and died. Behind it, he could see the door that led to the tower from which the very same parson's distant predecessor had plunged to *his* death. It was exactly as Henry Gough had described it, but the conjured images of the past seemed to gain new life by his very presence.

'And who might you be?' a sharp voice piped from the direction of the altar.

Jacob spun around to see two men before him. One was clearly a policeman and uniformed as such. The other was a balding, fidgety looking man of indeterminant age dressed in a rather untidy jacket and dusty shoes. Jacob suspected he must be the first man's superior, for it was he who had posed the question.

Jacob Jarvie had become so used to this enquiry being made of him, he knew exactly what to say in reply. 'My name is Jarvie, Mr Jacob Jarvie, recently arrived from Southampton,' he flashed back, 'to carry out a survey for the Ordnance Survey Office. I'm so pleased to make your acquaintance, sir.' He offered up his hand for what seemed like the umpteenth time that day. 'And you, sir...?'

There was a deafening crack of thunder, and a flash of light lit up the western window just a second later. The storm had finally arrived, and by the sound of it, the squall was directly overhead.

'I am Halwill, Inspector Austol Halwill Barton, to be precise, of the Cornwall County Constabulary.' Inspector Halwill paused and looked Jacob up and down. 'And you, sir, are an imposter!'

Chapter Eighteen

Henry Gough arrived in Albert Woodward's higgledy-piggledy office at the appointed hour. As Browning ushered him in, all compliance and glad-handing, he found his old friend gazing out of the window onto the high white stone battlements of the medieval Tower of London.

When Woodward failed to face and greet him, Henry decided to be provocative in return. 'I had planned a busy day trawling in Mayfair, Albert. It's all hands to the pump at this time of year, with money to be made on every street corner. I hope this summons of yours is justified!' he exclaimed with a hint of roguishness.

Woodward's shoulders remained obstinately turned against his visitor. 'I'm watching the peregrine, Henry,' he muttered. 'It's an amazing and most fascinating creature, all told. It misses often, yet its determination is peerless, and for certain, it will triumph in the end. The poor pigeons that crown the Tower are no match for it. At the finish, each will meet their own end. It's only a question of time… *vincit qui patitur*, as my predecessor oft repeated.'

'Albert, I have not come all this way to talk in Latin or

speak about falcons, though I know the latter is a subject that greatly fascinates you,' Henry chided gently.

Woodward twisted to face his old comrade. 'I apologise, Henry, but the perseverance of the bird gives me much food for thought. Our own actions should try to imitate it in every way. Persistence and tenacity will bring their own rewards. 'Tis but a moderately sized fowl, but it's heart must be large in comparison to others of similar stature. If we emulate the peregrine, the prey *we* seek must eventually fall into our own hands.'

'I take it there is news from Cornwall…' It was time for Henry to bring Albert to the point.

'There is indeed!' Albert said forcibly, as if to shut out his wistful reflections without further ado. 'And I have to say,' he resumed, 'I have misjudged young Jarvie, for he appears to have made his mark already. I called for you because his first report arrived yesterday, and it shows him to be making alarming progress. And now, this very morning, yet another missive arrived from him, which adds even greater weight to the evidence he has compiled. He is certainly making himself known to the folk of the village, your daughter included, but I do not wish him to overreach himself.'

'I quite agree.'

'You see, Jarvie remains a greenhorn – albeit a far bolder one than I imagined, I'll grant him that – but he is inexperienced, all the same. If he pushes too far, it will bring about his downfall. I have seen it all too often before. Now is the time to tread carefully – to regroup, so to speak, and share in the wisdom of others. In short, I think he needs your guidance, Henry.'

'That's very flattering, Albert—'

'And I believe you must bring forward the date of your return to Borwenstow, if not for Jarvie's sake, for your daughter's, who, from these reports, appears to be in the thick of things too.'

'I told you I saw some dash in that young man.' Henry tried not to sound smug. 'But are you suggesting my daughter might be in some danger? Pray, tell me, what has he uncovered?'

'Here, see for yourself. Read his despatches while I try to spot that plucky peregrine once more.' Woodward tossed a sheaf of papers in Henry's direction and returned to the bay window to resume his ornithological surveillance.

Henry snatched up the bundle, his eyes widening with every sentence he read. Part of him wished he had not spoken to Elizabeth to seek her covert help. By the look of things, she had more than warmed to the task, and he was proud of her courage and resourcefulness. But he had qualms also. By the time he had finished the last lines, his mind was made up. Albert was right. There was so much to discuss; he would have to return the following day. With luck, the wedding being but a week away, his reappearance in Borwenstow would not create any undue attention.

'It appears Jarvie is indeed doing a fine job,' he offered. 'The signs could not be clearer. Matters are coming to a head in Cornwall. This movement of boats along the coast is particularly interesting, and I have a hunch I know what it may concern—'

'I suspect we share the same thought, Henry...' Woodward replied before his friend could elucidate further. Swiftly halting his observations of the River Thames, he added quickly, 'The Honeys must be preparing the way for another smuggle. The tunnel you spoke of, the one blocked by Snuggs's revenue men, must be their target, and their aim is to undo the work of last September. They wish free and safe access into the church once more.'

Henry nodded in happy agreement, though he'd been

beaten to the punch. 'It must be so. I had the same inkling too.'

'Will you return, Henry, and see this through?'

There was no point in procrastinating any further. 'Of course I will, Albert!' Henry answered immediately. 'If it's your wish that I resume my enquiries and provide a steady hand for Mr Jarvie, then I wholeheartedly agree to it. In truth, it's not a difficult decision to make. The stakes are high, and with my Elizabeth circling the web, I should like to prevent her from falling in. Is there anything else you wish of me?'

'There is…' Woodward muttered. 'I should like you to bring Samuel Snuggs into your full confidence. Meet with him, tell him everything and allow *him* to take the lead. He has local knowledge plus the command of men and horses, which will be needed when the hour comes. Any lingering doubts I might have held about his integrity must be put aside. You have met the man, and your reports of him are positive. The courts continue to remain silent as far as his guilt of any crime is concerned, and Jarvie has uncovered nothing to say otherwise. Now must be the time to put our faith in Snuggs and lend him our full support.'

'And what of the bold Inspector Halwill? He will not be far away, either.'

'Ah, our Hasty Halwill will be pressing and nudging in from all sides, I suspect!' Albert chortled. 'Like a whippet off the leash, ha-ha! But now we must disregard his much-proclaimed impulsiveness – it's most important we bring him in too. I have given Halwill my word we will share our intelligence, and I must abide by it. I suggest you call on him in Launceston on your way to Borwenstow. Methinks we shall need all the bodies we can raise, for if there is to be an attempt on the coast, and the Honeys are cornered, I fear they will not come lightly. They have a formidable reputation and will want to slug it out. No, Henry, the more the merrier. I just wish

I could add some support from London, but 'tis out of the question.'

'Very well. I understand. I'll leave Paddington on the first train tomorrow. Can you send word to Halwill? Ask him to meet me the minute I arrive at Launceston Station. I can brief him there. It will save time that way, as I'll need to catch the trap across the moor while there is still daylight.'

'I will happily do as you ask. But my strong feeling is, it will be Samuel Snuggs, not Mr Halwill, who will hold the key to our future success. Once Snuggs is on board, he may be able to shed new light on Jarvie's revelations and, if necessary, obtain further reinforcements from Bude or Port Isaac, maybe some other nearby revenue office. He will know how to achieve it. To oil the wheels, I shall draft a letter assigning you to our cause. It will further demonstrate my support as head of the London detectives. You may use it as you wish. It may have some influence in those parts, it may not… but 'tis better than nothing.'

* * *

Jacob Jarvie did his melodramatic best to look daggers at the police inspector who stood scowling at him from the other side of the nave.

'Sir, pray withdraw your wicked assertion! Nobody may call me an "imposter" and get away with it, not even a man of your noble occupation.'

'I repeat my claim without fear, sir. Jarvie may well be your name, but an officer of the Ordnance Survey you most certainly are not. You may speak plainly to me. It is not my intention to do you down. 'Tis only Constable Marshgate and I alone in the church. Be not concerned, no one else need hear your justification for posing as a scholarly surveyor.'

'But… 'tis most irregular! Withdraw or—'

'Or "I shall inform Mr Albert Woodward" perchance?' Halwill spat back.

'Mr who?'

'Or maybe Mr Henry Gough… do you know him, eh?' Halwill was beginning to enjoy himself. 'A good friend and confidant of yours, is he, sir? Was that not his fine daughter I saw leave the churchyard just now? I hope you two have not been canoodling…'

'Certainly not! How dare you! I am a married man, and she is betrothed to another. What do you take me for, man?'

'Mr Jacob Jarvie of the London excise detectives,' Halwill fired back. 'That's *who* I take you for, sir. Down here to snoop for clues about the so-called smuggling and the unnatural goings-on hereabouts.'

Goodness! Self-confidence is a strange bedfellow – in one minute, out the next… Any equanimity Jacob might have gained from his lately finished conversation with Elizabeth Gough had now evaporated into a desert of self-doubt. He tried one last throw of the dice.

'Sir, I am most affronted!' It was a pathetic thrust, and he knew it.

Halwill knew it too and grinned back with a snide look of self-satisfaction. 'Come with us, Mr Jarvie, I have something to show you. It may interest you… and serve your purpose, to boot.'

The two policemen led a submissive Jacob to the vestry door, which Constable Marshgate opened ahead of them. Lighting candles, they proceeded beneath the portraits of long-dead parsons, crossed to a further door, through which they entered, and descended a short flight of cold steps into the underground crypt of St Piran's itself. Here, they weaved between the assorted raised tombs and time-scoured effigies towards the north-western corner of the chamber. Next to the tomb marked *Oliver Pococke – 1713–1777*, Halwill pointed to a wall of recently repaired rust-coloured brickwork, which revealed the outline of a low rectangular door at its heart.

'This is what you have been wanting to see all along, I suspect. Being a gallant officer of the Revenue, you will not need to guess long to deduce its purpose,' Halwill snorted with more than a hint of sarcasm. 'I showed the same to Mr Gough just the other day, and even he, being a mere amateur at our game, instantly recognised it for what it was. *You* should, therefore, have no difficulties at all…'

Any pretence Jacob had of maintaining his false persona had gone the minute they'd entered the crypt. He replied steadily, 'It is the bricked-up entrance of the tunnel that leads directly to the beach – the one they say is haunted.'

'Bravo! No longer the humble surveyor from Southampton, eh?'

'There is no need to mock me, sir. You have revealed my true identity and hurrah for your perspicacity! But what of it? Are our purposes not joined at the hip? If you have the patience to listen a while – for I understand you to be a *hasty* man – I will happily tell you all I have discovered.'

'Oh, touché! Mr Jarvie, you are indeed well informed,' Halwill sneered back.

Jacob uttered his next words with a deliberate sarcasm that immediately hit its mark. 'But… can I count on a pair of policemen to be discreet… honest, dare I say?' he said quietly. 'That is the difficult circle I must square…' Jacob made sure to glare while waiting for his answer, for he too could use contempt as a weapon, should he choose.

Inspector Halwill's eyes bulged at the intended insult, while Constable Marshgate shifted his not inconsiderable frame between large boots. Meanwhile, Jacob Jarvie towered over both of them and stared unblinkingly back.

At length, Halwill said, 'Mr Jarvie, I have no wish to be your enemy, but such sly accusations may not be conducive—'

Jacob knew when to let go. This time, he offered up a genuine smile of contrition. 'I wish to be your trusted associate, sir. If I have offended in some way, please accept my apology. I should add, for completeness, I have spoken to the village policeman, Constable Poundstock, on a number of occasions, without declaring my true identity or purpose here in Borwenstow, and he could not have been more accommodating.'

'I'm sure he will forgive you that, sir,' came the rather surprising yet steadfast intervention from Marshgate, as if he were speaking for the absent constable.

'If I deceived Poundstock, I assure you I did so with the best of intentions.'

'Very well, sir.'

'But now, we have work to do,' Jacob carried on. 'The three of us, if we are to get to the bottom of this matter, must work together. And to that end, I would be happy to give you my full report.'

Inspector Halwill, who had been surprisingly silent over the last few minutes, nodded in thoughtful agreement and indicated Jacob should continue.

'So, now seems as good a time as any,' Jacob pressed ahead, 'as we remain unseen and unheard in this rather melancholy place. What say you, gentlemen?' While Jacob had been speaking, the uneasy atmosphere had begun to lighten, almost with every word he uttered. When he'd concluded his explanation with an offer of cooperation, Inspector Halwill waited a while before making his own reply.

'Very well... perhaps I too could have been more friendly,' he said steadily. 'If so, I also apologise.' Then Inspector Halwill clapped his hands twice to show he wished the ending of all further discussion on the matter. 'Now to business. I have news and ideas which I am prepared to share also, but perhaps, as you have the floor, sir, I should like very much to hear your report first.'

Having just delivered a similar narrative a mere few minutes earlier to a spellbound, if mildly confused, Miss Gough, Jacob knew he had to get his facts properly ordered and conveyed with a clarity he had not achieved thus far. He spoke without interruption for a full fifteen minutes – it was obvious his audience was rapt, especially when learning of Elizabeth's overheard conversations at Pennycrocker Hall.

When Jacob had finished, Inspector Halwill asked just one question. 'Most enlightening, Mr Jarvie. Tell me, as an expert in such matters, what do you believe the Honeys are trying to achieve with their regular visits to Shrouded Cove?'

'Shrouded Cove?'

'It's the name the locals have given the place these last one hundred years, sir.' It was Marshgate who spoke in reply. 'On account of the inlet's cloak of invisibility from the land and the sinister legend that accompanies it.'

'An apt moniker, indeed, Constable,' Jarvie replied. 'My conjecture is a simple one. The Honeys are making preparations for a consignment of contraband to be landed at Shrouded Cove within the next week – on the twenty-fifth of May, to be precise, as Miss Gough overheard. My guess is the consignment will be, for the most part, smuggled whiskey. On that day, I suspect the tide will be high by around midnight, and the moon will be all but absent.'

'I'll need to check the charts with Poundstock, sir, but that sounds about right to me,' Marshgate said solemnly.

'These will be ideal conditions for such a covert undertaking. Given the Honeys' long-held familiarity with the coastline and the sea conditions in these parts, they should have no difficulties navigating their way ashore.'

'Why whiskey?' Halwill asked. 'You seem very specific on the matter.'

'I can be even more exact, if you wish… I believe it to be Irish whiskey, probably a cargo of the *Carrells* brand, maybe including some tubs of the illicit brew they call "potcheen". It will arrive across the Celtic Sea from County Cork, if I'm not mistaken. You see, everywhere I go there seem to be Irish connections hereabouts. The brand I spoke of, *Carrells,* was offered to me when I was up at the Hall. The kitchen was stacked with crates of the stuff as I passed through, and the stable yard was full of empty barrels that I suspect once contained potcheen. For some reason, *The Gauger's Return* sells no Scotch whisky – only Irish – this cannot be a mere coincidence. My firm belief is the Honeys, with the help of the innkeeper, Mr Trewint, and his lackey, Amos, are currently engaged in unblocking the tunnel at the seawards end of Shrouded Cove, as they await a large shipment to arrive.'

'Well, the evidence does seem to point to it, I grant you…' Halwill muttered. 'It appears most conclusive, in fact.'

'And I believe at least two of the staff at Pennycrocker Hall to be at the heart of the matter.' Jarvie was in full flow now. 'Miss Gough heard it all, didn't she? Mrs Hennessey, the cook, condemned herself with her own words and drew in the absent butler, Mr Patrick Wilks, for good measure. My guess is he's not in Plymouth at all! He must be in Ireland at this very minute, making the necessary preparations. 'Tis as plain as a pikestaff!'

'And what of Sir William and Her Ladyship? If Mrs Hennessey is to be believed, they must be culpable too – in some lesser way, perhaps, but guilty, all the same.' Halwill shook his head. 'What have things come to? Sir William stood as magistrate for some years, you know.'

'My suspicion is Sir William may have been involved at the outset – perhaps he put up the funds a while back to recommence the business of ancient times – but he has since had second thoughts. Something must have happened to change his tune. For certain, he has no time for the Honeys anymore, even if he ever did... Sir William conceded to me they had "an occasional acquaintance built around commerce", which may be some quaint way of referring to smuggling. But in the same breath, he called the Honeys "rogues". 'Twas in my very presence! To enrich things further, he named Cassius "a blackguard at heart". Those were his precise words. The squeaky innkeeper, too, seems to be no better, in Sir William's opinion; he called Trewint "a scoundrel". It all makes complete sense to me.'

'You mentioned talk of Sir William having "blood on his hands",' Halwill asked slowly.

Jacob sighed. 'I confess I do not understand the meaning of it, but there certainly appears to be some sort of a hold on Sir William. Maybe his money, once so important, is still required for the enterprise to succeed. Whatever the reason, it's clear he is railing against it.'

'We shall have to tread carefully,' Halwill said gravely. 'These are deep waters, indeed. Unproven accusations involving the gentry, and a former magistrate at that, can end an honest man's career in an instant. On no account must the facts we have just discussed leave this room. Marshgate, are you clear on the matter? You may not share this with *anyone*, not even Poundstock.'

'I am clear, sir. Not to a living soul...'

A strange gloom befell the dark chamber. One of the candles gutted, and the others looked close to death. Marshgate hurried off to find some more.

'Inspector,' Jacob tried to sound bright, wanting to change the mood, 'you tell me you have information you are prepared to share. I should be most interested to hear it, as I concur with Messrs Woodward and Gough that all matters before us, including the unexplained deaths, must be connected in some way.'

'That may well be the case…' Halwill replied drily, 'but my investigations concern murder alone, and now, if I include Ignatius in their number, it appears I have three to solve.' As Marshgate returned with fresh candles, which he lit from the fluttering wicks of their predecessors, Halwill commenced to describe the poisonings of Rosewarne and Polrunny that had occurred in mighty quick succession. The mystery of who had unlocked the church after he'd given strict instructions to the contrary had given him much pause for thought.

'I confess I am no closer finding the culprits or the method by which the poison was administered, let alone the motives for these twin crimes,' he ended with a miserable look.

'Three deaths in all, sir! All victims were connected to St Piran's in some way. The last two occurred within days of the other, both from the same cyanide poisoning. That cannot be a coincidence!' Jacob exclaimed.

'Of course it can't!' Halwill snapped back. 'But *who* would want to do such a thing? What would they have to gain?'

'Free access to the church, perhaps? You said yourself that Parson Rosewarne had his heart set against the Honeys. He declined to allow his church to be used to marry Cassius's sister, and he supported the Revenue's decision for the tunnel to be bricked up. He, too, wanted to prevent any further incursions of this "free trading". By all accounts, Rosewarne was the Honeys' bitter enemy. His refusal to allow the house of God to be used for smuggling meant a feud was the natural result. Maybe the parson's death was simply punishment from the smugglers for his obstinacy.'

'I agree 'tis possible... But why kill Polrunny too? It does not make sense. If all three are connected in some way, pray, tell me how?'

Chapter Nineteen

Once he'd prodded Joshua awake, Henry Gough greeted the coachman as if he were an old friend. The Paddington train had arrived in Plymouth in perfect time for Henry to make the connection to Launceston, and as he descended the station steps, it cheered him mightily to see the eternally disconsolate carriage driver once more. Joshua had been dozing on the seat of his now familiar trap in a grubby corner of the railway yard when Henry had spotted him. If he'd been pleased to see his old customer, he didn't show it. Perhaps the jab Henry had been forced to give the driver to bring him back to life had been a touch too sharp... Maybe Joshua had been deep into some pleasant daytime reverie and wished to remain within its dreamy embrace... Who could tell? But the first words he spoke to greet his former patron were not hospitable.

'I s'pose you'll be wanting me to take you that accursed Borwenstow ag'in, sir,' he'd grumbled as he rubbed the sleep from his eyes.

'Ah, Joshua! I was so hoping to find you here this afternoon!' Henry replied brightly. 'Yes, if it's not too much trouble. Carriage to *The Gauger's Return* is exactly what I desire – and perchance some hard-boiled eggs and milk at Hallworthy, on the way!'

The inn was reached slightly later than before, due to a rather longer stop to water the horse and take in some sustenance. Henry had used the time to press Joshua for any news from Borwenstow, but true to form, his driver had replied with little else than a scowl and a mock shiver of his shoulders. 'It's none of my business, sir, I've told 'ee before. I want no part in the dark goings-on down by there.'

There was no sign of Isaac Trewint, nor his strapping young son, when the carriage pulled up outside the inn, and Henry was obliged to carry his luggage into the hallway on his own. Joshua had not volunteered to help either, remaining resolutely on his perch, and it was with one of his confounded grimaces that he had flicked the horse into a trot almost as soon as Henry's valise had touched the cobbled courtyard. It was the agreeable Molly who eventually came to his rescue. She recognised him instantly.

'Mr Gough, how fine it is to see you.'

Was that a glint in her eye, he noticed...?

'But Mr Trewint made no mention of your coming, sir, so I fear your old room is occupied.'

Henry had half expected as much, knowing young Jarvie had taken up residence at the inn, but he decided to feign ignorance. 'Oh, you say my room is taken?' he asked innocently.

'Yes, sir, by a gentleman from Southampton, come to draw charts and suchlike.'

'But you have other bedrooms, do you not?'

'Yes, but none as nice as before. We have a police inspector from Launceston residing with us too, so the best now available is the one next to mine... right at the back. It's very quiet up there, very discreet, so to say, but 'tis much smaller and has no view of the sea. It's three shillings cheaper, mind!'

'I'll take it. It seems there is no alternative, and my needs are modest.'

'Very well, sir,' she grinned. 'I'll show you the way. Don't hesitate to knock on my door, if you need anything…'

* * *

Samuel Snuggs had not expected to see his future father-in-law so soon – and certainly not at this late hour. While alone in the diminutive and newly purposed Custom House, his staff having returned, hours before, to their homes and loved ones, he'd been jerquing the latest bundle of small ship cargo manifests when a sharp rap made him look up from his ledger. The softly ticking clock told him it was approaching 7.30p.m., and a glance through the shutters revealed that twilight was approaching fast.

Warily at first, Snuggs heaved at the solid oak door, which had recently been reinforced to deter unwanted intruders. 'My goodness, sir! It's a pleasure to see you. I hadn't—'

'No matter, Samuel, please let me in. I can explain all.' Henry started to press his way past.

Once ensconced in the paltry public meeting room, Henry was able to look Samuel in the eye and explain himself. 'There is much I must tell you, Samuel, and most of it is grave news.'

'Is Elizabeth…?'

'Elizabeth is fine, as far as I know, but I had to come to you first. I arrived in the village but a few hours ago, and on the off-chance you may be still burning the candle, I decided to pass this way. I'm glad I did, for the sooner I can tell you my story, the happier I'll be.'

'I have whiskey, sir. Would you partake with me? It will be dark soon and the liquor might smooth the cogs and help in the provision of your report.'

'Ha-ha!' Henry cried as soon as he spied Samuel pouring the glasses. 'It's Irish whiskey, by the look of it. *Carrells*, if I am not mistaken.'

'Yes, sir. For the life of me, I cannot seem to purchase Scotch whisky in the village at all. Even to find a bottle of it in Bude is most unusual. Impossible too in Port Isaac. It appears the local taste for whiskey has been Irish for a while now, since Christmas, at least.'

'Have you ever considered *why*, Samuel?'

'It is the price, for sure. This bottle can be purchased for a fraction of the cost of a Highland malt, and the palate soon becomes used to it. In fact, 'tis a very excellent recipe, and I would say I prefer it now, even to many of the Scottish brews!'

'But why should it be so cheap?' said Henry with unabashed eagerness.

'Because there is so much of it, I suppose... even *The Gauger's* sells only *Carrells* now.'

'Precisely! And what might that tell your *revenue* nose?' Henry was becoming mildly irritated by Samuel's apparent naivety.

The look on Snuggs's face as the penny finally dropped was startling to behold. 'You mean this whiskey might be smuggled?' he said at length. 'But it's always been brandy from France, tobacco, genever and suchlike... Why should anyone want to smuggle whiskey from within Great Britain itself?'

'Oh, Samuel, you are a fine, upstanding chap in all respects, and as the future husband to my beloved Elizabeth, please do not take any offence by what I am about to say... I fear your mind has become narrowed by local circumstances – the events, the gossips, feuds and suchlike. Your awareness of the wider world is inhibited by your over-long residence in this county, and in this very village, for that matter. Have you not heard of the Irish Temperance Movement?'

'No, sir. I regret I have not.'

'Then you need to understand that Temperance is a very strong cause. It's dedicated to lowering the consumption of alcohol in all of Ireland. I happen to know that new laws were passed in Ireland just a few short years ago to ban the sale of drink on certain days of the week. In short, while the appetite might be great, the consumption of Irish whiskey has never been less on the Emerald Isle. Distillers such as *Carrells* are struggling to keep afloat. My guess is there is undeclared excess production which finds its way here, thus satisfying the local market for miles around. Why, maybe all of Devon and Cornwall, for all I know!

'*Carrells* is a brand from just across the Celtic Sea. What better way for the business to dispose of their excess stock? And if, as I suppose, the whiskey is indeed from undeclared production, without any duty paid, the profits for all those who sell it would be huge. As you know, being a revenue man yourself, the true cost of liquor is tiny compared to the excise levies that are imposed. For good measure, I may bring your attention to the parlous state of affairs between Ireland and our own nation-state at this time, which means duty-paid Irish whiskey is shunned by many so-called patriotic Englishmen.'

Samuel gulped down a mouthful of *Carrells* and stared blankly back.

'You mustn't blame yourself,' Henry said soothingly. 'For my sins, I happen to know a great deal about the trade in illicit whisky. Indeed, my fall from grace was as a result of its pernicious grasp. I would not be seated before you now had it not been for my arrest by the excise detectives – so there is some silver lining to rejoice in. Our task must now be to ensure there is no repeat. One mistake can be excused, but to make the same error twice is unpardonable.'

'I see it now...' Samuel said miserably. 'So, you believe the smuggling that took place in September was of this very same Irish whiskey?' he asked, holding up the remnants of his drained glass.

'There can be no doubting it! There is a method of shipment often used by smugglers, according to Mr Woodward. He described it to me before I left London. He calls it "coopering". This is when a vessel of some size transports a cargo from afar and transfers the goods to another *smaller* craft when close in to shore. In this instance, I suspect the port of Cork, or thereabouts, is the most likely point of origin. On arrival off the coast, the larger ship will anchor in dead of night a short distance from the beach. Then, on some prearranged signal from a party of shore smugglers, smaller local vessels – in our case, Cornish in origin – will emerge from coves and inlets along the coastline. Each will affect a rendezvous and hand over the contraband at sea. Like this, the goods will be safely brought to land a little at a time. If the "mother ship" – that was Albert's expression – is truly capacious, a number of trips will be required by its inshore "daughter" vessels to bring the whole load to safety. The work may take many hours to complete. If my guess is right, and potcheen is part of the shipment, the daughter craft, while small and nimble in shallow waters, will need to be large enough to carry in the tubs.'

'I know well enough of coopering, mothers and daughters, and suchlike, sir...' Samuel chided while putting his head in his hands. 'But I searched for the contraband everywhere! I fairly ransacked Doubloons in my efforts to locate the stash.'

'You were looking for brandy and tobacco, were you not?'

'Why, yes, that's a fact. But bottles are bottles, sir, tubs are tubs.'

'Agreed. But, pray tell me, did you use your writ of assistance to rummage at Pennycrocker Hall, by any chance?'

'Why, no! Sir William is a former magistrate, after all. I could not justify such an affront as that.'

Henry drew closer. 'This brings me to the true reason why I have come to see you now, at this late hour. Matters have moved on apace, and Mr Woodward and I feel certain another attempt at the coastline will be made soon enough. Early next week, if we're not mistaken, just days after your wedding, in fact – the ideal time for owling, don't you think?'

'While Elizabeth and I are away in Bodmin enjoying our honeymoon, you mean?'

'Precisely! And if the moon-cursers have any lingering concerns about *my* continued presence hereabouts, I will have returned to London also.'

'"Moved on apace", you say. I have seen little here to suggest anything unusual.'

'That is because Borwenstow folk know you for who you are, Samuel, and baulk if they pass you in the street. Am I not right? Even the honest ones have no wish to be tainted by your acquaintance. But imagine if you had free rein to poke about unsuspected by others. Might that not reveal the true underbelly of the village and expose the veritable state of affairs hereabouts?'

'It might, I grant you...' This was proving to be a much more difficult conversation than Samuel had envisaged less than half an hour before. Unbolting the Custom House door to admit Henry Gough had certainly opened a can of worms in the process.

'Then listen carefully to me now,' Henry said steadily. 'I have much to tell, and you will not find any of it dull, I'll warrant...'

* * *

The next morning, being a Sunday, Henry sent word to Elizabeth at Pennycrocker Hall to inform her of his arrival and to ask when it might be possible for them to meet. He proposed to host a dinner at the inn that evening at seven, to which Samuel and his mother, Constance, would be invited. And, of course, Hannah must come too, for she was still his wife and Elizabeth's loving mother. As fate would have it, Hannah now had short-term lodgings at the Hall, which made arrangements all the easier. Then Henry went in search of Jacob Jarvie. He passed Molly clutching a stack of plates to her bosom.

'The gentleman you spoke of last night, Molly, the man from Southampton – I should like to meet him. His occupation sounds most absorbing.'

'You mean the handsome Mr Jarvie,' she replied shamelessly. 'He went out early, as is his custom, but he usually returns before nine thirty. He knows I always try to keep something special for him.'

'Special?'

'For breakfast, sir… He won't touch the pilchards, mind. Eggs is what he likes best. Fresh eggs.'

'Thank you, Molly. I'll wait in my room until he returns.'

'Shall I send him up, sir? After his breakfast, of course…'

Henry had counted the eighth of an expected ten strikes of the market square clock when a crisp clout on his bedroom door drowned out the sound of the ninth. Expecting to see Jacob on the threshold, he was surprised to find it was Molly on the other side of the door. She gave him a cheeky curtsey and said, 'If it pleases you, sir, Mr Jarvie says he'd be delighted to make your acquaintance, but asks if you'd meet him in *his* rooms. They are bigger, and he has some charts to spread out, if that would interest you, sir… so he says.'

Henry nodded his agreement with a wan smile, unable to

hide a mild sense of annoyance at the changed plan, but he knew it made sense and followed the delightful Molly through a maze of corridors and steps to his old room. Once her retreating footfall could be heard no longer, Henry greeted his new friend with a brimming smile and a vigorous shake of the hand. The next two hours were spent in hushed yet energetic conversation as each man reported his news to the other.

'We must work together, you are right, Mr Gough. I greatly value your support. But, pray tell me, where can we four meet without drawing attention to ourselves, so we may share our ideas and arrive at a plan? There should be all of us around the table to thrash things out, and no one is more important in that regard than Samuel Snuggs. He knows the lie of the land better than any of us.'

'I think I can solve that little conundrum, Jacob…'

'You can?'

'We shall meet at the new Custom House in Fore Street tonight at ten. It's very compact, I grant you, but it's as secure a place as any, and we shan't be overheard, especially on a Sunday night. I have spoken to Samuel Snuggs already on the matter, and he is in agreement. Samuel and I will arrive there after our dinner, at a few minutes before ten. We will unlock together, as we did last week. No one should suspect us if we are observed, as we are soon to become family, and the whole of Borwenstow knows it. Your job will be to get a message to Inspector Halwill this evening. You must invite him too. If he refuses out of some vain pride, then more fool him. You tell me you have made your peace with him. This offer to collaborate will prove it one way or another. Only *him*, mind… Marshgate will have to stay asleep while we debate the issues.'

'Marshgate has already returned to Launceston, alone. Halwill dispatched him this morning.'

'All the better, then. If Halwill agrees, you two will have to travel separately, of course – such an amalgam will certainly arouse mistrust if you are seen together. I shall ensure you are let in one by one, two minutes apart. Once inside, 'twill be just the four of us, and we can get to work to devise a stratagem which will deal with this matter once and for all.'

* * *

Dinner that night was quite a jolly affair. Hannah, blissfully unaware of the perilous machinations that entwined both her husband and daughter, was on top form, even laughing out loud, at times, while sharing her sentiments of all she had seen at Pennycrocker Hall since her arrival a week before. She had yet to meet Sir William, she informed the assembly, but had encountered Lady Kathleen on no less than two occasions – a woman she described as "one of the most charming personages I have ever encountered". Constance had been quieter and more docile as the exchanges crossed the table, sensing perhaps, like only a mother can, that some hidden melancholy seemed to lie beneath her only son's outwardly gay appearance. In truth, Henry thought he saw it too – the hint of a dark apprehension in his son-in-law-to-be, buried within, by his perhaps *over-lively* conversation. Samuel had drunk rather more madeira than was wise, Henry mused. He hoped this mild euphoria would not make the sober judgements that lay a few hours ahead more difficult to accomplish. The conversation flitted from place to place, but at its centre were thoughts of the wedding, now less than six days hence, and the joyful anticipation of countless years of happy marriage ahead. Even Henry and Hannah, who had been unsuccessful in that regard, clinked glasses to toast the future of the devoted couple.

All through the evening, Elizabeth was as steadfast as a rock and yet gracefully congenial too. She laughed at all the jokes, telling some of her own in return, but she still found time for an erudite discussion with her father on the scale of the universe, which she described as "beyond the ken of mankind". Goodness, how dearly Henry loved, admired and treasured his daughter! It was difficult for him to put into words how much he venerated her simple, unaffected elegance, her scholarly charms and the sheer love of life that beat within her fragile frame. As he watched her with a feeling of warm detachment – his very own Elizabeth, now all grown up – holding a conversation with Constance about the work of American missionaries in far-off Siam, his heart fairly swelled with pride.

But all good things must come to an end, and by nine thirty, the last course of treacle tart all consumed, it was time for the ladies to retire. They made their fluttering excuses and left Henry and Samuel alone with their port.

They did not dally long. 'Come, Samuel, lead the way,' Henry announced, downing his glass while raising himself with his spare hand from the armchair. 'It would be good to arrive a few minutes early. If I am not mistaken, we shall need our wits about us tonight.' He touched Samuel's arm and turned to face him.

'I only ask one thing of you… Do not, on any account, hold yourself back. If we are to succeed in this noble venture, we may only have one broadside to fire, and it is most unlikely you will see a better and more willing array of cannon assembled in Borwenstow in future. Our task this evening is challenging, though it may appear straightforward. We must all speak candidly and arrive at the very best strategy we can, given the resources we have in our possession. The last words Albert Woodward left me with yesterday were: "Remember *the five Ps*, Henry – *Proper Planning Prevents Pitiable Performance.*" Spoken with his Valleys drawl, it made quite a mark on me, I don't mind saying!'

Chapter Twenty

Elizabeth Gough had wanted to spend some private time with her father during their dinner at the inn. There had been so much to discuss, so much to divulge, and the prospect exhilarated her. This new world of intrigue she'd unintentionally entered was thrilling indeed! Alas, any conversation of consequence had proved impossible, as she was rarely out of her mother's or Constance's sight or earshot. Henry had tried to make it clear to his daughter, by mouthing a few surreptitious words when the others weren't looking, that he also wished them to have a couple of moments together before she departed. It was only as the three ladies were climbing into the coach that would take them back to their respective lodgings that the pair finally managed to snatch a few words together. On the pretence of returning to the dining room for her misplaced clutch, Elizabeth had left the other two ladies nattering happily in the carriage while she hurried back to fetch it.

'Oh, Papa, I cannot dally. Mama is waiting. But I see you wish to speak to me, and for all that is true, I wish it also.'

'Dearest Daughter, listen to me. I have heard what you have done and been told what you have discovered. I am so proud of you! Mr Jarvie has advised me of everything. But this caper has to stop here. There may be danger ahead, and I wish you to have no part in it. I never should have brought you into this in the first place.'

'But, Papa—'

'I will not take no for an answer, Elizabeth.' His words were firmly but tenderly delivered. 'My instructions to you are clear. You will *not* be meeting Mr Jarvie alone in future. 'Tis too perilous for you – for the pair of you, in fact. If you have something to share, and I beg you *not* to go looking for it, send word to the inn, and we can meet. It will be far safer that way. I will be your go-between from now on. If I have to come to the Hall, I will. After all, my wife and daughter reside there now, so a visit to finalise the wedding arrangements will not attract attention. I shall instruct Jacob likewise – that on no account is he to meet you alone. We are gathering tonight, anyway, to determine a way forward to resolve this state of affairs. You have done so well, Elizabeth, but here it must end.' He kissed her lovingly on the cheek. 'Now, run to your mother. I know how she hates waiting!'

'Very well, Father. I understand. It was certainly exciting while it lasted!' she gushed. 'Trust me, I shall take no risks, but the walls have ears at Pennycrocker Hall, and I shall remain listening and writing down what I learn.'

Before Henry could remonstrate, she was gone, blowing him another kiss as she hurried away to the waiting carriage. He watched her go with a grimace of paternal frustration, and vowed to speak to her properly the next time they met.

* * *

It was well past 10p.m. before the four protagonists sat down to chew the cud. Samuel had chosen the location for their gathering carefully. Situated in the centre of the new Custom House, it was a cleared-out storeroom – windowless and distinctly poky.

On ushering Inspector Halwill into the building, Henry made sure to shake him warmly by the hand. 'It's so good of you to join us, Inspector. Mr Woodward sends his very best regards from London.'

Candles were lit, and the little group took random places around a square table Samuel had arranged in the middle of the room. From here, each could touch the walls that pressed in from behind. As proposed by Henry en route to the Custom House, it was Samuel who fittingly commenced the proceedings with an introduction and a few words of welcome. He then invited each of the group to outline and explain their separate roles and involvement in the grave matters at hand. Once the brief narratives had concluded, Henry Gough offered to summarise events thus far. He suggested he might be the best placed to do this on behalf of the group, as he had knowledge of the complete picture, and the others readily accepted his proposal.

'I will not dwell on the ancient history of smuggling in these parts,' he started. 'It is known to all of us around this table, as are the many dread legends that accompany the events of the past. Instead, I intend to cut to the chase. Please excuse me if, in doing so, my remarks appear harsh or even accusatory. That is not my intention. I only wish to tease out all the facts so we can combine to form a solution.'

The others nodded in sober understanding, though in doing so, Halwill managed to look especially glum.

'In my eyes,' Henry continued, 'our story begins with the cruel and vicious murder of Ignatius Honey on the steps of St Piran's in September last year. His missing head has yet to be recovered. You, Samuel Snuggs, were falsely accused of his murder, were you not?'

'That I was,' Samuel replied grimly.

'And you, Inspector... have yet to find the culprit. Am I correct?'

'You are, Mr Gough. I would add, in my defence, that a curtain of silence, which is most common along this shrouded coast, has hindered all police efforts to uncover the killer... or killers.'

'Is it not also true that there is strong evidence that smuggling took place on the same night of the murder, not a few hundred yards from where we now sit? To add to that, all the efforts of the Revenue have failed either to capture the perpetrators or seize any contraband. Am I right, Mr Snuggs?'

'Yes, regrettably, 'tis so. The breaching of the Shrouded Cove tunnel that leads to the crypt speaks to it. I fear the wall of silence the inspector speaks of has undone me also.'

'There is no need to dwell any further on the disappointments thus far' – Henry did his best to sound buoyant – 'as we must move the story forwards by eight months and into the present... Two further murders have since been committed, each by poisoning, and both of officials from the very same church. I witnessed the death of Reverend Rosewarne myself. His verger, the man Polrunny, was to follow his master to the grave in very short order. My understanding, Inspector, is you are no further along finding *their* killer... or killers, either?'

Halwill returned Henry's question with a most disagreeable look. 'I regret not... though I do agree, the church itself links all these crimes.'

'Do you mean the church, sir, or perchance, the *tunnel* that lies beneath it?'

'I have my theories on that score. The fact that the reverend had set himself so strongly against one of the prominent families in the village may have caused his death. The fact that one of their number was found headless beside the lychgate of Rosewarne's church may also be pertinent.'

'Speak plainly, sir,' Henry interjected. 'Do you mean the Honeys – who have been branded as cut-throat smugglers for generations?'

'That is correct. And their motive must be revenge, plain and simple. For good measure, I will attach their desire to renew their free trading, unchallenged and unchecked by the obstinate parson.'

'And the verger... what of him? By all accounts, Penrose Polrunny was on friendly terms with your suspects. Some have said he was a sympathiser, indeed, who disagreed with the parson's view that all Honeys, including their sister, Prudence, were devils incarnate. Why should they wish to kill him also, if he was their friend? After all, in the scheme of things, his part is of no consequence – a mere verger, a man less concerned with men's souls than with maintenance.'

Halwill looked troubled. 'I have no answer to that. It still concerns me why Polrunny should have been so callously murdered. My only conclusion is that he held a set of keys to the church and had easy access to the crypt and its tunnel at all hours of the day and night...'

'We saw Trewint with Amos and Jago emerge from the vestry on the day of the parson's death,' Henry said. 'My guess is the innkeeper has a set of keys too. I'll wager a number have obtained copies, over the years.'

'Then I am truly flummoxed,' Halwill admitted.

'Very well, let's move on. A question for us all, gentlemen... Do we all agree that the suspected trafficking and the murders must be connected in some way?'

The awkward hush that followed gave Henry his answer.

'If so, allow me to bring our story fully up to date.' Henry announced, 'We have evidence that Sir William

Pennycrocker and the staff at the Hall may be complicit in this alleged smuggling also – even Her Ladyship seems to have been drawn in. Our intelligence, most bravely collected, I might add, suggests a plan is afoot for another attack on the coast, to take place at any day. Irish whiskey will be the contraband, and if my guess is correct, there will much of it. Mr Jarvie's excellent observations indicate work is being undertaken to clear the seaward end of the tunnel into St Piran's.'

'The twenty-fifth has been mentioned,' Jacob Jarvie piped up.

'Precisely! If that be the case, our simple task must be to prevent it. If our assertion that both crimes are connected is correct, we shall resolve the whole matter in a trice!'

There then followed a lengthy discussion on the ways of smugglers and the art of coopering, during which Samuel Snuggs took the lead. 'On the night of the twenty-fifth, the moon will be negligible and the tide at its peak at 1a.m. – perfect conditions for owling at Shrouded Cove.'

'But *which* twenty-fifth?' Halwill's question caused the others to frown.

'Of May, clearly... A week on Wednesday, if I'm not mistaken,' Henry replied for all of them.

'No, you miss my meaning,' Halwill sighed. 'Am I not correct that a conversation has been overheard that some event must take place on the twenty-fifth, or there will be all hell to pay... some words to that effect?'

'Yes, that was what I was told,' Jacob said.

'But my question is... will it be the night of the twenty-fifth... or in the wee small hours of the twenty-fifth? Now do you understand?'

'The inspector makes a good point,' Henry said, taking in a lungful of air. 'We shall have to plan for both nights. The state of the moon and tide will be much the same on each, I assume.'

'I have a question,' Jacob muttered. 'Is it true that Shrouded Cove cannot be accessed from the cliff?'

'That is correct; there is no path down to it,' Snuggs replied, 'unless a 150-foot rope is used. It's the reason why it is the ideal place to bring goods ashore, as it cannot be observed or attacked from the land – that is, as long as the tunnel is serviceable.'

'Then how do we confirm the seaward end of the shaft has indeed been unblocked? The evidence points to it, but how can we be sure?' Jacob pressed.

'It can only be done by boat,' Samuel answered.

'But we would show our hand if we attempted it,' Jacob replied while the others nodded.

'I could ask the revenue cutter to pass by in the next few days,' Samuel Snuggs offered. 'I happen to know the *Vigilant* is in Bude at the present. I could send word to Mr Geach, its commander. A passage at a quarter of a mile distant and a reasonable spyglass should tell us all we need to know.'

The group tutted in agreement. 'It would be better if you delivered the message yourself,' Henry suggested. 'Can he be trusted, this Mr Geach?'

'He most certainly can; I went to school with him! Jack Geach is a Cornish boy through and through and a very competent seaman, at that. He has been the hero of a number of tussles with smugglers over the years, and his cutter, though it has seen better days, is still one of the fastest along this coastline. I know Geach's hands are often tied by his superiors, who wish him to patrol further northwards into the Bristol Channel, but I'm sure he will do me this service, if I bring him into our confidence.'

This suggestion was approved by the group, and Snuggs was assigned to travel to Bude the following day. The discussions moved to the most effective way to intercept the smugglers on the night in question.

'How many staff do you have at your disposal, Samuel? Who can you trust to join us?' Halwill asked.

'I can call on just six riding officers, with horses, and a single clerk. That is all. A paltry group, to be sure. In answer to your last, I can put my faith in just four of them, if I am to be candid.'

'And the horses?' Jarvie hooted. 'What of them?'

'I can vouch for *all* of the horses, sir,' Samuel laughed back. 'It's only a couple of my men who cause me sleepless nights.'

'That's not a lot, for our purposes.' Jarvie shook his head.

'I can summon Marshgate back from Launceston, with another two or three men, with luck… and there is Constable Poundstock too. If we bring him into the plan at the last minute, he can bolster our numbers,' Halwill offered.

'That makes a dozen of us.' Samuel scratched his ear. 'It should be sufficient, if we dispose of our forces carefully. At most, we shall have to contend with six in opposition: the two Honeys, Trewint, Amos, Jago… and add another for luck. The last thing we should do is to flood the village with strangers. The word would soon go around.'

Samuel Snuggs spoke next. 'With ten men, we have enough combined to observe covertly from the cliffs above Shrouded Cove and use the rest to surround the church from a discreet distance. It will be dark, but for the smugglers it will be the same, and *they* shall need lights. Our plan should be to first conduct a lookout from the cliffs for signs of the mother vessel arriving off the coast. We will then watch as the expected daughters approach and depart from their mother. It will be a waiting game. Those who are tasked with surrounding St Piran's must strike only when they see suspicious movement from within the church grounds. In truth, if we could delay further, it would be better, as I am anxious to discover where the Honeys *stash* the contraband. If we had the resources to follow at a distance, it might solve the mystery. For I have searched high and low for the last consignment and never found it!'

'That might be difficult... Don't forget the almost moonless night,' Henry observed.

'The transportation of a sizeable load of whiskey will require a road. There are but three thoroughfares that lead from the church. We might consider stationing men along each route and at every crossroad. That way, the goods will be sure to pass by, one way or another,' Snuggs added, stroking his chin.

'That may be a good plan, if we had two squadrons of men!' Inspector Halwill interjected. 'But with our limited resources, I suggest we keep things simple. Your original stratagem is best. We use a handful to watch from the cliffs and the main force to surround the church. We strike only when we see figures emerge and know the goods have landed. We can then demand the truth from those we capture. I assure you – it will not take long for them to tell *me* the truth about the whereabouts of their hidey-hole! And when Pennycrocker is implicated, as I'm sure he will be, I will have men spare to pay him a visit before he wakes. I doubt he will be dirtying his own delicate hands in a haunted churchyard on such a midnight jaunt as this. It will be most entertaining to stir him *and* Her Ladyship from their slumbers, eh?'

Unable to fault this intervention, Jacob looked at Henry, who looked at Samuel, who gazed back at Jacob in return. It was Samuel who spoke for all of them. 'It will be a pleasure to join you, sir. I have a writ, so there will be no need to visit the magistrate for his permission at that late hour.'

Any tension that may have existed within the assembly

dissipated in an instant, as all four men laughed out loud at the thought of it. Their policy was settled there and then. With the masterplan formed, in outline at least, the group turned to discuss how best to use the remaining days before the night of the twenty-fourth. Unless their intelligence changed, this would be their first outing in force. Henry hoped this would be the correct moment, for he had doubts that these arrangements would survive if all had to be repeated the following day. Such were his fears. Like the others, he fervently hoped their designs would remain secret, but his experience told him the inclusion of hitherto unknown members of their party had the potential to compromise their objectives. Knowing who to trust, he mused, was the hardest thing of all.

Before each went their separate ways, it was agreed that Jarvie would continue his patrols of the coast and his casual chatting to locals in the manner of a fellow from the Ordnance Survey. He would make sure to steer clear of Doubloons and Shrouded Cove.

Gough would go about the business of preparing for the wedding and endeavour to visit Pennycrocker Hall – and Elizabeth, in the process – at least once, maybe more.

Snuggs would pay a visit to Commander Jack Geach in Bude and secure the services of the revenue cutter, and then on returning to Borwenstow, he would appear to go about his normal duties. The group tasked him with drawing up maps and lists of names and addresses for each to use on the night in question.

Halwill would make himself ostensibly busy for a couple of days. He would then retreat to Launceston with deliberate fanfare, only to return with reinforcements, under cover of darkness, a week on Tuesday. If important intelligence surfaced over the next week, it was conceded that this might be shared simply between Snuggs and Gough – even with Jarvie, if precautions were taken. But for Halwill, such exchanges would be impossible. He would have to rely on delayed word reaching him.

Finally, they agreed that their next meeting as a group would include all participants. This would take place at 9p.m. in the crammed Custom House on the very day Halwill resurfaced in Borwenstow. Here, all the troops would be briefed, deployments would be finalised, and weapons, ammunition and sundry equipment would be issued. By the time all had been concluded, Sunday had turned into Monday. Each thanked the other, and handshakes were exchanged.

'Before we depart, there is one matter we have overlooked,' Henry said, sucking his teeth and turning to the policeman at his side. 'You told me once, Inspector, that you had seen the spectral skull of Borwenstow, the very same that folklore claims is the spirit of Abel Snuggs which haunts the passage to the crypt. You said it was an experience you will never forget. Pray, can you tell us more? For if the church does possess a spirit, I'm sure all of us here would wish to know of it.'

The previous mood of hilarity halted in an instant, replaced by one of grim attentiveness, as the assembly strained to hear what Inspector Austol Halwill Barton might say in reply.

'What I told you was the truth, sir. And I was scared out of my wits by it. The memory has never left me. But I was just a boy at the time.' Halwill looked to his side to engage Samuel individually. 'Of course, the legend that your ancestor's ghost roams these parts had been handed down over many years. Do you mind if I ask if you have seen it too?'

'I have not, sir. Nor do I wish ever to do. But I have spoken to many who have sworn by it. On certain nights, I'll admit a strange shiver in my bones comes to me from within the church itself. In terms of a visual manifestation, I have never encountered such a thing; however, on two occasions, a chill of pure fear took my breath away as I passed by the outside wall of the nave. I avoid the place now, but I recall each time being left with an unexplained sense of abject loneliness and remorse – a feeling of inexplicable shame. My senses recovered soon enough, but the episodes left their mark, all the same. And you, sir? You say you have actually seen the phantom…'

'I believe I have, sir, or something purporting to be it… I first heard the story from my own grandfather when he tucked me into bed one night. What a thing to tell a child as one douses the candle!' He shook his head. 'The tale fair put the fear of death into me, I can tell you. I used to dream of the spectre just as my grandfather had described – the skull, teeth and eye sockets all blazing, as if in flames. Some years later, I must have been about ten years old, my family had reason to come to Borwenstow for a lengthy spell – a relative needed some succour, I recall – and they brought me. My grandparents came too. I used to lie in bed, in the self-same room I have occupied these last few nights, in fact, and reflect on the legend. For it was all the talk back then. The inn had a different name in those days, *The Pandora*, as I remember. You see, *The Gauger's Return* is recently named, less than twenty-five years ago. Gauger is another word for a revenue officer, of course, and now the inn names itself after your ancestor. But I'm sure you knew all that already…'

Samuel nodded that he did.

'Of course, the village became famous for it,' Halwill continued. 'The folk round here thrived on the legend, in fact, and people would come from miles around in the hope of seeing "the spectral skull"!' He raised his fingers to indicate imaginary quotation marks. '*I* was not to be disappointed either, for one eerie twilight, my grandfather took me by the hand straight into the churchyard, and there it was, gaping at me – just floating in the air under the eastern window. I turned on my heels and fled, screaming for all I was worth. My grandfather just hooted with laughter, in the manner of one who'd just played a wicked trick. But for me, at the time, it was no laughing matter. I was as scared as a little boy could ever be. Even now, all these years later, I struggle to enter that church, though deep down I know I must have been the victim of some prank. Remembering the experience makes me irascible – more than usual…' Halwill broke into a thin smile. 'These last few days have been very trying, I don't mind telling you.'

Chapter Twenty-One

Samuel Snuggs was confident he knew where to find his old school pal, Jack Geach, soon enough. Bude was fifteen miles distant, so if he left at first light, he'd be able to track his friend down and hopefully join him for breakfast. *The Bush Inn* would be his first port of call. If Samuel didn't unearth him there, he would try Her Majesty's Revenue Cutter *Vigilant* herself. She was sure to be moored alongside the harbour wall. One of the crew would be able to tell him where their commander was. Samuel knew the road to Bude like the back of his hand, and even though he'd travelled it many times, he nearly always enjoyed the ride – as long as the weather behaved. But on this fine May morning, with all thoughts of Atlantic thunderstorms now glimmers of the past, he saddled up "Lancelot" with such a hammering heart as to make him wonder what the cause might be. There was anticipation, of course, urgency also, but there was dread too… Setting an easterly course, the sun blinding him at first, he trotted Lancelot to the gate at the rear of the Custom House, and then, turning left onto the road, he raised the pace to a brisk canter.

In less than a mile, he passed the track that led to

Doubloons, and as his horse rose to the brow of a knoll, the farmhouse and outbuildings could be clearly seen about a quarter of a mile to his left. He half wondered whether he might catch a glimpse of an early risen Jacob Jarvie lurking amongst nearby trees, still intent on maintaining his lonesome watch over the starkly drawn line of coast. But it was not to be, fortunately Samuel thought, and he pressed on. At Treskinnick Cross, he pulled Lancelot to a halt, dismounted, and after leading him to a water trough, allowed the grateful animal to chew amongst the lush early summer grass. Here, Samuel stretched out full length and gazed into the sky. After trying vainly to make portentous shapes from the wisps of clouds, he reached for his pocket watch, which told him it was five minutes past seven. With barely five miles to go, he was confident of reaching his goal before eight.

He tried closing his eyes, and almost instantly an image of his beloved fiancée came smiling to him. The angst returned. It had been only on hearing the startling accounts of Jacob's twin meetings with her that he'd properly realised how much Elizabeth had achieved. To expose the scandalous conduct at Pennycrocker Hall had indeed been astounding. He chided himself for failing to entertain even a single suspicion of Sir William's now clear culpability. He'd been blinded to it. Perhaps Henry Gough was right. Samuel had been in Cornwall too long – in Borwenstow, maybe *far* too long... He had become stale, a man without imagination or ingenuity who just went through the motions, day in, day out. The people of Borwenstow must look on him as a fool...

Look what Jacob Jarvie has achieved in just a few short days!

Samuel folded his arms across his chest and sighed. He'd taken the morality of the gentry for granted, but he vowed he would never make the same mistake again. How could he have been so blind? He should have been more resourceful, much braver too… like Elizabeth had… Jacob, also. As the senior revenue officer for miles around, Samuel had possessed the power to search the Hall without recourse to another for permission. Why hadn't he used it? After all, he'd rummaged near everywhere else! In his heart, he knew the answer, plain and simple – he was not up to the job. His ancestors would be ashamed of him… and rightly so. Poor Abel…

The image of Elizabeth faded as the wind started to pick up. Samuel pushed himself up from the grass and got to his feet. Lancelot looked at him gloomily. The horse had not stopped his munching and wanted to continue feasting on the juicy green shoots all around. But it was time to go. Maybe the ever-jovial Jack Geach could alter Samuel's foul mood.

The Bush Inn drew a blank. The proprietor told him some of *Vigilant*'s crew, including their intrepid commander, had spent the previous evening drinking there, but all had returned to the cutter before midnight. It was just a short walk to the dock, so after booking a room for himself for one day, and leaving Lancelot in the hands of the inn's stable boys, Samuel made his way down to the quay. As expected, the single-masted *Vigilant* lay alongside, looking a good deal more ragged and time-worn than he'd expected. At a mere seventy-five feet in length, with a beam of twenty-three feet, she was smaller than most might have imagined too. As he approached the stern rail, Samuel hollered out to one of the deckhands who, back turned against him, was busily engaged amongst the rigging.

'Is your commander aboard? I have come to see Mr Geach.'

To his surprise, when the crewman turned to answer, the fellow was none other than Geach himself, appearing decidedly dishevelled, with hands covered in what looked like black pitch. 'Goodness! Why, if it isn't old Snuggsy! The man himself, come to pay his friend a visit,' he hollered back.

'Good day, Jack. I called for you at *The Bush*. Don't you usually rest there when you are in Bude?'

'Oh dear, Snuggsy, you need to keep your ear to the ground more. The revenue commissioners won't allow it now – not even for the commander of one of their mighty cutters! Times are hard. They tell me their purses are closed to such luxuries. No, old friend, I am obliged to stay on board these days to save the Exchequer from bankruptcy.'

'May I come aboard? I have much to discuss, and your advice would be most prized.'

'Best not, we are in quite a muddle below decks... This ancient hulk has seen better days, haven't you, old girl?' He caressed the end of the boom with a loving touch. 'Allow me and my men to clear up. I'll meet you at *The Bush* in an hour, if that suits. I have a lot to tell too, and none of it will be pleasing to the ear.'

It was after nine before the pair took up their conversation once more. Samuel had ordered bacon and eggs and mugs of hot tea to be brought to a table at the back of the inn. Jack Geach's eyes lit up when he saw the spread. 'Exactly what a man requires after three hours of solid work. I applaud your foresight, sir!'

'Three hours, already?!'

'Indeed, old chap. I have orders to begin decommissioning *Vigilant*. Your visit has caught me on the hop! I'm expecting to be posted to Bristol any week now. The Master of the Queen's Warehouse beckons, by all accounts.'

'But what of the marine service?'

'Gone to hell, as good as... The commissioners, in their wisdom, wish to cut back. There is no smuggling in these parts, so they inform me... nor any risk to the nation's security! I have told them otherwise, of course, most vociferously, in truth, but they pay no attention to a lowly fellow such as me. Our patrols are to cease as soon as my new orders come through from London. *HMRC Vigilant* has done me proud these last three years, but even she is on her last legs. You can't expect to be afloat for more than four decades without showing your age. She's past it, bless her, and so is the cutter service, if the commissioners have their way.'

'That is bad news indeed, for it is the use of *Vigilant* I have come to seek. I'd hoped you might conduct a patrol for me. I have reliable intelligence that a smuggle of contraband is being organised as we speak – the date is set, even.'

Commander Jack Geach placed a lump of bread in his mouth and drew closer. 'A smuggle, you say, and soon?'

'Why, next week. My information is second to none, I may add. We are expecting a mother ship loaded with whiskey from Ireland to anchor off Borwenstow on the twenty-fourth or twenty-fifth of this month. In just eleven days.'

'Which is it? Twenty-four or twenty-five?'

'I don't know precisely… The hour will be around midnight, hence our uncertainty, but each of the dates will be when the tide is high and there is all but the tiniest of moons.'

Samuel began to explain the situation in depth, with Jack asking many questions as he spoke, all of which were resolved to the commander's satisfaction. 'I wish you to conduct a daylight patrol along the cliffs by Shrouded Cove,' he told Geach. 'We need to know if tampering of the old tunnel has occurred. We want proof the shaft is open once more.'

'Ah-ha! The haunted place where phantoms are seen most nights, eh? I've never given that cave a second glance these many months, for 'twas you that sealed it up last year, was it not?'

'Will you do it, Jack? One final patrol…'

Geach's answer was immediate. 'I will!' he roared. 'There you have it. I need no permission, and there is no time like the present. The ship is prepared, and the tide is in our favour. If we leave now, we'll be back in time for a late lunch. Come, Samuel. This may be your last chance to ride on one of Her Majesty's valiant revenue cutters.'

* * *

Elizabeth Gough had grown to love her three charges – Wilhelmina, Clodagh and Maeve – as if they had been her very own children, and the prospect of being parted from them, even for a short period of leave, caused her not inconsiderable dismay. As the wedding date approached, she'd also realised that the planned five days' absence she and Samuel had set aside for their subsequent honeymoon was awkward, to say the least. It would come during a period crucial to the success of her future husband and beloved father's secret enterprise. She'd spoken to Samuel on the subject during their dinner at the inn, and he had readily agreed. Five days in Bodmin, under the circumstances, was too long. If the pair shortened their time away to just two days and nights, both would be back well in advance of the most momentous events that were slated to befall them all. They settled on it. Samuel needed to be in Borwenstow, as did she, but the conundrum lay in how to change the dates without arousing the suspicion of the Pennycrocker household. In this regard, her much professed love of Lady Kathleen's children would come to Elizabeth's rescue, providing her with a valid excuse to change her plans. When the opportunity arose to speak to Her Ladyship, Elizabeth seized it with both hands. She had been in the middle of conducting a lesson in French for the elder two, while Maeve had been playing happily with a pile of wooden bricks, when Lady Kathleen entered the nursery and swept the little one up in her arms.

'Come, Maeve, Cook and I have something to show you. She is making sponges and needs someone to lick the bowl. I'm sure Miss Gough won't mind me taking you from her for just a few minutes. Even *I* have to ask her permission, you know,' she laughed, 'as your governess has grown so attached to you all!'

This was Elizabeth's opportunity and she took it. 'I love them so dearly, Your Ladyship, that I have decided to cut short my honeymoon. Samuel has agreed. We will be away just two days instead of five, if that pleases Your Ladyship.'

'Ah-ha! I expect the expense of things must be a factor too. Grand hotels in Bodmin can cost a pretty penny these days.'

'Well, yes... 'tis something we have thought about also. I need to save for the future – and Samuel, too – but it is the loss of these three that weighs most heavily.'

'I am sure my husband and I can lend a hand, if money is a concern. An advance, perhaps? What do you say? Would ten pounds suffice?... twenty?'

'Oh, Your Ladyship is most kind, but I'd prefer to keep things as they are now. I do so hate owing money to others.'

'A gift, then. I shall ask Sir William this very evening. I am sure he will agree.'

The corner that Elizabeth had now painted herself into seemed to grow smaller with each sentence uttered. 'But... I feel sure my husband would disapprove, Your Ladyship. Your gift of the carriage and the pair of Arabs is already too generous. If there was more, I fear my Samuel would worry that folk would misunderstand.'

'They need never know! *I* shall certainly not tell them. Why worry about what folk say anyway? *I* never do.'

Elizabeth resisted the urge to reply that ordinary people had different rules to abide by. The class to which Her Ladyship so providentially belonged played a very different game. 'That is most generous… I shall certainly mention your kind offer to Samuel, but if I understand him as I think I do, I know what his answer will be.'

Lady Pennycrocker frowned benignly and tutted. 'Very well. If truth be known, I shall be grateful for your early return, as indeed the children will also… won't you, girls?'

Wilhelmina and Clodagh beamed up from the list of *Vocabulaire Français* they had been pretending to study. 'Oh yes, Mama, please say Miss Gough can come back to us sooner! We will miss her too badly if she's away for five whole days!' cheeky Clodagh cried as her elder sister nodded her vigorous agreement.

* * *

The weather changed dramatically early the following morning, in the manner it often does in England at that time of the year. The bright, warm days that had heralded the beginning of the month and had filled the verges with a host of spring blooms gave way to a period of prolonged wet conditions as an Atlantic depression tormented the coastline. The timing of this inclement shift was fortunate indeed for Samuel Snuggs, as his jaunt aboard *HMRC Vigilant* had been in the nick of time. Had they delayed by just a day, the vessel would have remained in port, with visibility so bad as to leave any surveillance patrol wholly meaningless.

As luck would have it, the sail-past was a roaring success. The increased wind from the north pushed the cutter along at a pace that disavowed her age. The lively performance brought broad ocean-splattered smiles to the faces of Samuel and Jack – and even to some of the weather-beaten, "seen it all before" crew on deck. Exhilarating it had been, but the true worth of the expedition occurred only when Shrouded Cove hove into view on the starboard tack. Samuel was not the only one training a spyglass from a distance of 400 yards at the grey sandstone cliff face and the gaping caves beneath. His observations – confirmed by Jack Geach's telescope, levelled on the same spot – showed the fissure under the prominent tower of St Piran's had indeed been breached. The evidence was clear. A dark hole, which Jack knew had not existed eight months before, now seemed to shout at them from the distant rocks. With some difficulty, as the ship was shifting under his body all the while, Samuel peered ever deeper into the crevice. Then, he'd seen enough. He was certain that the architecture of the cavern had changed. Jacob Jarvie's clifftop observations had indeed yielded fruit.

Now, their joint plans to thwart the assault on the coast could proceed apace.

That evening, at *The Bush* tavern, Samuel and Jack shared a hearty dinner – and more ale than either had consumed in a month – before the latter was forced to retire to the outdated relic that was once the proud flagship of the entire revenue fleet.

'Get word to me, Samuel, if you need my help again. If I have not been recalled to Bristol, my crew and I will do our best to respond. Rest assured, I have told my boys nothing of the intelligence you have shared with me, nor will I ever, not until the time is right. They are a fine body of men, but they need to know nothing at this moment. I regret my influence with the commissioners is now exhausted, and I cannot delay the inevitable. It's just a question of time, less than a week most probably, before I have to say farewell to my brave little craft. Until the time comes, you know where I am.'

The ride home the following morning should have been uncomfortable in the extreme for both horse and man. The wind and rain had fairly lashed at their heads throughout, and both were soddened to the core by the time the church tower of Borwenstow loomed, grey and imposing, ahead of them. But for Samuel, at least – he could not speak for Lancelot – his mood had changed, and hugely for the better. He felt surprisingly relaxed, carefree even. He had news to impart – good news, at that.

* * *

The next few days, while the storms ran their tempestuous course, were filled with hours of reflection. There was little anyone could achieve in conditions such as these. Inspector Austol Halwill Barton busied himself poking about the blustery churchyard for a while before announcing to all who would listen to him that he had completed his investigations and the church gates could be swung open to the congregation once more. He then made a great song and dance of his return to Launceston. Most were glad to see him go…

'About time too – the gadfly is no nearer to the truth of it…' one elderly woman was heard to say to another as they sheltered from the drizzle under the cover of the lychgate.

Jacob Jarvie stayed in his room at the inn most hours. In the interludes between the rains, he made sure he was seen chatting to harmless folk in innocent places about the village, his tripod and bag of assorted paraphernalia always close at hand.

Henry Gough broke out of his rooms on just three occasions in five days – once to take a breath of fresh air down at the harbour wall, where all the boats were tightly packed, secured against the storms; and twice, via the servants' gate, into Pennycrocker Hall. Here, he took tea with his wife and daughter in her upstairs rooms and discussed plans for Saturday's wedding. Henry had hoped he might bump into

Sir William on one of these visits, but it was never to be. It seemed the whole community, gentry included, had decided to lay low until the trough had passed through.

'I understand Reverend Studley has confirmed he will conduct the service, dear,' Hannah announced during one such tea party. 'He arrives in Borwenstow on Thursday, by all accounts. He will provide the congregation with a sung Eucharist on Sunday, so Mrs Polrunny told me when I ventured into town yesterday. It will give the choir a chance to raise their voices, at least.'

'They shall do so well before then – on my wedding day, too, in case you had forgotten, Mother,' Elizabeth had replied proudly. 'The choirmaster, Mr Bamber, has agreed to it.'

'We can be thankful for that, at least!' Constance, who had joined them, exclaimed. 'And grateful, too, there shall be no wedding rehearsal either! I wouldn't want to go through all that again. The pilchards have tasted decidedly unpleasant since that terrible day. I won't touch 'em anymore.'

On the Thursday before the wedding, as if to rejoice in the arrival of Clarence Studley – the new, albeit temporary, vicar – the weather cleared at last. Maybe it was God himself looking down with benevolence on the forthcoming nuptials that had caused it. Whatever the reason, the sun was greeted with a busy hive of village activity. But it was in the countryside that most change could be seen, as farmers, their bailiffs, shepherds and ploughmen took to the fields once more. Animals were returned to pasture, lambs counted before their tails removed and warm-weather crops sown – carrots, beetroot, beans and the like.

Samuel Snuggs had broken the news of his Shrouded Cove sighting from the *Vigilant* to Henry Gough on the day he'd returned, wringing wet, from Bude. He had been pleased to receive a resounding "Bravo, Samuel!" in reply.

Henry had shared the information with Jacob that evening and had managed to catch Halwill before he'd departed for Launceston. All agreed it was a most positive development, and each looked forward to their next proper encounter on the following Tuesday. Samuel then set to work to prepare the maps and papers which would be required on the decisive night that all now anticipated so much.

In these ways, the Cornish days drifted by, as if in service to the very weather itself. For Henry and the others, both anticipation and suspense were mounting. The hope that their courage would not fail them at the appointed hour became a constant companion for each. But for Henry alone, he had one single important task to perform before he ventured into the fray. First, he had to give his daughter away.

Chapter Twenty-Two

St Piran's had been the scene of much grander marriage ceremonies during its 900-year history. The Saxon church had hosted many modest services too. Had attendance records been kept over the centuries, the magnitude of the wedding between Miss Elizabeth Charlotte Gough and Mr Samuel Snuggs on the twenty-first of May, in the year of our Lord eighteen hundred and eighty-one, in terms of its guests alone, would have lain somewhere towards the middling ground.

For Henry Gough, the prospect of walking his eldest daughter down the aisle was the most enchanting thought he could imagine. Without doubt, it would be one of the proudest days of his entire life. There had been a time when he'd thought he'd never undertake such a loving task. Under the circumstances, the very fulfilment of it, perhaps the most fatherly of all duties, made the idea seem all the sweeter. But as he approached the imposing gates of Pennycrocker Hall, at the reins of the horse-drawn trap lent to him by the family of Constance Snuggs, he could not prevent his thoughts turning to other approaching events. However much he tried, darker images flooded, looming and unwelcome, into his head. Strive as he might to fill his mind with the purest visualisations of the happy events shortly to follow, his imaginings seemed inexorably drawn into this much bleaker place – a place of menace and foreboding.

As the little carriage passed under the majestic cedar tree that marked the end of the lengthy driveway, the grand house revealed itself to its fullest extent – Georgian architecture in perfect proportion with extensive sash windows under a wide hipped roof, topped by high brick chimney stacks. The classical columns adorning the facade made the house as impressive a sight as one might glimpse for at least fifty miles around. In front of the grand portico, Sir William's gleaming and monogrammed Shelburne Landau waited, all opened up to the sky. With the pair of fine grey Arabs at its head, the Hall as a daunting backdrop, the composition made a striking spectacle indeed. In a corner of the driveway, Henry parked the trap unobtrusively, close to a barrier of laurels that protected hidden gardens from the gaze of uninvited visitors.

As he descended from the driving seat, he heard the sound of clopping hooves approaching from the rear of the house. He looked across to see a powerful horse emerging from between a gap in the laurels. The rider was a young, tousled, auburn-haired woman, slight of frame. Despite the size of the horse, which was massive by any measure, she sat astride the saddle as a man would. Henry squinted to see more. The lady appeared to be engrossed; the look of concentration on her freckled countenance told its own story. She passed him by, barely three feet away, without saying a single word or even looking in his direction, her eyes fixed rigidly on the path that lay ahead. Henry didn't know who she was; he'd never seen her before. But he did recognise the horse… The unique snake-shaped blaze on its head marked it out as being one from the Honey stable, the very same creature he'd seen Gabriel and

Cassius riding weeks before. He paused to watch as she jolted the animal into an undignified gallop and sped off towards the front gates.

Why should one of the Honeys be visiting Pennycrocker Hall on this of all days? Maybe it was one of the household maids come to visit a servant friend at the Hall… But surely not on Cassius's horse!… He quickly dismissed his ruminations. It was time to take his daughter to the church.

As he approached the house, Elizabeth seemed to materialise, like a living apparition, in the shelter of the porch. It was as if some miraculous intervention had caused her to appear – she must have been hiding there, watching and waiting.

His daughter looked positively magnificent. In the wedding dress painstakingly stitched and lovingly fashioned by the hand of her adoring mother, the sight of her standing before him nearly made Henry's heart stop. Created from white satin and white brocade with full quilted trimmings, and a front of brocaded satin and velvet, the ensemble looked fit for a princess. The train looped slightly at the back and flowed away from her body like mist on a shimmering stream. The murky thoughts that had recently plagued Henry's brain vanished in an instant. There she waited before him, his very own Elizabeth, coyly clasping a corsage trimmed with lace and garlands of orange blossoms tied with satin ribbon. A veil of tulle covered her head, but not enough to disguise her face from him – his beautiful, brave and breathtaking daughter. Some of the lesser servants, those who were not already waiting at the church, had turned out, flattening hands against aprons, to watch her triumphal departure. They broke into spontaneous applause as Henry guided his daughter into the luxurious Landau seat and took his place beside her. Sir William and Lady Kathleen were nowhere to be seen, which was no surprise to Henry, as they had politely declined their invitation to attend the service many weeks before.

Barnaby Hawkes, Sir William's driver, dressed in full green and gold livery, took Henry's cue and flicked the horses forwards. Goodness, what a sight they must have made! Henry even found himself wishing he could be both passenger and bystander, so as to be able to watch from a distance as the carriage commenced its short journey to the church!

The voyage to St Piran's had been less than two minutes in progress before Elizabeth raised her veil and spoke directly into her father's ear.

'Papa, you must know,' she whispered, 'I saw *Flora Honey*, no less, as I was dressing, just an hour ago.'

'A strawberry-haired lady on horseback, perchance?'

'I saw no horse, Father, but yes, that sounds to be her. Cassius's wife – a fine-looking woman, so the men servants say… But it's most unusual to see her at the Hall. I have never witnessed it, in fact.'

'Maybe she has a friend in the servants' hall?'

'Not that I know… I'm sure I'd have heard of it. There is more… you see, she came into the main house. I saw her first from my window, arriving at the back door, and then a second time from the landing. Mr Heath escorted her along the corridor towards the morning room. Then I lost sight of her.'

'Is that the same passage that leads to Sir William's study also?'

'The very same. Jacob told me the Honeys and Sir William had some business together. Maybe Flora was—'

'That's most interesting, Elizabeth,' her father interrupted, 'but can we concentrate on today's events? This is *your* day, pure and untarnished, and it will never return. Enjoy it! I, for one, intend to relish every moment. Let's put the shadows of Pennycrocker Hall to one side, shall we?'

The sixteen-minute journey to the lychgate of St Piran's passed, for the most part, pleasantly enough and without incident, although Henry had to remind his daughter twice to halt all talk of the Hall's sundry intrigues and conspiracies that seemed now to fill her mind. She relented by the time they reached the village boundary, and the last mile was spent in enjoying the morning sunshine and in the holding of tightly gripped hands. The two bridesmaids, Samuel's pretty, young nieces, were at the lychgate to greet them, looking splendid in shimmering silk dresses of freshest pink. Constance's brother, Harold, was on duty at the church door, and sweating slightly, he ushered father and bride inside.

As the pair skirted the font, an image of the previous parson, unsolicited and awful, came to Henry, but he was able to push it out of his mind almost instantly. With Elizabeth on his left side, the couple began their short procession down the aisle towards the high altar and the expanse of stained glass that burnished in all its vivid colours directly ahead of them. There stood the familiar slight frame of Reverend Clarence Studley. With beaming face and open arms, he looked for all the world like a newly restored uncle – fortunately minus his butterfly nets. In this way, smiling and nodding at those they passed in the accepted benign fashion, Henry and his daughter headed, hand in hand, steadily ever eastwards. There were some amongst the congregation who Henry recognised. A few from the Hall had come, all seated on the left, including Esther and Thomas, the under footman, but there were no signs of either First Footman Heath or Mrs Hennessey. There, too, sat Miss Chadwick, nudging ever closer to Constable Poundstock. Ah, there was Dr Plymswood, who despite his yellow eyes, looked surprisingly well, and Mrs Polrunny too!

Henry was delighted to see Molly from *The Gauger's Return*. She gave him a cheeky wink as he passed. On the right were a gaggle of about twenty folk, all presumably from the Snuggs family or his revenue service supporters – some old, some young, some in the prime of life, but all unknown to Henry. They stopped two yards before the altar steps.

Henry lifted his daughter's veil, kissed her tenderly on the right cheek and backed away to join Hannah in the first row of pews. Here, they stood alone, surrounded by naked wood and empty seats, and his heart sank at the thought of it. According to Hannah, the prospect of a journey from London for Elizabeth's younger brothers and sisters had proved "problematic". She had not elucidated any further on the subject – she could be stubborn that way – but Henry guessed his own challenging presence may have had something to do with it. Hannah had blithely added that, in any event, the cost of travel for all of them had been exorbitant – "far too expensive to countenance". Instead, she told him, they intended to save the family coffers and to celebrate together when Elizabeth and Samuel next ventured up to Marylebone.

'You may come too,' she'd told her disengaged husband with an airy wave, 'providing you come alone...'

Henry had been compliant on the matter. Although he regretted deeply that he would not be reunited with his other children – on this occasion, at least – this was Hannah's decision to make alone. There was nothing to be gained by being combative. Best to let sleeping dogs lie and ensure any delayed wedding feast in Marylebone would be one to remember.

The service was but halfway complete; they had just listened to a reading from *1 Corinthians 13:4-8*, delivered by a still perspiring Harold, when a noise could be heard from outside. As Reverend Studley opened his address from the pulpit, the church door flew open with a noisy bang. At first, Henry imagined the wind must have caused the disturbance, but when he looked over his shoulder, the imposing figure of Cassius Honey stood, hands on hips, like the Colossus astride the Port of Rhodes. As far as Henry could see, Cassius was alone. As if in deference to the interloper, the parson halted his speech mid-sentence and stared down the aisle. Almost as one, the congregation, including both bride and groom, turned to face the western door. There was stony silence for a few moments as Cassius raised his chin and stood his ground, refusing to take a pew in one of the many vacant places at the back.

'Don't mind me, Reverend. Pray continue,' Cassius shouted down the aisle. 'I am not invited here today, I know well enough, but a man has a right to enter his church at any time, does he not?'

'You are most welcome, Mr Honey. I was just exploring the relationship between human love and the love of our Lord. God's love is for all of us, you know...'

'I have no doubt you are right, Reverend. You being learned and well versed in such matters. A humble farmer, such as I, must bow to your greater education.'

At this point, Constable Poundstock stood up. Before he could utter a word, Cassius Honey raised both his hand and his voice to stop him in his tracks. 'Please, don't stand on my account, Constable. I won't be staying long,' he boomed. 'I have no wish to scare this flock of yours, Parson – no more than I appear to have alarmed them already,' he snorted. 'Before I take my leave, Reverend, I wanted to remind *myself* of one thing, and *you* of another.'

As Poundstock resumed his place, Studley took up his oratory once more. 'The eyes and ears of the Lord are always turned towards those who seek the truth,' he hummed in the affected fashion so favoured by country parsons.

Cassius Honey was not to be deterred. 'For my part, I wanted to remind myself of how a holy wedding in this village of ours is actually conducted.' Cassius took a few steps down the aisle, sneering at each of the congregation he encountered. The assembly, stunned into silence, remained firmly fixed to their pews. The choirboys, straining for a better view, shuffled in their seats, causing Mr Bamber to wave an infuriated baton at them to keep them in their places.

'You may recall,' Cassius was now yelling, 'my family were refused right of entry here! We were *denied* when all my sister desired was the self-same sacrament that is taking place today.'

'Greetings, all ye who enter in the name of our Lord!' Studley cried.

'You have stolen my thunder, Reverend, for I do believe you have satisfied the second reason for my coming here today.'

'I have?'

'You assured me my family *should* always be welcome to receive the holy sacraments. To get married, to baptise our children, and to lay to rest our dead – to name but three. You told me this less than a year ago. Do you still hold to it, sir, now you possess the keys to St Piran's?'

The entire church remained as silent as the grave. Henry itched to say something, but he knew it was not his place as a mere guest of the parish. It was for the local worshippers to raise their voices in protest. But none did, and the rector of St Geraint's, too, seemed lost for words.

'I will leave this place only when I hear your reply...' Cassius said in a measured yet menacing manner. Despite the quiet intensity of his voice, all in that place could hear each deliberately spoken word quite well enough.

A subtle change seemed to come over Reverend Studley at that moment. Pursing his lips and making the sign of the cross from forehead to heart, his appearance altered markedly.

An aura of resolve – some said later it looked more akin to wrath – seemed suddenly to possess him. He replaced his notes quietly on the lectern and, without uttering a syllable, descended almost soundlessly from the pulpit. Raising his head stiffly, he then approached his inquisitor in a steady, unhurried march down the centre of the aisle. When he had reached less than a yard from Honey's massive frame, the priest tilted his head upwards to speak to his visitor. The fresh proximity of the two men's physiques served to exaggerate the difference in their sizes. Cassius now appeared to tower over the vicar by nearly two feet. A pin-drop silence enveloped the chapel.

'I do, Mr Honey... You have my word. What happened in the past was a mistake, and I feel your hurt more than you can imagine. You and your family will always be welcome in this church, at whatever hour or minute of the day or night. This is God's house and you are one of God's creatures, as we all are here assembled today. Pray, join us now in celebrating the marriage of these two wonderful people.'

The speech, so soberly delivered, seemed to set Cassius Honey back on his heels somewhat. This was clear to all, for the giant literally took a few paces backwards, faltering slightly as he did so.

Studley advanced another step forwards and reached out both hands in an act of obvious contrition. At the sight of it, Honey's confusion appeared to grow... For a moment, the two stared closely at one another. It was as if Honey was trying to search out some clue of intent in the eyes of the advancing vicar. As the others watched with grim stares, Cassius Honey blinked and shuffled back once more, his eyes now moist and flickering. Reverend Studley took another step in his direction as Honey's head started to rock from side to side, slowly at first but gathering pace with each tightening of the neck. Backing away still further, the interloper suddenly twisted his body and stumbled towards the door. Silently this time, as if he wanted to make as little noise as possible, he pulled the latch open and, with swelling eyes, stepped out into the sanctuary of the clear morning air. Almost as abruptly as he had entered, he was gone, and with his going, a low murmuring of both relief and triumph rumbled along the pews.

One might have imagined the remainder of the wedding would have been impacted by these shocking events. But surprisingly, perhaps, this was not to be the case, as thereafter the service went entirely to its convivial plan. The congregation appeared, on the exterior at least, to be hardly affected by the fearsome intrusion all had witnessed. On Honey's sudden departure, Studley's demeanour was completely unmoved, almost as if such interventions were commonplace in his profession, and he knew exactly how to deal with them.

For Henry Gough, who had remained glued to the spot throughout, the experience had been like nothing he'd ever witnessed in his whole life before – almost supernatural in its nature. The episode had felt almost as if some hidden hand had touched the moment, giving strength where strength was needed and doubt where doubt had never existed before. It felt as if the combined sway of all of St Piran's parsons, dead and alive, had amalgamated in a single moment to put down the ugly tormentor. Whatever had caused it, the outwardly mild-mannered Reverend Studley had become imbued, for a few short moments, with something bordering on the ethereal. The vicar had seemed possessed with such unyielding authority that folk later said they had never seen its like before. To have faced down so formidable an opponent as Cassius Honey in such a composed, almost tranquil, style simply beggared belief. The consequence of which, to all who had witnessed it, was the knowledge that Cassius Honey's dominion had been diminished to practically naught in just a few still, unalterable seconds. And this had occurred before their very eyes, to boot. No one could deny what they had seen. In that moment, another Borwenstow legend was born!

For Elizabeth and Samuel, the remains of their day were to be truly memorable. Hannah had organised a most marvellous wedding breakfast at the nearby church hall, to which all were invited. The mood had been especially lively after the events at St Piran's, which were the talk of everyone – for the first hour, at least... until the alcohol began to take effect... after which, conversations turned to less captivating subjects and became more ribald and humorous. This was especially the case between the revenue officers and some of the younger women, including a few of the female staff from the Hall, Esther included. Molly was always seen to be in the thick of it. The hilarity and banter in the church hall grew to such a level that at one point the new parson had been forced to intervene. A little decorum was required, he'd insisted. This intercession was most respectfully listened too and accepted by all, given the reverend's newfound reputation for bringing calm to all things.

Food had been prepared from a number of sources, all of which was gratefully received. The cook at *The Gauger's Return* had made a vast starry gazey pie, which Molly cut and distributed generously by hand, insisting all the guests should partake. Even Mrs Hennessey from the Hall contributed to the catering, producing four trays of Victoria sponge laced with last year's homemade strawberry jam.

Speeches of thanks and congratulation were given, none better received than Henry Gough's, during which the couple were showered with good wishes. But by three o'clock, it was time for the newly-weds to depart for Bodmin. At the appointed hour, the happy couple, full of kedgeree, assorted pies, roasted pork and plum duff, and having consumed more claret and ale than may have been wise, set off for Bodmin's finest hotel, *The Duke of Cornwall.*

Chapter Twenty-Three

Hannah Gough returned by train to London the next day, vowing to come back as soon as news reached her that a baby was expected. This, she confidently predicted to any who would listen, would be before Christmas. Henry left Borwenstow the same day, departing early on Sunday morning for Tintagel. At least, that's what he wanted everyone to believe...

Instead, Henry had made secretive arrangements with his son-in-law to borrow his coastal cottage – which lay in the hamlet of Trevalga, less than a mile to the south of Borwenstow – for the next few days. This is where Henry would remain, effectively hidden, until their late deployment meeting on Tuesday night, when all their plans would be revealed.

Before departing on his Bodmin honeymoon, Samuel had made all the necessary preparations, including Henry's transportation from the inn. Samuel's deputy at the Custom House, the loyal and long-serving Wilfred Gale, had collected Henry from *The Gauger's Return* at 10a.m. precisely in a modest closed waggon, property of Her Majesty's Revenue. Ensuring they were not being followed, Gale had driven him the relatively short distance to Samuel's cottage. Henry was left there, out of the sight of others, on the understanding he would remain until his son-in-law's return from Bodmin.

Before he departed the inn, Henry had made sure to pay his compliments to Isaac Trewint and thank him for his hospitality. As he settled his account, he candidly informed the hirsute innkeeper of his forward plans. These, he told Trewint, were motivated by his fascination for the story of King Arthur and his desire to know more. Tintagel, the fabled home of the once great king, lay along the coast about five miles distant, and here, he told everyone, he would spend a single night researching the history of the Knights of the Round Table, before returning to London on Monday morning.

'Very well. Safe passage, Mr Gough. If you come again, I 'spect we'll still be 'ere, God willing... By the by, they say Arthur 'tis but a legend and no more,' Trewint wheezed through a forest of broken teeth.

'Ha-ha, much like all the tall stories folk speak of hereabouts!' Henry could not resist the temptation to poke his man in the ribs. Trewint made no intelligible reply, just a shrill groan of sorts, and hurried off into the saloon.

Henry found time to thank Molly too, though she looked more than slightly ruffled, weary even, when he bumped into her on the landing. He wondered if her dishevelled condition might be the result of all the excitement and dissipation of the previous day – and night...

'Why, thank you, Mr Gough,' she stammered on receiving his more than ample gratuity of two shillings. 'I was thinking, sir... I'd like to come to London one day. Would you be able to find me work? I am an honest girl, at heart, and no trouble really,' she giggled, rubbing the sleep from her eyes.

'Molly, if you ever find your way to Alpha Yard in Marylebone, pray, ask for me. I will do my best.'

The cottage Samuel Snuggs inhabited on the edge of

Trevalga had once been his grandfather's – none other than tragic Abel's eldest grandson. Named, appropriately enough, *Starboard Rummager*, it was a sprawling affair, typical of old-fashioned country design. Properties with thick limewashed walls, modest-sized windows, low ceilings and skewed slate roofs were frequently encountered in the locality, but for all these reasons and more, Samuel's home seemed to embody the style more than any other. In every way imaginable, it was the archetypal Cornish cottage. The house, which was rather larger than most of its counterparts, faced the open sea, a mere 300 yards distant. It sat on a patch of raised ground close to an abandoned water mill and right at the centre of a pretty walled garden. At this time of the year, this half acre of land overflowed with colour and buzzing wildlife.

Letting himself in with the key Samuel had provided, Henry found himself straightaway standing on the cold slates of the parlour floor. He supposed the room, with its blackened fireplace, must have remained unchanged for nearly 200 years. Each chamber he encountered during his inspection was plain, much as he'd anticipated, but he was surprised by how many there were. Every corner he ducked around seemed to bring him to another, and the narrow passages upstairs that led this way and that were confusing in the extreme. Making sure it wasn't Samuel's own bedroom, Henry found himself an upstairs resting place that gazed out on the ocean. Here, he unpacked his modest belongings. In the pantry, he found apples, bread, cheese and beer, and settled down for the rest of the day. He yearned to walk along the cliffs, but he knew it would be unwise in the extreme. To be seen and recognised here might create all sorts of unwanted gossip, so he resolved to keep his head down and wait until nightfall before taking a stroll. Samuel's collection of books impressed him, and it wasn't long before he'd crawled into a cosy chair with a copy of *The Rime of The Ancient Mariner*, which he felt was entirely suitable reading, under the circumstances.

* * *

To describe Elizabeth and Samuel's brief escape to Bodmin as "disappointing" would not be entirely accurate. However, it might be said their honeymoon had not turned out in the way either of them had hoped or expected. The hotel was as well appointed as they could have asked. The rooms were plush, the bed sheets crisp, clean and comfortable, and the dining room fare was fit for the Duke of Cornwall himself. But from the early hours of Sunday morning, the sheer joy they had experienced at the outset of their stay seemed to diminish with every following minute. Even the rapture of their loving embraces tapered somewhat as the day advanced, moment by measured moment, and the hour of their departure loomed ever closer.

'Do you feel the same creeping anxiety, my love?' Elizabeth asked her husband as they took breakfast on their first morning as a married couple.

The heavy sigh in return told her all she needed. 'It's true, my dearest sweetheart,' he replied slowly. 'In the flesh we both remain here, yet I cannot contain my mind from drifting back to Borwenstow – to its ugly affairs that must soon be mended. I promise, my darling Bess, we shall take a proper holiday once this matter is settled… to London, perhaps… We've been invited already by your mama, so it will be an event to anticipate in earnest.'

When their final morning at *The Duke of Cornwall* arrived, both lingered contentedly in the marital bed before taking a late breakfast. Eschewing the lunch, which had been paid for in advance, they packed their bags and climbed aboard the eleven o'clock coach to Borwenstow.

Elizabeth's arrangement with the Pennycrockers meant she would continue to reside at the Hall after her marriage. However, her six-and-a-half-day working week would be reduced to six. To account for the change, a salary adjustment was enforced, which Elizabeth regretted but knew was inevitable. She was granted dispensation by Lady Kathleen to spend two nights of her choosing each week with her new husband, on the proviso she must return to the Hall by no later than 7a.m. the following morning. Elizabeth had chosen Fridays and Saturdays as her indulgence half days, meaning she was required to be at the Hall early every day to dress and supervise the children. This concession entailed a twice-weekly ride, each Saturday and Sunday morning, of some two miles from Samuel's cottage to Pennycrocker Hall. Although Elizabeth was an accomplished horsewoman, she was much relieved when her husband offered to escort her on these short journeys.

'I have to pass close by the Hall on my way to Fore Street, Bess. It will be but a minor diversion and a joy to accompany you – so nice to share the morning air together.'

This arrangement meant when, after their brief honeymoon, Samuel left Elizabeth at the portico of Pennycrocker Hall, it being a late Monday afternoon, she knew she would not see her husband for another four days. Not until one o'clock on Friday, in fact, when, with any luck, she might find him waiting eagerly for her arrival back at *Starboard Rummager*. In her heart, though, she knew the arrangements would almost certainly be different, for she had to accept his duties at the Custom House were many and could often delay his arrival home. In all probability, it would be *her* who waited for *him*...

When both had dismounted at the sculpted front entrance, she kissed Samuel with an undisguised passion which, frankly, he had not expected, given the public nature of the setting.

'Take care, my husband,' she sighed. 'I will be here, waiting. I long for Friday when, God willing, we shall be together once more.'

He returned the kiss with another, this time on the cheek, and caressed her neck. 'I have to remain safe, if only for you, my dear Bess.' His voice lifting a notch, he added with a jaunty cry, 'With luck, there will be much to discuss when we next meet.' Leaping back on his horse, Samuel blew her a final kiss and trotted Lancelot towards the distant gates.

Elizabeth watched as he departed, her stomach churning with a sudden inner loneliness. 'Pray, come back to me...' she whispered with tears in her voice.

Behind the open window of an upstairs room, Lady Pennycrocker observed the revenue officer as he took his leave. *Much to discuss*... She wondered what the new husband of her pretty governess meant by such a remark.

* * *

The children raced to her as soon as they saw their "long-lost" governess. Elizabeth knew she'd find them in the nursery, and her sudden appearance caused squeals of delight as the girls abandoned the hapless Esther, who'd been understudying in her absence. As Elizabeth embraced each of them in turn, starting with little Maeve, the nursery door opened behind them. It was Lady Pennycrocker silhouetted at the entrance, framed by the doorway and the well-lit corridor.

'Welcome back to Pennycrocker Hall, *Mrs Snuggs*,' Her Ladyship said brightly. 'I thought I glimpsed you in the drive with that handsome husband of yours.'

'It's wonderful to have returned,' Elizabeth beamed.

'You may leave us, Esther. Thank you for substituting these last few days.'

'Very well, Your Ladyship.' Esther curtseyed clumsily as she backed out of the door.

'Was your stay in Bodmin a good one?'

'Most enjoyable, Your Ladyship.'

'Then make sure to note down all the exciting happenings in that journal of yours. I see you jotting in it a lot these days.' She paused and laughed. 'Not *all* the news, perhaps! Some things are best kept between husband and wife! Just record the episodes that will be of interest to your grandchildren in years to come. I, like you, keep a journal. I find writing a diary a most satisfying way to occupy the afternoons. And I have a great interest in reading the histories of our ancestors, whose chronicles can be quite chilling at times.'

'Chilling, Your Ladyship?'

'Many of my lineage strove hard without much success. Others accomplished marvellous things, which have enabled those who have followed to make even greater strides.'

'I shall have to tell that to my father,' Elizabeth replied. 'He will have more than a few stories to recount of his life roaming London's streets and avenues. Some of the encounters he's experienced fairly make the blood curdle.'

'He is a cab driver, is he not?'

'A cab proprietor, to be exact, Your Ladyship. My father owns upwards of thirty horses now. He, like your ancestors, has seen some success in his lifetime, though he was born of lowly stock.'

'It is as I thought. Then you must tell him to write all *his* stories down too. Others may be the judge, in the future. Not all our history can be pleasant to read, at times. For my part, my family were once the victims of terrible crimes. Some transgressions beyond belief. Wrongs that will one day be put right... Only by the writing of words will we learn the lessons of the past and bring justice to those who deserve to be punished for their sins.'

The sudden edge in Her Ladyship's voice was hard to miss. Elizabeth tried to make light of it. '*My* petty history will be just childhood memories and the dull domesticity of living in Marylebone.' Elizabeth's face brightened. 'But at the moment, it's your children and their hilarious antics who take pride of place.'

'Hmm… you must show me your journal one day.'

Elizabeth made no reply, merely returning the comment with a shy, slightly uneasy grin, and the moment passed quickly enough.

'All the same,' Lady Pennycrocker cried, 'we have missed you, haven't we, girls?'

The three little ones looked at their mother and nodded avidly.

'We seem to be so short-staffed at the Hall these days. Half the servants are absent with one family matter or another to attend. Poor Heath is struggling to cope.'

Elizabeth coughed lightly. She had found her voice once more. 'I'm sure it won't be long before Mr Wilks returns from County Cork, Your Ladyship. Matters will return to normal soon enough. I assure you, I have no plans to disappear at any time soon' – Elizabeth raised a willing smile – 'other than on the afternoons and evenings we have agreed.'

'Yes, we are expecting to see our celebrated butler any day now. The overwhelmed Mr Heath will indeed be overjoyed…'

Elizabeth imagined she saw a trace of disquiet in Lady Kathleen's expression. A few moments elapsed with neither uttering a word until Her Ladyship picked up the conversation once more. 'Yes, he'll be back from Ireland, as you say… soon enough…'

'I hope his father has recovered.'

'We shall only know that when we see him, shan't we? It'll be by Wednesday, from all accounts. My husband tells me we shall set eyes on the vibrant Mr Wilks in just a few days from now.' Lady Pennycrocker clapped her hands to indicate the audience had come to an end. 'Very well... I'll leave you in the loving arms of my tumbling infants. Are you pleased to see Mrs Snuggs, girls?'

'Mrs Snuggs?' Wilhelmina looked bewildered.

'She is a married lady now. Her name has changed, as did mine when I married your father. I was called Keenan, once upon a time, before you three were born,' she laughed. 'You must now call her Snuggs, do you understand?' She gazed oddly at Elizabeth for a split-second, and then added in triumphant tones, 'You see, our Miss Gough is no more!'

* * *

By the time Samuel Snuggs reached *Starboard Rummager*, it was nearly five o'clock. He had called into the Custom House on his way from Pennycrocker Hall and was pleased to find all was in order. As he dismounted from Lancelot, he searched for signs of life inside the cottage, half expecting Henry Gough to appear and greet him at any moment. But it wasn't until he'd entered and closed the door behind him that he spied his father-in-law. In a deep slumber, there he sprawled, cosseted by the warmth of the south-facing window, the familiar copy of Samuel Taylor Coleridge's immortal poem spread carelessly on his lap.

'Mr Gough...' Samuel gently nudged the sleeping man.

Henry woke with a start, inadvertently throwing the book into the air. Samuel deftly caught it, preventing its fall to the floor. 'I was just thinking...' Henry cried, half dreaming.

'Good day, sir. I am returned in one piece, hearty and ready for whatever trials we may next endure. Your daughter sends her love. She is in fine fettle. I have just returned her to the Hall.'

'Goodness, Samuel, you gave me quite a shock. I am not the man I once was, clearly... Dozing in the afternoon like an old codger is unforgiveable when there is so much to be done.'

'Relax, sir. There is a time and reason for everything. I have brought whiskey, cheese and some rashers of bacon from Bodmin. There is a steak and kidney pie too, cooked in the kitchens of *The Duke of Cornwall Hotel*, no less.'

'Whiskey, you say. It will be more of that damned Irish brew, if I'm not mistaken,' he laughed.

'It is indeed! A bottle of the finest *Carrells*. Very serviceable it is too, especially at the price I paid.'

'But it is most probably smuggled, Samuel. Did we not discuss the matter?'

'Until now, I have no proof...' he winked. 'By tomorrow, I may have a different story to tell, but at this moment, I think we might be permitted to partake in a few grains. It may be the last time we enjoy a drink together – for the time being, at least,' he added with a hopeful gleam in his eye. 'So, let's enjoy the moment while it lasts, and anyway, it's mighty fine liquor.'

The two men cleared the decks, and while Samuel lit the oven, Henry arranged plates and glasses. The first whiskey was downed while the pie was still warming. The spirit tasted good, especially with the crumbly slices of nettle-wrapped cheese that Samuel brought to the table. By the time the steak and kidney was eventually served, the bottle of Irish was already a quarter drunk.

The talk inevitably fell on the strategy for the following night's adventure. The weather had been set fair for a number of days and looked to continue in a similar vein, probably until the middle of the week. Both agreed to propose a simple plan to the rest when they met in the Custom House. The design would be the same for each of the nights their intelligence suggested the smuggle might take place.

'With luck, this escapade will occur the day after tomorrow in the early hours,' Samuel observed deliberately, once the drink had given poetry to his voice. 'Throughout, we must act like the ghostly barn owl. We shall be silent hunters, inconspicuous yet deadly. Woe betide us if the enterprise is delayed…' he shook his head, 'and we have shown our hand to any night-time wanderers.'

Samuel had decided to call on his four best men to be in attendance the following night, complete with their horses. He told Henry the pocket-sized armoury in the Custom House would be brought into special use for the operation, and each officer would carry one of the six Martini-Henry Mark 1 rifles it held. Although not the latest model, it was a fine breech-loading weapon, capable of fast loading and accurate firing. They agreed their forces should be split into two parts. The first group, an unarmed surveillance team of three men, would be covertly positioned on the cliffs above Shrouded Cove. Henry knew the landscape, as did Jacob Jarvie, so it was proposed they would take on this role. The second group would comprise the assault team. They would be carrying fire arms and be led by Samuel. It would consist of his own revenue officers, plus any policemen Halwill had managed to bring up from Launceston.

'If the police are armed, all to the good,' Samuel observed, spreading out a chart. 'My task will be to find hidden positions surrounding the church grounds.'

'And mine is to send you word as soon as we see lights moving at sea. Am I right?' Henry replied.

'Quite… It will be all but dark, the moon is minimal, but the smugglers will need their own lights. That shall be their downfall. Your communication of a sighting will be essential to our success. I will deploy one of my men to act as your messenger. If there is a further message to relay, you can send

Jarvie. I will keep the remaining force in reserve at the Custom House so as to minimise the risk of being seen. As soon as we receive news that a sighting has been observed offshore, our task will be simple. I shall disperse my men, and with Halwill's support, we shall cut off all the roads and pathways leading into the church, thus preventing any escape.'

'And when will you strike?'

'I will delay any advance on the smugglers until we have observed them leaving the churchyard. Such movement by them will indicate their load has been landed, concealed and will be awaiting further transportation when the time is right. With the church empty, that should be a straightforward task for Honey and his men, providing it is organised properly.'

'Do you think they will be in possession of the whiskey when they leave the churchyard?'

'Of that, I am unsure. My guess is the Honeys will try to get as much away as they can on the night. They will need horses and waggons if they attempt it, and we should be on the lookout for them both. Their appearance on the scene will tell us the game is afoot.'

'There may be much to carry, I agree.'

'If the consignment is substantial, as we suspect, much of it may have to remain in the tunnel itself, to be brought out piecemeal over many nights and got away to the final stash when the coast is clear.'

'We should strike quickly then?' Henry asked.

'Yes, but only when I hear there is movement from the church. That will be the time I shall call for the knock.'

'Knock… I have heard Albert Woodward use such a term. It means the moment of the strike. Am I correct?'

'It does indeed. And on this occasion, we shall not be knocking politely!' Both men laughed and took another splash of *Carrells*.

'And what of their boats – the daughters, so to speak? Do you believe it will be their plan to row them back to Doubloons once they have completed their task?'

'That is a very good observation, sir. We may have to consider that eventuality when the moment arrives, but my guess is no. Time will not be on their side. My belief is they will haul their boats into the tunnel and conceal them alongside their booty, to be recovered at some future high tide. With much to bring ashore, it may require many sorties to and from the mother ship. They will want to complete the task of ferrying and stacking the goods in a single night and will only have a few hours to achieve this. By 2a.m., or thereabouts, the water will be in full retreat, effectively cutting off any escape by boat. Their only route to safety will be via the church.'

'I understand. So, they will be trapped, Samuel.'

'Precisely! For all practical purposes, once the tide has abandoned them, they will be like fish in a barrel – there for the taking!'

Chapter Twenty-Four

Lady Pennycrocker had suspected all was not quite as it seemed with Elizabeth for a number of days. At first, the change of honeymoon plans had appeared strange. Despite the generosity of the Pennycrockers' offer to fund the newly-weds' trip to Bodmin, Elizabeth had been resolutely against accepting it. She'd wanted to curtail the holiday from the original five to just two days, and that was that.

Why would she do such a thing? It was her honeymoon, after all... It had not gone unnoticed that by returning early, so also would her revenue officer husband. But he was a complete nincompoop, as far as Her Ladyship was concerned; he posed no true threat to their plans... surely not...

The excuse that Elizabeth missed the children did not really ring perfectly true either. But on the other hand, the girls adored their governess and she them, so perhaps there was some substance in it. After giving the matter a lot of thought, Lady Pennycrocker had decided to let matters rest. She told herself that her doubts were misplaced; it was just a coincidence, and her sweet-looking governess was indeed just that – an innocent who knew nothing of the momentous matters that were slated to take place within the next few days, matters which, for a while, had consumed the inner workings of Pennycrocker Hall.

But then Lady Pennycrocker was forced to rethink her perhaps hasty judgement. It had been a casual, almost throwaway, remark made by her governess that made Her Ladyship ponder again. Elizabeth's assertion that "Mr Wilks would return from County Cork soon enough" created real misgivings. The whole household had been told Wilks was in Plymouth tending his sick father. County Cork and Ireland had never been mentioned, not to a soul – save Mrs Hennessey, of course, but surely *she* would not have let the matter slip. How then had Elizabeth learned of the butler's true destination? And if she knew that, might she also be aware of his true purpose there?

Lady Kathleen first consulted the cook, who'd flatly denied she'd been indiscreet, and between them, the pair thought through the implications. Her Ladyship had still been keen to give Elizabeth the benefit of the doubt, but Colleen Hennessey disagreed. She was adamant. They had to find a way to test the girl's guilt, or otherwise. Matters would soon be coming to a head. Nothing should be left to chance, and they must discover the truth before it was too late. In this way, the couple conjured up a little trap for the wayward governess – a snare, that if Elizabeth fell into, might show her hand completely. The idea was to lure the governess away from the Hall so a search of her room could safely take place. The hope was it would reveal the contents of her journal, which both imagined might be quite enlightening…

* * *

Elizabeth Snuggs woke before four the following morning, just in time to meet the rising sun. She had slept very badly indeed, hardly a wink, in fact – not more than a few disjointed episodes since ten o'clock, when she had brought *Alice Through the Looking Glass* to accompany her to bed. The book may have contributed to her restlessness, for images of a ghastly Red Queen – for some reason in the form of Lady Pennycrocker – kept returning, uncalled for, into her head. She missed her husband too, that was undeniable, but the true cause of her insomnia lay in her frantic anticipation of the day which was yet to unfold. As she drew back the curtain, the sun temporarily blinded her, having already crept over the agrestic gate that bisected the eastern wall of Pennycrocker Hall. She flinched and raised a hand to shield against the slanting rays. The other, she placed over her sternum, which felt as if a gigantic rock had crept under it during her sleepless night.

The children were on bouncing form, as usual, and their frolics helped to assuage the feelings of unease. For a few pleasant hours, she forgot all about haunted Shrouded Cove, the menacing boats arriving there in the dead of night, and the desperate men ready to do her husband and father down. But by the early afternoon the feelings of anxiety had returned – so much so, she couldn't enjoy the afternoon tea that Mrs Hennessey had prepared for her. Indeed, the very thought of the conniving cook now brought shivers down her spine. There was no doubting it, the brave face Elizabeth bore with such fortitude was becoming ever more difficult to maintain.

'You don't look well, Mrs Snuggs…' These words, spoken so gently by Lady Pennycrocker, came as Elizabeth had just finished bathing and dressing the children for bed. Her Ladyship's observation made her stomach turn somersaults once more. 'Cook tells me you have lost your appetite as well,' she continued. 'Now, that simply won't do. Is there something troubling you?'

'It's nothing, Your Ladyship. A touch of indigestion,

perhaps. We over-indulged in Bodmin. Too much rich food – I'm not used to it!' She tried her best smile.

Lady Pennycrocker indicated she wished to have a private conversation. The girls were playing contentedly, so Elizabeth followed her into an anteroom and out of earshot of the children. 'Why don't you take some air?' Lady Kathleen started. 'You have been locked in most of the day. I can take over from here. A walk to the village and back will do you good. It's a lovely evening. The last colours of sunset will be a wonderful spectacle, I expect.'

'Why no, Lady Kathleen. That's a kind thought, but I don't have the strength for such a thing. You are right, I am not on good form. A walk would bring me down even further. Maybe an early night to bed will bring its own reward.'

For a moment, Lady Pennycrocker looked disappointed. 'Are you sure? The walk might be just the ticket.'

'Oh no, madam. I think I'll rest here.'

'Did you know Mr Wilks is returning soon?' Her Ladyship changed the subject with more than a hint of excitement in her voice. Her mood seemed to change in an instant. The rigid formality had all but disappeared. 'If you continue to feel unwell, I suggest you go to him. He's from a family of apothecaries back in County Cork, you know. Patrick Wilks is quite a man, of that there is no doubt. A man of many hidden talents...'

'I had not realised Mr Wilks knew about medicines and the like. That's the first I've ever heard of it.' Elizabeth was beginning to sound interested. The lump in her stomach was shrinking fast.

'Oh yes. He doesn't like it widely known, but he's familiar with all the best remedies and keeps a stock of medicines, should the need arise. I'd rather go to him than drunken old Plymswood any day.'

'You must have known him a long time, Your Ladyship… Mr Wilks, that is.'

'About a dozen years or more. He and I do go back in Ireland a long way.' Lady Pennycrocker looked vaguely whimsical at that moment. 'He has healing hands, does Patrick… I mean, Mr Wilks. You are a married lady, Mrs Snuggs, you may now appreciate that a man's touch can revive like nothing else – speaking woman to woman, you know.' Lady Kathleen gave her a look of distinct confidentiality. 'I can tell you, his touch can cure all of *my* ailments at least… each and every one!'

Elizabeth was not quite sure what to say in reply. That whimsical look of Lady Pennycrocker's had returned – this time much more powerfully than before. It was almost as if she'd drifted into a trance. *What on earth is Her Ladyship trying to tell me?… Woman to woman…?*

At length, Elizabeth replied, 'You will be pleased to see him back, then…'

'Yes, that is my happy expectation. He will be home tonight, all the way from County Cork… He should have already started his journey. He must be on the high seas as we speak.' Lady Pennycrocker touched her neck and approached closer. She put up a hand as if to whisper. 'I intend to wait up for him… Please don't tell Sir William – or even hint of it. My husband can be a touch possessive. With luck, Patrick will be here around midnight… maybe an hour or two later.'

'Goodness, that is good news, and if I still feel under the weather tomorrow morning, I will definitely seek him out. Now, if you will excuse me, Your Ladyship, I can hear the children squabbling. I'd better return to them.'

'You may tell Patrick I sent you but, pray, keep this to yourself.' Lady Kathleen caught Elizabeth's arm. 'The others may misconstrue. And now, I too must away. Things to do, matters to prepare…'

With the children safely tucked up and sleeping soundly after a shorter than normal bedtime story, Elizabeth resolved to take up Lady Pennycrocker's suggestion that she might take the evening air. She had a message to deliver. She found Esther in the scullery and told her of her plan to walk into the village to clear her head. Esther promised to keep a sharp ear open – she loved the children more than she could say and never seemed disappointed when her affections were so rarely returned.

'With luck, I may still catch the sunset,' she told Esther. 'I shall be back before eight. It will be nearly dark by then, but I'll find my way home. Trust me.'

Elizabeth had but one thought in her mind – she had to warn Samuel that Patrick Wilks was returning that very night. The scandalous rest could hold until another time. The smuggle was going to take place within hours, and the sooner Samuel and the others knew of it, the better.

As she hurried away from the Hall, little did she know she was being watched from one of the highest windows of the house by two pairs of Irish eyes.

'Our little scheme has worked well, Your Ladyship. Poor creature is but a child abroad,' Colleen Hennessey mocked. 'Look at her go now, all bristling with newfound energy and brimming with falsehoods that are set to trap her.'

'Very well, Mrs Hennessey, you may let the search begin.'

It did not take them long to find the journal. It was Mrs Hennessey who, squeezing her not inconsiderable frame under the bed, discovered a pretty vanity case, which she managed to force open with a knife brought from her own kitchen. Inside lay a tiny notebook covered in attractive cloth of duck-egg blue. The cook handed it directly to her mistress.

'You had better read it first, Your Ladyship.'

After she'd scanned the pages for less than thirty seconds,

Lady Kathleen Pennycrocker was obliged to seek the support of Elizabeth's bedstead. She could hardly believe her eyes. The sentences that unfolded, most written in the full, round hand so typical of London-trained governesses, made her knees tremble.

'My God, Colleen.' Lady Pennycrocker slumped onto the narrow bed. 'You were right to press the matter. Our discovery changes things mightily. This harmless girl is not who she says she is. She has been keeping her ear to the ground, it seems, and has been conspiring to bring about our downfall these many weeks. Her father, too… and the young man from the Ordnance Survey is part of it! The information is all here in black and white. Look at this! She even knows the date! Her malicious eavesdropping has undone all our work.'

'Let me see!' Colleen Hennessey snatched the journal from her mistress's hands.

Lady Pennycrocker looked decidedly flustered. 'It's just as well I told her Patrick was returning tonight and not tomorrow. This false information will confound them all. It still gives us time to remedy the situation, providing we move quickly.'

'You must tell Sir William, madam,' the cook urged, having read but a few of the incriminating sentences.

'Take the book, Colleen. I wish you to copy these two pages as proof,' she indicated with her forefinger. 'I may need to show the lines to my husband if he baulks. They are damning enough. Go to it quickly, put down the words in your own hand while I speak to him. Then replace the journal in its rightful position. It's important our governess doesn't know we have been in her room.'

Minutes later, Lady Pennycrocker slid into the study through the hidden library door to find her husband hunched over his desk, a half-empty bottle of Madeira at his side.

'We have a crisis, William,' she burst out. 'Tomorrow's landing is compromised. You must inform Honey. We have to change our plans.'

'I do wish you wouldn't use that damned concealed door so often. It fair puts the skids under me.'

'Listen to what I have to say, damn you! Put your wine down and listen!'

Once the story of the last hour had been told – it took Lady Kathleen less than two minutes to complete the narrative – Sir William slapped his desk and rose to his feet.

'This is your doing, Kate. I told you this would be dangerous, but no, no... you would not listen to me. You insisted. When I refused to help, you threatened me. Now you have got your just deserts. Go and solve the problem yourself. I wish no further part in it!'

'William, stop this nonsense. You must help me. This will be the last time I ask anything of you.'

'I'm sorry, but no more. Under the greatest of duress, I spoke to that wretched woman... her name escapes me—'

'Flora.'

'Yes, as sour a female as I have ever met, and that's saying something! I did as you asked. She took my money and your instructions back to her husband. As far as I am concerned, the matter is now settled. The boat arrives tomorrow night with your cargo aboard. The Honeys know what to do. I have paid them enough, have I not? Two hundred pounds is a pretty price to give to support your damnable conspiracy.'

'But if they proceed as planned, they will fall into the ambush that is now being prepared for them, and Wilks will be captured too...'

'Your precious Wilks,' he sneered. 'Don't think I don't know about you two and all the goings-on. Apothecary's son, indeed! A good enough excuse for your philandering. You sicken me! All this is your fault. Why did you tell the girl that your paramour was returning tomorrow in the first place? 'Twas sheer foolishness.'

'You are not listening, William. I told her Wilks would be returning *tonight*! I wanted to see her reaction.'

'I still would have said nothing!'

'Don't you see? I have read her journal, and thank goodness I have! If I had not taken the initiative, we would most certainly be sunk in a matter of days. I had to draw her away from the Hall. It was bait to arouse her interest, and she fell for it.'

'Very well, but I want nothing to do with it.'

'William, I had no idea she knew so much. As a result of my courage, we have discovered the journal and the truth of it. It's most fortunate too, for we still have time to save the day. Our governess may know some of it, but not all. Her journal tells only a fraction of our story, and the true secret of our purpose has yet to be uncovered.'

'*Our* story? *Our* purpose, Kate? 'Tis yours and Wilks's alone... and that damnable leprechaun in the kitchen,' he added, clenching his fists so the knuckles whitened. 'I will play no further part, do you hear?'

'Please, William, listen to me. Take your horse and ride to Doubloons immediately. Speak to Honey. Tell him he must find another landing spot for tomorrow. The boat will have departed from Cork by now. We cannot change the date, but we can change the place they disembark. There is still time to avert a disaster.'

'Ha! Look at me! I'm in no fit state to ride a horse at this hour. And for absolute clarity, I refuse to go tomorrow as well. My hands have been bloodied enough. Do what you will. Go and run to Mr Honey. As long as you take sufficient money, he will do what you want. Honey and money, eh? Like twin brothers. That's all the man's interested in – the filthy lucre.'

'If you force me to go, I will tell him the truth about Ignatius,' she replied with a steely look.

If Lady Kathleen thought this threat would make her husband think again, she was mistaken. He was in full angry flow. 'Go to the bounder – see if I care!' he screamed. 'You will find him a fine fellow. A large man, a tad daunting, perhaps, but if you ask him nicely and flutter your eyelashes as you hand over the gold, I'm sure he will find a way to oblige.'

'You must do it, William!' she yelled back. 'I cannot be seen in that man's presence. You and he are business partners.'

'We might have been once, my dear, but not anymore. Not since you intervened with your unholy plot. Our arrangement was never worth a fig anyway. I am set firm. You have made your own bed; now you may lie in it!' he snarled.

'I mean what I say about Ignatius. I will tell them the full story.'

'Ignatius got what he deserved. I had to protect Rose; you know that.' Sir William let out a hearty laugh. 'If you tell Cassius the *full* story, as you put it, then you will be damning yourself. You and Wilks played an ugly part too, don't forget – some might say more dreadful than my own. For a single bullet is an honourable way for a man to die. Cutting the head from a corpse, on the other hand, is macabre in the extreme. Such a foul act cannot have been a pretty matter to undertake, nor easy to explain. Did you and Wilks take pleasure in it?'

'It was done to save you from the gallows!' she screeched.

'It was done to further your loathsome agenda!' he retorted. 'Cassius will want to know the *whole* truth, and if you don't tell him all, I shall have to provide him with the details, in the fullness of time.'

'We had a pact. I have played my part. Wilks and I covered up for your wickedness. Now, will you do as I ask?'

'I will not,' Sir Willam replied flatly. 'Go now,' he said with a dismissive flick of his hand. 'This is becoming tiresome...'

'Believe me, William, I will tell all.' She stared at him with an intensity he'd never witnessed in his life before.

'Do you know what...?' Sir William glared back. 'I don't think you will... Consider the matter properly for a moment, sweetheart. By revealing all to the very devil himself, you will achieve quite the opposite of what you now desire. Such a story would gain one thing only – his incontrollable wrath! Sometimes sleeping dogs are best left untouched. You don't have the courage for such a fight anyway,' he scoffed. 'Not at this moment, at least... If you want to save your precious Patrick from the hangman's noose, you'll have to ask Honey to change the plans yourself, and mark my words, the brute will have to be compliant. If you reveal to him how his brother really died, woe betide you. I'll wager the fury Honey will fly into will shake the foundations of that miserable farmhouse of his. Go now.' He brushed another disdainful hand in her direction. 'Do what you will. I shall await your return with interest.' Grinning like a Cheshire cat, he poured himself another glass of Madeira.

Lady Pennycrocker cursed him as she flew out of the room. After slamming the door, she heard her husband cry out to her, 'Take care, dearest Kate. If you choose to go now, beware – there may be vagabonds abroad at this dark hour...'

* * *

Elizabeth Snuggs knew where she would find her husband at that hour. The market square clock had not long chimed seven when she rapped on the door of an insignificant looking building in Fore Street.

'My goodness!' Samuel gaped when he saw her. 'Come in quickly, before someone sees you.'

'I had to come,' she said breathlessly. 'I have important news. The butler, Wilks, is returning tonight from Cork, no less. Lady Pennycrocker told me herself, just an hour ago. I came as fast as I could, as I know you will be making your preparations later tonight.'

'Whoa! What did she say?'

'That Mr Wilks is returning to the Hall tonight – he is already on his way, by sea – and that she would be waiting up for him. She expects him around midnight... or maybe a few hours later.'

'Elizabeth, you have done well. How can we thank you? This intelligence will help us greatly, but if you will excuse me, my dear Bess, I will still have to tread carefully. The last time I received such information from you, I was sent on a wild goose chase.'

Elizabeth looked indignant. 'That may be so, but there is no doubt in my mind that Her Ladyship was telling me the truth.'

'But think of it, Bess, why should Her Ladyship bring you into her confidence – and on such a night as this? We know she has some part in the matter. Why reveal herself to you in such a way?'

'She has an affinity for Wilks. It all spilled out from her like a lover's confession. "Woman to woman", she called it. She is quite taken by him. I fear he has some hold over her.'

'Did she see you leave the Hall tonight?'

'I have no idea. I wasn't aware of her watching.'

'Now I have a conundrum, my dearest...' Samuel took her hand in his.

'Why so?'

'Shall I allow you to return to the Hall tonight? That is the problem. If Her Ladyship has laid a trap for you, it may not be safe for you to return.'

'I insist on going back! I told Esther I would return by eight. If I do not appear by then, it will surely raise suspicions. No, I will not hear otherwise. You may drop me close to the Hall, if you like, so I might arrive back all the sooner. If there are doubts about me, I will confound them. A walk to the village and back is what I said, and I'll keep my word. Come now, saddle your horse and take me back; Lancelot is strong enough for the two of us.' Her voice was strident and persuasive.

'Very well, if you insist. I will discuss this bulletin with your father and Mr Jarvie only. The others do not need to know of it. 'Tis my hope you are correct, for if we have to extend our campaign by a further night, I fear for the consequences…'

Chapter Twenty-Five

Elizabeth and Samuel's ride back to the boundary walls of Pennycrocker Hall took less time than either of them had expected, and she was back in the kitchen well before the appointed hour of eight. She made sure to speak to Esther and enquire about the children before she retired. Then she busied herself for a while in tidying the nursery, hoping her presence would be noted, but all around seemed quiet, and not a soul did she encounter. The Hall had gone to sleep, and now, it was her turn to do the same. The events of the day had been extraordinary.

While she prepared herself for bed, try as she might, she could not get the strange conversation with Her Ladyship out of her consciousness. Elizabeth's mind was still swimming by the time she touched her head onto the pillow. At ten minutes after eleven o'clock, she could bear it no more. She would have to take steps to relieve the tension. Lighting a candle, she reached under her bed to search for her journal. Pulling out the vanity case, she fumbled for the catch, which came open in an instant.

It was in that moment she knew unseen visitors had been in her room…

* * *

The tiny Custom House could not have seen so many conspirators collected within its rustic stone walls as it did on that night. When all had assembled, Samuel Snuggs made the introductions. There were eleven present, all told, gathered under the low ceilings of the simple meeting room. Halwill had brought three men with him from Launceston – Constables Marshgate, Newmills and Hill. Samuel had selected four of his most trusted staff – Officers Wilfred Gale, Nat Copplestone, Paul West and David Wendholt. Henry Gough and Jacob Jarvie made up the numbers. On advice from Inspector Halwill, it was decided to exclude Constable Percival Poundstock from their number, not because any held suspicions against his good character, but rather that his absence from normal duties might create adverse attention and attract unwanted questions from inquisitive local folk who knew him and his daily activities so well.

'Our purpose tonight is to finally bring an end to the wicked trade that has cursed this shrouded coast for over a century,' Samuel opened with his back against the cold inglenook. 'Before I furnish you with the facts, I must command all here to keep what I am about to say close. You have all been chosen because I believe you can be trusted to hold your tongues. Does everyone here understand? Gale, what do you say?'

'All is clear, sir.'

'Copplestone?'

'Sir,' he nodded.

In this manner, Samuel Snuggs asked every man present to pledge his allegiance to the cause, which all, including Henry Gough, did most forcefully.

Once the round was completed, Samuel continued thus... 'We expect contraband, a sizeable shipment of Irish whiskey, to arrive on these shores within the next twenty-four hours. The landing will take place either tonight or tomorrow night, though our strong presumption is 'twill be this very night. Our intelligence tells us the old tunnel into St Piran's will be brought into use once more by the smugglers. Our strategy is a simple one. As soon as we have indication of activity outside the church, we shall pounce.'

'Beg pardon, sir...' – it was officer West who spoke – 'we spent nearly a week last year blocking that shaft up.'

'So you did, Officer, and a fine job you all made of it, too. But I have seen with my very own eyes, in the last few days, the tunnel debris has been secretly removed. I believe the only task remaining for the owlers to clear the way fully is to break down the final wall into the crypt. When they do that, and we see them appear above ground in the churchyard, we shall know they will have completed their task. That will signal the time to strike.' This speech was accompanied by low murmuring among his audience, made all the more resonant by their close confines, where all stood cheek by jowl.

'Mr Gough and Mr Jarvie will form our advance party,' Samuel resumed when the mutterings had subsided. 'They will secrete themselves on the cliffs above Shrouded Cove.' Turning to the huddle of revenue men, he said, 'Officer Wendholt, your physique and youthful vigour demands that you accompany Messrs Gough and Jarvie to their position and bring word to us as soon as they see lights or movement out at sea.'

'Very well, sir,' Wendholt smirked, clearly pleased with the flattery.

'For the rest of us, it will be a waiting game.'

'My officers are armed,' Halwill announced. 'Each of us carries Enfield revolvers.'

'Thank you, Inspector. That is comforting, and I'm sure your men will use their weapons prudently... My officers will carry their rifles, so between us, we shall present a formidable force.'

'As long as we don't shoot one another…' West grumbled.

'I have further news – good tidings too,' Samuel announced. 'We shall have the assistance of the cutter tonight also!' A round of ironic cheers rose up from the group of revenue officers. 'I have received word from Commander Geach in Bude. The *Vigilant* will conduct a patrol for us – it may even be her last. With luck, the crew will sight the mother ship, which we believe hails from the port of Cork – a distance of some 200 miles. *Vigilant*'s orders are to intercept any vessel she sees on a north-westerly course from the bay, which will indicate its return to Ireland, having already shed her supplies. If *Vigilant* engages with another vessel, we shall hear of it. They will signal the shore by ship's lamp, using Captain Colomb's Morse code method. Both Mr Gough and Mr Jarvie are familiar with the language and will send word, as necessary.'

'Mr Snuggs, can you remind the assembly of the tide and moon conditions tonight?' Jacob Jarvie requested.

'A very important factor, sir. High tide tonight will occur at six minutes past midnight. The moon will be but a thin crescent, but will provide light enough for our purpose. I estimate the sea conditions will allow shallow-draught boats to approach the cave entrance for about two hours either side of the tide. By half past two tomorrow morning, the water will have retreated, meaning access by any daughter vessel, or vessels, will be impossible. The owlers must complete their task between ten o'clock tonight and the wee hours or risk being stranded. But, make no mistake, four hours will be time enough to bring a substantial cargo ashore. I intend to let them do the donkey work, carry in their goods, and only then will we make our presence felt. In that way, we shall seize both men and cargo in one fell swoop.'

By nine o'clock, all questions had been answered and every man knew his job. It was time for the advance party to secure their positions. Henry Gough, Jacob Jarvie and David Wendholt took their leave, accompanied by murmured voices wishing them "good luck" and encouraging them to "keep 'em peeled". The familiar walk to the cliff edge above Shrouded Cove was briskly undertaken and did not take the trio long to accomplish. Jacob led the way, and they encountered no one on the march. A flawless firmament, dotted with myriad stars greeted them as they rose up the rutted track, the celestial bodies made all the more spectacular by the low-lit moon. To the west, bright Venus could be seen dipping against the horizon, while overhead, titanic Jupiter shone with familiar lustre – plenteous enough light, once their eyes had adjusted, to make their way without the lighting of lamps. A light breeze fanned their faces as they took their positions low against a sturdy gorse that served to further camouflage their presence. Out to sea, the outline of Cow and Calf rocks could be made out, adding dusky shape to the flat horizon.

Jacob took out his spyglass and scanned the ocean, tutting all the time. 'The glass may not help us much tonight,' he muttered. 'Despite the stars, it's too dark to focus on anything clearly, except the sliver of moon.'

The little group fell into hushed silence, listening and watching – each occupied by their own inner thoughts. An hour went by with nothing to report, except the progress of the ever-climbing moon and the gentle shifting of the heavenly panoply westwards. Eleven o'clock came and went. Henry thought he heard a noise from beneath and crawled closer to the edge to peer down. But all was blackness, save for an occasional shimmer from below as the glow caught the tops of the rippling tide.

'I would have expected to have seen something by now,' he grumbled as he returned to the huddle.

'I also,' Jacob replied gloomily.

'Look there, sir.' It was Officer Wendholt who spoke.

It was difficult to gauge distances, given the conditions of darkness and the vast swathe of unbroken water before them, but sure enough, a dim light had suddenly become visible in the north-east quadrant. As they watched, the glimmer appeared to move from their right to left, approaching the Cow and Calf at an agonisingly slow pace.

'Whatever she is, the vessel is approaching from the north. Not the way we expect of our mother ship,' Henry observed after he'd peered through the trembling spyglass.

After twenty minutes, the light disappeared with a flicker behind the outline of the Calf, only to reappear once more, a few minutes later, at the head of the Cow, still on a determinedly western course.

'It's the cutter!' Jacob announced with a chuckle. 'By Jove, surely it can only be that. 'Tis *Vigilant*, on her promised patrol, if I am not mistaken.'

By midnight, the dot of light had disappeared once more – this time, behind the headland that guarded Borwenstow itself.

'The tide will turn soon,' Henry announced. 'Damn! I fear our vigil has been in vain. It is too late now to bring anything ashore. Do you agree Jacob?'

'I do, sir.' The frustration in his voice was clear for all to hear.

'Wendholt, please take the following message to Mr Snuggs: "There have been no sightings, save for the cutter itself. We intend to remain here another hour and then stand down to the Custom House." Please give him the message and wait for his reply. We shall hold our positions until you return.'

Officer Wendholt scurried away, happy to feel movement in his aching limbs once more.

'I fear we shall have to resume this game tomorrow,' Henry said. 'If nothing else, this has given us a taste of what to expect.'

Suddenly, the once vanished point of light reappeared again from behind the headland, this time moving steadily eastwards. The cutter had clearly decided it was best to return to port also. And to confirm any doubts of their intentions, the same light began to skip and dart before them in a series of distant flashes:

_ _ _ _ _ ... .._ _.. . *To Bude*

Samuel Snuggs and the others huddled in Fore Street received the news in a resigned fashion.

'Another day will make no difference to us, men! We shall regroup at nine tomorrow evening,' he announced, trying to sound optimistic. 'Before you depart to your loved ones, please remember what I told you earlier. Not a word to a soul until this matter is concluded. Then you can chatter all you like and tell whatever tall stories you wish of your derring-do. Understood?'

'UNDERSTOOD!' came back the singing reply.

* * *

Elizabeth Snuggs was in the nursery, with a map of the British Empire spread out on the Baluchistan carpet before the kneeling girls, when Michael Heath entered. Esther followed shortly behind him, looking strangely sheepish.

'Her Ladyship asks if you can join her in the morning room, Mrs Snuggs,' the first footman said through his nose and without a hint of emotion. Elizabeth had spent yet another fretful and sleepless night, and her tiredness and anxiety may have been the reason why her knees faltered slightly as she rose from the rug.

'Make a list of all the countries marked and coloured in pink, girls. Have it ready for when I return, for I shall tell each of their stories, one by one.'

Elizabeth followed Heath down the grand staircase. She wondered what Lady Kathleen wanted at this early hour. She hoped there would not be a repeat of the previous day's revelations, for she wasn't sure how she might react to further outpourings of the heart. There was something different in the manner of Heath, as he led her down the second corridor, that struck Elizabeth as odd. Heath was normally an ebullient man, especially when amongst the staff, but today he seemed staid, formal and stiff. When Elizabeth enquired after his health as they crossed the landing, he made no reply whatsoever. Maybe he hadn't heard... *Strange, though...* she thought.

He led her towards the morning room door, which they entered without first knocking.

'Mrs Snuggs, Your Ladyship,' Heath announced. He bowed and then left the room, closing the door behind him.

'I'll come straight to the point, Mrs Snuggs,' Lady Kathleen spoke quickly. With the light from the huge bay window behind her, it was difficult for Elizabeth to discern her expression. 'Sir William and I have decided we no longer require your services here at Pennycrocker Hall. We have made alternative arrangements and ask that you leave today – this morning, in fact. I have arranged for a carriage to take you and your belongings to your marital home in Trevalga. Barnaby will meet you in the drive at noon.'

The tremor in Elizabeth's knees returned as soon as Her Ladyship uttered the first words. It was as if they knew before she did what was about to be revealed. 'My goodness... this comes as a shock,' she stammered in return. 'Have I done something to offend, Your Ladyship? If so, I apologise unreservedly.'

Lady Kathleen replied with a cold stare. Without answering the question, she said, 'Sir William and I are as one on the matter. You are a married woman now, who soon will be hoping for children of your own. We wish to give you every chance to fulfil that dream, as Agnes did before you.'

'But... I—'

'Our mind is made up. I will leave you with ten pounds to cover your immediate expenses until you get another position. I can do no more, I'm afraid. My husband was quite insistent.'

'If I have hurt—'

'You may say goodbye to the children. I will have the carriage ready at twelve. Barnaby will have the money for you. And now, if you will excuse me, Mrs Snuggs, I have pressing business to attend.' Lady Pennycrocker pulled the cord behind her and, almost instantly, Heath appeared once again; he must have been waiting immediately outside for the inevitable call.

The tremor in Elizabeth's legs curdled into an onslaught of violent quivering as she rolled, head swimming, towards the door. The audience with Her Ladyship was all over in a matter of seconds. The simple act of walking now took place as if in a numbed dream. As they rounded the corner, Heath took pity on her, at last. He took her by the arm and steadied the now former governess up the grand staircase.

'I am very sorry, Miss Elizabeth. I had only the vaguest idea... The gentry can be cruel at the best of times. We are all at risk of losing our positions at any moment. All I can do is help you with your luggage.'

By the time they reached the landing, Elizabeth had recovered enough of her poise to speak. 'Tell me, Michael, has Mr Wilks returned?'

'Not that I am aware. Cook tells me we may see him

sometime soon. I, for one, wish it could be today. The weight of my duties has more than doubled since he's been away in Plymouth.'

'In Plymouth... of course...' Elizabeth said in return. 'Pray, remind me, why has Mr Wilks gone to Plymouth?'

'To attend to his sick father. That's what Mrs Hennessey told me. Poor man was dying, last we heard.'

A cold and clammy sweat broke out on Elizabeth's forehead as she gathered up the few meagre belongings from the room at the top of the house. She recalled the night she'd eavesdropped, from that very same chamber, on Mrs Hennessey's conversation with Her Ladyship with all the talk of Patrick Wilks's trip to Cork. A moment of unbearable realisation swamped her as she suddenly understood how careless she had been. For it was *she* who had unwittingly repeated the overheard exchanges with Lady Pennycrocker, thus revealing a fact unknown to the rest of the household. Wilks had been in Plymouth, not Cork, as far as the servants knew. How could she have been so reckless? As she thought through the furrowed connections, she began to appreciate the true gravity of her situation. She realised the sooner she left Pennycrocker Hall, the better, and started to wonder if a carriage ride with the dreaded Barnaby, Sir William's notoriously taciturn coachman, was such a good idea.

Where might he take me? Is a trap being laid? Surely, she was overreacting...

She wanted so much to see the children one final time, but the prospect of their tears, mixed with her own, was too much to bear. She packed all the essentials she could into a single bag. The rest would have to wait until matters had blown over.

Am I being paranoiac? she asked herself one final time. *No!* came back the firm, if rather frightened, reply.

In that moment, she resolved to leave the house on her

own terms – alone and immediately. She threaded her way to the ground floor, silently poking around corners and relieved to encounter not a single soul on the way. She contemplated making her escape via the kitchens and rear entrance, but she knew the servants' hall would be a hive of activity at this hour, and the thought of seeing Mrs Hennessey turned her stomach. There was only one thing for it – she would have to run the gauntlet of the inner hall and the grand front entrance. Picking up her skirt, her valise in the other hand, she hurried to the heavy oak frame, opened the door and peered out into the morning air. Happily, there was no sign of the daunting Barnaby or his carriage – her appointment with him was over an hour away. It was time for her to leave, and without further ado, she skipped out onto the warm gravel.

The valise suddenly felt heavier than before. By the time she reached the arched gateway that marked the commencement of 200 yards of gritted driveway, half running and half stumbling, she was wholly out of breath and in considerable pain. The weight of the bag tore at her shoulder and judging from the burning of both her biceps, they were hardly up to the task. She let herself onto the lane and found the footpath in short order. Once under the cover of the oak trees, she laid her bag down and turned to face Borwenstow.

She was a free woman, and the feeling that swamped her was one of sheer joy.

Chapter Twenty-Six

Elizabeth Snuggs found a swathe of soft grass under a spreading bough and, crossing her legs, sat down for a while. She needed to gather her strength for the walk through the woods that would lead her, in about twenty minutes, to the outskirts of the village. With her heavy load and aching limbs, the prospect would normally have been most unappealing, even though the ground was dry and most of the journey would be downhill. But today, in her current mood of exhilaration, she felt confident she could have walked to the moon and back, had she been forced into it. As she gathered her thoughts, she heard the sound of a horse and trap approaching down the nearby lane from the direction of Pennycrocker Hall. She left her bag and went to investigate. Peering through the leaves, her heart leapt when she saw who it was – the amiable and bibulous Doctor Plymswood, no less – flicking a pretty piebald pony forwards while descending towards Borwenstow. Elizabeth broke cover, ran into the dappled sunlight and waved him down.

'Whoa!' Plymswood cried, pulling on the reins as the trap slid to a halt at her feet. 'Mrs Snuggs, what on earth…?'

'Could you carry me to the village, Doctor? I have an

urgent appointment and no one to take me, as you see.'

'Old Pennycrocker can't spare a carriage, eh? I get the drift... Typical of the skinflint!' He shook his head. 'Come, climb aboard. I'm on my way to attend to Mrs Polrunny. You can ride as far as the square, if you like.'

'I have a valise,' Elizabeth said quickly as she hurried back into the copse under the watery eye of a bewildered-looking Plymswood. With her luggage heaved in, the doctor geed up the horse, and the pair were soon on their way.

'I trust Mrs Polrunny is not serious,' Elizabeth asked as soon as they had rounded the first corner.

'A touch of dyspepsia, I believe. She has an appetite for pilchards like no other woman I have ever met. The fish and her fondness for Trewint's cider brew has brought about another attack. I've lost count of the times I've told her to stick to sausages and clean distilled drinks. Whiskey is a much better beverage than the *Gauger's* cloudy mulch. I am living proof of it!' Plymswood cried.

Elizabeth fixed her companion with a critical stare. His blue-streaked nose, salivating lips and reddened cheeks were impossible to disregard. 'Living proof indeed, Doctor...' she mumbled, trying to disguise her amusement. As they clopped forwards, it was time to ask another question. 'And what of Mrs Polrunny's husband? Had you ever seen a case like it before?'

'Cyanide, the post-mortem reported,' Plymswood responded with another shake of his head. 'I suspected it, of course, but it's not an easy substance to come by these days, so I was not sure at first. You have to know your business if you dabble with such dangerous preparations. How it arrived in a place like Borwenstow heaven only knows... Poor old Polrunny was always a physically strong man – a rogue, without doubt, despite his late calling to the church –

a likeable fellow in full vigour, even with his single leg.' The doctor breathed out heavily and looked pensive. 'It must have been a hideous way to die...'

'But cyanide has a reputation for killing quickly, does it not, Doctor?' she pressed.

'If ingested, that's correct. But Polrunny had the smudges of it on his hands – the fingers and palm on the right were particularly noticeable in their cherry-red rash. He must have touched the poison somehow, and it absorbed through the skin – probably only a small quantity, mind, for there was no sign any had been swallowed. Once the substance gains a hold, there is nothing will stop its natural course. A breathless and terrible death is inevitable.'

'Do you have any suspicions of who might have killed him, Doctor?'

Plymswood laughed. 'In fact, I do, dear lady, but no one will listen to me... That inspector from Launceston is a fool, all bluff and bluster, chasing hither and thither and not harking to others.'

'You think you know the identity of the killer?'

'I do.' Plymswood took his yellow eyes off the road ahead, beheld Elizabeth directly and chuckled. 'The people around about consider me a sot, you know. Maybe you do, too. And not without cause, perhaps, I will admit... But I *am* a qualified man, and I know the ways of folk in these parts. If you want my opinion as a physician – and I believe I'm not mistaken, Polrunny killed himself.'

Elizabeth gaped back in shock.

'Not deliberately, you understand...' he added quickly. 'My belief is the verger came across some traces of the substance by accident; he must have handled it, and it killed him.'

'Goodness, that is quite a theory,' Elizabeth frowned as the horse led them into the village.

Dr Plymswood brought the trap to a halt outside the post office. He laid down the reins and turned his bulging face towards her. 'I have more, if you are prepared to hear me out.' Elizabeth felt mildly uncomfortable all of a sudden, but nodded thoughtfully to show she wished him to continue. 'My guess is the poison that did for the verger was the exact same as accounted for the parson. There is a difference though. In my view, the death of the vicar was a deliberate, wicked act brought about by another who wished him harm. Polrunny's demise, on the other hand, was an accident – collateral damage, so to speak... The truth of it all must lie within the walls of St Piran's, but for the life of me, I cannot imagine where...' Dr Plymswood sighed again in the manner of one who had, maybe, revealed too much. 'Now, if you will allow me, Mrs Snuggs... Mrs Polrunny will be waiting.'

Elizabeth wanted to question him further but decided to leave the matter there. She thanked the doctor as she got down from the trap, and on retrieving her valise, she walked the short distance along Fore Street to the Custom House, where she hoped she would find Samuel and news of last night's adventures.

On seeing her at the threshold, her husband drew her behind the door and greeted her with the warmest of embraces – of a type which would have been most improper had they met in the street. 'My love, you are indeed a sight for tired, sore eyes. I hadn't expected to see you for days!' he exclaimed.

'I have grave news, my darling,' she replied as he released her. Elizabeth swiftly recounted the events of the morning. The news of her sudden dismissal as governess of Pennycrocker Hall was greeted by Samuel with a look of pure horror. When he pressed her for more details, she answered him firmly. 'That's the bones of it. I can tell you more later, but there are more important matters to occupy us. What of last night's events? Did you capture Wilks and the whiskey? The butler has not surfaced at the Hall, for sure.'

Samuel looked glum. 'I fear I have nothing to tell you. We were busy until nearly three o'clock, but there was no movement at Shrouded Cove, nor at sea… nor the church, for that matter. We plan to set ourselves in readiness again tonight. Your father is still here, in fact, upstairs resting, as we speak – as is the inspector, whose men are accommodated in the stables. We cannot hide them for long. One day more, maybe two at the most, and then we shall have to withdraw our forces and admit defeat.'

Elizabeth slumped into a chair. 'So, my reports were defective once again… I am so sorry, Samuel. It seems I have set another hare running.'

'Nonsense, dearest sweetheart. Last night's efforts were not wasted. I view them as a dress rehearsal for what must surely take place soon enough.'

'There is more… I fear I may have been discovered. My journal with all my notes – I think it was found… I think it has been read… I'm sure it's the true reason for my summary dismissal.'

Samuel paused before responding. 'So be it. Let them burn in hell. I'm mightily glad to see you here, at least. You did right by absconding under your own steam when you did. Who knows what they had planned for you! I made a dreadful mistake allowing you to return to the Hall in the first instance. At least Almighty God has been merciful, and I shall not have to pay for it. You are safe now, and here you shall remain. That's all that matters to me.'

* * *

The remainder of the day was spent in virtual hiding within the thick walls of the Custom House. Elizabeth was reunited with her father, and between them, they examined every facet of her time at Pennycrocker Hall, searching for clues and ideas about the household's future intentions. Elizabeth was brought to tears on more than one occasion at the thought of the much beloved children she had left behind.

By dusk, the Custom House's waiting task force began to stretch their bodies and stir from their resting places. One by one, the revenue officers returned from their homes, each bringing provisions – mostly bread, cheese and eggs – to share. Beer found its way into the building too, and by the time Samuel assembled all and sundry into the cramped meeting room, a few had started talking brashly of how they were going to confront the challenges that lay ahead. His address was brief and to the point.

'Gentlemen, we live to fight another day. Your orders are the same. Our plan is the same. Commander Geach and his crew will be in attendance offshore, as before. *Vigilant* will be sailing from Bude within the hour.'

He reminded the assembly of the grave undertaking which they were about to commence before instructing a few of their number to desist their drinking, the latter drawing a low grumble of protest from certain quarters. Then he gave the signal for Gough, Jarvie and Wendholt to take up their forward positions. By nine thirty, and in near complete darkness, all was set. The moon had waxed by a few degrees but, for practical purposes, it shed very little extra light over the clifftop scene. The weather was kind once more. A mild inshore breeze ruffled the tops of an otherwise flat, calm sea and another cloudless, starry night beckoned. Samuel announced that high tide would occur at forty minutes after midnight, meaning, by three o'clock in the morning, Shrouded Cove would be cut off from the sea to all shipping, however large or small the craft.

Henry Gough and his little band took the now time-honoured walk, unchallenged, to the clifftop, where they dropped into their familiar positions, roosting like hens, lying low, with backs against the giant gorse. Here they hunched, a light breeze exploring their faces, and here they waited. As before, Jacob Jarvie peered through his spyglass, only to reach the same inevitable and bitter conclusion that his eyes were more suited than any other contraption to scan the expanse of black. The trio sank into a contemplative silence, gazing as one into the abyss.

Just after ten, Henry nudged Jacob in the ribs. 'I think I see a light – a single light,' he whispered. 'Look to the east, close by the bluff.'

'I see it! Exactly as we expected.' The note of youthful exhilaration in Jacob's voice was clear to all.

'It's moving very slowly…'

'Would you like me to report the sighting, sir?' Officer Wendholt asked.

'No, Officer, I don't want you running about unnecessarily. We will be patient and observe a while. There is a long night ahead of us.'

As they squinted into the gloom, the speck of light moved steadily westwards from their right. After ten minutes, Jarvie noticed something which he thought surprising. 'Whoever she is, the craft seems to be following the same course as the cutter did last night.'

'Surely it can't be *Vigilant*; she's moving much too slowly. But I agree, 'tis most interesting. She could be just transiting along the coast… a fisherman perhaps…'

'Not at this hour! She must be heading for a rendezvous.'

'But I can't see anything else out there…'

Another five or so minutes passed as the spark inched its way across the horizon's dark curtain. And then, as quickly as it had appeared, it disappeared.

'She's hidden by the Calf,' Jacob observed, 'just as the cutter was last night.' The trio maintained their vigil, expecting the object to reappear at the head of the Cow, but after a full twenty minutes, the light had still not resurfaced, and its non-appearance was beginning to cause consternation. Then suddenly, there *was* a flicker exactly in the spot they had predicted.

'She should have appeared many minutes ago, even at that slow crawl. Something must have delayed her on the other side of the island,' Henry said slowly.

'I have it!' Jacob exclaimed with a stifled cry. 'The mother ship's guiding lights must be hidden from our sight by the Cow's craggy rocks. The vessel must be anchored close in, behind the islands. My guess is mother and daughter have come together and the first load has been transferred.'

'You may be correct, sir. If you are right, we should see the daughter approach us soon enough.'

'I'm surprised we have seen just one daughter vessel,' Jacob observed. 'The Honeys have two jolly boats. For the size of load we're expecting, surely they would use both to ferry in the cargo.'

'Maybe this consignment is smaller than we imagined. We were only speculating, after all.'

In silence, the trio watched the distant light as it moved away from the head of the Cow. But something was still not right… After a few minutes, the craft's direction of travel confounded them once more. Instead of heading inland towards them and into the jaws of the cove, the vessel continued snail-paced ever westwards.

'Maybe it is the cutter's lantern we can see after all.' Henry sucked his teeth. 'Any daughter craft should have turned inshore by now. This is all very perplexing…'

Now it was Jacob's turn to elbow Henry in the side. 'No,

look! *That* must be the cutter!' he said, pointing eastwards. 'A light yonder, over to the right, has just emerged from behind the bluff. For my money, it looks identical to the one we saw last night – it's brighter than the first, and it's moving much faster, exactly as *Vigilant* did yesterday.'

'She's on the same course as before too…'

'At her speed, she will be on top of the other in less than twenty minutes.'

Henry decided it was time to inform the others. 'Wendholt, please relay this message to Mr Snuggs: "We have movement. The cutter is sighted. It appears to be in pursuit of another craft, heading south-westwards. No landings have yet taken place in Shrouded Cove." Do you understand?'

'Yes, sir.'

'Run to him and return with his reply immediately. We are sure to need your services again tonight.'

After the young revenue man had departed, Henry rose to his haunches. 'I need to get a closer look at the cove – just to be sure. Stay here, Jacob, and don't take your eyes off the lights. I need to know whether there is a shore party lurking beneath us. There's a ledge that juts out, about twenty yards from here. If I crawl and crane my neck, I may be able to see better. Give me the spyglass.'

Jacob did as he was asked. Before Henry slithered off into the darkness, he caught his sleeve and whispered, 'Take care, Mr Gough. It's a tricky spot by there and a long drop if you slip…'

The area Henry had in mind was right on the cliff edge where a narrow patch of ground extended out only to curve back on itself. If he could reach it, he imagined it might provide an improved angle from which a clearer view of the cave entrance could be obtained. The thought had suddenly occurred to him that part of Honey's gang, Trewint perhaps, might have gained access to the beach directly from the land side of the tunnel by breaking down the wall from within the crypt itself. It was an eventuality they should have considered, and he cursed himself for the lapse. He knew there was no one watching the churchyard at that time, so a landing party might have already let themselves in, arrived at the sea entrance, and were now waiting for the first boat to land. If so, he imagined he would see something, for the night remained as murky as Hades itself and the smugglers would have to be carrying tapers or lanterns.

There was barely enough glow to discern the outline of the clifftop, and feeling his way, Henry approached it cautiously. When the soft grass under his body was replaced by a patch of dry, crumbled stone, he knew the ledge was close, and sure enough, as he shuffled forwards on elbows and knees, he reached it. He could go no further. His hands now dropped into thin air as the clifftop fell away beneath them. A sudden gust of frigid air swept over his neck, sending a shiver down his spine. He tried to manoeuvre his body to face the direction of the cave entrance. Imagining his head was at the centre of a cartwheel, he moved the spokes, his feet and legs, in a low circle across the brittle stones. In this way, feeling every inch of the ground as he went, he managed eventually to rotate his body by a full ninety degrees. When his right elbow slid briefly over the edge, he caught his breath, only just able to keep his balance. He could tell he was now lying parallel with the brink and could move no further. With luck, he'd now be facing the opening to the tunnel. Craning his neck like a feeding giraffe, he peered ahead, hoping to see some lights from below. But there was nothing… only the smudged outline of rocks under the starlit sky met his eyes. He lay a while, breathing in shallow draughts, hardly moving a muscle and blinking into the void. He turned his ear to the breeze and strained to hear. Perhaps the sounds of rising voices could be identified… But again, there was none – just the soothing rumble of the high tide lapping against the rocks hundreds of feet below.

Damn. He emptied his lungs, lay his head on the cold rock and closed his eyes. *It had been worth a try, at least.*

As he contemplated his retreat from this precarious crow's nest, he felt the ground under him move slightly. He held his position, stiffly praying the shifting earth would settle, but seconds later, his knees dropped by at least an inch. He began to panic. He would have to leave, and quickly! He tried to roll away, but as he spun on his shoulder, the whole shelf seemed to crack asunder. In an instant, amid a flurry of crumbling sand and stone, his legs slid away from the once solid, scarred surface. Plunging violently away from his upper body, as if attached to a hanged man dropped from the scaffold, they plummeted downwards through the thin night air. The spyglass went tumbling out of his grasp and spiralled onto the rocks below. Henry had no time to cry out, such was the speed of the collapse. With arms and hands flailing, searching desperately for purchase, he managed somehow to find a jagged outcrop that still held firm. He held to it for dear life, the rock cutting deep into his palm and ripping the fingers of his right hand, while his feet dangled helplessly beneath him. Knuckles white, and with every sinew screaming in agony, here he hung, writhing in mid-air. If only he could find a place to grasp with his other hand, there might yet be a chance… But try as he might, the spare hand just thrashed the empty air. With one final lung-bursting effort, he reached out once more and managed to feel the sliding rock face, but his fingers slipped away almost as soon as they had touched it. There was simply nothing to clasp.

This was it, and he knew it… the moment all men never dream will come to them – and for him, too soon… An image of Caroline sewing quietly in the bright parlour at Alpha Yard came to his head, and with it, a bizarre calmness enveloped him. He wasn't afraid anymore and steeled himself for the inevitable fall into the chasm and eternal peace...

On the point of releasing his unbearable grip, he suddenly became aware of a strange glimmer that shone directly from above him. Too tired to think clearly, he imagined it must be the ethereal light people sometimes spoke of – come to bring him to his god. With the radiance came an abrupt pressure to his once floundering hand. Then his whole body jerked. Surely this was it, his final moment had arrived. But no! He gazed upwards to see his hand had been grasped by another. Cold ebony fingers now wrapped around his own, and in an instant, he felt his frame rise up as if some hidden force was propelling it from both above and beneath at the same time. The hand that gripped his was long and bony – there was a prominent ring of bright ruby borne on the fourth finger. The force drawing Henry upwards was one of unimaginable power, and within seconds, he found himself lying prostrate amongst the cushioning grasses of the clifftops once more. He stared across the ground, expecting to see the shape of a smiling Jacob, but the place was completely deserted.

Resting his head on a tuft, he fixed his eyes on the heavens. *The stars seem all the brighter for the emptiness...*

He inhaled a gulp of sweet air, and readied himself to cry out. But in the nick of time, he remembered he was at the centre of a clandestine mission and managed to stifle the shout. Instead, arms aching and hand bleeding, he crawled back towards his earlier position. Here, much to his relief, he saw the silhouette of his friend sitting, as before, with his back to the mighty gorse.

'Well, did you see anything?' Jacob asked with disturbing nonchalance and without even turning his head towards him.

'My God, Jacob, you saved my life. What strength you have! I would be a dead man now, if it were not for you.'

'I don't understand…' came the puzzled reply. 'Tell me, did you see into the cave?' he repeated.

'Jacob, stop this fooling. You are a hero. You just saved my life. You pulled me from the brink.'

'What are you saying, Henry? I have not moved from this spot.'

'Then Wendholt… Where is the man?'

'Not returned yet from the Custom House. Give the fellow a chance, he's been gone less than ten minutes.'

'My God,' Henry replied with a low growl. 'This is no time for a jape. Look at me!'

'A jape? I don't understand. What are you talking about, Mr Gough?' Jarvie whispered, his voice replete with innocence.

'My God, Jacob, if not you, then who…? Do you not feel the cold?' Many seconds of silence followed before Henry spoke again. 'Jacob – I think I have just seen an apparition… Do you have any whiskey in your bag?'

Chapter Twenty-Seven

Henry resumed his sentinel position alongside the impassive form of Jacob Jarvie, and took a nip of whiskey from his friend's rucksack. His hands were trembling. Despite his fiercely beating heart, the cold Henry now felt after his dice with death would not leave him. An unquenchable chill seemed to envelope both mind and body, and when, sporadically, the wind gusted in from the ocean, needles of ice drilled into his very bones. The two moving lights at sea had vanished. Jacob reported in low tones that the first boat had disappeared behind the bluff that shielded Borwenstow from their view, while the other, *Vigilant* they'd presumed, had become obscured by the Cow and Calf.

'She must appear again soon, by my reckoning,' Jarvie announced, trying to sound buoyant.

Henry, who remained dazed by his recent experience, found sufficient energy to ask a faltering question. 'Remind me, Jacob... why is the second light the one you believe to be the cutter?'

'It must be *Vigilant* – she was travelling on the same course as last night and at the same speed as before. I expect to see her round the Cow's head at any second.'

But after ten minutes, they were still waiting… and there was *still* no movement after a further five long minutes.

Eventually, Jarvie broke the silence. 'I am utterly confounded, Henry. Where has the damned cutter disappeared to?'

'Perhaps she is hiding behind the rocks… maybe at anchor… maybe she has seen something out of our view and is giving chase,' Henry ventured, not entirely sure whether his fleeting understanding of nautical matters gave him the right to offer an opinion.

Just as Officer Wendholt reappeared through the gloom to join them their questions seemed to be answered. A soft light glimmered into view to the right of the Calf, and then, as if to confound them once more, another lantern could be seen almost touching the first. From the leading craft, a series of the unmistakeable flashes announced the arrival of a Morse signal. Henry translated it instantly:

To Bude with prize

And then, after a delay of ten seconds, the dots and dashes were repeated:

To Bude with prize

'With prize!' Jacob yelped. '*Vigilant* must have made a seizure!'

'Stay here with the officer, Jacob. I will go and report the news to Samuel. He will know what to do. If I'm not mistaken, a trip to meet the cutter in Bude will be required, and he is the best man to do it. Don't take your eyes off the sea. What time is it?'

'Ten minutes before one.'

At the new Custom House, Samuel Snuggs greeted the information with a raised fist. 'Good old *Vigilant*!' he cried. 'I suspect that signal marks an end to tonight's adventures. Henry, can I ask you and the inspector to hold the fort a while? I will take Gale to Bude. We need to speak to Jack Geach and examine his catch. Stay for an hour, and if all remains quiet, you can stand the men down. I will return as soon as I can – by noon, if at all possible.'

* * *

The mother of Constable Percival Poundstock, Borwenstow's lone policeman, found her son's recent fascination for planet-gazing hard to fathom, at first. As Percival had grown through boyhood into a man, the only pastime that had ever captured his interest was the sport of wrestling. Since the age of ten, it had dominated his waking hours to the exclusion of everything else. Unhealthy perhaps – certainly, some folk muttered as much – yet with this youthful fixation came rewards. For by the time the lad had turned twenty, he had become a local champion – winner of the Launceston Middleweight Cup, no less. Joining the police force had been a mere formality after that. So, when her beloved Percy, who had never shown the slightest interest in the stars or planets, started to talk of nothing else, his mother was forced to consider what had brought about this great change in him. The orbits of the spheres and the movement of miscellaneous celestial objects meant nothing to her, so why should they to him? What could have aroused her son's sudden interest? These days, he seemed to speak of practically nothing else – unless the topic concerned the scholarly Miss Eliza Chadwick...

And then, the penny dropped. Percy's newborn love of heavenly bodies was precisely that... It was all the young postmistress's doing. The girl had poisoned his mind; she had drawn him into her own well-documented passion for all things astronomical. Suddenly, the thought of losing her only son scared the older woman. She told herself she needed her son above all things. Her husband had died nearly eighteen years before, heroically drowned while trying to save another from the surf. Percy had become the centre of her life; he was all she had. How could she allow him to be taken from her?

Jemima Poundstock decided a firm hand was required. She announced to her son she wanted him to have nothing to do with Eliza. She gave only the slightest explanation too…

'She is a most unsuitable girl, Percy. I will not have her in the house. You deserve better than that flighty madam; she is far too clever for her own good. An honest country lass will find you soon enough. And you have your mother, who alone brought you into this world, to consider.'

When Percival remonstrated, his mother closed the conversation down and the young policeman was left to rue the day he'd mentioned Eliza's name. But the truth was, he'd fallen in love with the coy, bespectacled postmistress, and the more he brooded over it, the more he imagined his feelings were reciprocated. His only course was to find clandestine ways to continue their relationship. He told himself he wanted to reach a point where he was certain of their mutual affection, and then, when his mind was made up, he would tell his mama, and she would simply have to wear it. If his mother would not entertain Eliza Chadwick, he would have to do it himself, and what better than a starlit assignation to stake his claim?

It had been Eliza's idea, in truth… 'The night sky is beautiful at this time,' she had declared. 'Saturn and Jupiter are high and brilliant, and with my father's field glasses, I can see the swirling Jovian moons quite clearly. Come with me one night when it's clear,' she'd told him with a suggestive smile, 'I will show you everything…'

And so it was that Constable Percival Poundstock and Miss Eliza Chadwick found themselves alone and unwatched on the promontory above Borwenstow at midnight. And this, on the very day that secret ambushes were being planned less than a mile away along the northern coastline. Beneath the feet of the closely seated pair, the shadowy outline of the thick-walled harbour stretched out like a dormant anaconda below them, its curved jetty and the dim shape of the adjacent fish market unmistakeable in the murk. The church tower of St Piran's could be seen, prominent against the grey sky, as were several of the half-lit houses in the sleeping village. From their vantage point, on a clear day, the gabled corners of *The Gauger's Return* would have been visible, but despite the parade of stars and the faint crescent moon, it was not possible to discern their shape on that particular night. Beyond the harbour wall was the old Custom House, square, stolid and stubborn, looking for all the world like a pocket-size fortress. Percival noticed, with mild interest, the light of a candle flickering from one of its upper rooms.

Having satisfied themselves with the rings of Saturn and the glittering moons of Jupiter – whose sight through the glasses moved Percival to cry out, 'My goodness, Eliza, I could never have imagined such a thing!' – the couple had drifted into idle chatter about considerably less cosmic matters. This was the lull in conversation Percival had been waiting for. He knew he had to say something or he would burst, and he grabbed the opportunity with both hands – quite literally.

'I like you most uncommonly, Eliza!' he blurted, grasping her shoulders.

Any reservations that his love was unrequited were dismissed in an instant as she pulled him towards her and uttered, 'My love, I have been hoping for this moment for longer than I can say.' It seemed to young Percy that the heavenly bodies he'd just been gazing upon had fallen from the sky and were now dancing in his heart. He touched his lips to hers, and she kissed him back with a force he thought quite remarkable in a woman of such slim physique. He took her head in his hands, and together they slid onto the soft grass, where he kissed her again. As he caressed her forehead, his eyes were drawn to a movement from below, and then the unmistakeable sound of oars dipping in and out of water entered his ears. Disengaging for a moment from his amorous embrace, he dragged himself onto an elbow and strained to see better. It was a small boat, for sure, a lantern in the prow, rowing steadily towards the harbour wall. As he tried to make sense of what he saw, an impatient Eliza drew him playfully back towards her. He gently resisted her advances, putting a finger to his lips – they should try to keep quiet for a few moments. The arrival of a jolly boat at that early hour puzzled him, and being a policeman, he knew it was his duty to get a better look.

The craft moved deliberately, almost noiselessly, towards the quay, the only splash coming from the rhythmic pair of oars that slid unhurriedly through the flat, dark water. Constable Poundstock fumbled for Eliza's set of brass binoculars, which he found close to her now prone and inviting face. He could not resist kissing it tenderly once more before raising the glasses to his eyes. As the vessel passed directly under their bodies, he counted five seated figures. The pair working the oars he recognised instantly. They were none other than Cassius and his brother, Gabriel, of that there was no doubt. As for the remaining three... they were men, most assuredly, but... The craft tied up close to a set of stone steps and all but one alighted onto the wide harbour wall. Percival noted that the three men who trailed in Cassius's unmistakeable wake were carrying shoulder bags, each of which took some effort to lift, such was the apparent weight of their burdens. Without making a sound, Cassius led the others along the stone pier to a point where they moved out of Percival's sight, disappearing right under the cliff face. Meanwhile, Gabriel sat alone in the boat, stiffly holding both oars a few inches out of the water, as if primed to scurry back out to sea at any given moment.

Percival kissed his lady once more, this time ever more lustily. Then, with another secretive indication for her to remain still, he pushed himself forwards to get a better view. His efforts were rewarded instantly, for the sight of the four men returned to him as they reappeared from under the cliff and back into the open. He watched as the group approached the old Custom House on the southern corner of the harbour. Much to his surprise, Cassius, still at their head, appeared to open the grand front door without any knocking. Had there been a rap, Percival would have surely heard it. Then the quartet disappeared, without any ceremony or greetings from the inner sanctum, directly into the bowels of the building. Less than a minute elapsed before Cassius re-emerged from the entrance, this time alone. Retracing his steps along the jutting pier, he was soon reunited with his younger brother. Within seconds, both had cast off and were heading back out to sea. Constable Percival Poundstock frowned and stroked his chin as he watched them go. Desiring to return to his sweetheart's embraces without further ado, he decided to give the matter no more consideration; he made a mental resolution to note down the events when he arrived at the police office the next day. But for now, all he wanted was to take Eliza back into his arms.

* * *

The previous evening, Lady Kathleen Pennycrocker, forced to contemplate her next course of action, had stood alone in the stables to think things through. She had never spoken to Cassius Honey in her whole life, and the thought of it made her go weak at the knees. But her husband's drunken intransigence and the critical need to alter existing arrangements had given her no alternative. For one thing, Patrick would never forgive her if she didn't intervene. Indeed, his life may even be endangered if she refused to act… There was simply no way out. Her vulgar and blundering husband had refused to help her, so she knew she had to take matters into her own hands. She reflected how a few minutes before, while in high dudgeon and the course of storming out of Sir William's study, he had callously called out to her, 'Be careful, dearest Kate. There may be vagabonds abroad at this dark hour…'

She'd brushed off the derisive warning at the time, but as she saddled her horse, her head became filled with irrational images of night-time spectres of the sort the local fools believed haunted their so-called shrouded coast. But Her Ladyship was made of sterner stuff – more determined, in fact, than most who thought they knew her could have ever imagined. She told herself she had to be practical, logical and resolute. Lighting a lantern, she mounted her mare, and dismissing all thoughts of imaginary highway ghouls lying in wait to intercept her, she set off into the night for the two-mile journey that would take her to Doubloons and into the arms of the dreaded Honey clan.

If Cassius Honey had been surprised to see her, he didn't show it. 'You'd better come in,' he said in his practised amiable fashion on opening the front door. 'I am alone, Your Ladyship,' he bowed slightly, 'so you may speak plainly. I assume that wastrel husband of yours has sent you. He has lost his courage once more and wishes to duck out of our bargain. You are here to pass on the bad tidings… am I correct?'

'Not to abandon the contract, Mr Honey, rather to *adjust* it – slightly… Sir William wishes me to speak with you concerning some minor alterations in the details.'

'Changes of plan come at a price. I hope you have brought gold.'

'You will find us generous in that regard, and I believe the trifling amendments will be to your liking. For you shall be doing less work for more money.'

'You intrigue me, Your Ladyship.'

'The collection will take place at the location and time as arranged.'

'I'm pleased to hear it.'

'The Irish vessel – her name is *Skibbereen Princess,* by the by – will meet you close to Cow Rock tomorrow night at the appointed hour, when the tide is rising to its maximum.'

'Very well.'

'You will need just one boat and two men to row the cargo ashore. It will take you just one trip from the Cow and Calf.'

Cassius Honey returned with a sneering grunt, 'One trip, indeed! The tubs and bottles your husband has promised will take six visits to the cave, at least – maybe as many as eight. My men are standing by with a second boat to ease the load.'

'The cargo will *not* be Irish whiskey tomorrow, Mr Honey. It will be men – four men, to be precise.'

'Men!' Cassius Honey cried.

'You brought in men the last time, did you not?'

'But with them came whiskey – a great load too. Where's the profit in just men?'

'We shall be the judge of that. I have an extra 250 pounds in gold and the assurance from my husband that the whiskey trade will continue, once this work is done.' Lady Kathleen knew she was making promises she could not keep, but she told herself she had no alternative. *This man Honey has to agree!*

'One trip, you say?'

'Precisely. You shall have no need for the second boat,

nor its crew. The delivery should take you less than an hour. There will be more of this gold to share between you and your brother.' She dropped a bulging silk purse onto the table. 'One hundred gold sovereigns, sir – split them as you will. The remaining 150 will follow, when the delivery is complete.'

'And the whiskey? We have customers aplenty.'

'They can wait. There will be two cases of *Carrells* for your personal use. In that way, you may sweeten your tea...'

Cassius Honey laughed out loud, and this time, the mocking tone had disappeared. 'Is there anything else I should know, madam? These *men*... tell me, who are they?'

'That is not your concern, sir.' Before Honey could protest, she added quickly, 'There is another detail. You will not be using Shrouded Cove to deliver the cargo. We have reason to believe it is being watched. Your job will be to bring our passengers directly into Borwenstow. I shall be waiting at the old Custom House to greet them. Bring them to me. I shall have the second payment ready. What could be simpler?'

'You say Shrouded Cove is being watched?'

'I believe so. You must understand that by visiting you tonight, I have come to warn you also. This is a lucky day for you, indeed. For you shall have more money than originally agreed for less work to perform *and* the benefit of all my intelligence. Fear not, Borwenstow harbour will be the safest place along this coastline tomorrow night. Snuggs and his revenue fools will be occupied elsewhere.'

'And the cave tunnel? We have worked hard to clear it.'

'You have been well rewarded already, and the tunnel may be used for future consignments once the coast is clear. My guess is the Revenue will close their offices hereabouts soon enough, and then it will become open season once more.'

'And what of these mystery men? Are they your friends?' Cassius persisted.

She gave him a lethal look. 'Mr Honey, do you agree to our new contract, or do I have to find another to bring these few men ashore?'

He replied at length, his voice firm and businesslike. 'I do, madam. If it pleases Your Ladyship, I shall collect your cargo from the *Skibbereen Princess* at Cow Rock tomorrow night and bring the whole damned baggage directly to your doorstep at the old Custom House.'

* * *

The sun had crept above the eastern trees by the time Samuel Snuggs and Wilfred Gale arrived at the docks in Bude, where Her Majesty's Revenue Cutter *Vigilant* lay at her moorings. Tied up alongside, trapped between the cutter and the jetty, was another, slightly smaller, twin-masted ketch, on which the inscription *Skibbereen Princess* was proudly borne. Commander Jack Geach greeted his old friend with a flashing smile and an invitation to come aboard.

'My, what fun we had last night, Sam!'

'Bravo, Jack!' exclaimed Snuggs. 'You have seized our Irish mother ship, by the look of things. We had no contact with the shore party at all last night, so nothing was landed, as far as we could see. I hope your prize was fully loaded, as we hoped.'

'A case of *Carrells* whiskey. That's all, I'm afraid.'

'A single case?'

'I agree, not much to show for a night's work, but there is more to it than that. It's possible I may have captured a better prize after all.'

'Tell me, Jack...' Samuel Snuggs said with a slump of his shoulders.

'We have detained a stranger – a very sick one, at that. A mystery man, a young fellow who refuses to tell me the truth about his purpose on board. He is certainly not a sailor. A most unseaworthy fellow, I should say. A landlubber indeed.'

'Who is this mystery man then, if not a member of the crew?'

'There's the rub… He gives his name as Sean O'Connor. He says he's a deckhand, all the way from Dublin. But the fellow is a liar. His hands are soft; he dresses like a junior clerk – a minor official, at best. And to top it, he carries a prescription for tonic wine and lithium from a Cork physician in the patient's name of Michael Hennessey, born 6 September, 1859. The age fits; our man is less than twenty-five years old, I'll warrant. Hennessey must be his true name, unless I'm very much mistaken.'

'Lithium?'

'I believe it is a metal substance consumed to treat insanity.'

'And what of the other crew? What do they have to say?'

'Very little. Believe me, we have done our best to prise out the truth. The captain is a drunken madman by the name of Whelan O'Brien. He just screams back at us when we challenge him. His coxswain must be a mute, for all I know. He has refused to utter a single word – all we get from him are sulky looks and white knuckles. Just Murphy, the young boatswain, has spoken to us, and then only when we brought him ashore and plied him with brandy. He says he thought he was on a trip to deliver linen to Swansea. He is lying, of course. Of Hennessey, our mystery man, he told me the fellow was a passenger who joined the boat in Cork two days ago. There were three others with him, who disembarked last night into an open boat, just before we intercepted the *Skibbereen Princess*. He didn't know their names, and the descriptions he has given are of the vaguest: very young men – dark-haired, middling stature, downy complexion – save for one – an older cove who might have been their leader, a fellow in his mid to late-forties. According to young Murphy, our unknown "clerk", the fellow I'll call Hennessey, became seasick from the moment they left port and remained so for the whole voyage. In the end, so ill was he, the fellow was unable to disembark with the others and opted to be taken back to Ireland.'

'Does he have any other papers, bar the prescription?'

'Nothing... The absence of documents speaks volumes of a man's desire to remain anonymous. I suspect the medical prescription was an oversight on his part. It was found lodged deep in his top pocket. There is more... One of my crew saw a man answering Hennessey's description throw a bag into the sea just before we boarded. My guess, it was our clerk destroying the evidence.'

'Evidence of what? What was he trying to hide?'

'It certainly wasn't whiskey,' Geach replied with a chortle. 'But something smells. I have a nose for it. We are still rummaging the ship. Trust me, Samuel, we shall find something to incriminate them before the day is out.'

'And the bag that went overboard?'

'I am casting off in an hour. With providence, it will float, and we may still recover it close to the Cow and Calf. The tide was still rising when they surrendered, and we were very close in to the beach. There is a good chance the sack has gone aground on the rocks. If it's there, we shall find it.'

'Hennessey, you say... I know that name from somewhere,' Snuggs muttered.

'It's a common enough name in Ireland,' Geach replied. 'My talk of "tongue-loosening brandy" may have stirred something up in you, too,' he laughed.

'Beg pardon, sir...' It was the taciturn Wilfred Gale who spoke next. 'You told me once that your wife spoke of the cook at Pennycrocker Hall in such terms. Is her name not Hennessey also?'

Chapter Twenty-Eight

Henry Gough waited with Inspector Austol Halwill Barton until they'd heard the second peal from the market square tower. Only then did they release the others from their call to duty. The Custom House contingent of revenue officers and policemen had fallen into a moody silence during the previous three hours – some men sleeping fitfully wherever they could lay their heads, others fidgeting with their weapons. When news of their emancipation arrived, it was greeted with desultory groans – a show of displeasure for yet another night wasted.

'Cooped up like hungry chickens, we are,' Officer West muttered when out of Henry's hearing, 'just pecking around for a delivery of imaginary millet.'

As Halwill Barton briefed his policemen in one corner of the meeting room, Henry Gough took the troop of revenue officers to another. 'Before you stumble back to your wives and children,' he told them, 'Mr Snuggs has ordered that you all return here by ten o'clock. His guess is there will be much work to be done. Your master will bring word from Bude soon enough and, God willing, we will know our consignment has been intercepted. Then you will have some local calls to make.

Bring your best rummaging skills, for I believe we shall need them.'

Once all had shuffled away, and the three police constables had returned upstairs to their makeshift cots, Gough took Halwill outside for a smoke. The tranquillity of the slumbering village felt strangely overpowering as each lit pipes and settled to watch their circling fumes waft into the balmy night. Henry wanted to offer up a little speech of encouragement but couldn't find the right words. It had been another long evening and perhaps enough had been said already... Clearly, Halwill felt the same, for he made no effort to commence a dialogue either.

As the pair gazed aimlessly down the lane, which ran past the front entrance of the Custom House, a noise of approaching footsteps could be heard coming across the cobbles from the general direction of the post office. Instinctively, both men drew back into the shadows and waited.

'Goodness, it's young Poundstock,' whispered Inspector Halwill as the figure approached on the other side of the road. 'What on earth is he doing at this hour?'

'His wanderings will be coupled to the lovely Miss Chadwick, I'll warrant,' Henry chuckled back.

'Maybe, maybe not... Whatever his purpose, there is only one way to find out.' Before Henry could answer, Halwill burst from their nook and cried out, 'Constable! May I have a word?'

The unexpected voice from the darkness clearly surprised the young man, for he visibly jumped and halted in his tracks almost immediately. Poundstock peered across the road, obviously confused, trying his best to locate the author of the summons. He half wondered if it might be an agent of his mother's, come to spy on him.

'It's Inspector Halwill. Come over. Join us, if you please.'

'Inspector...' Poundstock repeated hesitantly. 'Oh, and Mr Gough...' he said on observing Henry lurking in the shadows.

He touched his hat and approached them. 'How good it is to see you both.'

Halwill did not beat about the bush. 'What are you up to, young man? It's very late to be conducting a patrol – and with no uniform, either.'

There was no reason to perjure himself, but Percival Poundstock found himself wavering.

'Speak up, man. We will not bite!'

'I was visiting my sweetheart, sir.'

'At this hour?'

'Yes, Miss Chadwick... You see, she wanted to show me the planet Jupiter. Look, sir, you can observe it from here.' Poundstock pointed almost directly upwards.

'Jupiter?' Halwill craned his neck.

'Yes, sir, and its four moons. We have just returned from the headland. From there, the night sky is even more impressive.'

'You'll struggle to see the moons of Jupiter, Poundstock,' Henry offered. 'By Jove, even Signor Galileo could not spot them without a telescope.'

'But Eliza had one, you see! Her father's field glasses were sufficient, as long as we had a steady hand.'

'For how long were you watching the stars, Constable?'

Poundstock began to look shifty, as if he was about to tell a lie. 'Well, err, it has been a lovely night, sir. There was Saturn too...'

'I'm sure it must have been most enlivening for you both...' It was clear Halwill wanted an answer to his question.

'About an hour... maybe more...' Poundstock replied at length.

Henry could not suppress a chuckle. 'Did you see any others up there engaged in this "stargazing"?'

'Well, sir... actually, yes. There *were* others. But not with us, you understand, for we were all alone.'

'How do you mean, "others"?'

'In an open boat. Five men, in all. The two Honey brothers were amongst them.'

The self-indulgent expressions and childish grins that had characterised Halwill's and Gough's faces for the last few minutes were wiped away in an instant. Suddenly, there was a flurry of questions from both men – so many, in fact, Constable Poundstock was forced to raise his hands in surrender.

'You had better come inside,' Henry suggested in an effort to end the confusion. 'You can tell us all over a cup of whiskey.'

* * *

'Have I got news for you, Samuel!' Henry exclaimed as his son-in-law dismounted his horse at the rear of the Custom House later that morning.

'If it tops my own, I shall offer you a gold sovereign,' came the cheerful reply. 'I have had a most profitable conversation in Bude, and I shall need your help, Henry. You and Mr Woodward have contacts in the War Office, I understand. I would like them to check their files. It appears *Vigilant* has indeed captured a prize, and I have a hunch your friends in London will be most interested.'

Together with Inspector Halwill and Jacob Jarvie, who had lately returned looking somewhat dishevelled from his clifftop vigil, the quartet convened to discuss the momentous events of the previous night. It was not long before they agreed they required a new plan of action.

Immediately on hearing the news that the old Custom House had received a trio of night-time visitors, Halwill had taken steps to control the situation. He'd woken his sleeping men and dispatched them to watch over the building until reinforcements arrived. By ten o'clock, there had been no reported movements or sightings, and Snuggs was able to deploy his freshly arrived officers in support. Between them, they were tasked to guard every entrance and departure point of the old Custom House, thus preventing any escape by the nocturnal interlopers.

'This is a mystery indeed,' Snuggs summed up. 'Who are these strange fellows who go to such lengths to be brought secretly ashore in the dead of night?'

'They must be connected to your mysterious Irishman, I'll be bound – this fellow Hennessey,' Henry observed.

'There is only one way to find out,' Jarvie cried. 'We must knock on the door of the old Custom House and ask them directly!'

'I've telegraphed Nathaniel Hope at the War Office, as you asked,' Henry offered. 'I've supplied him the names of the men you've captured in Bude. We should know soon enough if any has come to their attention.'

'Jack Geach and his cutter crew are searching the Cow and Calf for the abandoned bag as we speak,' Samuel replied. 'He says he will bring *Vigilant* into Borwenstow when he has any news.'

'That's all well and good, sir, but these initiatives may take hours to resolve – maybe days. I say we strike now!' Jacob exclaimed. 'I have a hunch these fellows could be dangerous. Now they lie like rats in a trap. We cannot let them escape. We should move before they do.' Jarvie was clearly in the mood for immediate action.

'Do we all agree?' Samuel asked. 'Mr Jarvie's call to arms has merit, I believe.' All, save Halwill, nodded in harmony, and the group turned their heads as one to look at the police inspector. At length Snuggs said, 'Halwill, what say you?'

'This is not my kind of enquiry,' the detective replied in low tones. 'I am here to investigate two murders. The art of capturing smugglers remains in your bailiwick, gentlemen, so I will happily submit to your judgement. If you believe we should strike quickly, so be it. But Mr Jarvie has also implied a degree of menace, and I am forced to concur. There is something here that nags. These could indeed be ruthless men. Have you not noticed how a connection to all things Irish keeps repeating itself? If it's not Irish whiskey, then it's Irish boats, Irish sailors and Irish men. Indeed, Lady Pennycrocker is originally from Cork, as is her cook.'

'Not to mention the enigmatic Mr Wilks,' Jarvie added, nodding vigorously.

'This affair,' Halwill continued, 'could be something far more sinister than mere whiskey smuggling – more disturbing than my simple murders, even… I will say no more until proof arrives, save to add that if we *do* decide to move on them now, we should be on our guard and be prepared for a fight, if necessary.'

'Very well,' Snuggs answered after a moment's contemplation. 'We *will* pay our unwelcome visitors a call and do it *now*! Spread the news and ensure the inspector's wise words of caution are heeded by all. Despite our want of sleep, I'm confident we have sufficient mettle to take this forward. And sheer adrenaline will account for any lacking vigour! Are you all with me, men?'

'We are!' came the bellowed reply.

As the others dispersed, Samuel Snuggs reached into his pocket and pulled out a gold coin, which he handed to his father-in-law. 'Your reward, sir. Your intelligence has indeed topped mine, sir. The sighting of unknown visitors to the old Custom House has turned this matter on its head. I was never much one for gaming or cards, sir – though Three-Stake Brag was once my favourite. Had we been playing, I fear my prial of kings would have been trumped by your three aces! And let me tell you… I could not be happier for it!'

'Thank you, Samuel. I'm content to accept your payment. Let that be a lesson not to make rash wagers in future!' Henry wagged his finger. Then, turning to the inspector, he said, 'I owe you ten shillings, Halwill. Ours was a joint effort!'

Their plan was simple. The target was now the old Custom House. Samuel was familiar with every inch of the place – every nook, every entrance and passageway, every hidey-hole and every room. From his many hours spent jerquing manifests and gauging barrels within its thick walls, his knowledge of its structure and fabric was unmatched.

He also knew of a way to get inside unseen...

Three years before, when it had been his unpleasant task to transfer ownership of the historic building to Sir William Pennycrocker, Samuel had the foresight to withhold a bunch of keys. Quite *why* he'd done it, he couldn't explain, at the time. Maybe it had been his fondness for the place, a nostalgia borne out of his and his ancestors' many years tramping the passages and oak-panelled rooms that had prompted him. The ancient set of keys had no value in monetary terms, he knew that, but their worth to him was priceless. When, from time to time, he came across the clanking bundle at the back of his bureau, he would slowly turn them around in his hands, wistfully remembering each door and cupboard they opened. Images of his father would come to him, seated on a tall chair under a high window, quill pen in hand, counting pennies and shillings while entering the details into a dark archaic ledger.

When all had reassembled, Samuel Snuggs addressed them.

'Our moment has come, and we must seize it with courage. We must bring an end to this affair once and for all. At five minutes before eleven, I shall take two of my men, armed at the ready, and we will gain covert access to the Custom House via its rear door. I have the writ of assistance, and I have the keys, so our entrance will be a silent one. With luck, we shall surprise them before they have a chance to put up any resistance or destroy evidence. The remainder of you must assemble outside, conceal yourselves as best you can, and wait for the clock to strike the hour. Then, at eleven precisely, you will enter by the front.' Samuel handed the main door key to Officer Gale. 'If at any time before the appointed hour you hear a hullaballoo from within, come to our aid immediately, and we can let battle commence. Once we have secured the building, the search will begin in earnest. I want all the rooms thoroughly examined, every inch of every cubby-hole. Do you understand? Rip up the boards. I want the place rummaged from head to toe.' Samuel turned to his father-in-law. 'Henry, will you join me in the forward group?'

'I will bring my revolver,' came the immediate reply.

At precisely ten minutes before eleven, Snuggs, Gough, West and Wendholt let themselves out of the new Custom House for the short walk to the old. There was rain hanging in the air, but none fell to dampen their progress. By five minutes to eleven, Samuel had navigated his little squad around the back of the stout building, and they were facing its single rear entrance. Squeezing the key into the familiar lock, he could not help but hold his breath – *What if the locks had been changed?* Much to his relief, the well-oiled mechanism turned effortlessly between his fingers, and the old oak door swung open with just the slightest protest from its bone-dry hinges. He knew this route would lead them directly into the old Queen's Warehouse.

'West, stay here and guard the door,' he whispered. 'Wendholt, come with us. I want to search upstairs first. My guess is that's where we'll find our visitors, and I want to surprise them. We have less than five minutes before the others descend on us.' He spoke next to his father-in-law. 'Henry, withdraw your revolver and follow me...'

Samuel had expected to find the interior of his old workplace much changed. They moved quietly out of the old Queen's Warehouse and through the maze of sundry other storerooms into the main building, and he was surprised to see that very little had altered. The hall, which had once served as the Long Room, remained almost exactly as before. As they began to creep upwards, he noticed the wooden treads of the old, curved staircase were now enveloped in a rich burgundy carpet. Samuel rejoiced in the fact, as it made their stealthy approach all the easier to disguise. But apart from the comfortable rugs strewn here and there and expensive drapes that adorned the walls and windows, all seemed much as before.

As they mounted the staircase, both he and Henry were struck by the complete absence of any noise. Though it was late morning, neither could detect a single sound that came from within. It was as if the whole building was enveloped in aspic. Either that, or it was empty – void of any life. Samuel brought his party to a halt at the top of the stairs. Here, two narrow yet well-lit passageways led away on either side towards eight tightly closed doors, four on each side of the building. Samuel knew that half of the entrances protected rooms that faced the open sea, the nearby harbour and St Piran's tower, while the others overlooked the market square, assorted village dwellings and open fields beyond. During the early hours that day, Constable Poundstock had described a candlelit room at the top of the old Custom House. Samuel suspected this must be the double-aspect chamber at the far northern end that overlooked both the harbour and the church. Samuel knew this particular room better than any, for not only was it the largest on the first floor but it had once been his own office.

He started to move towards it. Turning briefly to Wendholt, he indicated silently for the officer to cock his rifle and position himself as a blocking force on the landing. Samuel's fingers began to tighten on his revolver and, as if walking on plovers' shells, with Henry Gough in line astern, the two approached the door. As lightly as he could manage, he turned the handle. There was no resistance, and the door pushed open smoothly. The market square bell started to strike…

At the moment of their stepping into the chamber, muffled noises could be heard from downstairs, which meant only one thing – Jarvie and the others had gained entrance below and were now in the building with them.

Samuel gazed into the relative gloom, trying to make sense of the unfamiliar scene. The heavy drapes obscured any useful sunlight, which made his task all the more testing. Then, his body recoiled slightly. The emerging sight of his old study, now adapted into what appeared to be a luxurious bedroom, complete with four-poster bed and dainty furnishings, made his heart sink. *This must be the marital suite,* he thought. After a few seconds of inching forwards, with every sinew straining to detect some movement, he realised he needed to see better and took a decisive step towards the curtains. But Henry Gough had beaten him to the punch and was already holding the tassels. There was a sudden whoosh of costly fabric, and the room was promptly bathed in the dull light of an overcast May morning. They soon grasped they were not alone…

The bed was occupied – not by one, but *two* gently stirring bodies. The nearest was a woman, dressed only in a thin cotton nightdress. Henry recognised her instantly. It was Lady Kathleen Pennycrocker. Next to her lay a naked man who, clearly confused, was struggling to rouse himself.

'What on earth…?' Lady Pennycrocker gaped, fixing her bleary eyes on the intruders that towered over her bed.

'I have a writ, madam.'

'Get out of my house!' she screamed. 'Patrick, tell them!'

Henry moved quickly around the bed to confront the awakening man. Pointing his revolver towards the bared chest and with disarming self-assurance, he said quietly, 'Please stay where you are, sir – for the present, at least... This is Senior Officer Snuggs. He is in the service of Her Majesty's Revenue. Please listen to what he has to say.'

Samuel obliged in an instant. 'By the power of Queen Victoria, I have a legal writ to search this house. My men are at their work as we speak.'

'But—' said the man, scratching his eyes.

'And, who are *you*, sir?' Samuel enquired abruptly. 'You are certainly not Sir William, that is plain enough...'

'This is all very embarrassing...' the man replied. That was when Samuel recognised him. It was the appealing lilt in his voice.

'You are Mr Patrick Wilks, are you not, sir – the butler at Pennycrocker Hall?'

'You have discovered me, Officer,' Wilks returned with a scathing smile, 'and in most awkward circumstances, it must be said... But whatever you may imagine concerning my liaison with Her Ladyship, it does not give you the right to burst into her house and point guns at us.'

'I am on Queen's business, sir. Please get out of bed and get dressed. I will have some questions for you once my search is complete.' On a shout from Snuggs, Officer Wendholt hurried in from the landing. 'Wendholt, keep guard on this man. Allow him to dress and hold him here.'

'If I am not mistaken, Officer Snuggs,' Wilks called out as he pulled a shirt over his shoulders, 'you have a writ of assistance to search for uncustomed goods. I believe that is the expression, isn't it – "uncustomed *goods*"? You must know such a legal instrument does not apply to the detention of people, whatever their blighted circumstances. The law is very clear on the matter. You are acting illegally, sir!'

'Put Mr Wilks in irons, Wendholt!' Snuggs cried. 'I will deal with him later.'

Wendholt did exactly as ordered – hastily and none too sweetly, either. Once the grumbling Wilks had been secured, Henry, relieved from his duty of shielding the man, found a silk dressing gown and offered it to Lady Pennycrocker. Chalk white and visibly shaking, she could not look him in the eye as she took it from him. The feisty contempt had been sapped out of her slim frame in a few short moments.

Just then, a shout went up from outside, and Officer Nat Copplestone came running in. 'We have them, sir,' he said breathlessly. 'Two of 'em – just boys, in truth – hiding in the closet of one of the back bedrooms. And they must have brought heavy bags with them, sir. We found three lying in the old QW. They're packed to the brim. You had best come and see for yourself, sir.'

Samuel Snuggs knew what contraband was. Despite his fairly modest years in the service of the Crown, he'd measured countless tubs of captured brandy in assorted Queen's Warehouses. He'd seized hundreds of cases of stacked-high port from the insides of abandoned barns. He'd trundled a myriad of barrels of detained rum along the rocky edges of lonely beaches and had uncovered bales of tobacco hidden under the deck planks of three-masted schooners. But never in his life had he seen anything like this before. At first, the stiff brown parcels of waxed paper gave him little idea what they might contain.

'How many of these packages have you found, Copplestone?'

'There are six, in all. There were two parcels in each bag.'

'What are they? It's certainly not tobacco.'

It was Henry Gough who was able to venture a theory. 'I have seen this kind of thing before – back in seventy-nine, when Russian anarchists were running amok in London... If I'm not misguided, Samuel, these parcels contain sticks of dynamite.'

Snuggs ordered the first to be unwrapped, and it took just a few seconds of artful cutting for Henry's speculation to be proved correct. Tumbling out of the box like a cascade of great fat cigars came twenty tubes sealed with waxed paper. Each was about an inch in diameter and twelve inches in length. They were marked with the inscription *Nobels Extradynamit, Stockholm.*

'Great Scott, what do we have here?' Samuel exclaimed, taking an instinctive step backwards.

'Unless you have any better suggestions, gentlemen,' Henry ventured, 'I suggest we have uncovered a nest of Fenians.'

'And with their hideous cargo, by the look of things... If my arithmetic is correct, we must have 120 sticks! Are they dangerous to touch?'

'Not if we are careful,' Henry soothed. 'But we must remove them to a place of safety, and at all costs, we must refrain from smoking. A naked flame might blow us all to kingdom come.'

Snuggs gave Nat Copplestone orders to remove the parcels to a dry corner of the old Queen's Warehouse. In less than five minutes, the officer returned to greet the stunned assembly with something clutched in his hands. 'I thought you might like to see what I have found, sir.' Copplestone handed his master a brown bundle of torn waxed paper. 'There is plenty more on the cellar floor, sir.'

It was Jarvie who spoke next. 'By the blazes, this cannot be their first trip... The discarded paper is proof of a previous consignment. Look, they even bear the same marks.'

Henry took it on himself to reply for all of them. 'We may have the wrappings, gentlemen, and the evidence of foul play, but where in God's name are the sticks of dynamite these scraps once enfolded?'

Chapter Twenty-Nine

Samuel Snuggs knew he had to act fast. The trail was still fresh, and there was much to do. The interrogation of Patrick Wilks, Lady Kathleen Pennycrocker and the pair of young Irish intruders would have to wait until he'd gathered as much evidence as possible. Now he needed facts to beat them with. He gave instructions for the prisoners to be separated and held apart within the old Custom House lock-ups. There were many such rooms in the basement which, like the rest of the building, had remained largely intact, bolts and all, since its sale.

Such was Lady Pennycrocker's hysterical state of mind, Mrs Polrunny was called in to sit with her. It was vital Her Ladyship did not harm herself before her interrogators arrived.

'We must speak to Sir William and find his cook – that woman Hennessey,' Samuel told Henry. 'They will have much light to shed on this matter. I'm certain of it.' Leaving Jacob Jarvie and three of his men to continue their search and guard the captives under lock and key, he and the others mounted horses and made straightaway for Pennycrocker Hall.

A surprised-looking Michael Heath was there to greet them when the breathless party arrived. 'Take me to Sir

William,' Snuggs announced, 'and then go with the inspector and his men. Mr Halwill wishes to speak to Mrs Hennessey.'

'But Sir William has asked not to be disturbed. He has business—'

'Take us to him this instant. I have a Crown writ. Sir William's business this morning will be with one of Her Majesty's commissioned officers.'

'You will find him in his study. He has been there all morning.' A distinctly apprehensive-looking Heath pointed along the western passageway. 'It's the second door on the right.'

'Come, Henry, you must be at my side.'

Seconds later, the pair, accompanied by Wilfred Gale, having sped to the study entrance, found the door locked tight from the inside. Samuel rapped smartly on the polished wood. 'Sir William, this is Officer Snuggs from the Revenue. We wish to speak to you. It is a matter of the utmost urgency. Please open the door and let us enter.' They craned their heads for a reply. Samuel rapped again, this time louder and with the handle of his riding crop. 'Open the door, Sir William. Your wife has been arrested. We need to talk with you.'

This seemed to prompt some action from within, for suddenly there was the sound of movement… 'I saw your advance from my window, Snuggs,' the distinctive vowels of Sir William could be heard yelling from inside, 'but you are all too late!'

'Open the door, sir!'

The unmistakeable crack of a revolver blast confused Samuel, at first. His initial reaction was to turn towards Henry in case his friend had inadvertently discharged his own weapon… But then, it was rapidly clear to all what had occurred. All three leant their weight to the door, and after a series of hefty collisions, the hinges gave way, and it tumbled open. Through the dust, the bright afternoon sun flooded into the dim corridor.

Stretched over the bureau, with arms spread out like a great spatchcock turkey, lay the bloodied body of Sir William Pennycrocker. The corpse was instantly recognisable, though the head had been all but blown apart. The crown and hair were completely missing. Only the still gawking eyes, hooked nose and blackened mouth remained to show who had once lain beneath. Clutched in one hand was a single sheet of paper. In the other, hanging limply from the tip of his index finger, was the Webley pistol that had blasted him into eternity.

'He's shot himself in the mouth,' Gale observed in his typical deadpan way.

Henry prised the document from the clenched fist and peered at it. 'My God, it's a confession, by the look of things,' he murmured as he released a mouthful of pent-up air through pursed lips.

'Does he admit to the smuggling?' Samuel asked.

'I'm not sure… it's just a few lines, but I can't see anything about whiskey or free trading. He says he was the one who killed Ignatius Honey, and he wishes to be forgiven for it… murdered to protect his sister, apparently.'

'Is that all? Is there nothing about his wife? Nothing about the Irishmen?'

'Nothing. See for yourself!' Henry handed him the paper.

After a brief inspection, Snuggs put the suicide note in his pocket and shook his head. 'Come, Henry, we can do nothing more. I want to hear what Mrs Hennessey has to say for herself.' He turned to his second-in-command. 'Gale, stay with the body and search the study as best you can. I will get the footman to send for Dr Plymswood.'

By the time the two of them had made their way to the kitchen, the place was already in a state of high dudgeon. A flour-dusted Colleen Hennessey had been kneading dough when Inspector Halwill and his men marched into her domain, and it had taken a good while and a lot of waving arms to calm her down. The distant gunshot from the direction of the study had not helped to ease her foul mood either. The whole kitchen was in uproar.

'You have no right!' the cook screamed repeatedly at the hapless Halwill. 'You have no right to burst in here, you and your damnable monkeys... Sir William will clap you all in irons for it!'

'Sir William is *dead*, Mrs Hennessey!' interjected Snuggs shortly after entering, his voice rising above the melee. On seeing her indignant reaction, he added for good measure, 'And your son will die too, unless you steady yourself, madam, and tell us the truth of the matter.' Samuel had no firm proof that the Irishman captured in Bude was the cook's son, save for the remark made days earlier by Elizabeth, which had lodged in the back of his mind. His warning to the cook, however, seemed to strike home instantly, as the screaming woman was suddenly lost for words. Samuel persisted. 'Your son is the one clapped in irons, madam, and he does not look well on it! He's in custody aboard one of Her Majesty's revenue cutters in Bude.'

'My son?'

'Your very own son... Michael...' Samuel was gambling again.

'You have *my* Michael...?' Colleen Hennessey replied softly. In a matter of seconds, she had become a changed woman – open-mouthed and incredulous, all the hot air taken out in an instant. 'May the saints be forgiven...' she frowned back. 'How could they let that happen?'

'Maybe it was St Daniel who led their number!' replied Samuel with a sarcastic gleam in his eye. He then leant towards the somewhat bewildered-looking inspector and whispered, 'Halwill, I suggest you clear your men out of here. Take the rest away, too. Sir William has killed himself. Your expert hand is required in the study. You will need to call for Dr Plymswood. Then I suggest you and your men search the Hall and question the other staff. With your approval, Mr Gough and I would like to have a quiet word alone with this lady. Her son's arrest by our man Geach may work well for us. It may loosen her tongue, if we speak nicely to her… but alone. If she divulges anything about your murders, I shall call for you directly.'

Inspector Austol Halwill Barton nodded his instant approval; he did not need any persuading. The thought of interrogating such a shrieking woman was too terrible to contemplate, and anyhow, he knew his way around dead bodies better than most. The kitchen was cleared of all in less than a minute, save for the continuously sobbing Colleen Hennessey and her two inquisitors.

'Time is short, Mrs Hennessey. I will speak plainly.' Samuel Snuggs addressed her in a voice of the utmost sincerity. 'I came from your son this morning. He is not a well man – sick from his voyage across the sea from Cork. He will recover soon enough, but whether he will escape the noose on a charge of sedition is another matter. It is in your power to save him – and to save yourself, if truth be told… You see, I have proof of your own involvement in this matter. If you answer my questions truthfully, there may be hope for you yet – and for your boy, who lies in the brig, spilling his guts into the bilges.'

'My boy…' Hennessey moaned. 'He is just a wee man and would not hurt a fly.'

'Then tell me, how did he fall into the clutches of Patrick Wilks, for it is Wilks who has clearly led him astray, has he not?'

'Where is Wilks?' She looked at him uneasily.

'You have no fear on that account. He is safe in our custody. We captured him this morning, with Her Ladyship.'

'Her Ladyship!' Hennessey spat out the name in the manner of one trying to dislodge a piece of gristle from a troublesome tooth. 'I told Patrick all along she would be his downfall. Until he started warming her bed, all had been well with Sir William. We held him in our sway.'

'*Our* sway? Mrs Hennessey... surely you mean *his* sway.' Samuel tilted his head to one side and offered a look of affected reassurance. 'After all, you and your son had nothing to do with this, did you...? This was all Mr Wilks's doing, was it not?'

The cook blinked and pressed her floured, fat hands onto her apron. 'Well, yes, of course, if that's what you say...' she mumbled back at length.

'Then you must tell us all,' he said with the most benign smile he could muster. 'Start at the beginning. Mr Gough will make us all some tea while we chat, won't you, Henry?'

It did not take many minutes after a pot of Assam had been brewed before Colleen Hennessey's story started to pour out faster than the tea itself.

'It all started with Ignatius Honey!' she exclaimed. 'When he began to court Miss Rose, we all knew of it, you know. I think all of Borwenstow knew of it, save for Sir William. You must understand Sir William is very protective of his sister... and a proud man, too. He can fly into terrible rages.'

'He *was*... Mrs Hennessey. May I remind you, Sir William has taken his own life. I have his last confession. He killed Ignatius, did he not?'

'He did, sir,' she nodded vigorously. 'And what a stir it created! Sir William shot him between the eyes when he came to ask for Rose's hand. He must have flown into a rage at the young man's impudence. That's when Patrick saw his chance.'

'His chance?'

'Yes. Patrick offered to take the body away and clear things up. But first, Sir William had to agree to help with his plan.'

'His plan?'

'You see, Mr Patrick Wilks and I go back a long way; we virtually grew up together in Cork. We had been in service with Her Ladyship's family for more than ten years. Patrick had held a candle for that woman for as long as I can remember, even though he was already a married man with his own babies. I warned him not to deceive himself – not to rise above his station – and now look where it's got him. When Lady Kathleen became betrothed to Sir William, she wanted us to join her here in England. I think it was Patrick who put her up to it – put the idea into her head. *My* employment was merely to make the arrangement look like a business one, when all along it was his infatuation at the root of it. So, it was agreed the both of us should accompany Her Ladyship to Cornwall and enter service here.'

'And Sir William, did he not have a voice in the decision?'

'Oh, he was so desperate to seal the knot, he'd have agreed to anything. She was a desirable woman, you know – still is… "the loveliest in the whole county", many said, and the old man fell for her. Slavering, he was…'

'And Lady Kathleen – was she in love too?'

'What a question!' Hennessey laughed. 'Of course not!' she shrieked. 'Not with Sir William at least, but he was rich – 'tis the age-old story – a match made in hell between Mr Lust and Madame Lucre. Her father pressed her too, for he was near bankrupt at the time. Sir William fixed it all – he even sacked his existing staff in favour of us. You can imagine the fuss *that* caused…'

'Very well, pray continue. I want to hear about the plan you speak of.'

'Patrick had no guilt about leaving his wife and babes. I told him it was wicked, but he said he would visit them whenever he could and send his wages to keep them in shoe leather.'

'And you?'

'My husband had died years before, and I was never going be married again, even if I'd desired it… I had no living parents, just my poor wee boy…' She started to weep again – this time, in a most affected way.

'How could you leave him then, if he was so important to you?' Henry asked plainly.

Colleen Hennessey's tears dried in an instant. She glared back over her handkerchief. 'Because, sir, the position here as cook and the money Lady Kathleen offered made it an easy decision for me. I sent money to Michael every month; he went to proper school as a result, and has even visited from time to time.'

Samuel changed the subject. 'I don't wish to be indelicate, Mrs Hennessey, but do you know if Mr Wilks and Lady Kathleen had been lovers at that time, back in Ireland?'

'Ha! You must be jesting, sir! Of course they were – Patrick was into her skirts whenever he could manage it. He bragged to me about it! It was sickening to hear, of course… but I pretended to sound interested…' Mrs Hennessey cleared her throat in a culpable manner the others found most revealing. 'When in drink,' she continued, after glancing at them as if seeking their approval, 'Patrick would talk of nothing else but their embraces – her sweet lips, her soft skin and lustrous hair, her—'

'We have the picture, madam…'

'Why, he told me once she'd even declared her own love for him!' the cook cried.

'And then?'

'Their romance, as it existed in Ireland, did not last for long in Cornwall. In fact, it ceased the day we arrived here. It was Lady Kathleen who ended the affair – she must have felt some guilt for her transgressions and wanted to redeem herself. Shortly after, the babies started to come, and then she only had eyes for her little ones. Patrick tried his best to win her back, but she would have none of it, and this made him morose and all the angrier to see how a wealthy man could take his sweetheart from him. He felt misused – he'd come all this way, just to be put in his place. But he refused to blame Her Ladyship for his woes. I think he truly loved her and hoped she would return to him one day. But matters only got worse with the birth of each child. That was when Patrick started to think of ways to exact revenge on the "Bastard English".' The cook halted for a moment and put her hands up. 'They were his words, not mine… please excuse me, sirs…'

'We are used to it,' Henry smiled. 'But now we need to hear of this "plan" you have talked of. What was it, madam?'

'You see, Mr Wilks fell into ever darker moods,' she went on, 'and the drink made him spiteful. When Sir William warned him about his drunkenness, Patrick took it very badly. He started to resent the English race for everything – and not just for his *own* troubles, either. He became interested in politics – he talked of nothing else – and turned his anger against the power of England over Ireland. That's when he started talking to the Fenians…'

'So, it *is* the Fenians who are behind all this.' Samuel turned to Henry Gough and nodded. 'We thought as much.'

'Please believe me, I had nothing to do with it,' Mrs Hennessey blurted. 'I just passed messages from Patrick to Her Ladyship when he was away in Ireland.'

'Of course not! Nor your poor sick son, Michael, either…'

Samuel soothed, patting her arm like an avuncular bishop. 'Now, pray continue with your account.'

'Eventually, Patrick could stand it no more. He told Her Ladyship he had a plan to become rich by smuggling whiskey, and he needed Sir William's help. He wanted an advance of money for his plan and to use Sir William's local contacts. Patrick warned her he would tell all to Sir William about their previous affair unless she persuaded her husband to take part. He dragged me into it too, and to my shame, I agreed. He is a very charming man, at times, is Patrick – he could twist any woman around his little finger.'

'So, Patrick wanted Sir William's financial help, and he needed Lady Kathleen to press his case for him. Is that right?'

'It is, sir.'

'But it wasn't whiskey at all, was it? It was dynamite he wanted brought in,' Henry advanced.

'I wasn't aware of it, sir…' Mrs Hennessey's talent for playing the innocent victim was clearly growing by the minute. 'All I knew,' she replied with a bold grimace, 'was Patrick thought Sir William would agree to his plan if Lady Kathleen merely fluttered her eyes at him – but he was wrong. Sir William would have none of it – not at first, at least… This made Lady Kathleen exasperated, angry even, and it's my belief she took it into her head to punish her husband – that's my opinion, for what it's worth.'

'And then?' Henry asked.

'She was so distraught that she could not bend him to her will. The two of them would have flaming rows, and then she'd make up to him, all kisses and flirts. But Sir William refused to fall for her charms, and that's when Lady Kathleen's romance with Patrick flared once more. I think she did it to wound her husband more than for any love she might have had for Mr Wilks. She's a real schemer is our Lady K! The pair of 'em, her and Patrick, used to meet in the old Custom House. When Sir William was in London, sometimes she would stay with Patrick for days on end. She was quite unashamed by it.'

'That's all very well, but tell us why the murder of Ignatius was so important,' Samuel pressed.

'And the plan... tell us about this plan,' Henry urged.

'Because after the shooting, Mr Wilks could then control Sir William by himself. Sir William was horrified by what he'd done, and mighty scared of the consequences.'

'Of hanging, no doubt,' Samuel offered.

'More so the wrath of Cassius. He was in awe of the man – terrified, if truth be told. He ran to Lady Kathleen, of course, and she sought Patrick's help. He offered to dispose of the body for her husband in a trice... and offered to make it appear *you* had done the murder, sir.' She stared at Samuel Snuggs. 'I'm sorry if that caused you any offence, sir...'

'It was discomforting at the time, madam. But I have survived it.'

'What of the plan, Mrs Hennessey? You must tell us all,' Henry pleaded.

'Ah, the plan... Well, Patrick's idea was to bring the consignments in from Ireland, and he knew the Pennycrockers had been involved in the smuggling around these parts for centuries. When Patrick learned of the old tunnel into the church, that was the icing on the cake. He wanted Sir William to get it reopened. He thought to get the Honey family back into business once more, and they would all become partners in the venture. He had the whiskey contacts at *Carrells* in Cork, Sir William would provide the finance, and the Honeys would bring it in. All profits to be split three ways. When Sir William first turned him down, he was shocked. I was surprised also – utterly amazed that Patrick had not been instantly dismissed for making such a proposal. But Patrick was like that – a man who rode his luck with a four-leaf clover tattooed on his heart.'

'And then?'

'Then, a month or so later, Sir William's rage got the better of him, and he killed Ignatius. Once he'd accepted Patrick's offer to remove the corpse, he was trapped and had no choice but to fall in with his wishes. Sir William just did as he was asked and approached the Honeys, who readily agreed to recommence the smuggling. This time, Patrick told me the profits would be shared between him and the Honeys. Sir William would get his vow of silence in return. Of course, Cassius had no idea his young brother, Ignatius, was already dead. Anyways, all the Honeys are ever interested in is gold.'

'And the cargo?'

'Irish Whiskey was the cargo, sir – cases and cases of *Carrells*. So, Mr Wilks told me...' She put a finger to her lips and sucked on it as she said the words. 'All was arranged very quickly, in just a few days. The night the goods arrived, he and Barnaby dumped Ignatius's headless body, all secret-like, on the steps of the church. It was part of Patrick's idea to convict you, sir...' Hennessey looked guiltily at Samuel once more.

'And the dynamite, madam?' Henry pressed. 'We have evidence of dynamite.'

Colleen Hennessey turned her head away as if trying to shield the guilt writ large on her face. 'I have told you. I know nothing of *dynamite*, sir... only whiskey...'

'Who cut off Ignatius's head?' Henry broke the awkward silence.

'It was Patrick,' she replied steadily. 'He paid Barnaby five pounds to help him do it. They took knives from my kitchen, so I learned later. The skull had a bullet in it, so I suppose it had to be removed anyway, or others would have noticed – even old Plymswood would not have missed that!' she sniggered. 'Then they kept the body as cool as they could in the cellars before taking it to the church on the night. They wanted Cassius to find it when the first cargo was brought ashore.'

'But the body can't have been fresh – Ignatius being dead for a number of days.'

'They bargained Doctor Plymswood would not notice as long as they took the head off and did it fast enough, and they were right. The old drunkard never batted an eye!'

'So, what happened next?'

'When he saw his brother minus his head, Cassius was spoiling for a fight, by all accounts. And when folk started speaking of the false sighting of you, sir, and the way you were "lifted up into the air", they were ready to believe it.'

'Who told them?'

'Patrick and Barnaby spread the word in the first place. Their tall story was quickly believed. So much so that other witnesses came forward to say they had seen the whole thing too! The fools! All folk believe in demons around here. Once people have a story they want to believe, the gossip spreads as quickly as fire in a hayloft.'

'What do you know of the parson, Mrs Hennessey? Did he know of it? Did he allow the tunnel into the crypt to be used?'

Colleen Hennessey stopped her talking and regarded them both for a while. With ever-moistening eyes, she said at length, 'My boy… you say you will protect him. Do you give your word he will come to no harm if I tell the truth of it all?'

'We will do our best for him,' Henry replied, to which the cook's shoulders seemed to slump once more.

'Tell me, madam,' Samuel interjected, 'what is your son? Is he a man of dynamite with designs against the state, or is he a simple smuggler of Irish whiskey?'

'Of *whiskey*, sir…' she hesitated… 'I'm sure he knows nothing of anything else…'

'That's what I hoped to hear. Listen to me… If he will testify against the others, I will go further than my friend, madam. I will give you my word Michael will escape the gallows, if he is as obliging as his mother. When we have concluded our business here, I will take you to him, so you can explain all. You will have your chance to save his life. How does that satisfy you?'

Hennessey thought a while before answering. 'It does, sir… I trust you. My poor boy wouldn't hurt a worm, let alone a fly,' she whimpered.

'So, tell me about Parson Rosewarne. Do you know who killed him?'

'I do, sir,' she replied, her voice suddenly becoming triumphant.

'It was Cassius Honey, was it not?' Henry advanced. 'For the insult the parson gave for not marrying his sister?'

'No, sir. It was not Mr Cassius.'

'Then who?' Henry looked puzzled.

''Twas the verger that did the deed, Penrose Polrunny. But it was Wilks who paid him to do it. He gave him the poison, too.'

'The verger? But he is dead – poisoned also!' Samuel said impatiently. 'How can it be?'

'Wilks told me his story just before he left us for Ireland. He was in drink, and boasted about it for hours. He was proud of it! He said no one would ever discover the truth.'

'But how? Why?' Henry asked.

'Why? To clear the way, of course! When the parson heard of Ignatius's death on his church steps and that the crypt had been used once again for smuggling, he vowed to stop it. He even told a few that he'd seen Forrabury's ghost, who had actually spoken to him – told him it was his duty to prevent it. Naturally, most folk round here thought it was a terrible warning – a voice from the grave, no less – and from that day, the vicar swore smuggling in his church would never happen again.' She stopped and addressed Snuggs directly. 'But you know that already, sir, don't you, sir?'

'Rosewarne was genuinely upset, and 'tis also true he mentioned the apparition to me…' Samuel's voice tailed off. 'I'll admit I was perplexed… But one thing is certain – the parson was adamant; he wanted us to block the tunnel from the sea,' Samuel said with force. 'He told me he wanted no part in the trade, and I believed him.'

'And Forrabury's ghost?' Henry nudged him. 'Did *you* imagine he'd actually seen a spirit? It's most important I know…'

Samuel looked distinctly uncomfortable and made no answer. Instead, he addressed Mrs Hennessey once more. 'So, madam, tell us, what happened next?'

'Well, after the first consignment had been so successful and good money was made by all, Patrick and the Honeys wanted more. But you see, the parson would have none of it. He swore to protect the crypt at all costs. He used to keep a watch on it, and old Polrunny was brought into the duty as well. Rosewarne tasked him to walk patrols at night and raise the alarm if anything strange was seen. But after some weeks, the verger made it known he was tired of it, and that's when Wilks approached him. He offered him money. Polrunny was a rogue at heart, though he tried to look godly. Twenty-five pounds, it was. Patrick gave him the poison, too – he is an apothecary, you know. He knows of such matters.'

'But where… how? We both witnessed the parson's collapse.'

'I know the answer to that, too,' the cook replied, now speaking with some enthusiasm. Clearly, she was enjoying being centre stage. 'You see, Parson Rosewarne was in the practice of drinking holy water. Everyone saw him do it. It was his daily habit. Folk used to remark at it. Before each service, he would take the christening spoon, scoop up a serving, put it to his lips and swallow the lot. Then he'd make the sign of the cross. Patrick had heard of it, though he'd never seen it done, as none of us Catholics ever ventured inside St Piran's. He bribed Polrunny to put the poison in the font, to mix it with the holy water. The next time the vicar attended the church was your wedding rehearsal, sir. And you saw what happened. 'Twas quite a sight, apparently.'

The others were visibly stunned. 'But how did Polrunny die?' Samuel asked at length. 'It makes no sense, unless he took his own life. The guilt for killing the parson must have weighed heavily, perhaps…'

'I think I have the answer to that…' Henry replied. 'It was Polrunny's job to maintain and tidy the church. Good Doctor Plymswood told us Polrunny had signs of a rash on his hands, notably to the right. The verger also had a key. He must have entered the church when all had departed and cleaned up the font to destroy any evidence. Yet he didn't realise the potency of the substance he'd placed into it earlier that day. My guess, it was the holy water that did for him too. Contact with the skin was enough. The effects were felt more slowly, don't you see, for the contamination must have been considerably less – fatal, all the same. That's maybe why it took him so long to expire.'

'My God, you could be right, Henry… Listen, I think we have heard enough, for the time being. I promised to call Halwill if the matter of the murders was raised.' Samuel Snuggs rose to leave.

'We are grateful for your openness, madam,' he said to Hennessey, 'but we must depart now. It's time for us to speak with Mr Wilks and Lady Kathleen. They have a lot to explain. Inspector Halwill will take our place here with you. He will want to ask you questions about the deaths of Ignatius Honey, Parson Rosewarne and Penrose Polrunny. I ask you to be as straightforward with him as you have been with us – tell him exactly what you have told us. We will take you to meet your son once our business is concluded.'

'Please keep my darling Michael safe, sir.'

'We will do what we can. I have made a promise, and I would like to hold to it. But before we depart, I have one final question for you, madam… Tell us, where is the head of Ignatius Honey?'

'I can take you to it, if it pleases you, sir. I helped Patrick bury it.'

'You mean you *saw* Patrick bury it… do you not, Mrs Hennessey? The inspector will want you to be absolutely clear on the matter.'

'Err… of course, sir. I *saw* him do it – from afar, as it happens…'

'And its location?'

'We took—' She caught her breath. 'Sorry, I mean to say, *he* took it to the walled flower garden. I believe the head lies beside the Victorian rose bush – he dug it in deep. Patrick thought it fitting for Ignatius to find his Rose, at last – even in death.'

Chapter Thirty

The news that Patrick Wilks had escaped from Custom House custody was the mightiest of all body blows for Snuggs and Gough as they dismounted their horses. Samuel was especially affected and blamed himself for the lapse. The guilt borne from his perceived incompetence came instantly. If only he had stayed and guarded his prize capture himself, none of this would have happened.

Then he found Jacob Jarvie and rounded on him for an explanation. 'My God, Jarvie, how could you let such a thing occur?' he raved.

'I'm sorry, sir. I had been called away to assist Mrs Polrunny. She had been trying to restrain Her Ladyship, who had started to tear out her hair. While I was away, it seems Wilks overpowered his guard. He must have drawn the officer into the lock-up on some pretext – perhaps on the subterfuge of needing water, or maybe feigning illness – but either way, there was a struggle, and the fellow has made his escape. It was about fifteen minutes ago. He's stolen a horse, too.'

'And his shackles?'

'Unlocked, sir. He took the keys from the officer.'

'Who was guarding him?' Samuel looked like he meant business. 'He shall feel the lash of my tongue.'

'It was Officer Copplestone, sir… but…'

'What does Copplestone say?' he cried. 'How could he fall for such a greenhorn ruse?'

'Nat Copplestone is dead, sir. His own bayonet stuck deep into his eye.'

'I'll be damned!' Henry exclaimed. 'Oh, my dear Lord, the poor fellow… have you sent men in pursuit?'

'No, sir. I had none to send, as I feared I might lose one or other of my captives.'

'He is long gone by now, damn him!' Samuel put his head in his hands. 'Henry, come with me. We must speak with Her Ladyship this instant.'

Lady Kathleen Pennycrocker looked to be a broken woman when they arrived in her makeshift cell. Still clad in the thin nightdress and with one leg chained to a chair, a stained gown half untied at the waist, and her hair in disarray, she made a pitiful sight indeed.

'She won't stop her wailing, sir. Look, she's even pulled these clumps from her scalp. I couldn't stop her. I'm sorry, sir,' Lena Polrunny explained, presenting a bloodied tangle of dark tresses.

'Your Ladyship, I will be brief.' Samuel sat down and clasped his prisoner's shoulders in his hands. 'Forgive me, madam, but I must tell you… your husband is dead – killed by his own hand.'

'Dead, you say?' She looked at him with a strange curiosity, as if weighing up a series of competing thoughts.

'Yes. He used his own pistol. We were too late to save him.'

'So, there is a god after all!' she replied implacably. 'If the Lord has any remaining mercy, he will take me too.'

'I have some questions.' Samuel came straight to the point.

'What do you know of dynamite, madam? It is of the utmost importance that you tell us.'

'Ha-ha! Ask Patrick. That is *his* game.'

'We have seized 120 sticks of dynamite today. Tell me – what were they to be used for?'

'Leave me to die,' she moaned. 'I know the way of things… Patrick will tell you all – then you will hang him. That will be the cycle of affairs, will it not?'

Before either could make another enquiry, Lady Pennycrocker's face brightened inexplicably. 'You may hang me too, if you like…' she declared with an emerging smile. 'Becoming a martyr to the cause appeals to me – it must be better than dying as a broken-hearted, silver-spooned nonentity, don't you think? People would remember me then, wouldn't they, Mr Snuggs? The grand lady who fought for the cause…'

'Which cause do you speak of, madam?'

'A free Ireland, of course – is that not good enough for you, sir?'

'Is that your motive… Irish independence from Great Britain?'

'Is there a nobler project? It was Patrick's campaign; he believed in it with all his heart, and I loved him, even though I wronged him so badly. So, perhaps I should now fully embrace the cause to express the unity I once denied him…'

'I fear she is delirious, Samuel. Her ramblings make no sense.'

'Madam, you must tell us.' Suddenly the lines of blood that forked down Lady Kathleen's ice-pallid countenance seemed more extravagant than before. 'Tell us about the dynamite,' Snuggs persisted. 'What do you know of it?'

'I have no other reason to be alive now. My dearest love is doomed to swing for his principles.' She gazed upon them through clouded eyes. 'So perhaps I shall adopt his politics for my own.' Lady Pennycrocker got to her feet as renewed energy seemed to seep into her. With outstretched arms, she cried out as if in exultation. 'Yes! 'Tis better to be a campaigner than a callow woman! What do you think, Officer Snuggs? And you, sir… Mr Gough, you are a man of the world. What is your opinion?'

'Some might agree with you, madam,' Henry replied slowly. 'I am sympathetic to the idea of it, but Irish Independence divides us all. I draw a line at killing others to achieve it, however… We cannot allow that to happen. So, tell us about the dynamite. Where was it intended to be used?'

'Will it make me famous if I tell you both? Will I become a heroine for the cause, a rebel who will be remembered for ever? The infamous Patrick Wilks and his aristocratic paramour, bonded for eternity, two lovers who died for their beliefs?'

'History will be the judge, not us,' Henry replied gently. 'But now you have the chance to save people's lives. *That* may go down in your history as an act of self-sacrifice like no other.'

'Ha-ha! Fine words indeed, Mr Gough. Very well…' She slumped back onto the chair in a clatter of chains. 'I might as well be hanged for a sheep, as they say. I will tell you! The dynamite is to destroy Dartmoor Gaol, gentlemen.'

'How do you know this?' Samuel frowned.

'Because when I asked Patrick, he told me,' she replied simply. 'At the time, I was concerned for the deaths it might cause, but he assured me the blast would only allow the prisoners to escape, some of them Irishmen too – the ultimate act of liberation. It would send a signal to the world that liberty must be achieved at all costs. The dynamite would not kill. Instead, it would knock down confining walls and bring freedom to the downtrodden and subjugated.'

'And the dynamite that has already been brought in?'

Samuel continued. 'We have evidence a previous consignment contained explosives. Where is it now?'

'All got away... In Dartmoor, I expect,' she said carelessly. 'The blast is to be a big one.' Lady Kathleen paused a second and her eyes brightened. 'There is something else, gentlemen... You may not know it, but last year, along with the whiskey and dynamite, came brave Irishmen too – ready to fight for the cause.'

'Like the two we have in our custody today, you mean?'

'Precisely. I never saw them, mind you, but there were three in September, so Patrick told me. There should have been three more last night, had it not been for Hennessey's son, who clearly got cold feet,' she said with contempt in her voice.

'Are you saying Mrs Hennessey's son, Michael, was sent with the others to explode a bomb?'

'Not one bomb, sir, many! Patrick insisted on him joining the party. It gave him further leverage. Patrick likes to be in control. Young Michael's presence made our Colleen all the more eager to help, such is her love for the "wee boy", as she calls him.'

'Dartmoor Prison, you say...'

'Yes, but you had better hurry, the pair of you,' she crowed, 'as I fear you may already be too late. Once the others get word of Patrick's capture, they will know what to do. It may not be the fireworks Patrick had hoped for, but explosions are explosions, and who knows how many convicts might escape into the night, some never to be caught again...'

'Do you have any names, madam? We need the names of the Irishmen who are here, present and ready to do their wicked work... any details you can give – so we may find them before they kill others,' Henry pleaded.

'Enough of this!' Lady Kathleen cried out in reply. 'I have told you all I know. Please leave me now. I will happily hang with the others. I have said my piece. The next words I speak will be to my beloved Patrick, in the sight of God, when we parade together in heaven.'

Samuel and Henry looked at one another... Without speaking a word, each knew it was time to end the interview. Samuel turned to address Lady Kathleen's lay custodian. 'Mrs Polrunny, please stay with Her Ladyship a while. I will fetch someone to replace you as soon as I can. For now, please take care she doesn't hurt herself any more than she has already.'

'Where do we go from here?' Henry asked as soon as they had joined forces with Jacob Jarvie in Samuel's old office – now Lady Pennycrocker's boudoir and the scene of much excitement earlier in the day.

'I will return to the new Custom House and send a message to the authorities at the gaol,' Snuggs declared. 'Get a despatch with Wilks's description to Halwill at the Hall, would you, Jacob? He can spread the word through his own channels. I just hope we're not too late to avert a disaster. At least others can be forewarned and may take some extra precautions.'

'Has anyone talked to the pair of Irishmen yet? Surely they will have something to tell us,' Gough advanced.

'They are hardly men, Henry.' Jarvie shook his head. 'Just mere lads – they can't be more than fifteen or sixteen. Neither was carrying any documents, none at all, not a shred, not even a weapon of any kind... and they refuse to give us their names. They're frightened, though, and will talk to us once they know their captain has abandoned them.'

'We have to find him, this elusive Patrick Wilks. He holds the key to all this.' Henry sounded exasperated.

'He could be anywhere by now,' Snuggs replied, 'but my guess is he will make his way to Dartmoor. If the gaol is the target, he will want to be there to see it all. That's our best chance.'

There was a sharp knock on the bedchamber door and Wendholt entered. 'Commander Jack Geach is here to see you, sir. He brings news from the *Vigilant*.'

* * *

Patrick Wilks had never killed a man – at least, not until an hour ago. On performing the act, the feeling of conquest had been stronger than he'd imagined. There was no remorse – no revulsion either. This surprised him somewhat. He had expected to feel a trace of sympathy for his first victim, who he knew must show himself soon enough. But there was none... no guilt whatsoever. The emotions he experienced were all triumphant – pleasurable, even. He imagined this absence of regret was something he would have to get used to. Even while he was riding to safety and the image of the dying revenue officer came back to him – the long knife stuck with one fist into the man's head, the other wrapped around the fellow's throat – it had not affected him, save for a smile of satisfaction for his achievement. He had made his path, and there was no turning back...

It had not taken the officer long to die, which was perhaps fortunate. The blade must have entered the brain effortlessly, and he thanked his luck for it; it had made his escape all the easier. Finding a horse, already saddled and tied up outside the old Custom House, had been opportune too. Maybe his fortunes had turned after all.

His first port of call had been *The Gauger's Return*, where he'd surprised the shapely Molly in the kitchen's larder as he helped himself to as much food and drink as he could carry.

'Oh lawks, Mr Wilks! Shall I get Mr Trewint to help you with your bags?' she'd cried on seeing him stuffing horse satchels with provisions. Patrick thought about killing the nosey temptress on the spot, but he knew it would just waste valuable time, and anyway, he'd always taken a fancy to her comely manner. Maybe he still retained an ounce of compassion, he told himself, but soon dismissed the thought once he realised he could use the girl to his advantage.

'Tell your master I will be taking a fresh horse from his stables – one of the four he promised to bring to me at dusk. Tell him one horse is all I need, for the time being. Explain to him I have to go to Dartmoor on urgent business and will pay my debt with interest when I return in a few days. Do you understand, girl?'

Just after six-thirty, Patrick Wilks, his horse trotting quickly, was well established on the road to Launceston. By the time the sun began to shroud itself behind the low western clouds, he'd already travelled the near twenty miles required to reach the city's railway station. There, he tethered Trewint's sweating horse, and with the satchels slung over his shoulders, he bought a first-class train ticket from a cheerless railwayman. It had all been so easy, he thought, as he arranged himself in the otherwise empty compartment. Admittedly, the twenty minutes' wait before the locomotive had pulled the line of carriages away from the platform had been an anxious one, but it had given him a silent opportunity to reflect on the momentous events of the last couple of days.

All had gone well until a few hours into their journey from Ireland. After the gang of four had joined the *Skibbereen Princess* from a distant jetty in the port of Cork, Patrick had assembled his band of brothers in the claustrophobic forward cabin. Out of the hearing of the captain and crew, he explained their mission once again, and together they toasted their forthcoming success. While downing copious quantities of *Carrells,* Patrick had laid out the final details of their assignment. Using the abbreviated notes he'd written himself, he provided all the necessary facts, which hitherto he'd kept from them. Included amongst these was the most important information of all – the designation and location of their target, and the names of the men who would join them in their endeavour.

'You must commit what I am going to say to memory, in case I get separated from you all and can no longer be your nanny. Don't forget, or you won't know where to go and who to meet,' he'd urged them, wiping his mouth after yet another slug of whiskey. 'These are the final facts you need to know. You must implant them into your thick skulls, lads. Listen to me. Nothing may be written down. That way, if you are stopped by the peelers, you will have nothing to show them – except for your Irish wit and good nature!'

It was shortly after the sermon that Michael Hennessey started to complain of seasickness and began to puke on everyone. Wilks had immediately snatched the whiskey from his grasp and sent him up on deck to stare at the horizon. But this only seemed to make matters worse, and for the rest of the voyage, the lad had been as sick as a dog – spewing and retching; the whole business was nauseating and utterly repulsive. By the time Captain O'Brien had announced the boat had anchored at their handover point, Patrick thought his fellow collaborator might actually die. And so, it was agreed by all, Michael would have to remain on board and return straightaway with the crew to Cork. Patrick could not afford to carry a sick man, especially during the dangerous few hours it would take them to stumble ashore through the unfamiliar Cornish night.

'You will have to return alone, Michael. Maybe next time, eh? But only if you can find a cure for this fecking blight of yours. There are other ways to help the cause. You're only a "wee boy", after all, or so your mam keeps telling me,' he laughed.

'We three can manage. With the others already ashore, there'll be more than enough to scare the living daylights out of the fecking bastards. I'll just have to carry ashore your bag of surprises! We'll see you back in Cork when this adventure is over. Perhaps some dry land under your feet will allow you to celebrate with us!'

The jolly boat had arrived on cue, close to the Cow and Calf. Patrick knew Cassius and Gabriel Honey more by reputation than personal contact, and they did not disappoint – murderous looking, largely uncommunicative, yet ruthlessly efficient. Cassius had announced their change of landing point immediately they had clambered aboard. He gave no explanation for it, and Patrick hadn't asked.

When he found Kathleen waiting for him at the old Custom House, he was overjoyed. It was late; they had a lot to talk about. Their first embrace had led to one of the most wonderful nights of his life. But then things had started to go awry...

The sudden arrival of the Revenue in their bedroom had come as a complete surprise to them both, as had the amount of information the officers seemed to possess. Perhaps he had underestimated them after all. *But what complete fools they'd been to leave him alone,* he chuckled inwardly. And now, with one dead man behind him, here he was – a first-class gentleman on a first-class train – one that would lead him to his ultimate calling.

His arrival into the world of Fenian politics had come late in his life, but now he absorbed it totally. He believed himself to be a true freedom fighter, yet he knew one day he would have to show proof of his credentials. Today, he was on the cusp of achieving it, too. Nothing could stop him – he felt impregnable. In less than two days, the sought-after badges of battle would be writ large whenever his name was spoken.

He would become an instant legend – strangely, he realised, to both Irish and Englishmen alike. And deprived of the men he'd had to leave behind, he would triumph almost single-handedly – the underdog against the full might of Great Britain. How his kinsmen would marvel at it! And the woman he longed for would love him all the more, and all would be in the name of Irish freedom. Yet, she could wait… This was *his* time, and he knew exactly what he had to do next.

* * *

Commander Jack Geach was not a man to beat about the bush. His arrival in Borwenstow had been delayed by the outward running tide, and he was clearly in no mood to apologise.

'We missed it by ten minutes, Samuel. Our search at the Cow and Calf took longer than I'd imagined, and by the time we'd finished, the water was running hard against us. We just had to wait it out.'

'Better late than never, eh, Jack. And how was the search? Were you successful?'

'In part… I have come in person to bring you the treasure. I want you to see for yourself. We found the bag after a little searching – the tide had dropped it amongst the shingle on Calf rock, but I fear the contents are all but unrecognisable. I didn't want to bring the papers to you for fear they would disintegrate further. So, if you will oblige, I'd ask you to accompany me aboard *Vigilant*, where you can sift through the traces.'

'Are there many documents?'

'Hardly any, and most are unrecognisable, all sodden and breaking apart like a dollop of mashed turnips. There is a loaded pistol too – a very old design, mind. And also an assortment of queer-looking glass bottles. They look like tinctures of some kind, I'd say… Come, bring the others, if you like. There is room on board and a glass of rum for those who have a thirst.'

It was but a short walk to the berth where *HMRC Vigilant* lay at her lines, gently swaying as the northerly breeze pressed against her gunwales. Henry Gough decided to accompany his son-in-law. He wanted to see the evidence for himself, and the thought of boarding an armed cutter in Her Majesty's service also appealed to him.

The bag, when it was produced, still dripping from its stitched seams, was of a sturdy leather structure with a rigid internal frame of a type instantly recognisable to members of the medical profession.

'It looks like a bag Mr Gladstone might own – a smaller version of it, at least,' Henry observed.

'The thought occurred to me, too,' Jack grinned, 'but I doubt our prime minister would be carrying a pistol inside.'

'It's certainly quite sturdy.'

'I agree. Most other bags might have sunk without trace. At least this had enough buoyancy to keep it afloat long enough to allow it to become beached. I have removed the papers as best I could. They are drying over here.' Geach led them to a table where half a dozen blotchy documents had been spread out for inspection. 'Most appear to be ledgers of some kind, with a list of items and numbers against them, but I cannot decipher much detail. This one caught my eye,' he said, pointing at a single piece of tarnished paper that appeared drier than the rest. 'I noticed it because it bears a date much in my mind at the moment – the twenty-seventh of this month – this Friday, in fact. There are some numbers and letters beneath which could be read with a little imagination. Here, have a look.'

The paper was clearly handwritten and took the form of a ten-point numbered list. Items one to four could be clearly seen running in order down the page. Five to nine had all but disappeared, drenched in seawater; item ten reappeared at the bottom, having somehow survived the flood. Item one contained the date, as already identified by Geach. The other readable entries were as follows:

2. *South Yard W8*

3. *16, Paradise Cot* (the rest illegible)

4. *CD, ST, LF*

It was just possible to decipher item ten... *Swansea 1/6 5p.m.*

'Intriguing indeed...' Henry advanced. 'I wonder if "South Yard" could relate to Dartmoor Prison and "W8" to a cell number – we should try to discover the name of its occupant.'

'*Cot* could be cottages. I will enquire if there are any "Paradise Cottages" in Dartmoor,' Samuel offered. 'Maybe they provide housing for prison warders.'

'And Swansea?' Jack asked.

'There is a ferry service from Swansea to Cork,' Henry replied. 'Jacob found a shipping timetable in Sir William's desk. I'll wager it's a reference to the date and time of a departure to Ireland. We'll need to check for reservations.'

'I only know of one set of Paradise Cottages,' Jack Geach said casually. 'I walk past them every time I take *Vigilant* into Devonport. In fact, I shall be passing them again on Friday, if all is well. I can have a look in at number sixteen, if you like. From memory, they are occupied by dock workers, for the most part.'

'Are you taking this old tub all the way to Devonport?' Henry asked. 'You'll have to hurry, as it's a mighty fair distance from here by sea – all around Land's End and the Lizard.'

'No, sir!' Jack Geach looked mildly affronted at Gough's description of his beloved cutter. 'I shall be going by train, as it happens, and paid for by the Crown, to boot! I have an invitation to the launch of Her Majesty's spanking new warship, *HMS Cromwell*. She is to go into the water on Friday at 2p.m. precisely. I have the invitation here.' Jack Geach pulled a card from his uniform pocket. '"Your presence at the launch..." blah, blah, blah... Yes, let's see... I have a seat reserved for me – number 212, on the second tier. It says I have to be at berth W8 in the Southern Yard before one o'clock.'

Chapter Thirty-One

It took a few seconds before Geach's words properly sank in, and when they did, the trio realised their magnitude at the same time. But it was Jarvie who beat the others to the punch. 'We must alert the Royal Navy immediately!' he cried. 'The blackguard must have designs to spoil the launch.'

'Worse than "spoil", sir! He means to blow the dock to kingdom come – with *HMS Cromwell,* to boot!' Samuel fired back. 'Have we received any news from your man at the War Office, Henry? Was he not jerquing his files for information about young Hennessey?'

'No reply has come yet. Such things take time, and 'tis late. I expect we'll have to wait a while before we hear from Mr Hope.'

'Very well…' Samuel replied steadily while rising from his chair. 'It's of no consequence now, as I believe we have diagnosed the problem ourselves – at least, in part. Now it's up to us to find the cure. The matter lies in *our* hands, gentlemen, and we must act on what we know – and move quickly, too.' He turned towards Commander Geach. 'Jack, when did you plan to travel to Devonport?'

'By the last train from Launceston tomorrow, at eight

twenty-five. I have reserved a room at *The Lugger*, in Albany Street. It's but a stone's throw from the docks.'

'I fear we must depart sooner than that – and arrive in the fastest way possible.' Addressing his father-in-law, he said, 'Henry, will you accompany us to Devonport? We'll need to tell our story to the Navy and track Wilks down before he wreaks havoc.'

'First, I suggest we send urgent telegrams to the War Office,' Henry replied. 'We must inform them of all we know: the names, addresses, everything we have learned, and give them news of our intentions. They can share our knowledge with whoever needs to know – no doubt that will include the Admiralty. Then we should try to get some sleep… If we saddle up at first light, we can catch the early train tomorrow and be in Devonport by ten. That will give us a full day to make contact with the Navy, find Wilks, and with a fighting chance, we'll stymie his wretched plans.'

'I know just the man who can help us!' Jack Geach interjected. 'I have an old friend; we studied navigation together. He now works in naval intelligence. He'll know what to do – Commander David Franklin is a true man of action. As luck would have it, I'm slated to drink with him on Friday morning before the launch, but I'm sure he won't object to an earlier assignation.'

'Jacob, I wish you to remain here with Mr Gale and the others,' Snuggs told him. 'Pray continue your search, and see what you can get out of the two Irish lads. Tell them Patrick Wilks has confessed, if you like. That might swing them round. 'Tis not a lie either, as by his despicable actions, Wilks has done just that.'

'And what of Dartmoor Gaol?' Jarvie asked.

'The governor has been advised there may be a threat. That's as much as we can do. He has the men to snuff it out.

But I'll wager Devonport is where this matter will be settled.'

The sun rose into a blessedly clear sky the following morning, and the road to Launceston was deserted when the threesome set out. Clipping along at a fast trot, with the horses behaving impeccably, they arrived at the railway station a full hour before the scheduled departure of the train. After stabling their animals and being unable to purchase first-class tickets, they climbed aboard a surprisingly busy train thronged with animated gaggles of sailors' wives on their way to greet their husbands just returned from Singapore. By ten minutes before ten, after an otherwise uneventful journey, the locomotive pulled into Devonport. An eager fifteen-minute stride took them to *The Lugger*, where they found rooms for the night.

'You're in luck, gentlemen, I have three rooms... but one night only, mind,' the grizzled innkeeper announced as they laid down their money. 'We're fully booked tomorrow, what with all the folk attending the launch of *Cromwell*.'

'You two can bunk in with me tomorrow, if needs must,' Geach said with a huge grin. 'It might cramp my style, but Great Britain must come before I do!'

After depositing their bags, they went in search of Commander David Franklin. In less than an hour, they had tracked him down and were telling their story in his airy office overlooking the Southern Yard. Franklin was a genial, back-slapping type of fellow, a youngish man, who, much to Samuel's relief, asked a string of pertinent questions to show he was closely following their narrative. At its conclusion, he called for his assistant, a bearded and rather portly petty officer.

'Chiltington, ask the registry to check these people.' He handed his subordinate a sheet bearing the names of Wilks, Hennessey and the others. 'Tell them to find out all they can.

Give them this address too, would you? I want to know who resides at Paradise Cottages. Be quick about it, man! Double up, there's no time to lose!'

When Chiltington had departed, Commander Franklin addressed the others. 'This is indeed a fine yarn. I'll have to inform Admiral Davidstow, of course.' He rose and adjusted his uniform buttons. 'I will return as soon as I can.'

'He may wish to delay the launch, in view of the risks,' Henry Gough offered.

'I very much doubt he will agree to that, knowing his temperament as I do, but we shall see…' Franklin hurried towards the door. 'Make yourselves comfortable, gentlemen. One thing's for certain, I will not be long. The admiral takes decisions quickly. Our problems arise only when we have to live with the results.'

A strange silence fell on the company as they waited. A mandatory copy of Lord Horatio Nelson's portrait gazed down on them, steel shining from his eyes. Standing beside the high Georgian window, they could see the great battle hulk soon to become *HMS Cromwell* resting on the slipway. The ironclad turret ship was of the latest design and loomed leviathan-like less than a hundred yards distant. Surrounding the ship on three sides was a latticework of platforms, tall gantries and timber frames, some rising higher than the ship itself. Along the decks and amongst the tangled web of encircling wood, workmen swarmed like carpenter ants over a gigantic side of stringed beef. At the giant vessel's prow, the final touches to a vast scaffold, designed to seat the invited dignitaries, was nearing completion.

The door swung open suddenly and in strode Commander Franklin. It felt to them he had been absent for less than ten minutes.

'It's as I expected, gentlemen, the admiral won't have it. He's well informed, I'll grant him. He knew of the matter already – he'd received two messages on the subject this morning, one from Whitehall and another from Marlborough House. His mind is made up. The launch will proceed as planned and Princess Alexandra will graciously perform the rituals, as arranged. I fear my audience with the admiral was even shorter than normal. He says he will give orders to increase the guard and urges us to "take whatever other precautions necessary".'

'But surely the threats are too great for that? Princess Alexandra may be our queen one day, and we may have only twenty-six hours to save her skin!' Samuel exclaimed.

'Admiral Davidstow is not a man for turning. He was once first lieutenant on *HMS Bombay* when it was destroyed off Montevideo, back in sixty-four. He saved many from the fire by his heroic actions and promotion came fast after that. His gung-ho reputation has since been burnished by his strong-minded style. The admiral's exact words to me were, "I feel I have invested half my life in this, Franklin. I won't have it squandered by a few Irish hooligans."'

Petty Officer Chiltington knocked and entered holding a slip of paper. 'Sir, the registry has no record of the names you gave me. They say Paradise Cottages are Admiralty properties, reserved for dock workers and shipbuilders. They gave me this – it is a list of those currently residing at number 16.'

Commander Franklin snatched the paper from him. 'Very well, Chiltington, I'll call you if I need you.' After a cursory glance, he handed the note to Jack Geach. 'Does this mean anything to you?' There were ten names listed alphabetically, with occupations against each. Geach passed the slip to Snuggs, who ran a finger down the lines.

'I think I have it, gentlemen,' Samuel said at length. 'Look... the third name is "Connor Donagher GF welder", the fifth is "Liam Fitzgerald GF riveter" and the ninth reads

"Sean O'Toole GF welder". The names match the initials on Hennessey's sodden list, bar an "O" rather than a "T" for O'Toole, but we can forgive the author that.'

'Bravo, Mr Snuggs!' Franklin cried. 'They are all in the same room, too. The annotation GF against their names means "Ground floor/Front". We have them!'

'Not quite, sir... certainly not Wilks...' Henry Gough responded crustily.

'My guess is he will be not far away,' Franklin replied. 'I can task my men to watch the cottage, front and back. We shall see who arrives and leaves. I will circulate the man's description. If we see him enter or depart, we shall capture him on the spot. If he runs, we'll shoot him. I have men everywhere. He will not evade us!'

* * *

Patrick Wilks had never felt better in his entire life. The journey from Launceston to Devonport had passed without a hitch, and by eleven the previous night, he'd been reunited with his compatriots. Connor had let him in through the scullery door, and the joy was plain to see when Patrick presented his friends with a side of smoked ham and two bottles of *Carrells*, lately the property of the *The Gauger's Return*. The quartet had talked and drunk until the small hours before retiring. By six, they were awake again and ready to implement their plan.

For the last four months, Patrick's three companions had been employed as shipbuilders working on the great warship that lay on the BS3 slipway, waiting for the seawater to touch her sides for the first time. This shadowy group had to hold fast a while, spending nearly five months in idleness until their names had been called – Liam first, then Connor and finally, Sean. All knew their business. Despite their Catholic faith, each had been once employed by Harland & Wolff in Belfast. Their summary dismissal, two years earlier, following an ugly period of sectarian violence in the shipyard, had left them wounded and keen for revenge. Now, with Patrick Wilks calling the shots, they were within tantalising reach of achieving their goal.

For the last two weeks, they had carried, concealed amongst their clothes, no less than 180 sticks of dynamite onto the mighty ship. Here, they had concealed the explosives within the forward bow section of the boat, where, over time, they had connived and bribed a supervisor to allow them to work together. Under the giant windlass and heavy anchors, amongst the legion of chain links, they carried out their work – welding and riveting for twelve hours every day under the increasingly casual eye of the same overseer, who, once he thought he knew his men, had become more interested in Scotch than security.

Today was the day they would set the charge, calculated to ignite tomorrow at 1.58p.m. precisely – the time when the great and the good would be assembled at the bow to wave the Goliath into the dock basin. They had hoped to plant a bomb under the scaffold too, just for good measure and to ensure maximum damage amongst the English ruling classes, but the unfortunate events of the last few days in Borwenstow had prevented that. Wilks had explained all, making light of the Revenue's intervention, describing the setback as "nothing more than an irritation, lads". All was set, he told them, nothing could go wrong if they remained bold. He would take personal responsibility for installing the detonator and setting the timer. He would take Fitzgerald's place on board today. Armed with the necessary ignition devices, he'd ensure the fireworks would be the most memorable in all of Devonport's long history.

Liam Fitzgerald, who in age and appearance bore a striking resemblance to his leader, wiped the sleep from his eyes, dutifully handed Wilks his identity papers and wished them luck. He was going back to bed, he told them, to nurse his hangover and would see them for supper.

A short stroll to the slipway took them to the long columns of more than 200 morning shift workers, who passed obediently along the lines, each with papers held high for inspection. Although he could not deny a twinge of anxiety as he passed the gate with the bomb-making equipment strapped around his waist, Patrick Wilks found himself on board sooner and easier than he'd imagined. Once on deck, he followed his shipmates along one gangway after another into the bowels of the vessel. His task was a straightforward one. Once they had arrived in the bow section and were sure the coast was clear, Connor took him to the area directly under the prow where the dynamite had been concealed, jammed into tight-fitting, welded compartments. It was now a waiting game until the time for all to disembark. Patrick found a hidden corner and a place to lie down with his private thoughts, whilst the others carried on their banging and scratching all around. He could hear the ship's plates groan from time to time, and tried to imagine the sound they'd make when all were blown asunder.

As the end of their long shift drew closer, Patrick set to work. It took him less than three minutes of shuffling wires and fixing ties to lodge the detonator and set the timer for nineteen hours and fifteen minutes. With seconds to spare before they were obliged to leave, Connor returned to cover the exposed devices with another sheet of steel. This, they decided, should be loosely fitted, as any welding at that stage would probably kill them all. The plate was chosen for its weight, and it took two of them to lay it. The job complete, they shook hands and made their way to the gangplank, where they trundled down with the throng; by 7p.m., all had arrived safely onto the quay.

'Time for a drink, lads!' Wilks hollered once they'd reached *The Lugger*. 'Go fetch Liam from his pit, would you, Sean? We'll meet you both in the bar. The first round is on me. We'll have a party tonight, for sure!'

* * *

'No sign of Patrick Wilks, I'm afraid,' Samuel observed gloomily as they sat around the table in Commander Franklin's office. 'I've been with your men all day outside number 16, and I'm certain none of the callers at the front was him. He could have crept in at the back, of course.'

'There was not a single sighting at the rear, I'm reliably informed,' Franklin replied. 'And you saw the comings and goings at the front yourself.'

'I did. A crowd of shipworkers arrived after seven. But that is usual, once the shift is complete. We counted eight in all, but none fitting the description of our man. One fellow who left after seven looked quite similar, and I had to squint carefully, but it wasn't him,' Samuel sighed.

'Jack and I have searched every hostelry, every inn, every shop, every resting place in the town. We've been high and low, and my feet will answer for it in the morning,' Henry groaned.

'We still have nearly eighteen hours. Cheer up!' Franklin cried. 'The surveillance will continue through the night, and I have doubled security for tomorrow's launch. Everybody, all those coming and going, including the VIPs, will be subject to rigorous searches – the Princess of Wales and her party will be exempted, of course,' he laughed. 'If we can't find this Wilks fellow tonight, we'll pay a visit to Paradise Cottages first thing in the morning. They'll all be sleeping like babies, if we call early enough. We'll sort the weeds out from there. What do you say?'

The others, while looking reluctant, nodded their assent. 'They keep a fine table at *The Lugger*, so I'm told. I can ask the landlord, if you like,' Samuel suggested.

'Nonsense, we can do better than that dreary old inn. I have the very place. Be my guests, gentlemen. I shall take you all to the *Royal Clarence Hotel*, as fine an establishment as you will find in these parts. The roast quail is particularly to my liking, and if you prefer fish, the turbot cannot be beaten.'

'And tomorrow?' Henry asked. 'What time tomorrow shall we pay a visit to the cottage?'

'No need for you to dirty your hands, sir. I shall get my men to crash in at dawn. I'll have all the brigands in cells, lined up and awaiting our inspection, by seven. Come to me here at that hour, and I'll have all their names neatly listed and their possessions arranged for review. What say you, gentlemen? Is this a plan?'

'Seven it is, sir,' Samuel said thoughtfully. 'We shall breakfast at six and be with you at the appointed hour.'

* * *

The Lugger had been Patrick Wilks's favourite watering hole during the days in September last, when he had brought his compatriots into Devonport for the first time and settled them into their new cloak-and-dagger assignment. Together, the four had spent many bibulous hours under its oak-beamed ceilings, guzzling rum and touching the women, while decrying the English in veiled mutterings. But alas, the time eventually came for Patrick to leave them and return to his duties as butler of Pennycrocker Hall.

Wilks also liked Lucy well enough, *The Lugger*'s maid

who served drinks so coquettishly. She reminded him in many ways of young Molly in the village, but that's where the similarity ended. For he had enjoyed Lucy's pleasant company on a number of occasions during his previous two-week stay, and he intended to do so again that night. She greeted him like a long-lost lover when she first clapped eyes on him, and within minutes, a deal had been struck. She had a tiny room at the top of the inn, and she would allow him in at eleven, not a second before. She would have to make her excuses to the landlord, but he was used to that – and twenty per cent of her earnings always sufficed to keep him pliable. And so it happened that Patrick said farewell to his drinking companions at five minutes to the hour, swearing to see them at noon the following day so they could "enjoy the fireworks together".

* * *

Henry Gough had done his best to enjoy the extravagant fare of the night before, but in truth, he was concerned – deeply concerned. Despite all the precautions and safeguards promised by the admiral and Commander Franklin, who seemed to have untold resources to call on, he could not help thinking the worst. One thing was for sure, he told himself as he washed for breakfast, he was not stepping onto the VIPs' scaffold until Wilks had been caught.

He turned the poached egg over on his plate and wondered what the day would have in store. Less than eight hours separated them from potential pandemonium. As he sat in *The Lugger*'s bright morning room, with Samuel and Jack either side of him, he raised his head to talk to them. Both seemed much the worse for wear after their indulgences at the *Royal Clarence Hotel*, but through the fog, he wanted to discuss what more could be done. As he moistened his lips in readiness to speak, he caught sight of a man shambling past in the narrow corridor beyond the morning-room door. He looked to be hastening towards the inn's front entrance. Henry imagined the fellow to be unduly crouched for a gentleman who otherwise appeared fit and strong. There was something amiss about his manner. It was as if the fellow was hiding his face, either from some guilt or to protect a hideous facial imperfection from the sight of others. The departing man slammed the inn door behind him with a thump and was gone in an instant.

And then it struck Henry like a bolt from the gods. He was on his feet, napkin flying, before the others could say a word. 'It's him, Samuel! Wilks has just left the inn – unless I am a monkey's uncle, which I know I'm not. The man has just walked past us, easy as you like. Quick, we mustn't let him out of our sight!'

Samuel Snuggs and Jack Geach wiped their mouths and stared back in disbelief. But quickly seeing Henry was not in jest, they threw down their forks, leapt to their feet and followed their friend out onto the street.

'My God, you're right, Henry,' Samuel exclaimed as soon as he focussed on their retreating prey. 'Can we take him… just the three of us?'

'We have no choice,' Henry replied. 'We must do it before he gets away. It looks like he's heading towards the *Cromwell*. That could mean danger for all of us. I only have my swordstick. Do you have your revolvers? He may be armed.' It became swiftly evident that none of them was carrying their pistols.

'He's walking, not running…' Jack observed. 'He doesn't know we've seen him. Let's approach either side of him and take him alive, before he gets too close to the ship.'

The others nodded silently and quickened their pace. Seconds later, they were on him, Jack and Henry on either side, while Samuel ran ahead to face him head-on. On feeling the touch to his arm, Patrick Wilks made no attempt at a tussle. He stopped dead in his tracks and allowed his assailants to grasp his arms. From the front, Samuel said, 'You are under arrest, sir. The game has ended. You must come with us.'

'As you wish,' Wilks replied casually. 'I wondered how long it would take you. For the murder of your gaoler, I presume. I killed a man, and I am sorry for it. But…'

'No buts, Wilks… We shall get the truth out of you if we have to drag it from your body.'

At the perimeter of a cordoned-off area, Henry noticed a pair of uniformed sailors on guard duty over the slipway. Each stood smartly at ease, with rifles to their sides.

'Samuel, call one of them over,' he cried. 'They are armed; they can help us put this man in chains.' Samuel nodded he understood and waved towards the sailors, who were about fifty yards distant.

'You'll have to go to them. They won't come unless you speak to them. We'll hold Wilks here until you return. Go quickly now,' Henry added, tightening his grip on his prisoner's arm. At the moment Snuggs turned his back on them, Wilks, who until then had acted like a lamb, suddenly became a lion.

Chapter Thirty-Two

Without any warning, Patrick Wilks dropped his shoulders and fell to his knees, dragging his two captors with him. Henry Gough lost his grip as his elbow hit the hard surface, the swordstick clattering out of his hand in the process. Wilks had somehow transformed into a fist-waving distillation of raw energy. From the ground, he bounced back up in an instant, and with his now free arm, he shoved with all his might at Jack Geach. Losing his balance, Geach fell abruptly to the floor. Seeing Henry's stick close by, Wilks picked it up and ran towards the slipway for all he was worth. Samuel Snuggs made a valiant attempt to stop him, but the Irishman sidestepped the lunge with the verve of an international fly half.

'After him!' Samuel cried as the three gave chase. The commotion raised the attention of the two ship's sentries, who brought their rifles to the ready as they watched the pursuit begin. 'Help us in the name of the Queen! He is under arrest!' Samuel yelled as he raced past them. Out of instinct, the nearest of the pair left his partner and joined in the hunt.

Wilks had a ten-yard start on all of them, but with each passing second, the distance lessened as the energetic Geach, the fittest in the hunt, gradually made his ground. Wilks smashed his way through the cordon of ropes and placards and drew ever closer to the matrix of gantries and platforms that surrounded the enormous hulk. Suddenly there was nowhere to go. Others, recently alerted to the confusion, were approaching him from all sides, and the vast ship seemed to blot out everything ahead of him. He was cornered; the only possible escape was upwards. Slotting the stick into his belt, he grabbed the rungs of a nearby ladder and started to climb. He'd reached the first platform before Geach had put a foot on the third step.

And so, the chase continued. Ever upwards, Wilks climbed the scaffold. The sheer vigour of the man was remarkable to witness. As soon as he'd conquered the second stage, he leapt towards the third. By the fourth, his eyeline was level with the ship's uninhabited main deck, cleared of all its workforce for the launch. After reaching the fifth, and now horizontal with the funnels, he kicked the ladder away from behind him. On arriving at the sixth, he did the same. The effect was merely to delay his hunters, as it was only a matter of time now. Frantically, he scoured the topmost platform for another exit, but there was none. His journey had ended high above the warship he'd come to destroy. The only way was down, cradled in the sharp arms of his tormentors, and the thought of it sickened him.

'If you approach any further, I shall cut you to pieces,' he cried out, waving the swordstick at Jack Geach, who was fumbling with the discarded ladder.

Geach paused his work and stared up at his quarry. 'You have nowhere to go, Wilks,' he panted. 'Throw down the stick and come quietly.'

'I will not give you the pleasure!' came the screamed reply. 'I'd rather die than see your hand on my collar once more.'

One by one, the others, including the sailor equipped with a rifle, reached the platform. The last to arrive was a thoroughly exhausted Henry Gough.

'We have a gun trained on you now, sir. I insist you step down and put yourself at our mercy,' Snuggs shouted up. 'We know you have dynamite. Lady Kathleen has told us all.'

'Ha!' Wilks screamed. 'She knows nuthin, save a silly story I conjured up to keep her close. That means *you* know nuthin too! NUTHIN!' he yelled down at them. 'Burn in hell and be damned, you fecking bastards!'

Jack Geach put his foot on the first rung, only for Wilks to kick the ladder away again. 'If you do that once more, I'll order the able seaman to fire. Do you understand?' yelled Snuggs.

'He'll have to come down soon enough,' Henry observed as they watched Wilks pace the deck above them. ''Tis a waiting game now.'

'Let's shoot him where he stands. He deserves nothing better,' Geach replied.

'No, I want him in one piece,' Samuel insisted. 'Only he can tell us what we need to know.'

It was as if Wilks had heard their whispers – maybe sound drifts upwards better than sideways – for his next remark seemed to confirm it.

'You wish me alive, don't you…' he taunted. 'Otherwise, you would have shot me in the head by now. I have the better of you, and you know it. I have played you as fools all these months and enjoyed every minute. And now you want me to talk nicely to you. Ha-ha! What monkeys you all are. The English could never take a joke, let alone tell one! Well, this will make you laugh and cry at the same time… My final gift to you all,' he sneered.

Wilks turned away from his accusers, and facing the hulk beneath him, he inched forwards. Steadying himself on a stanchion for a brief second, he made the sign of the cross from forehead to heart. Next, Patrick Wilks opened his mouth wide and produced the loudest and last scream of his entire life.

'Bás do Chromail – Saoirse d'Éirinn!'

Then, like the Reverend Jerimiah Forrabury had done a hundred years before, he jumped – headlong into the abyss…

The head struck first, smashing against the edge of the hull and bursting open on impact. The limbs and body, spiralling and bouncing off the iron cladding, came to a rest directly under the giant black keel. Wilks would have died instantly at the first impact. The effect on the watching others was immense. No one spoke for nearly ten seconds, and when the first words were heard, it was the uniformed sailor who uttered them. 'Where would you like us to bring the body, sir?'

'He is of no use to us now,' Snuggs said grimly. 'Do with it what you will. We have no further interest in him. Let him rot in Hades.'

'What was that he shouted before he leapt?' Jack enquired. 'I did not understand a word of it. Sounded like a foreign tongue to me…' The others looked blank and shook their heads.

'If I may be of assistance, sir…' It was the sailor who spoke once more. 'I understood his words – they were Gaelic, Irish Gaelic…'

'If you know, then tell us.' Samuel sounded irritated.

'"*Death to Cromwell*", sir, "*Freedom for Ireland*".'

'Thank you, my man. What's your name? I should like to thank you for your sterling help to us today. I'm sure your superiors would like to know of it.'

'Byrne, sir. Able Seaman Keegan Byrne.'

* * *

'Apologies for our late arrival, Commander. There were matters beyond our control, I'm afraid,' Samuel announced on arriving in Franklin's well-appointed office.

'I understand you let your man Wilks slip from your grasp, sir. How unfortunate...' Franklin replied with more than a touch of coldness.

'My, news travels fast!' Henry exclaimed. 'We have come straight from the spot.'

'Worse things happen at sea, eh? Well, we still have nearly four hours before the launch. But with Wilks gone to meet his maker, I suspect any danger – if it ever existed – will have passed when his skull was shattered. And I have more good news for you all – my men have corralled your suspects, as I promised, and laid out their meagre belongings. We have ten of 'em, in all. What a fuss they made! Biting and spitting, some of 'em – so much so, you might find a few unconscious still. But they'll live to tell their tale soon enough. In your absence, I have asked my men to commence questioning those that can still stand.'

'The three, Fitzgerald, Donagher and O'Toole, are of most interest to us,' Snuggs said quickly.

'Exactly. All of 'em are true fighting Irishmen, and all are still alive and kicking. That's why I have put them into separate cells, and we have started speaking to them first. They haven't said a blind word, mind you, apart from proclaiming their innocence of all things – not so far, at any rate. We've tried to loosen their tongues using the ways we know best, but they've resisted all our brutal overtures... Maybe you three will have more luck. Why don't you take one each and see what you can squeeze out of 'em? Time to try a different tack – offer them money, eh? That can work sometimes!'

'Did you recover anything of interest from the cottage?' Henry asked.

'Normal, run-of-the-mill effects for men such as these.

Your three fellows are all from Cork, as you suspected. They are bona fide shipbuilders, all of 'em – used to work in Belfast, at Harland & Wolff, it seems. All got dismissed for laziness a couple of years back – hardly surprising, perhaps. There was one matter of interest… The man Fitzgerald could not produce any identity papers. He said he lost them in a public house last night. He'll be laid off for that, whatever happens.'

'It's the missing dynamite that worries me…' Samuel sighed.

'Let's be honest, gentlemen,' Franklin started, 'the explosives you speak of could be anywhere in Devonport… anywhere in the country, for that matter! We've searched everywhere. Are we sure they actually exist? No one has ever seen them!'

'We have the wrappings, David…' Jack Geach did his best to sound reasonable.

'The way I see it, gentlemen,' Franklin continued, 'maybe Patrick Wilks was planning something… maybe he's just another smuggler… Who knows? But whatever his motives, he's a dead man now, and the others, who may or may not be linked to him, are currently in Her Majesty's comfortable embrace. So, tell me… what can happen now? If I am wrong, you still have a few hours to prove it. If you must, go talk to your suspects and wring the truth out of them – if you can.'

A knock announced the arrival of the hirsute Petty Officer Chiltington once more. 'Sir, I have been asked to give you this. It was recovered from the body of the gentleman who fell from the gantry today.' The commander snatched it from him.

'I'll be damned!' Franklin cried on unfurling the paper. 'This must be our missing link – it's Liam Fitzgerald's identity document, complete with his signature. At least that's one mystery solved.'

'Goodness… but how was it found on Wilks's person?' Henry asked.

'It seems strange indeed...' Geach looked puzzled.

'Unless... of course... Wilks was posing as Fitzgerald,' Henry said slowly.

'Indeed – to gain access to the ship, perhaps.' Samuel Snuggs scratched the end of his nose. 'This Fitzgerald must have been the fellow I saw after seven last night, leaving the cottage. I had to look twice before ruling him out, so much did he resemble Wilks.'

'Tell me, Commander,' Henry took up the narrative, 'can we establish where Fitzgerald worked on the *Cromwell* – which part of the ship? If Wilks used Fitzgerald's papers to get on board, he must have done so for a reason. In fact, I should like to know where every man living in Paradise Cottages works on board.'

'Fitzgerald, Donagher and O'Toole are all welders and riveters,' Franklin responded. 'They could labour anywhere, for all I know. 'Tis a huge vessel – nearly the largest in the whole Navy!'

'All the more reason to narrow down our search,' Henry replied.

'My men have searched the ship already,' Franklin came back, 'every damned corner of it, and found nothing!'

'With respect, they are not rummagers, David,' Geach protested. 'They're not versed in the art of finding hidey-holes and secret compartments inside vessels, as we are.'

'I agree with Mr Gough, Commander,' Samuel declared, adding fuel to the fire. 'Surely the supervisors will have a record of some sort. We must pursue this with the utmost potency. It may lead us to the truth of the matter.'

'Very well, I will ask...' Franklin answered wearily and at length. Appearing distinctly disinclined, he nevertheless reached for his bell. When Chiltington re-entered, the commander gave out his orders crisply and left his petty officer in no doubt of the gravity of the matter. 'This is of *extreme* importance, Chiltington,' he concluded. 'Press as many men as you have to. I want an answer within the hour, do you understand?'

'Very well, sir. The chief shipwright will know, if anyone does.'

'All of 'em on the list, mind, but start with these three.' He underlined the names. 'As soon as you know where they work, come to me instantly.' When Chiltington had departed, Commander Franklin took up his pen and spoke to the others. 'Gentlemen, forgive me, but I have pressing matters to attend. I will send word as soon as any news reaches me. One of my staff will escort you to the cells, if that is your wish.'

It took longer than they'd hoped to reach the prison wing – it being located in a distant part of the naval block – and by the time the first of their captives, a chained and bowed Liam Fitzgerald, had been presented for inspection, it was already past eleven o'clock. Samuel chose to commence his interrogation immediately. He took Jack Geach with him, while Henry waited for O'Toole and Donagher to be brought up. Unsurprisingly, their first question, which concerned their man's freshly found identity papers, was received with a sullen and openly hostile glower. The swollen, bloodied mouth of their prisoner perhaps told its own story. When their third and fourth demands for information were met by equally hostile gapes, delivered through broken teeth, it was clear that the wall of silence would take them many days to break down – and they only had *hours*.

Just as Samuel was making another attempt to elicit a response from his reluctant captive, Henry Gough arrived and pulled him outside. The expression on his father-in-law's face told him he had important news to impart.

'We have it, Samuel!' Henry cried when he knew he was out of earshot. 'Come, we cannot waste any more time on these rascals. Fetch Jack, we have a search to make – it will require as many as we can muster. Franklin has offered us half a dozen men; one of them – a certain Lieutenant Clubb – knows about dynamite and suchlike.'

Horses were waiting to carry all three of them the short journey through the accumulating crowd to the slipway and the ship's side. As they mounted the freshly lowered gangplank, Henry looked down on the wharf. He winced as he recognised the spot where Wilks had plummeted to his death just hours before –betrayed by spatters of congealed blood spread like discarded paint under the keel.

Clearly, Commander Franklin could arrange almost anything at short notice had he a mind to it, for a squadron of men was waiting for them as they arrived.

'Take us to the bow, Officer,' Samuel directed the handsome young Lieutenant Clubb. 'The forward section is where all three of our men have worked these last four weeks. That is where we shall find our cache!'

Henry Gough had never been aboard a warship before, let alone a half-finished one, and the entrails of the soon-to-be *HMS Cromwell* fascinated him – narrow gangways, halted by stout bulkheads, with protruding frames and low beams at every turn. At various junctures, new passages seemed to lead off in all directions. As he stooped his way behind the others, he wondered how anyone could possibly navigate around the inner workings of such a craft. When the vessel was tossing and turning on the high seas and in the dark, it must have been nigh on impossible. A florid, weather-beaten man arrived from nowhere and breathlessly announced himself as Noah Hardwick, the works supervisor of the forward labour force. He explained he knew Fitzgerald, O'Toole and Donagher well enough and led them to the area where they'd been working for the previous few weeks.

The space was much larger than Henry had expected and covered more than one deck, each accessible via metal spiral staircases. With the revenue officers at the fore, lamps lit and held low, they set to work. It was not long before Jack Geach barked out something that Henry could not decipher at first, though clearly it was a shout of triumph. He squeezed past the sailors to get a closer look.

'The plate here is not welded. I can see a gap around the edge,' Geach cried. 'I can't budge it, mind – it's exceedingly heavy – but there is something beneath which appears most unnatural! Where is Mr Clubb?' he yelled. 'He needs to come and look.'

Lieutenant Clubb pushed past Henry and got down on his hands and knees, peering all the time into the cavity above which Geach now hovered. He shone a lamp onto the plate.

'Clear the decks, gentlemen!' Clubb exclaimed almost instantly. 'Get out of here, all of you. Leave this to me. I'll have this fixed in a trice, but not until *all* are absent from my sight.'

'Is it a bomb?' Samuel could not resist asking as he and the others backed away.

'I believe it is, sir. And now, please leave me – as fast as you can, gentlemen.' Clubb looked as cool as a January evening. 'I will give you ten minutes to clear the ship, and please inform those on the launching scaffold too. If this goes up, so shall we all, unless you disperse everyone to at least a hundred yards' distance – more, if you can. Do you understand? You have ten minutes, mind – just that. Now go, and do as I say.'

Henry hung back awhile and was the last to leave the cramped space. 'God be with you, and thank you, sir.' He clasped the young lieutenant's hand and bade him farewell.

As he retreated, ducking under a low bulkhead, Clubb called out to him. 'Sir, I fear I need your help. This plate is mighty heavy – I find I cannot budge it alone. Can you assist me?' Henry needed no further entreaty, and in a few seconds, he was at the young officer's side.

'Now do exactly as I say and no more – do you understand, sir?'

'I will.' Much to his surprise, Henry found his outstretched hands were level and still – not the slightest hint of trembling.

By the time Samuel had reached the quay, it was already being cleared of scurrying folk. The scaffold, too, had become a hive of activity, as the sprinkling of dignitaries, who had already taken their seats, was dispersed. Having been listening to the band of the Royal Marines and the first sonorous rendition of *Rule, Britania*, they were now scrambling as fast as their ladies' dresses would allow.

But where on earth was his father-in-law?

For Samuel, with Jack at his side, a full fifteen minutes elapsed in an agonising, almost silent, vigil. Henry's continued absence had become a matter for real concern…

What the hell was he up to?

An image of his new wife came to him – in a meeting when he was recounting and explaining her beloved father's last actions on earth. He knew he'd need to tell Elizabeth of their final seconds together, the precious moments before Henry had been blown to smithereens. He'd have to explain his reasons for watching on helplessly from the sidelines, like a coward and common deserter. The thought of it made him want to retch. A cold sweat broke out about his neck; his hands felt clammy and his feet would not stop moving.

Practically the entire population of the dock had been evacuated in less time than it took to drop an anchor. Clubb's orders had been followed to the letter – the stage, stalls and circle had been stripped of people. Then, with just a few of the foolish peeking from behind makeshift barricades, the excruciating interlude had passed. The pressure was released in the blink of an eye. For suddenly, the man of the moment appeared on deck, directly at the top of the gangplank. Lieutenant Clubb waved to the crowd. In the other hand he appeared to be clasping some unidentifiable artifacts.

At his side, looking distinctly edgy, stood Henry Gough.

Commander David Franklin, having arrived late to take charge of the evacuation, climbed up from his squatting position and exclaimed, 'Hurrah!' and threw his hat in the air. 'The Royal Navy has once again triumphed!' he whooped. 'The day is saved! Three cheers for the brave lieutenant! Hip, hip…' he roared, 'hip, hip, hooray!'

* * *

The scene in Borwenstow when Messrs Gough, Snuggs and Geach returned from Devonport was one of the utmost joy.

Jacob Jarvie and Inspector Austol Halwill Barton greeted them as they dismounted outside the old Custom House. 'What an adventure! What an outcome! May the Lord be praised!' Jarvie gushed.

Halwill, managing to curb any obvious elation he might have felt, gave a sober account that Michael Hennessey had admitted to his unwilling part in the affair. Halwill could not resist a smile, however, when he was forced to add it had not been *he* who had extracted the confession, rather the strident tongue of the lad's mother.

'The other young fellows in custody have remained silent,' he adjoined for good measure. 'They have an appointment with the magistrate on Monday.'

'And what of Lady Kathleen Pennycrocker?' Henry asked as Elizabeth rushed to be at his side.

'She has spoken much, in truth,' Jarvie replied with a twinkle, 'but only in the middle of the night… and in the midst of her maddened wails of anguish. It seems she has lost her mind completely.'

'Have you seen hide or hair of the Honeys since we've been gone?' Samuel enquired with a broad grin.

'Not a peep. And I doubt we will, unless they show their faces tonight.' Jarvie sucked his teeth. 'As providence would have it,' he continued, 'the Reverend Studley arrived from Trevilla only yesterday and has opened the church once again. On hearing the glad tidings, now widely broadcast, he wishes us to join a service of thanksgiving this very evening. The reverend says all may attend. He's insistent this is a time not just for exultation, but one for absolution too.'

'We shall be in the congregation, shan't we, gentlemen? Absolution as maybe, but there is a lot to rejoice too!' Samuel could hardly contain himself.

'After which, I propose we celebrate in a more bucolic fashion,' Geach cried. 'I'll show you how we mariners let our hair down on *Vigilant* whenever we capture a prize!'

As the western sunlight bathed the tower in its evening ochre light, the service at St Piran's got underway in a church with standing room only. As Reverend Clarence Studley raised his arms to welcome the congregation, the main door flew open with a crash. Standing at the entrance was the massive figure of Cassius Honey, his wife, Flora, and his brother, Gabriel, at his side.

'Come, in the name of the Lord, blessed are all ye who enter here.' Studley beckoned them forward in a repeat of his earlier invitation, so sorely refused. 'All are welcome in God's house.'

This time, Cassius did not back away. Taking Flora's hand, he removed his hat, and together with Gabriel at the rear, they advanced respectfully into the middle of the nave. Despite the crush of people, spaces were found for them, and they took their seats at the centre of the congregation.

The service was one the residents of Borwenstow would never forget. It was as if an exorcism was taking place simultaneous to the thanksgiving, and by its conclusion, the spectres and ghosts of the past had finally been laid to rest. It felt to Samuel Snuggs, whose family had been a part of the village for as long as anyone could remember, that the curse had been lifted at last. The eerie events of bygone times were now all explained by a mixture of hard evidence and the new spiritual strength that flowed in their veins. When he remarked as much to Henry Gough in the vestry, as the vicar's wife served tea to a chosen few after the service, Henry's reply came as a surprise...

'Some of the apparitions have been exposed as conjuring tricks, Samuel, I grant you – but not all... You forget the moment I was saved from falling from the precipice on the second night we imagined the smuggle would take place. No one has come forward to claim the credit for saving my life – not a living soul... Apart from Jarvie, the clifftops were utterly deserted, and he is adamant he did nothing and saw nothing. It was as if I had been protected that night by some force bent on doing me good. I could not explain it at the time, but now, I believe I have the answer...'

'But we know the answer, Henry! Since time immemorial, generations of Honeys have played their supernatural tricks on honest folk to deter them on the nights they brought contraband ashore. The curse of Abel Snuggs was just a myth – a bizarre fabrication created by their ancestors to terrify people away from observing their sinful actions.'

'You're not listening, Samuel,' Henry chided gently. 'That's as maybe. 'Tis true enough, and *your* reported spectral ascension to the heavens was vile propaganda, created to convict you of Ignatius's murder.' Henry paused and took his son-in-law's hand into his. 'But *who* saved me, young man? Tell me, if you can – do you have an answer to that?'

'I confess, I do not, sir,' Snuggs stammered, shaking his head in puzzlement. 'It is indeed an abiding mystery…'

'Allow me to show you something, Samuel. I believe I may have the solution to our little conundrum, yet I must warn you, a mystery it shall no doubt remain… I have kept this to myself until now, for fear of ridicule, but today I shall let you in. Follow me.'

Henry escorted Samuel to the other side of the vestry, where portraits of previous parsons gazed down benevolently onto the happy assembly. He led him directly to the likeness of the Reverend Jerimiah Forrabury. Together, they gazed up into the century-old eyes, which seemed to scrutinise them in return – in a strange, enquiring, sorrowful way.

'Do you see the parson's hand, Samuel? May God strike me down if those are not the cold fingers that reached out to me that terrible night and saved my earthly body from tumbling onto the rocks. That is the hand, sir, that protected me, pulled me from the brink, permitting me to carry on. It is my belief, were it not for the spirit of Jerimiah Forrabury, I would not be standing here beside you now. Neither, I suspect, would our enquiries have continued. Nor would we have found the answer the reverend wanted us so desperately to uncover. Old Forrabury has finally found his peace. His guilt is now expunged, and I'll wager no one will ever see his ghost again.'

'But why *that* particular hand, Henry?' Samuel felt a chill run down his spine.

'It's the ring, my boy! The ruby ring on the fourth finger. It's the very same I saw that night – perfect in each detail, every glimmer of crimson – exactly as I witnessed it. I am not a man to speak openly of my belief in phantoms, Samuel. But I vow, for the rest of my life, I shall never decry those who do… In private, I shall hold my thoughts close. I shall tell no one… but I know my instincts well enough, and they have never let me down.'

EPILOGUE

Henry Gough returned to London to the love of his life, Caroline, and their children, where he continued to run his business as a cab proprietor. He went on to have a further eight children with Caroline, who he eventually married on the death of his wife, Hannah, in 1894. Called on regularly by London's law enforcement community to assist their enquiries, he had many more adventures.

Samuel Snuggs returned to Borwenstow a changed man. He and Elizabeth went on to have five children. Their eldest boy was christened "Henry". The new Custom House in Borwenstow was closed down by the revenue commissioners a year after our story ends, and Samuel was offered a post on promotion in Padstow, which he accepted. He ended his career in 1914 as the collector of customs for Bristol and the south-west of England.

Elizabeth Snuggs resumed her duties as governess at Pennycrocker Hall under Rose Pennycrocker, who inherited the estate on her return from Italy. Elizabeth retained the position for a further year before becoming headmistress of Padstow Junior School. Later, she followed her husband to Bristol, where she became a leading figure in the suffragette movement which sought and won votes for women in the United Kingdom.

Inspector Austol "Hasty" Halwill Barton returned to Launceston and continued to be one of the most effective and admired detectives in the Cornish Constabulary. Despite this approbation, he never sought or was offered promotion, retiring in 1901 still as a detective inspector. He never married and died of heart failure less than two months after he left the police service.

Jacob Jarvie was not discharged by the head of the excise detectives. He returned to London, where he enjoyed a successful career specialising in intelligence. At the outbreak of war in 1914, he was attached to army intelligence and survived two years on the Somme with just a burst ear drum. He later conducted speaking tours entitled "Swinging the Lamp", and his audiences were never disappointed by the stories he told. He published a book about Cornish smuggling in 1921, which sold over 2,000 copies.

Commander Jack Geach persuaded the revenue commissioners to keep his beloved *Vigilant* until a successor, the sixth cutter to bear the name, was built. He captained the new cutter for a year before promotion took him to Bristol to join his old friend, Samuel. He retired in 1913 as head of maritime operations for HM Customs and moved back to Bude, where he taught sailing to the Sea Scouts for many years.

Cassius Honey remained in Borwenstow and, along with his family, became a regular churchgoer. With Flora, he had a son – an only child – who they named Ignatius. The boy was to grow as tall as his father, and the Honey line of farmers continues to this day. Neither Cassius nor Gabriel were charged with any offences as a result of "The Shrouded Cove Incident", as it became known, partly due to lack of evidence and partly because Samuel Snuggs did not wish to proceed with the matter. Cassius sought forgiveness from Samuel for falsifying his evidence of the murder of his brother Ignatius and the pair remained in amicable contact for the rest of their lives. In 1893, Cassius became verger of St Piran's Church. He died in 1911 when his boat overturned in a squall off Shrouded Cove.

Lady Kathleen Pennycrocker never returned to Pennycrocker Hall. She died, aged forty-seven, as a private patient in the Cornwall County Asylum in 1895 – some said of a broken heart. Due to her extreme mental condition, she was never charged with any offences and remained mute until her death. Her children, Wilhelmina, Clodagh and Maeve, were brought up by Lady Kathleen's sister-in-law, Rose Pennycrocker, and her husband, Massimo, after their return from Italy. The children's upbringing was assisted for over a year by Elizabeth Snuggs, who resumed her duties as governess shortly after Lady Pennycrocker was confined to the asylum.

Colleen Hennessey was given a two-year prison sentence for whiskey smuggling at Bodmin Crown Court. Following representations by Samuel Snuggs, charges of sedition were never brought against her, and following the completion of her sentence in 1883, she returned to Ireland, where she set up a meat pie business with her son, Michael (who was never charged with any crime). This was to prove highly successful. She died in 1909 as the joint owner of the *Hennessey's Ale and Pie Company*, estimated to be worth in excess of 10,000 pounds at the time.

Reverend Clarence Studley split his duties as rector of St Geraint's, Trevilla, and parson of St Piran's for a further two years, until a new rector was found in Trevilla. Deciding to remain in Borwenstow, he was the parson at St Piran's until he died of pneumonia, aged eighty-nine, in 1918. He had a butterfly named after him, the *Studley Fritillary*, but was never successful in finding a specimen of *Phengaris arion* in Cornwall.

Molly Goodhead left Borwenstow for London three months later. After a brief spell working for Henry Gough at his stables in Alpha Yard, Marylebone, she joined a theatre company and became a popular music hall performer, once playing the part of Kate in *The Pirates of Penzance* at the Savoy Theatre in 1888. She married the impresario, Cuthbert Kennacott, in 1890. They had three children, each of them girls, all of whom grew up to tread the boards in the West End of London.

Isaac Trewint was charged with selling uncustomed liquor and received a fine of fifty pounds and the loss of his licence for six months. He continued to own *The Gauger's Return* until his death in 1889 from alcoholic poisoning.

Constable Percival Poundstock married Eliza Chadwick the year after his mother, Jemima, died from a fall in her cottage during the harsh winter of 1881. Reverend Clarence Studley conducted the service. Poundstock remained as the village constable for a further twenty years before he took up a position as a Royal Mail cashier, following his wife's transfer to Tintagel, where she had been made postmistress. Together they had seven children. His twin sons, Samuel and Jacob, grew up to become revenue officers in Padstow.

Albert Woodward continued as head of the Excise Detective Branch until his retirement in 1890. He moved to Pentrych in South Wales with his wife and spent his pensionable years in the pursuits of birdwatching, growing leeks, and telling tall stories about his many exploits as an international spy.

Commander David Franklin was promoted to the rank of captain the following month and given a Distinguished Conduct Medal (DCM) for his actions in Devonport on the day the bomb was diffused. His career flourished thereafter; he was promoted to rear admiral in 1894 and knighted in 1895. He lost his life when a sniper's bullet struck him in the heart as he disembarked *HMS Hood* during the Cretan rebellion of 1896.

Lieutenant Christopher Clubb was killed nine months later while defusing a Fenian explosive device in Portsmouth.

Liam Fitzgerald, Connor Donagher and Sean O'Toole were convicted of possessing explosive substances without lawful purpose under the Explosive Substances Act 1875 and were imprisoned for life. In 1883, following a bomb-induced breach of the outer walls of Dartmoor Gaol and the resultant break out, all three escaped and returned to Ireland, where they remain undiscovered to this day.

The young lads who'd travelled to Cornwall on the *Skibbereen Princess* were eventually identified as Seamus and Ronan Wilks, nephews of Patrick Wilks, who killed himself in Devonport on 27 May 1881. Neither was charged with offences against the state and both were released after four days in custody. They returned to Cork on 1 June aboard the 5p.m. ferry from Swansea.

The Shrouded Coast – cast of characters

(IN ALPHABETICAL ORDER)

Agnes – former governess at Pennycrocker Hall
Amos – friend of Isaac Trewint
George Atkinson – official of Ordnance Survey
Arthur Atkinson – George's son
Liz Ayling – tea lady to the excise detectives
Bernard Bamber – choirmaster at St Piran's
Caroline Buchan – Henry Gough's mistress
James Buchan – Caroline's father (deceased)
Isaac Browning – assistant to Mr Woodward
Able Seaman Keegan Byrne – Royal Navy
Miss Eliza Chadwick – postmistress, Borwenstow
Petty Officer Chiltington – Royal Navy, assistant to Commander Franklin
Lieutenant Christopher Clubb – Royal Navy
Nat Copplestone – revenue officer
Admiral Horatio Davidstow – Royal Navy, Devonport

Connor Donagher – shipworker, Devonport dockyard

Edward – coachman in Henry Gough's employ

Esther – housemaid at Pennycrocker Hall

Liam Fitzgerald – shipworker, Devonport dockyard

Reverend Jerimiah Forrabury – parson of St Piran's, Borwenstow, 1780

Commander David Franklin – Royal Naval Intelligence, Devonport

Wilfred Gale – revenue officer

Commander Jack Geach – captain of Her Majesty's Revenue Cutter *Vigilant*

Chief Superintendent Jack Grieve – Scotland Yard detective

Molly Goodhead – servant at *The Gauger's Return*, Borwenstow

Henry Gough – cab proprietor from Marylebone, London

Hannah Gough – Henry's wife

Elizabeth Gough/Snuggs – Henry's firstborn, wife of Samuel Snuggs

John Gough – Henry and Hannah's youngest child, aged seven

George Gough – Henry and Caroline's son, aged three

Arthur and Walter Gough – older brothers to George

Inspector Austol Halwill Barton – police inspector, Launceston

Noah Hardwick – works supervisor, Devonport

Harold – Constance Snuggs' brother

Barnaby Hawkes – coachman at Pennycrocker Hall

Michael Heath – first footman at Pennycrocker Hall

Mrs Colleen Hennessey – cook at Pennycrocker Hall

Michael Hennessey – Mrs Hennessey's son

Constable Hill – police officer, Launceston

Captain Jake "Heartless" Honey – smuggler king, Borwenstow, 1780

Cassius Honey – descendant of Jake, resident of Doubloons Farm

Flora Honey – Cassius's wife

Ignatius Honey – brother of Cassius and Gabriel

Gabriel Honey – brother of Ignatius and Cassius

Prudence Honey – sister of Cassius, Ignatius and Gabriel

Nathaniel Hope – head of War Office Intelligence Branch

Gabriel Jago – friend of Isaac Trewint

Jacob Jarvie – excise detective, Tower Hill, London

Jim Jones – revenue constable, Tower Hill

Joshua – carriage driver from Launceston

Doctor Lesnewth – surgeon, Launceston

Lucy – barmaid, *The Lugger Inn*, Devonport

Constable Marshgate – police officer, Launceston

Murphy – boatswain, *Skibbereen Princess*

Constable Newmills – police officer, Launceston

Captain Liam O'Brien – captain of *Skibbereen Princess*

Jock O'Keefe – head groomsman in Henry Gough's employ

Sean O'Toole – shipworker, Devonport dockyard

Sir William Pennycrocker – landowner in Borwenstow, owner of Pennycrocker Hall

Lady Kathleen Pennycrocker – William's wife, née Keenan

Rose Pennycrocker – William's sister

Daniel Pennycrocker – Rose and William's cousin

Wilhelmina, Clodagh and Maeve Pennycrocker – William and Kathleen's children

Doctor Plymswood – physician, Borwenstow

Penrose Polrunny – verger of St Piran's, Borwenstow

Lena Polrunny – Penrose's wife

Constable Percival Poundstock – village policeman, Borwenstow

Mrs Jemima Poundstock – Percival's mother

Reverend William Rosewarne – parson of St Piran's, Borwenstow, 1881

Samuel Snuggs – senior revenue officer, Borwenstow, husband to Elizabeth, née Gough

Constance Snuggs – Samuel's mother

Abel Snuggs – revenue officer, Borwenstow, 1780, great-great-grandfather of Samuel

Reverend Clarence Studley – rector of St Geraint's parish church, Trevilla

Colonel (retired) Rupert Studley – Clarence's brother

Thomas – under-footman at Pennycrocker Hall

Isaac Trewint – innkeeper of *The Gauger's Return,* Borwenstow

David Wendholt – revenue officer, Borwenstow

Paul West – revenue officer, Borwenstow

Sir David Whittington – deputy chairman of the Board of Excise, London

Patrick Wilks – butler to Sir William Pennycrocker

Seamus Wilks – passenger on *Skibbereen Princess*

Ronan Wilks – passenger on *Skibbereen Princess*

Albert Woodward – head of the excise detectives, Tower Hill, London

Acknowledgements

My thanks go once again to Clive Woodward MBE for his constant support, encouragement and inventive plot ideas, to Lauren Dennington – www.lcdediting.com – for her professionalism, dedication and creative suggestions while leading the editing process, to Helen Thurlow and Mary Dickinson for their scrupulous proofreading, to the sublime artist, Susy Dixon-Jones for her brilliant cartographic portrayal of Borwenstow, and to Murray Bealby for his superb work in building and maintaining my social media presence – www.frankhurst.com.

FH
West Sussex
March 2025

About the Author

Frank Hurst, who writes under a pseudonym, started life as a novelist after spending a long career as a criminal investigator and intelligence officer for the British Government. He travelled widely during his work for the Crown, including many years living and working in India, the Eastern Caribbean and South East Asia. Hitherto, his novels have been historical crime adventures, the last two of which are set in Victorian England.

The Shrouded Coast is the third book in his *Hansom Cab* series, all connected to his great-grandfather, Henry Gough.

Frank has retained his appetite for travelling, and when he's not living the quiet life in West Sussex and Chiang Mai, he loves nothing better than to return to his old haunts and visit stirring new places around the globe – hopefully stumbling into new adventures in the process.